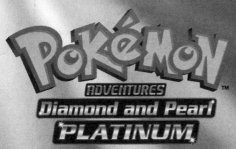

POKÉMON ADVENTURES:
DIAMOND AND PEARL/
PLATINUM
Volume 8
VIZ Kids Edition

Story by HIDENORI KUSAKA
Art by SATOSHI YAMAMOTO

© 2013 Pokémon.
© 1995-2013 Nintendo/Creatures Inc./GAME FREAK inc.
TM and ® and character names are trademarks of Nintendo.
POCKET MONSTER SPECIAL Vol. 8 (37)
by Hidenori KUSAKA, Satoshi YAMAMOTO
© 1997 Hidenori KUSAKA, Satoshi YAMAMOTO
All rights reserved.
Original Japanese edition published by SHOGAKUKAN.
English translation rights in the United States of America, Canada,
the United Kingdom and Ireland arranged with SHOGAKUKAN.

Translation/Tetsuichiro Miyaki
English Adaptation/Bryant Turnage
Touch-up & Lettering/Annaliese Christman
Design/Yukiko Whitley, Shawn Carrico
Editor/Annette Roman

The stories, characters and incidents mentioned
in this publication are entirely fictional.

No portion of this book may be reproduced or transmitted in any form or
by any means without written permission from the copyright holders.

Printed in the U.S.A.

Published by VIZ Media, LLC
P.O. Box 77010
San Francisco, CA 94107

10 9 8 7 6 5 4 3 2 1
First printing, June 2013

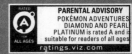

PARENTAL ADVISORY
POKÉMON ADVENTURES
DIAMOND AND PEARL
PLATINUM is rated A and is
suitable for readers of all ages
ratings.viz.com

vizkids
www.vizkids.com

VIZ media
www.viz.com

Our Story So Far...

A STORY ABOUT YOUNG PEOPLE EN-TRUSTED WITH POKÉ-DEXES BY THE WORLD'S LEADING POKÉMON RE-SEARCH-ERS. TOGETHER WITH THEIR POKÉMON, THEY TRAVEL, BATTLE, AND EVOLVE!

Pearl

Dia

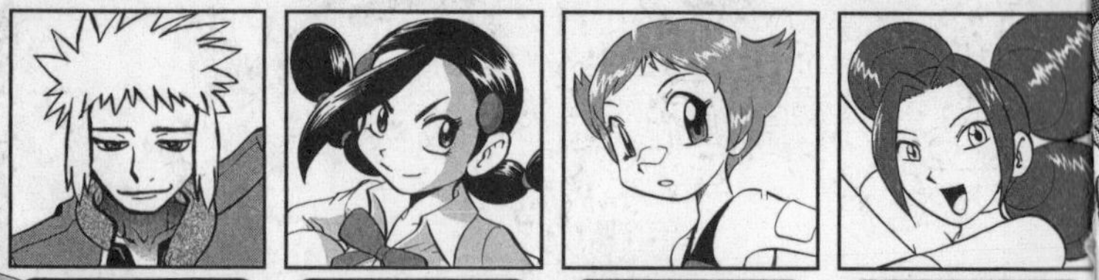

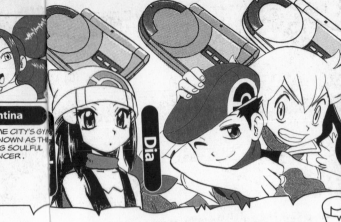

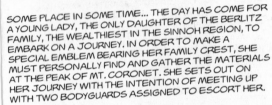

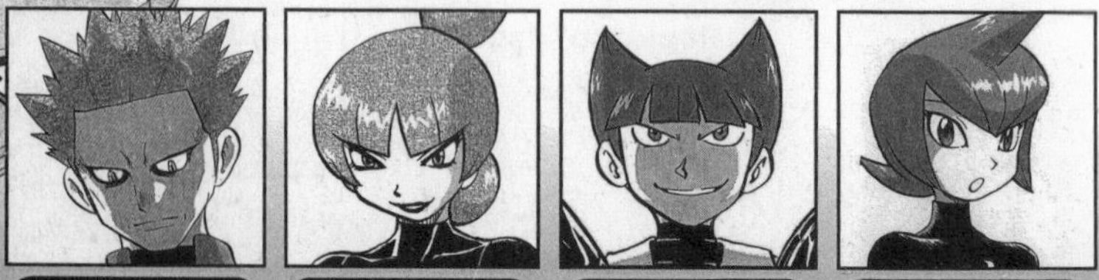

SOME PLACE IN SOME TIME... THE DAY HAS COME FOR A YOUNG LADY, THE ONLY DAUGHTER OF THE BERLITZ FAMILY, THE WEALTHIEST IN THE SINNOH REGION, TO EMBARK ON A JOURNEY. IN ORDER TO MAKE A SPECIAL EMBLEM BEARING HER FAMILY CREST, SHE MUST PERSONALLY FIND AND GATHER THE MATERIALS AT THE PEAK OF MT. CORONET. SHE SETS OUT ON HER JOURNEY WITH THE INTENTION OF MEETING UP WITH TWO BODYGUARDS ASSIGNED TO ESCORT HER.

MEANWHILE, POKÉMON TRAINERS PEARL AND DIAMOND, WHO DREAM OF BECOMING STAND-UP COMEDIANS, ENTER A COMEDY CONTEST IN JUBILIFE AND WIN THE SPECIAL MERIT AWARD. BUT THEIR PRIZE OF AN ALL-EXPENSES PAID TRIP GETS SWITCHED WITH THE CONTRACT FOR LADY'S BODYGUARDS!

THUS PEARL AND DIAMOND THINK LADY IS THEIR TOUR GUIDE, AND LADY THINKS THEY ARE HER BODYGUARDS! DESPITE THE CASES OF MISTAKEN IDENTITY, THE TRIO TRAVEL TOGETHER QUITE HAPPILY THROUGH THE VAST COUNTRYSIDE.

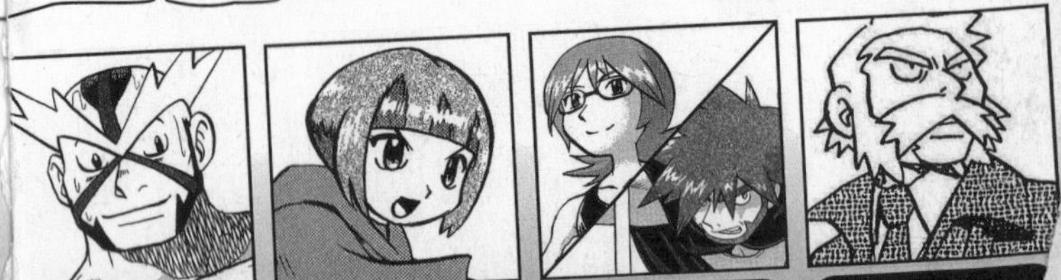

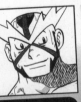

Wake
STORIA CITY'S GYM ADER. A WRESTLER KNOWN AS THE ORRENTIAL MASKED MASTER.

Gardenia
ETERNA CITY'S GYM LEADER, WHO SPECIALIZES IN GRASS-TYPES.

Roark/Byron
A FATHER AND SON TEAM, WHO ARE OREBURGH CITY AND CANALAVE CITY'S GYM LEADERS, RESPECTIVELY.

Professor Rowa
A LEADING RESEARCHER OF POKÉMON EVOLUTION. HE CAN BE QUIT INTIMIDATING

Volkner
SUNYSHORE CITY'S GYM LEADER. A LONER WHO SPECIALIZES IN ELECTRIC-TYPES.

Candice
THE SNOWPOINT CITY GYM LEADER. A POWERFUL GYM LEADER WHO USES ICE-TYPE POKÉMON.

Maylene
THE VEILSTONE CITY GYM LEADER. HER EXPERTISE IS FIGHTING-TYPE POKÉMON.

Fantina
HEARTHOME CITY'S GYM LEADER, KNOWN AS THE ALLURING SOULFUL DANCER.

THE TWO BODYGUARDS ENTRUSTED WITH ESCORTING LADY ARE AWARE OF THE MIX-UP AND SET OUT TO CATCH UP WITH DIAMOND, PEARL, AND LADY. BUT THEN THEY GET MIXED UP WITH MYSTERIOUS TEAM GALACTIC, WHO ARE BUSY CREATING TROUBLE IN THE SINNOH REGION. THEIR DEVIOUS PLAN IS TO CREATE A GALACTIC BOMB.

DIAMOND AND PEARL FINALLY REVEAL THAT THEY ARE NOT LADY'S REAL BODYGUARDS, AND THOUGH IT SHAKES HER UP FOR A MOMENT, LADY (WHOSE REAL NAME "PLATINUM" HAS NOW BEEN REVEALED) RESOLVES TO STICK BY HER FRIENDS AND TRUST IN THEM AGAIN. BUT THEN THE TRIO SEPARATE AND EACH SETS OUT ALONE FOR ONE OF THE THREE SINNOH LAKES WHERE THREE POKÉMON OF LEGEND—UXIE, MESPRIT, AND AZELF—SLUMBER.

UNFORTUNATELY, OUR HEROES ARE DEFEATED, AND THE THREE LEGENDARY POKÉMON ARE CAPTURED! IN THE MIDST OF THIS CHAOS, DIA—KNOWING ONLY THAT THE DIABOLICAL GOAL OF THE ENEMY HAS SOMETHING TO DO WITH "OUTER SPACE"—SNEAKS INTO ENEMY HEADQUARTERS TO INVESTIGATE FURTHER...

Cyrus
TEAM GALACTIC'S BOSS. AN OVERBEARING, INTENSE MAN.

Jupiter
A BATTLE-LOVING THIRD TEAM GALACTIC LEADER WHO DEPLOYS POWERFUL ATTACKS.

Saturn
HE IS IN CHARGE OF THE BOMB AND RARELY STEPS ONTO THE BATTLEFIELD HIMSELF.

Mars
A TEAM GALACTIC LEADER. HER PERSONALITY IS HARD TO PIN DOWN.

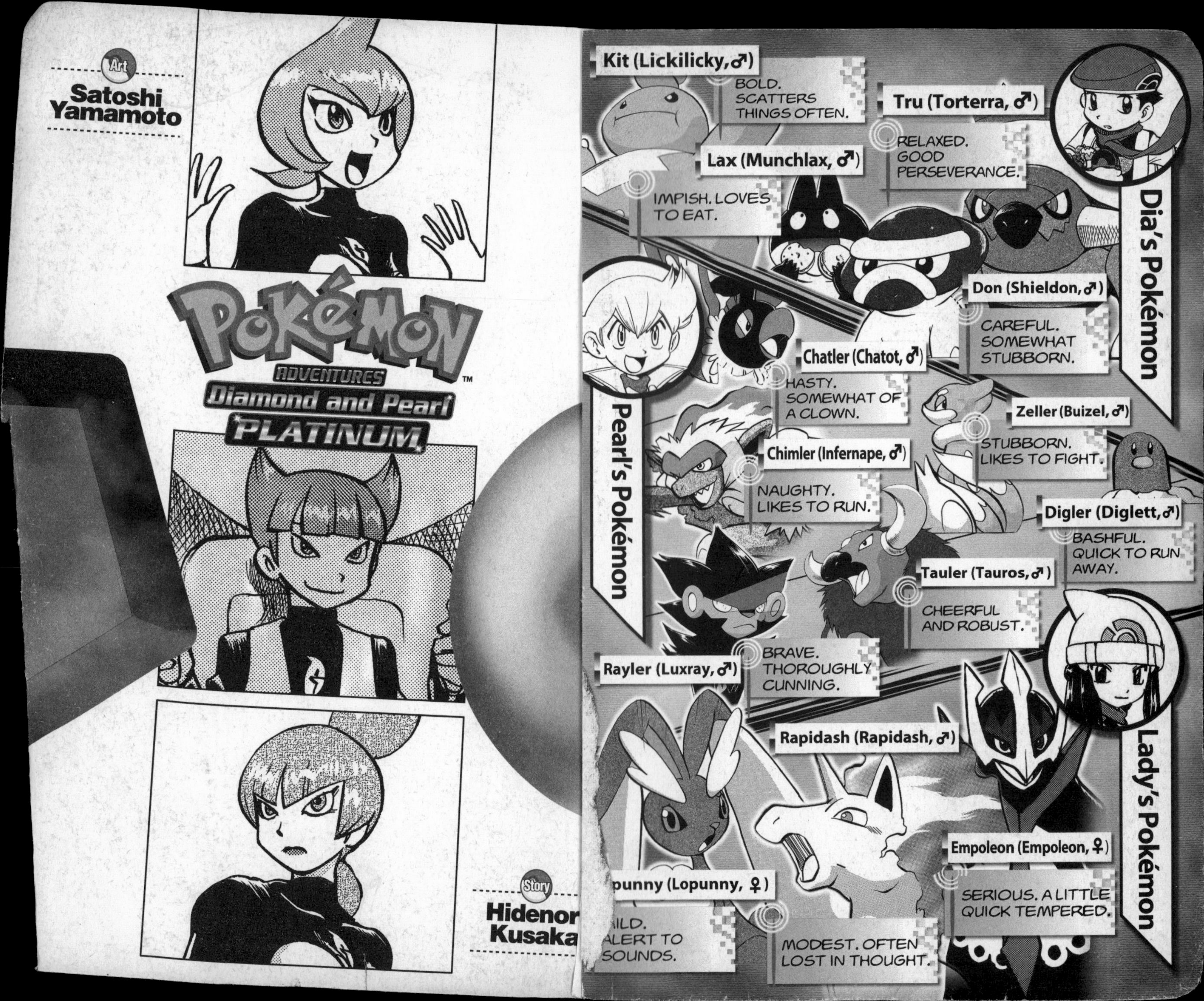
Art
Satoshi Yamamoto
POKÉMON ADVENTURES™
Diamond and Pearl
PLATINUM
Story
Hidenor
Kusaka
Kit (Lickilicky, ♂)
BOLD. SCATTERS THINGS OFTEN.
Tru (Torterra, ♂)
RELAXED. GOOD PERSEVERANCE.
Lax (Munchlax, ♂)
IMPISH. LOVES TO EAT.
Dia's Pokémon
Don (Shieldon, ♂)
CAREFUL. SOMEWHAT STUBBORN.
Chatler (Chatot, ♂)
HASTY. SOMEWHAT OF A CLOWN.
Pearl's Pokémon
Zeller (Buizel, ♂)
STUBBORN. LIKES TO FIGHT.
Chimler (Infernape, ♂)
NAUGHTY. LIKES TO RUN.
Digler (Diglett, ♂)
BASHFUL. QUICK TO RUN AWAY.
Tauler (Tauros, ♂)
CHEERFUL AND ROBUST.
Rayler (Luxray, ♂)
BRAVE. THOROUGHLY CUNNING.
Rapidash (Rapidash, ♂)
Lady's Pokémon
Empoleon (Empoleon, ♀)
SERIOUS. A LITTLE QUICK TEMPERED.
punny (Lopunny, ♀)
ILD. LERT TO SOUNDS.
MODEST. OFTEN LOST IN THOUGHT.

POKÉMON
ADVENTURES
Diamond and Pearl
PLATINUM

8

CONTENTS

68

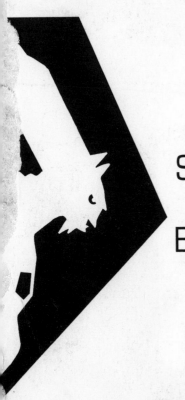

Shorting
Out
Electivire

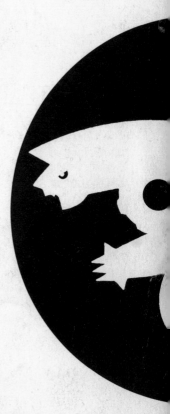

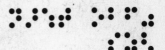

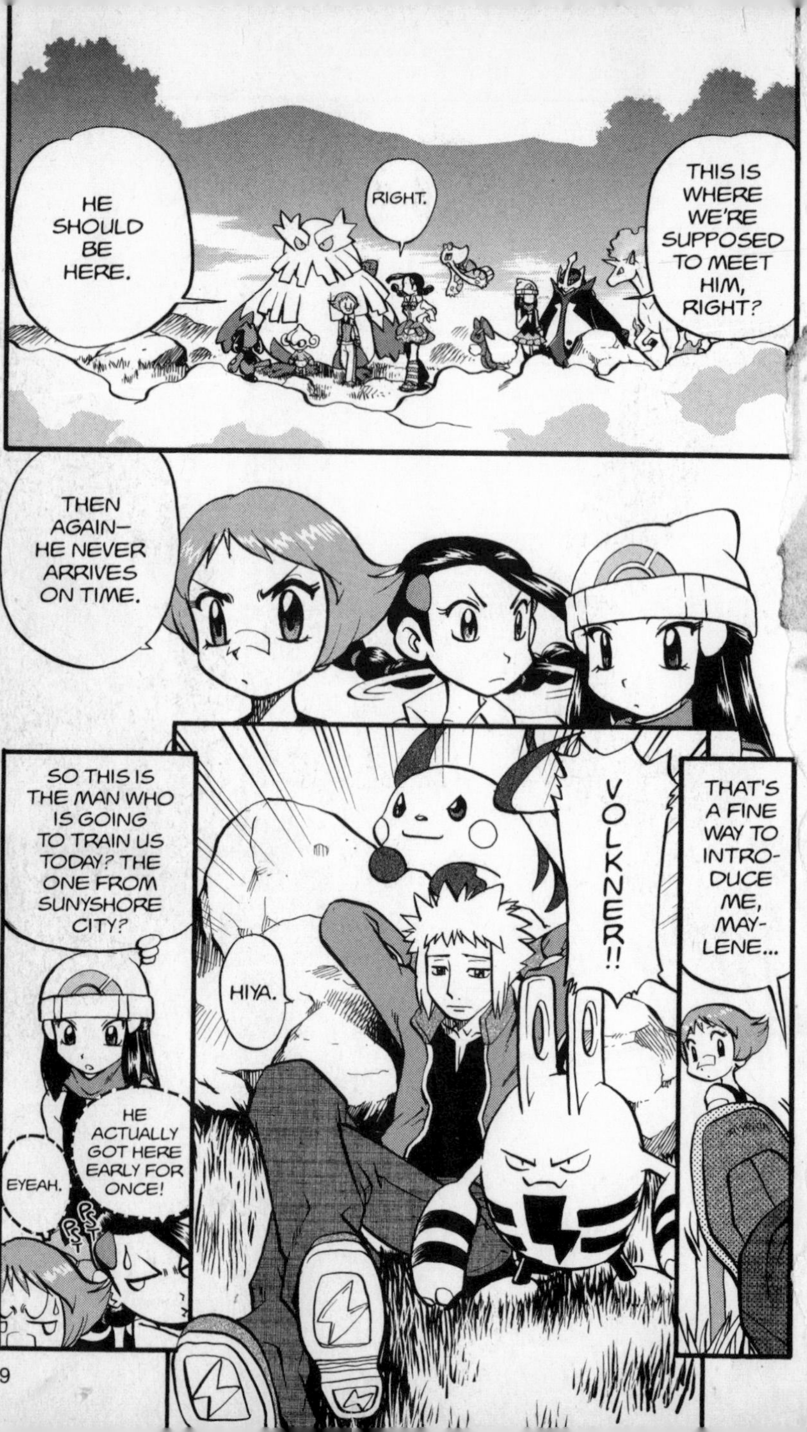
THIS IS WHERE WE'RE SUPPOSED TO MEET HIM, RIGHT?
RIGHT.
HE SHOULD BE HERE.
THEN AGAIN— HE NEVER ARRIVES ON TIME.
THAT'S A FINE WAY TO INTRO- DUCE ME, MAY- LENE...
VOLKNER!!
HIYA.
SO THIS IS THE MAN WHO IS GOING TO TRAIN US TODAY? THE ONE FROM SUNYSHORE CITY?
HE ACTUALLY GOT HERE EARLY FOR ONCE!
EYEAH.
PST PST

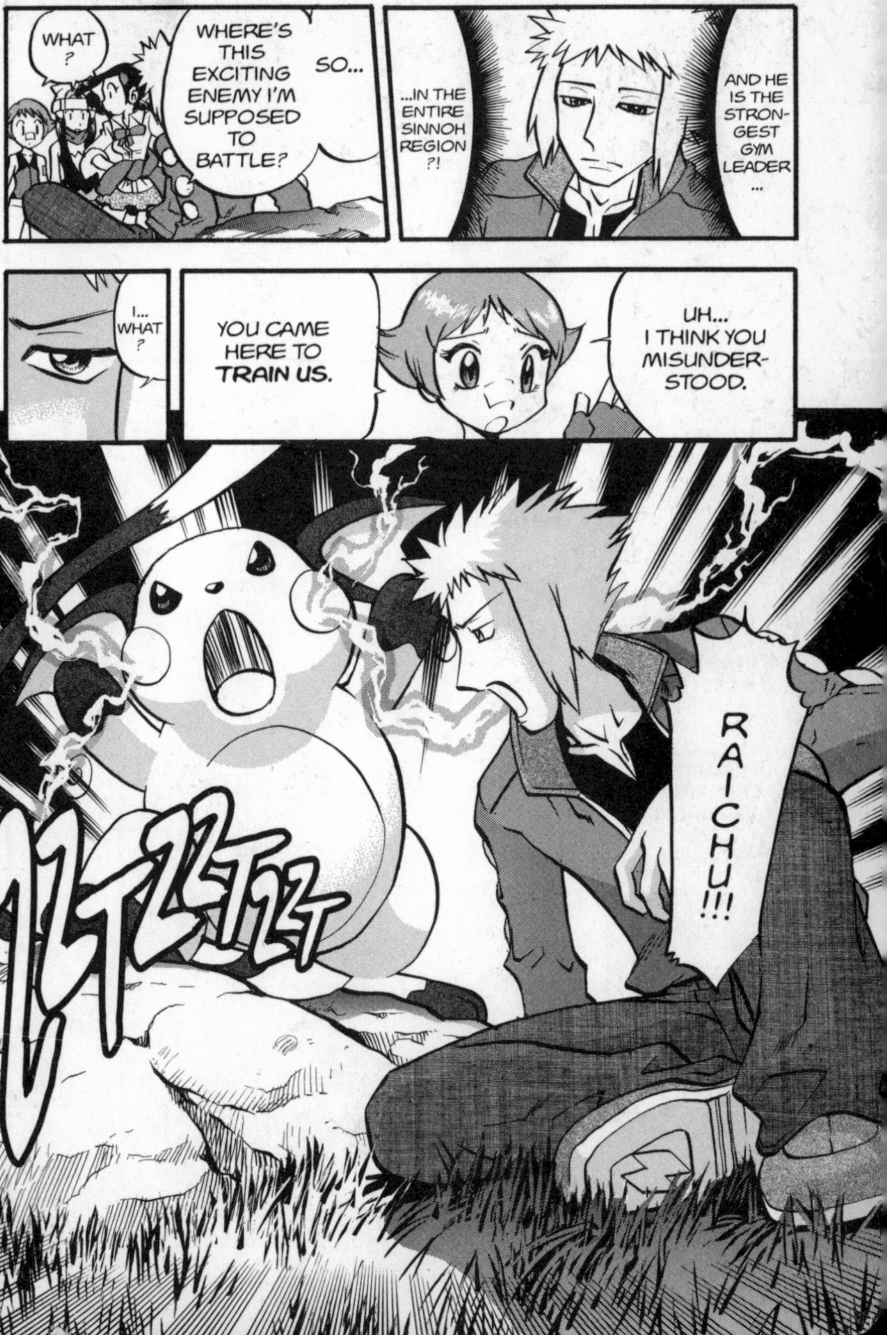
AND HE IS THE STRONG-EST GYM LEADER...
...IN THE ENTIRE SINNOH REGION?!
SO...
WHERE'S THIS EXCITING ENEMY I'M SUPPOSED TO BATTLE?
WHAT?
UH... I THINK YOU MISUNDER-STOOD.
YOU CAME HERE TO TRAIN US.
I... WHAT?
RAICHU!!!
ZZTZZTZZT

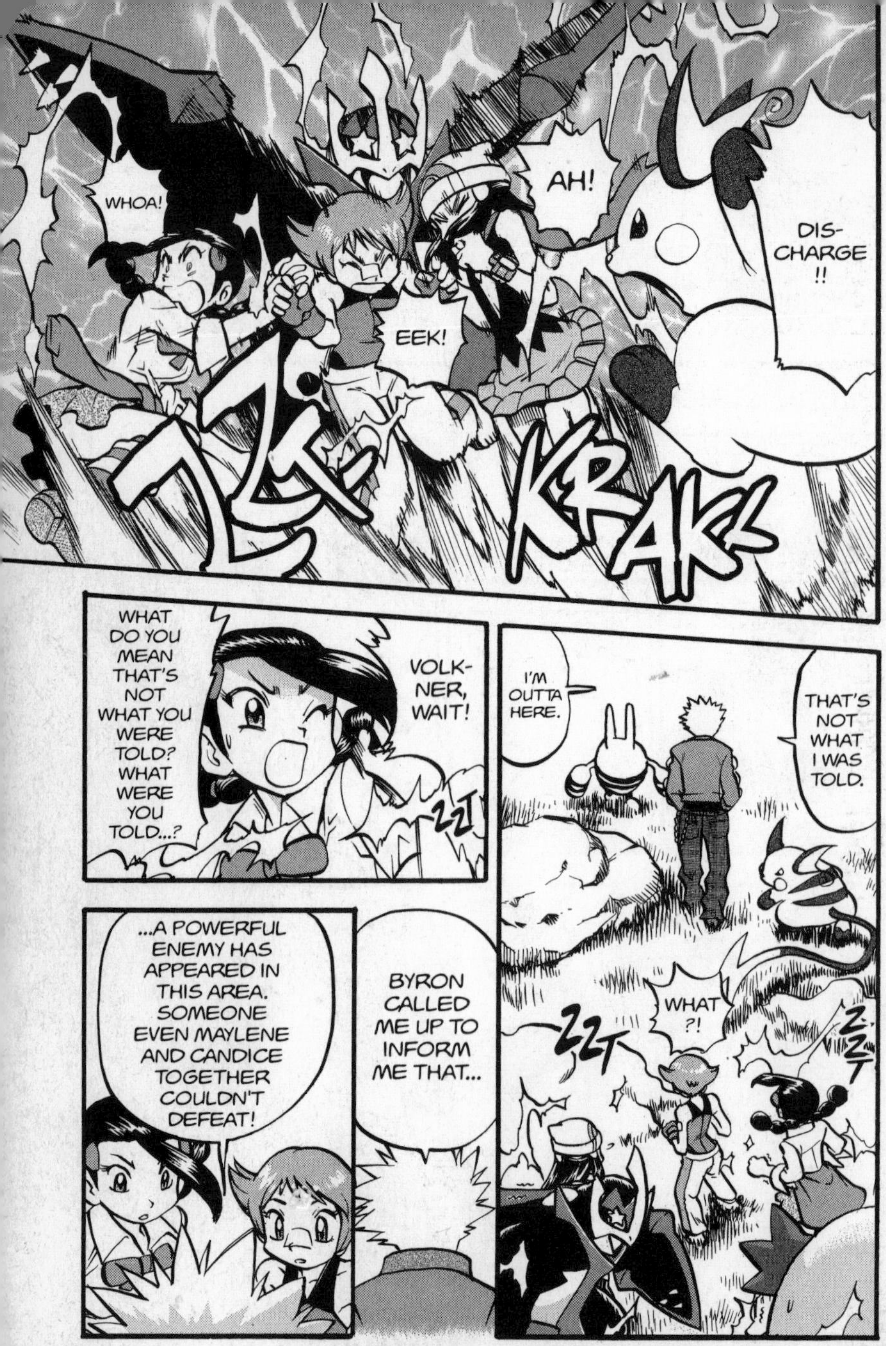
DIS-CHARGE!!
AH!
WHOA!
EEK!
KRAK!
THAT'S NOT WHAT I WAS TOLD.
I'M OUTTA HERE.
WHAT?!
ZZT
ZZT
VOLKNER, WAIT!
WHAT DO YOU MEAN THAT'S NOT WHAT YOU WERE TOLD? WHAT WERE YOU TOLD...?
ZZT
BYRON CALLED ME UP TO INFORM ME THAT...
...A POWERFUL ENEMY HAS APPEARED IN THIS AREA. SOMEONE EVEN MAYLENE AND CANDICE TOGETHER COULDN'T DEFEAT!

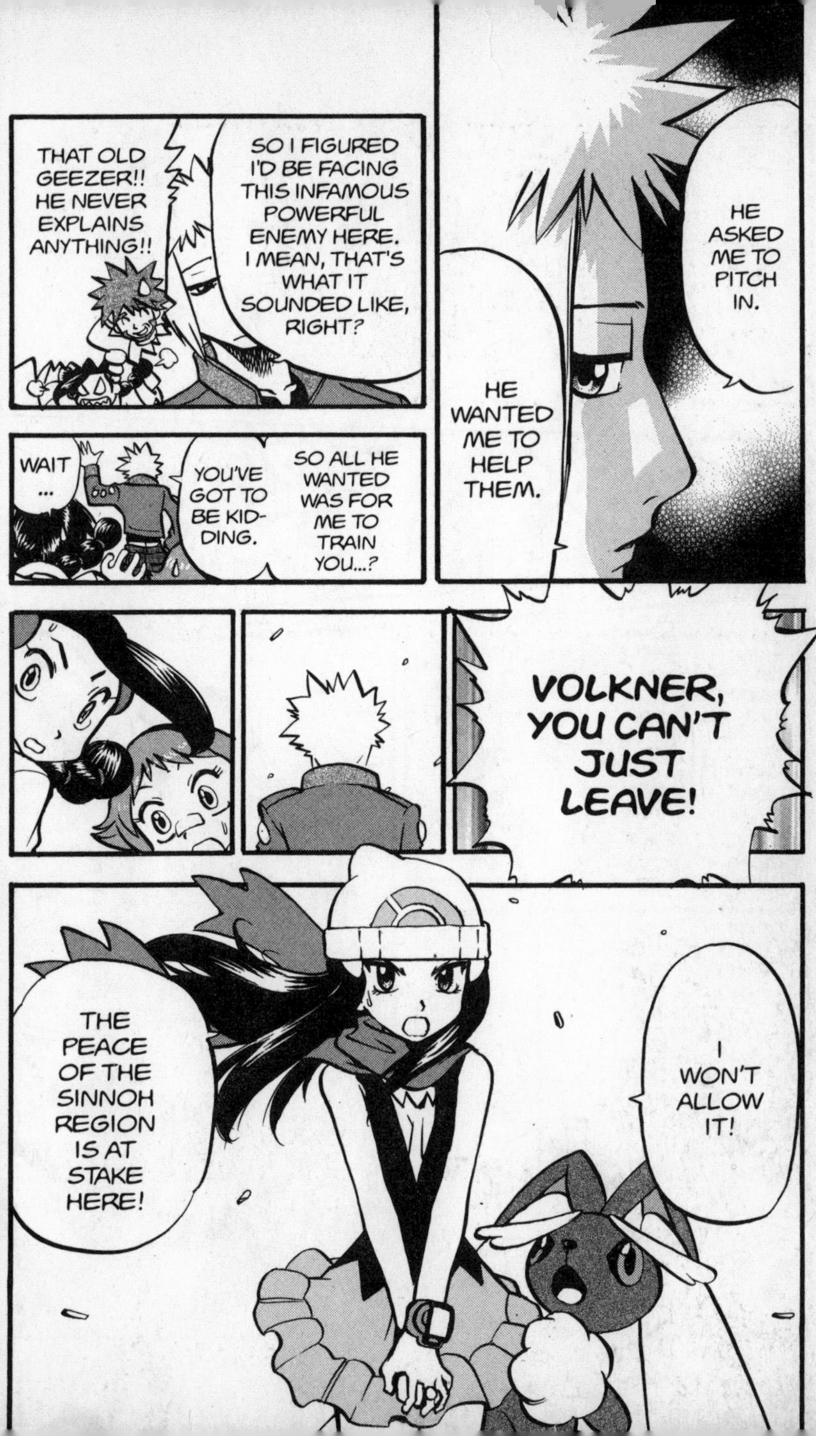
HE ASKED ME TO PITCH IN.
HE WANTED ME TO HELP THEM.
SO I FIGURED I'D BE FACING THIS INFAMOUS POWERFUL ENEMY HERE. I MEAN, THAT'S WHAT IT SOUNDED LIKE, RIGHT?
THAT OLD GEEZER!! HE NEVER EXPLAINS ANYTHING!!
SO ALL HE WANTED WAS FOR ME TO TRAIN YOU...?
YOU'VE GOT TO BE KID-DING.
WAIT ...
VOLKNER, YOU CAN'T JUST LEAVE!
I WON'T ALLOW IT!
THE PEACE OF THE SINNOH REGION IS AT STAKE HERE!

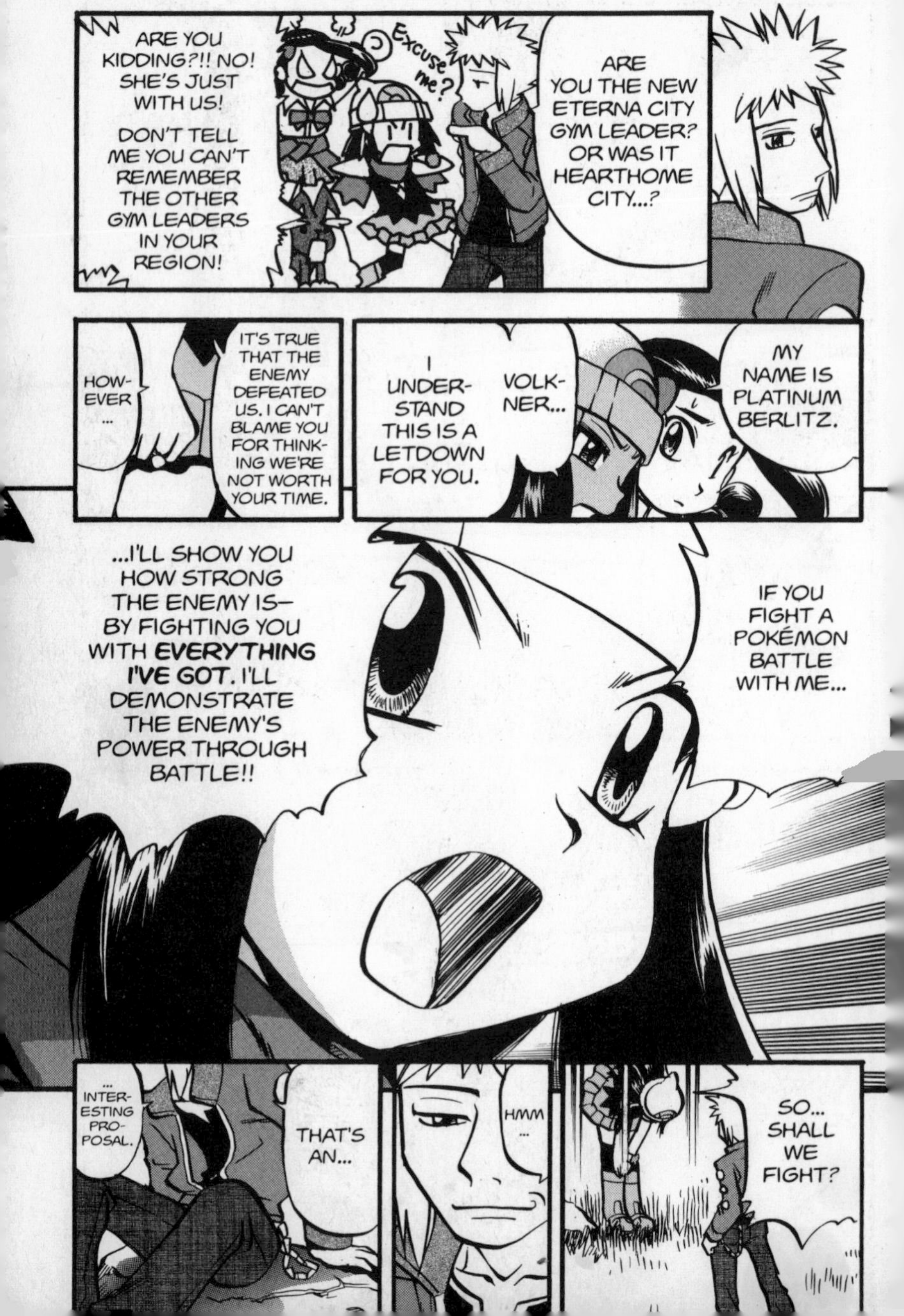
ARE YOU THE NEW ETERNA CITY GYM LEADER? OR WAS IT HEARTHOME CITY...?
Excuse me?
ARE YOU KIDDING?!! NO! SHE'S JUST WITH US!
DON'T TELL ME YOU CAN'T REMEMBER THE OTHER GYM LEADERS IN YOUR REGION!
MY NAME IS PLATINUM BERLITZ.
VOLKNER...
I UNDERSTAND THIS IS A LETDOWN FOR YOU.
IT'S TRUE THAT THE ENEMY DEFEATED US. I CAN'T BLAME YOU FOR THINKING WE'RE NOT WORTH YOUR TIME.
HOWEVER...
IF YOU FIGHT A POKÉMON BATTLE WITH ME...
...I'LL SHOW YOU HOW STRONG THE ENEMY IS—BY FIGHTING YOU WITH **EVERYTHING I'VE GOT**. I'LL DEMONSTRATE THE ENEMY'S POWER THROUGH BATTLE!!
SO... SHALL WE FIGHT?
HMM...
THAT'S AN...
...INTERESTING PROPOSAL.

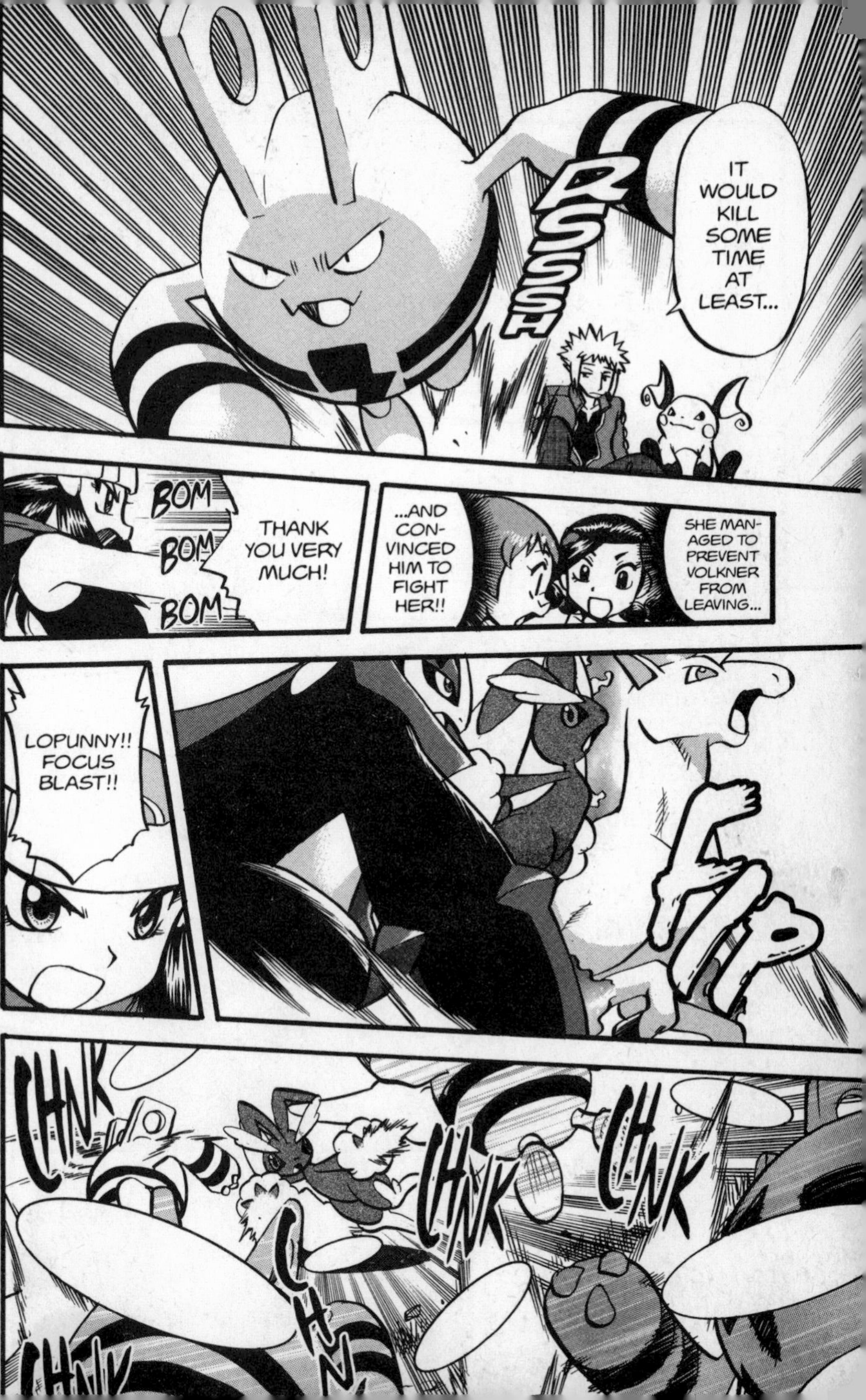
IT WOULD KILL SOME TIME AT LEAST...
SHE MAN-AGED TO PREVENT VOLKNER FROM LEAVING...
...AND CON-VINCED HIM TO FIGHT HER!!
THANK YOU VERY MUCH!
BOM
BOM
BOM
LOPUNNY!! FOCUS BLAST!!
CHNK
CHNK
CHNK
CHNK

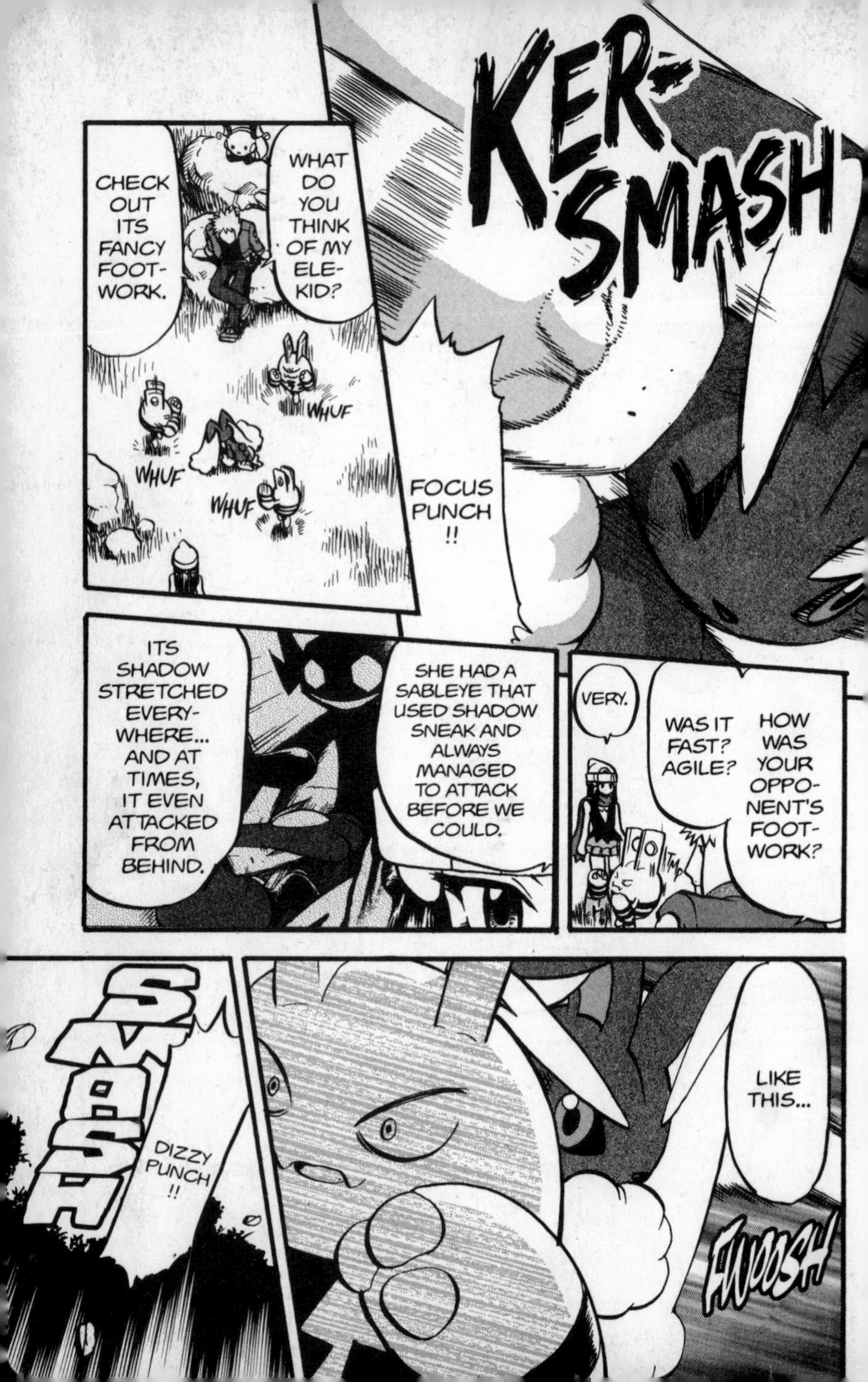
KER-SMASH
FOCUS PUNCH !!
WHAT DO YOU THINK OF MY ELE-KID?
CHECK OUT ITS FANCY FOOT-WORK.
WHUF
WHUF
WHUF
HOW WAS YOUR OPPO-NENT'S FOOT-WORK?
WAS IT FAST? AGILE?
VERY.
SHE HAD A SABLEYE THAT USED SHADOW SNEAK AND ALWAYS MANAGED TO ATTACK BEFORE WE COULD.
ITS SHADOW STRETCHED EVERY-WHERE... AND AT TIMES, IT EVEN ATTACKED FROM BEHIND.
LIKE THIS...
FWOOSH
DIZZY PUNCH !!
SMASH

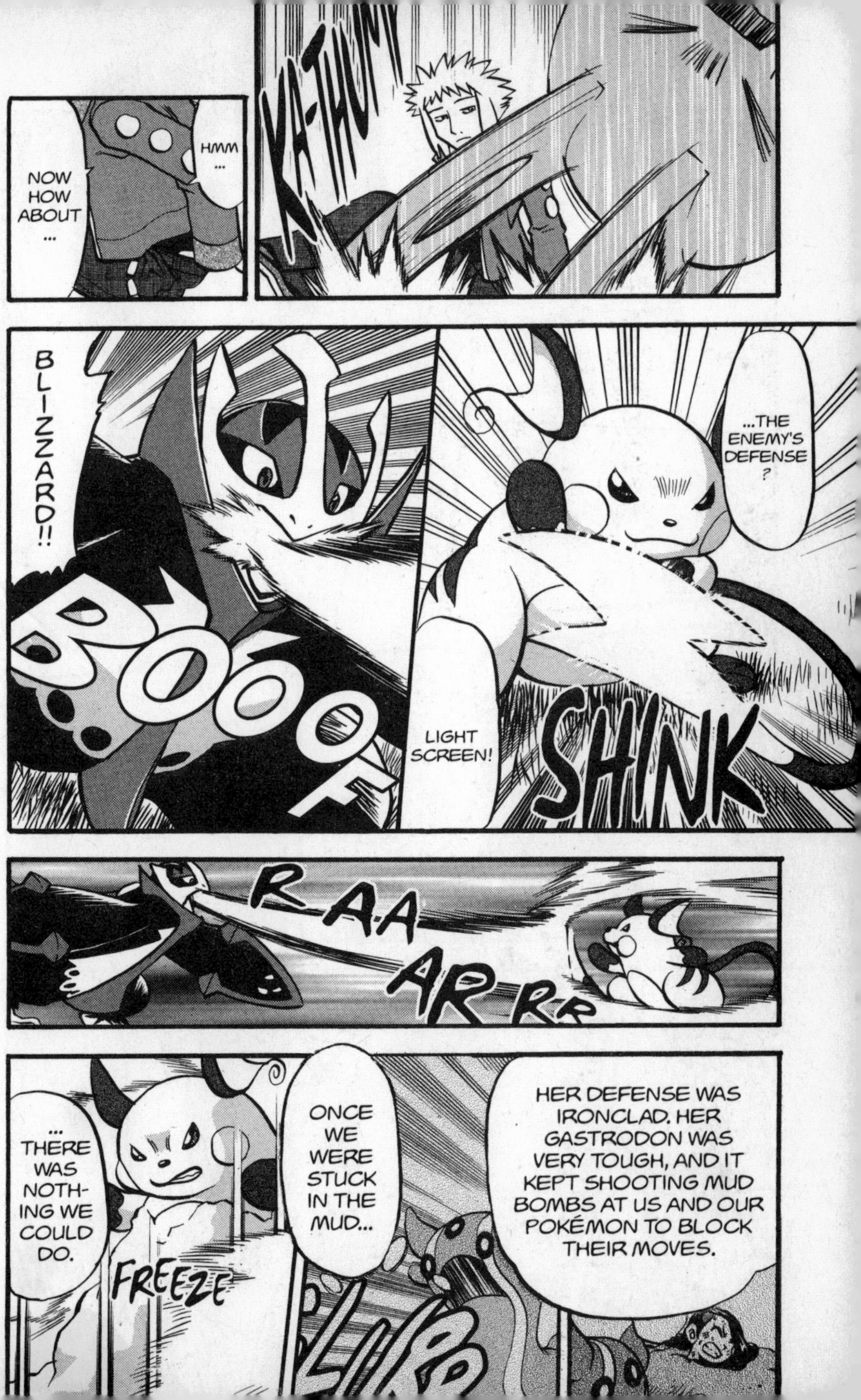
KA-THUN
HMM ...
NOW HOW ABOUT ...
...THE ENEMY'S DEFENSE ?
SHINK
LIGHT SCREEN!
BLIZZARD!!
BOOOF
RAAARRR
HER DEFENSE WAS IRONCLAD. HER GASTRODON WAS VERY TOUGH, AND IT KEPT SHOOTING MUD BOMBS AT US AND OUR POKÉMON TO BLOCK THEIR MOVES.
ONCE WE WERE STUCK IN THE MUD...
... THERE WAS NOTHING WE COULD DO.
FREEZE

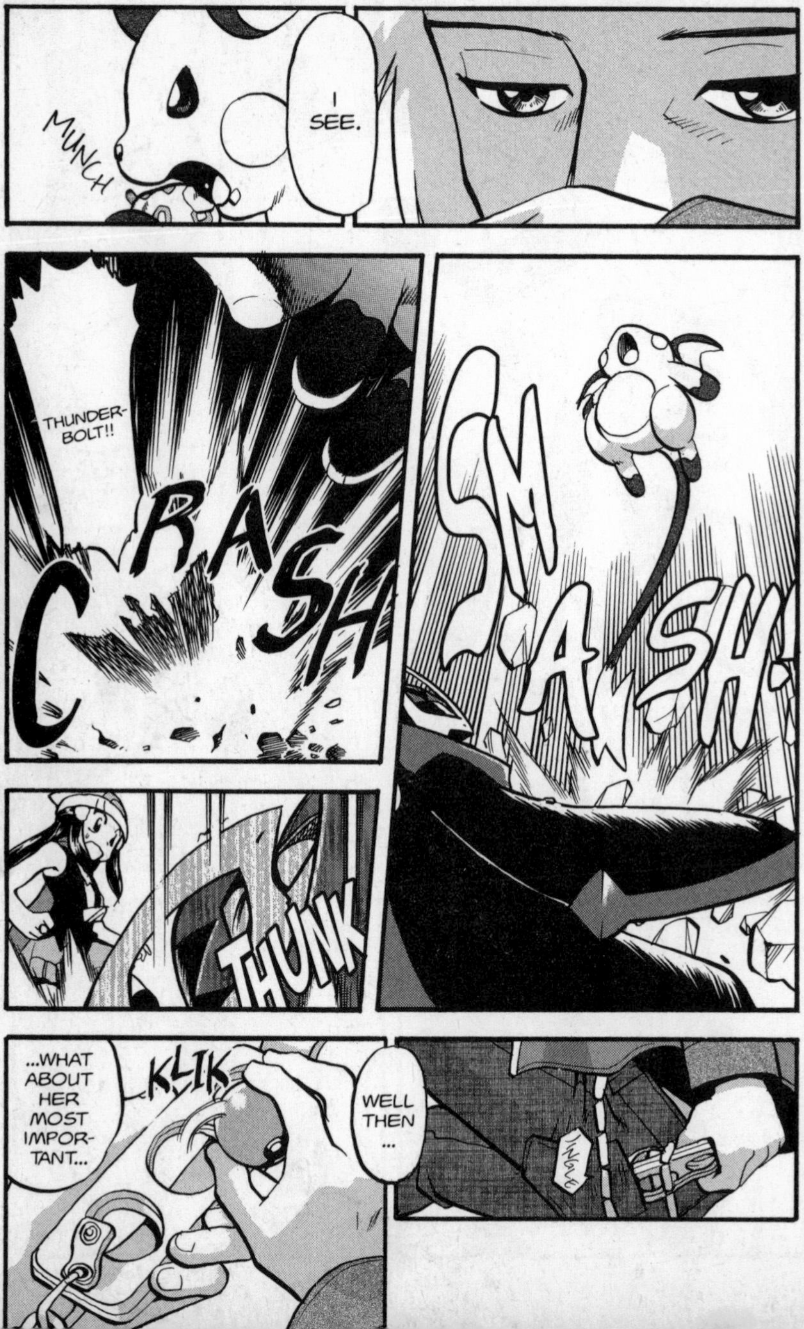
I SEE.
MUNCH
SMASH
THUNDER-BOLT!!
CRASH
THUNK
WELL THEN...
JINGLE
...WHAT ABOUT HER MOST IMPORTANT...
KLIK

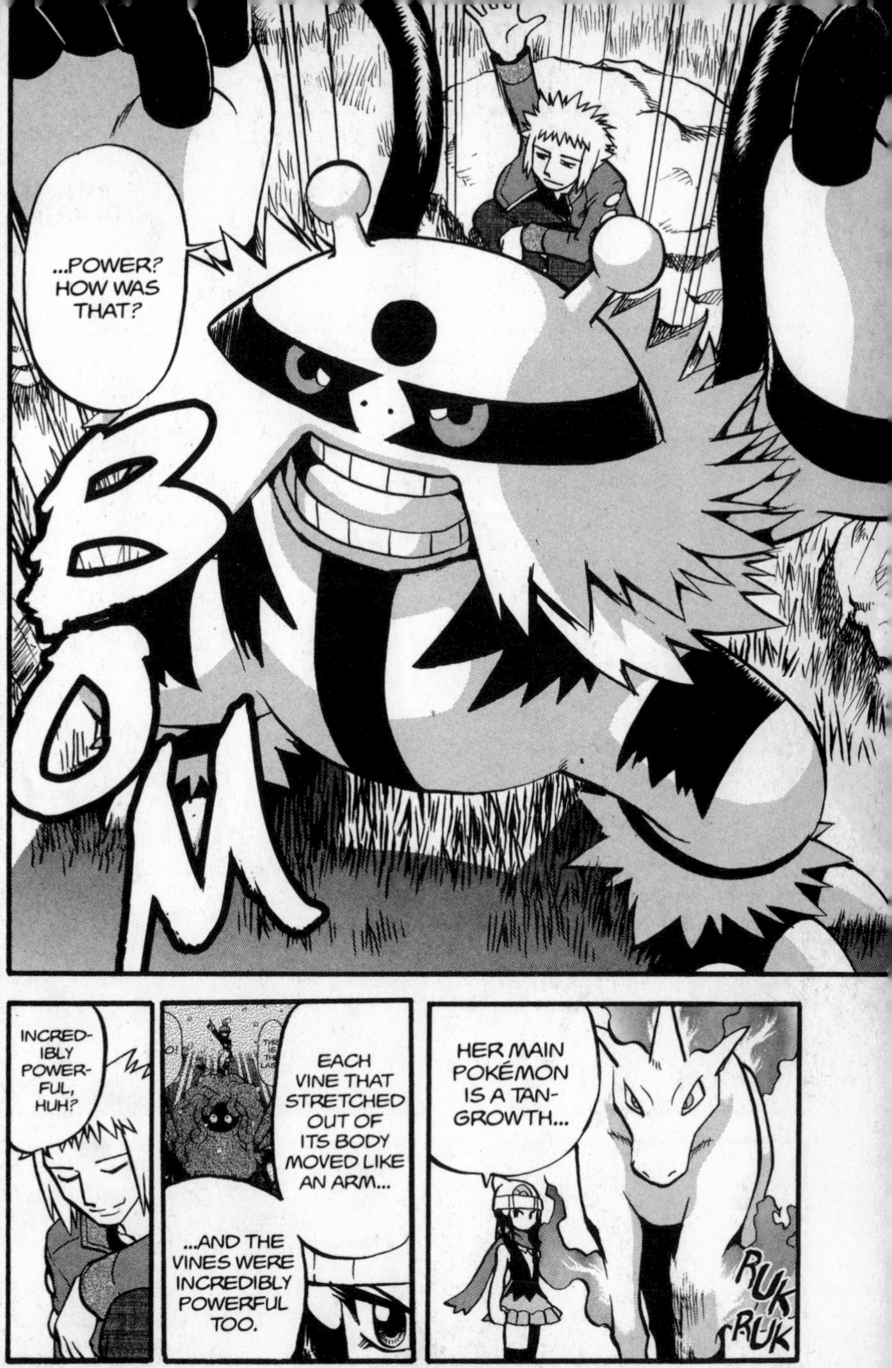
...POWER? HOW WAS THAT?
HER MAIN POKÉMON IS A TAN-GROWTH...
RUK RUK
EACH VINE THAT STRETCHED OUT OF ITS BODY MOVED LIKE AN ARM...
...AND THE VINES WERE INCREDIBLY POWERFUL TOO.
INCRED-IBLY POWER-FUL, HUH?

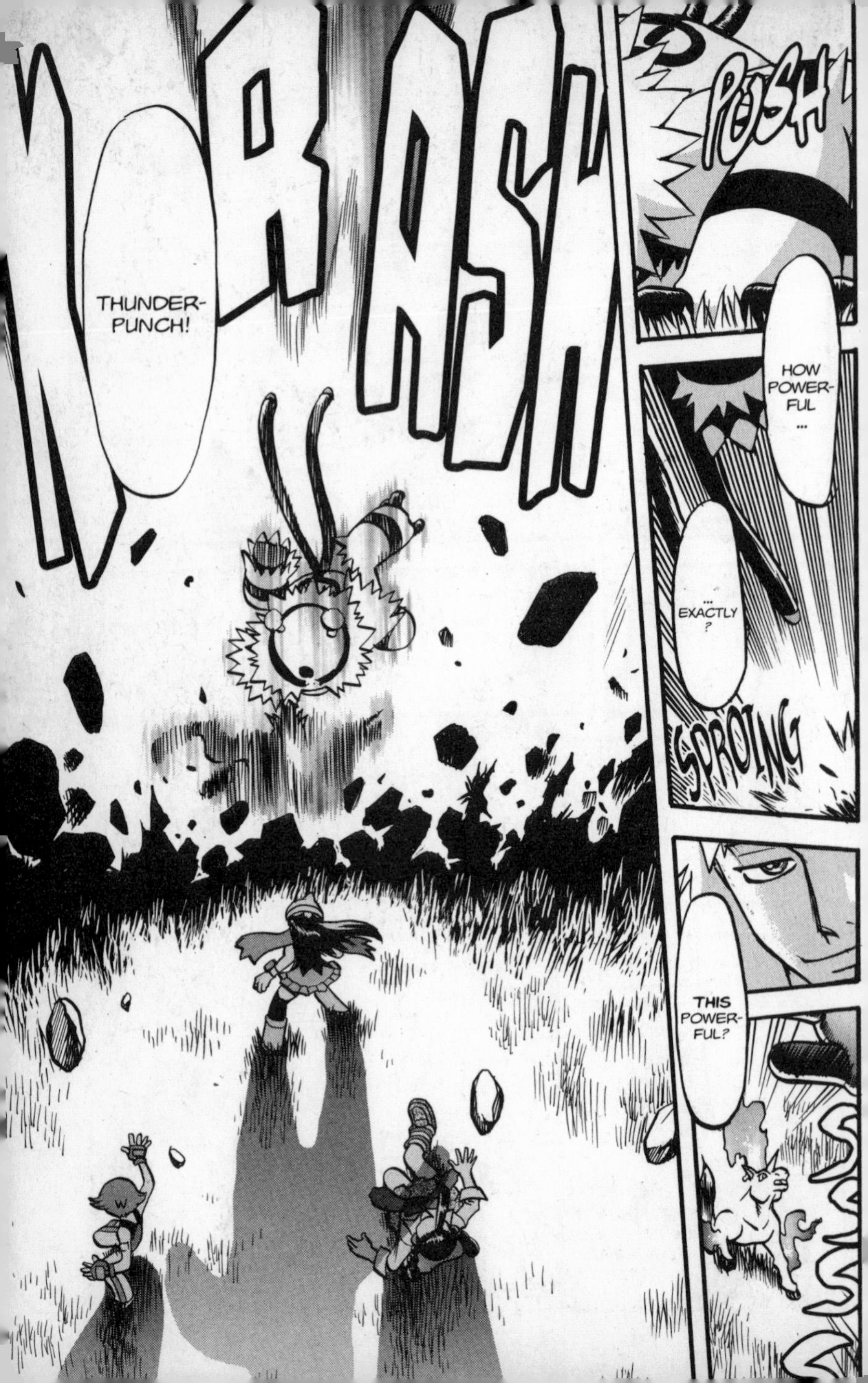
POSH
HOW POWER-FUL ...
... EXACTLY ?
SPROING
THIS POWER-FUL?
THUNDER-PUNCH!

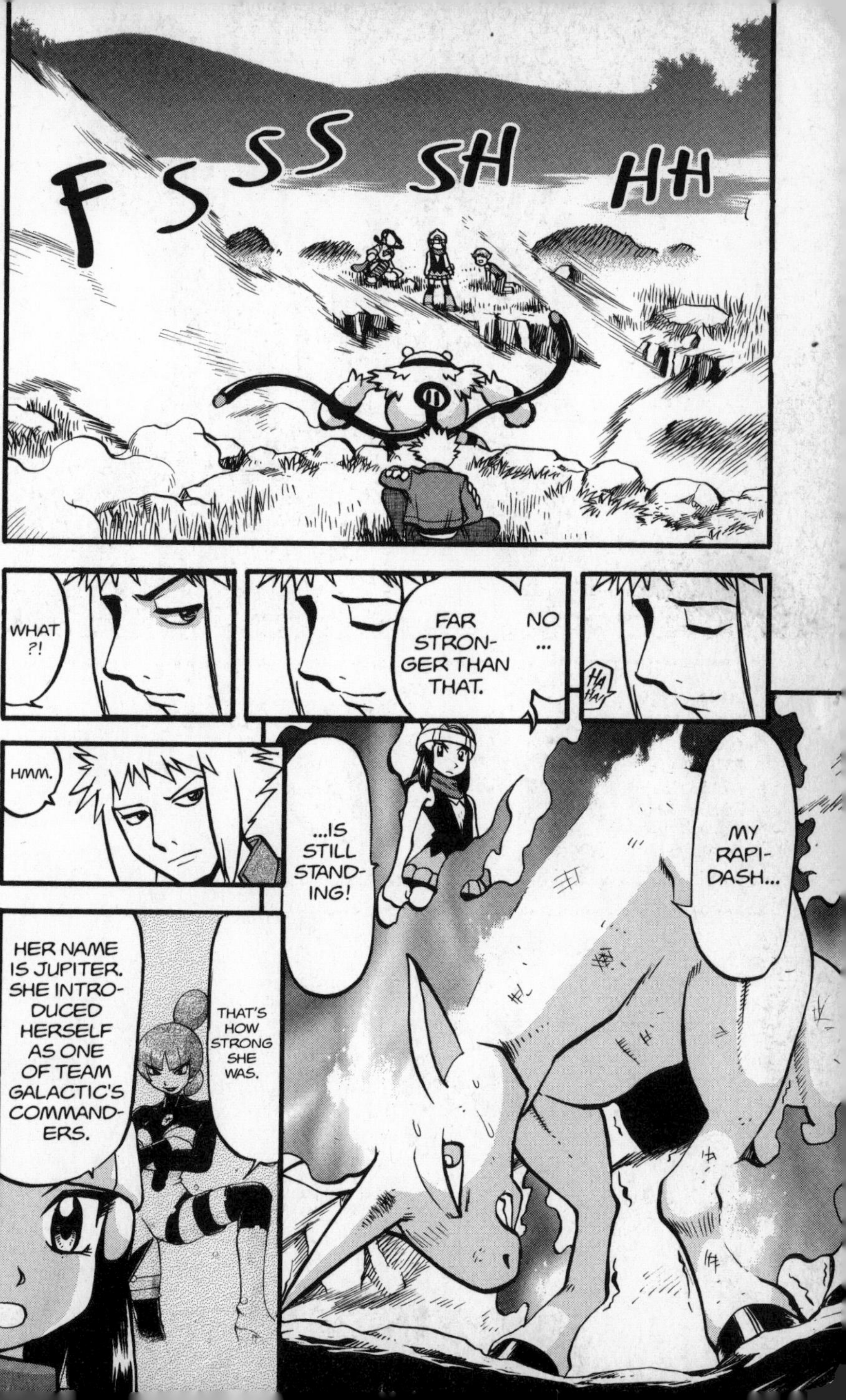
FSSSSHHH
HA HA
NO...
FAR STRONGER THAN THAT.
WHAT?!
MY RAPIDASH...
...IS STILL STANDING!
HMM.
THAT'S HOW STRONG SHE WAS.
HER NAME IS JUPITER. SHE INTRODUCED HERSELF AS ONE OF TEAM GALACTIC'S COMMANDERS.

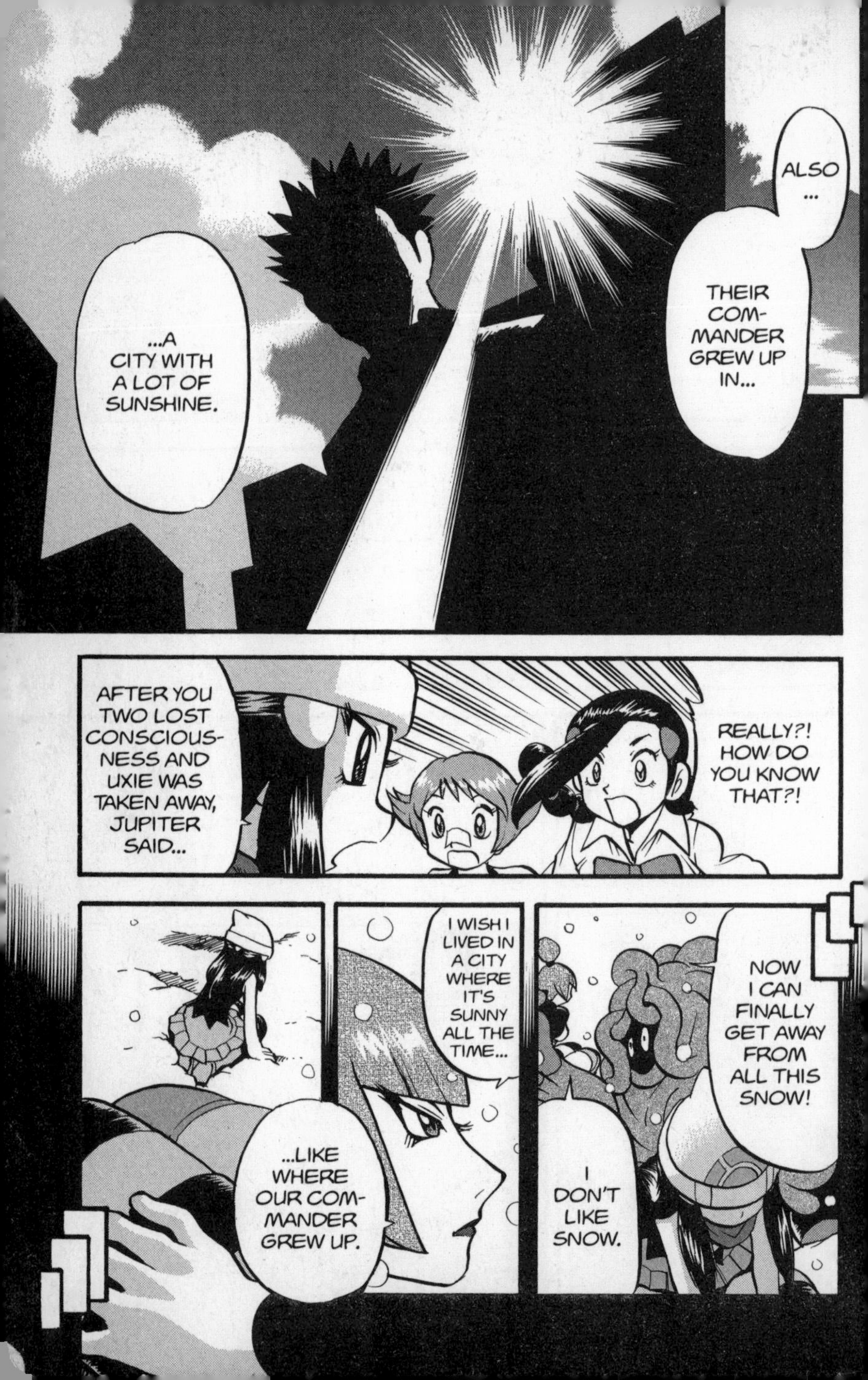

ALSO ...
THEIR COM-MANDER GREW UP IN...
...A CITY WITH A LOT OF SUNSHINE.
REALLY?! HOW DO YOU KNOW THAT?!
AFTER YOU TWO LOST CONSCIOUS-NESS AND UXIE WAS TAKEN AWAY, JUPITER SAID...
NOW I CAN FINALLY GET AWAY FROM ALL THIS SNOW!
I DON'T LIKE SNOW.
I WISH I LIVED IN A CITY WHERE IT'S SUNNY ALL THE TIME...
...LIKE WHERE OUR COM-MANDER GREW UP.

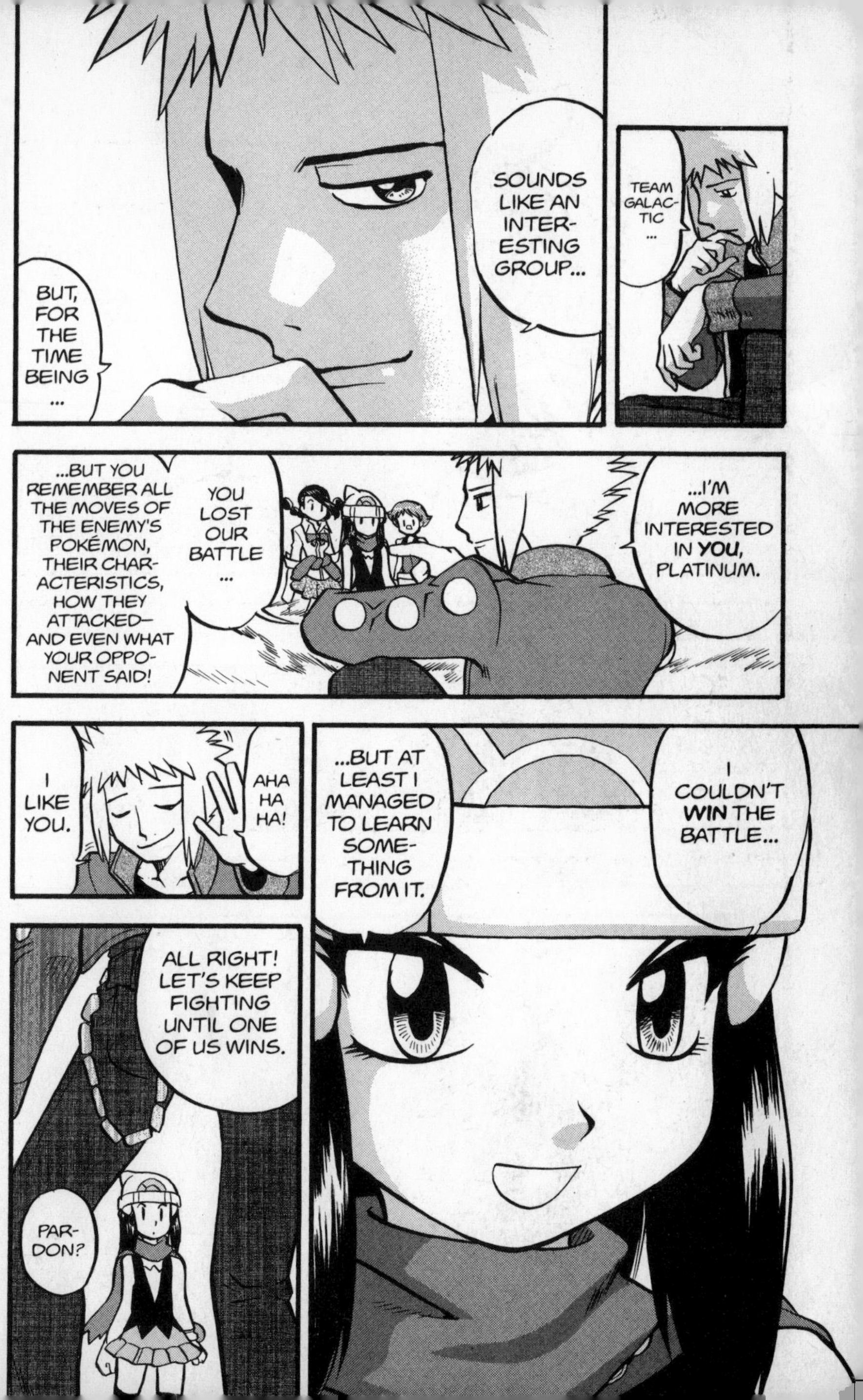
TEAM GALACTIC...
SOUNDS LIKE AN INTERESTING GROUP...
BUT, FOR THE TIME BEING...
...I'M MORE INTERESTED IN **YOU**, PLATINUM.
YOU LOST OUR BATTLE...
...BUT YOU REMEMBER ALL THE MOVES OF THE ENEMY'S POKÉMON, THEIR CHARACTERISTICS, HOW THEY ATTACKED—AND EVEN WHAT YOUR OPPONENT SAID!
I COULDN'T **WIN** THE BATTLE...
...BUT AT LEAST I MANAGED TO LEARN SOMETHING FROM IT.
AHA HA HA!
I LIKE YOU.
ALL RIGHT! LET'S KEEP FIGHTING UNTIL ONE OF US WINS.
PARDON?

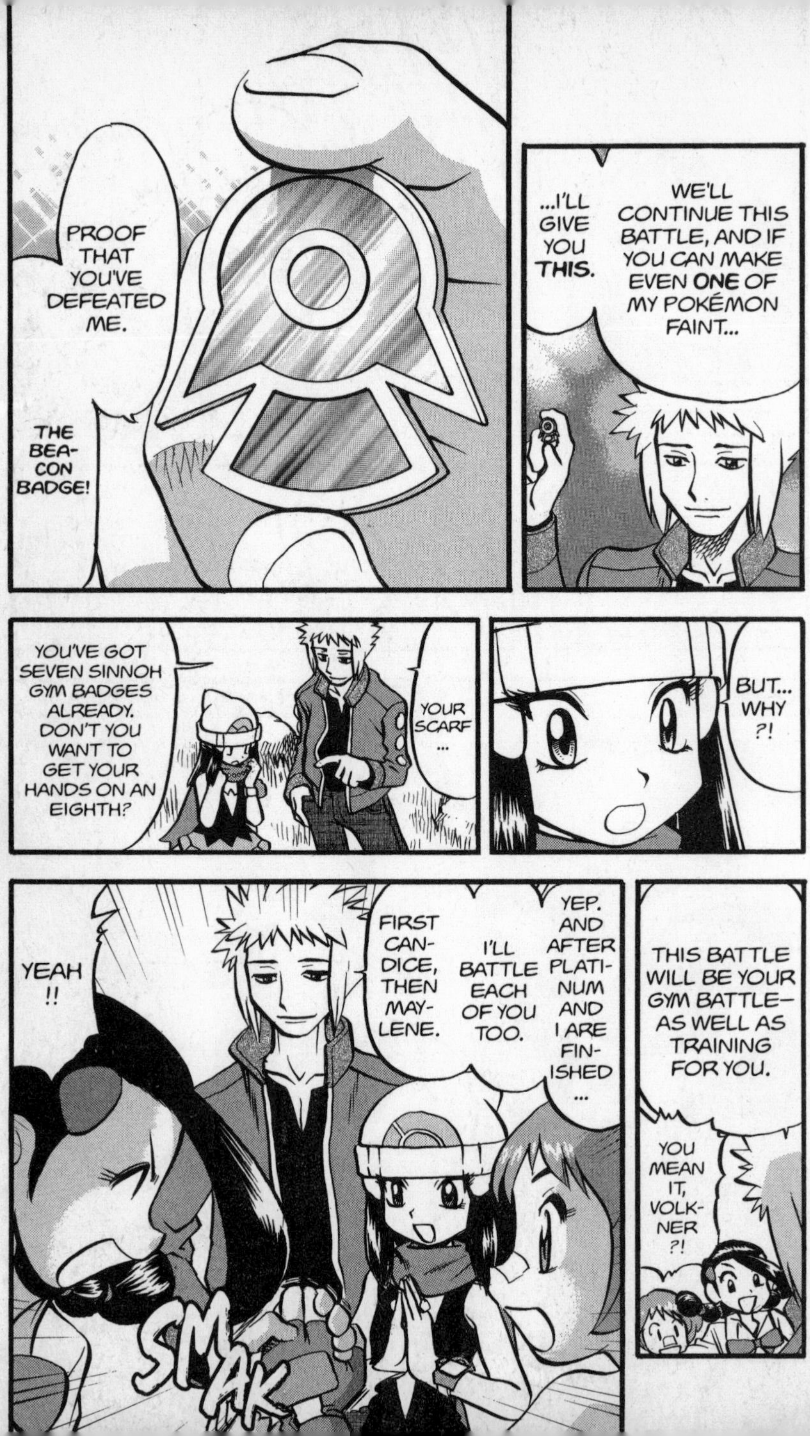
WE'LL CONTINUE THIS BATTLE, AND IF YOU CAN MAKE EVEN **ONE** OF MY POKÉMON FAINT...
...I'LL GIVE YOU **THIS.**
PROOF THAT YOU'VE DEFEATED ME.
THE BEA-CON BADGE!
BUT... WHY?!
YOUR SCARF...
YOU'VE GOT SEVEN SINNOH GYM BADGES ALREADY. DON'T YOU WANT TO GET YOUR HANDS ON AN EIGHTH?
THIS BATTLE WILL BE YOUR GYM BATTLE— AS WELL AS TRAINING FOR YOU.
YOU MEAN IT, VOLK-NER?!
YEP. AND AFTER PLATI-NUM AND I ARE FIN-ISHED...
I'LL BATTLE EACH OF YOU TOO.
FIRST CAN-DICE, THEN MAY-LENE.
YEAH!!
SMAK

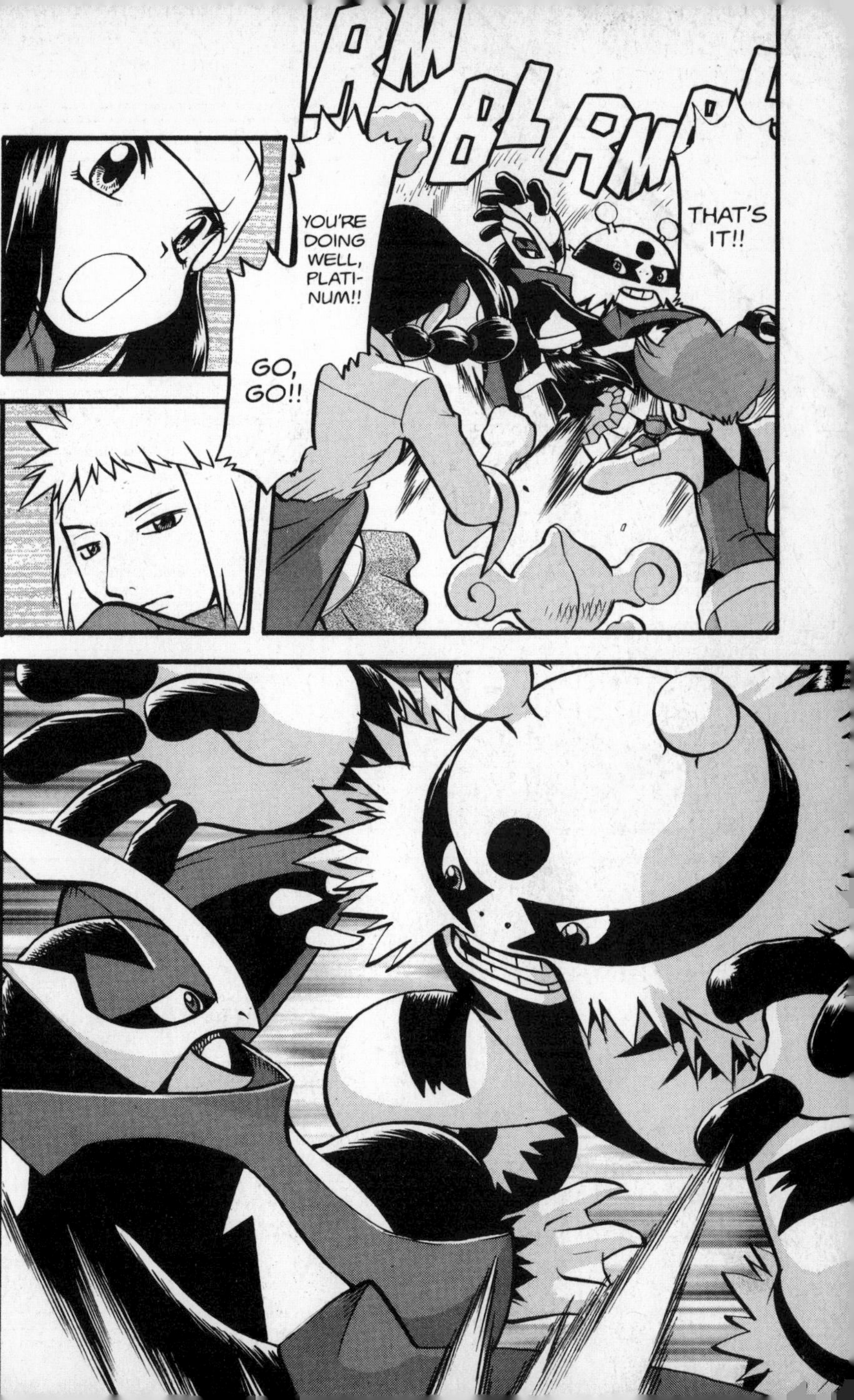
THAT'S IT!!
YOU'RE DOING WELL, PLATINUM!!
GO, GO!!

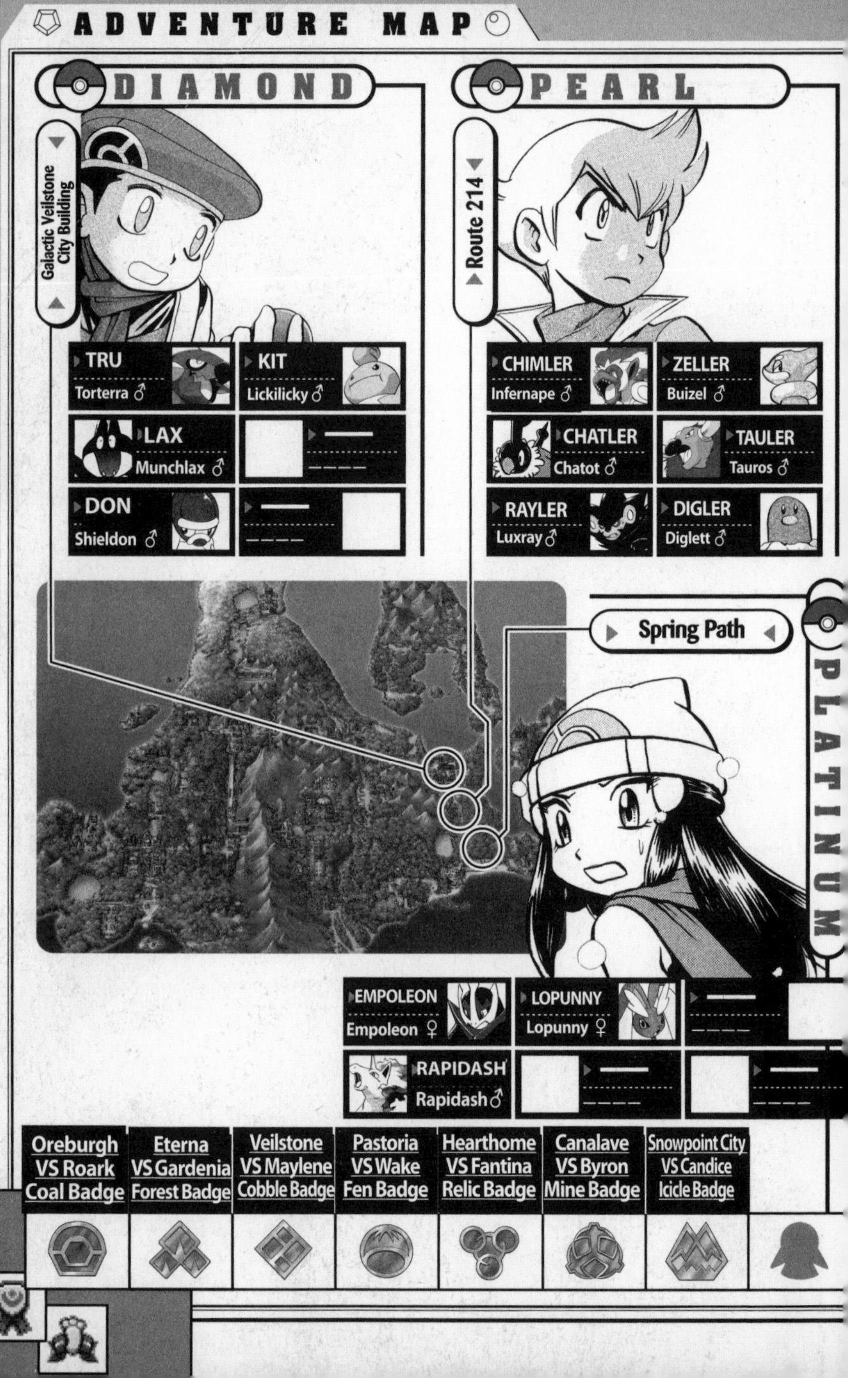
ADVENTURE MAP
DIAMOND
Galactic Veilstone City Building
TRU
Torterra ♂
KIT
Lickilicky ♂
LAX
Munchlax ♂
DON
Shieldon ♂
PEARL
Route 214
CHIMLER
Infernape ♂
ZELLER
Buizel ♂
CHATLER
Chatot ♂
TAULER
Tauros ♂
RAYLER
Luxray ♂
DIGLER
Diglett ♂
Spring Path
PLATINUM
EMPOLEON
Empoleon ♀
LOPUNNY
Lopunny ♀
RAPIDASH
Rapidash ♂
Oreburgh
VS Roark
Coal Badge
Eterna
VS Gardenia
Forest Badge
Veilstone
VS Maylene
Cobble Badge
Pastoria
VS Wake
Fen Badge
Hearthome
VS Fantina
Relic Badge
Canalave
VS Byron
Mine Badge
Snowpoint City
VS Candice
Icicle Badge

69

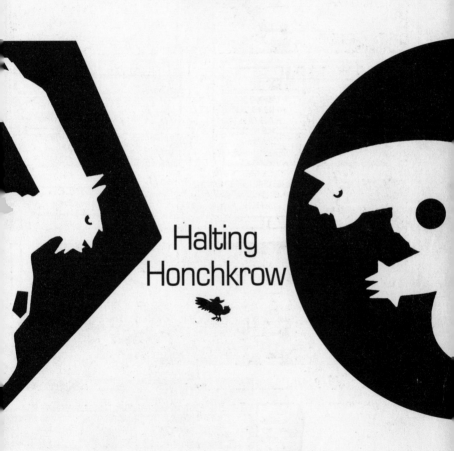

Halting
Honchkrow

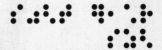

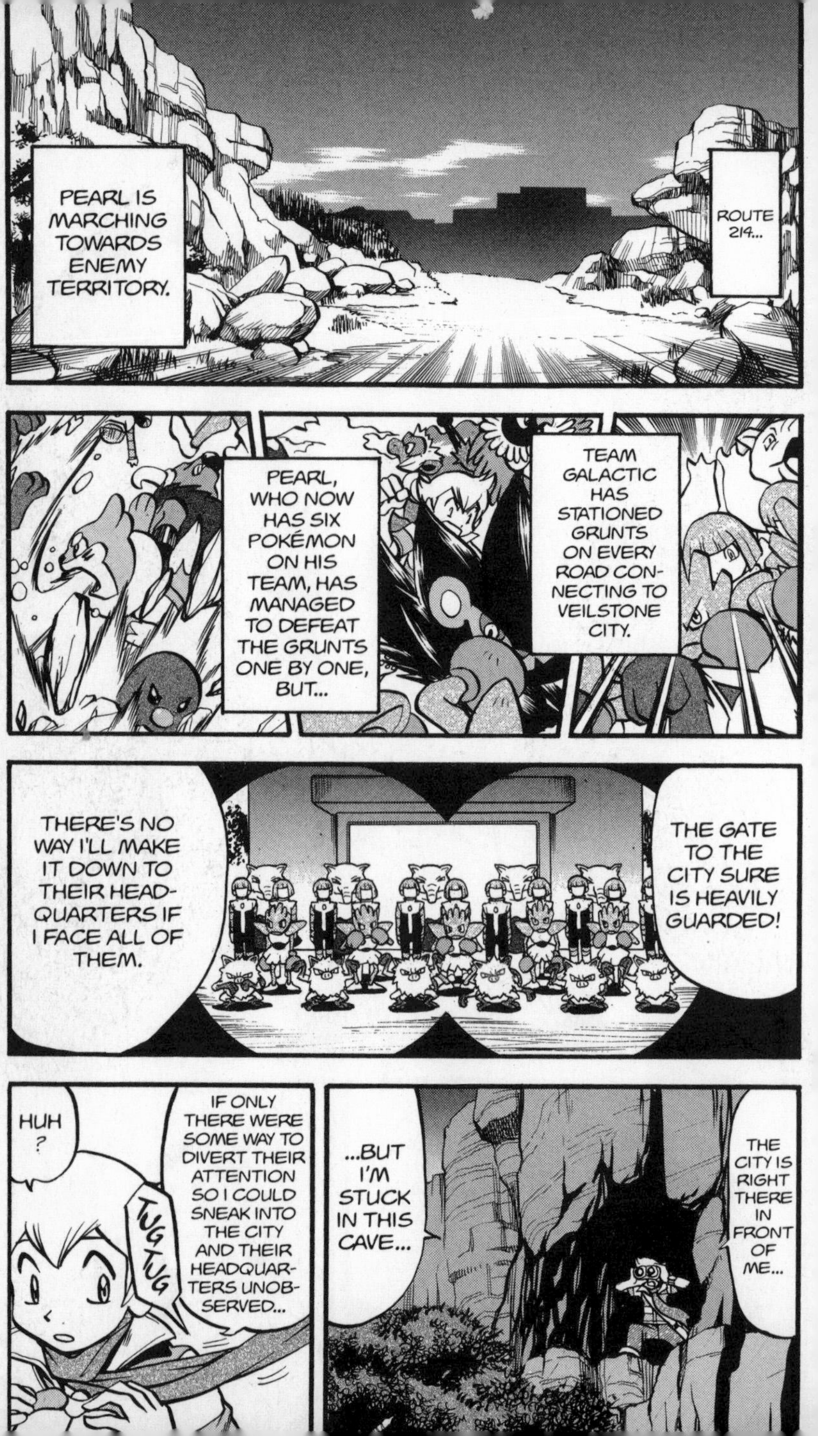
ROUTE 214...
PEARL IS MARCHING TOWARDS ENEMY TERRITORY.
TEAM GALACTIC HAS STATIONED GRUNTS ON EVERY ROAD CON-NECTING TO VEILSTONE CITY.
PEARL, WHO NOW HAS SIX POKÉMON ON HIS TEAM, HAS MANAGED TO DEFEAT THE GRUNTS ONE BY ONE, BUT...
THE GATE TO THE CITY SURE IS HEAVILY GUARDED!
THERE'S NO WAY I'LL MAKE IT DOWN TO THEIR HEAD-QUARTERS IF I FACE ALL OF THEM.
THE CITY IS RIGHT THERE IN FRONT OF ME...
...BUT I'M STUCK IN THIS CAVE...
IF ONLY THERE WERE SOME WAY TO DIVERT THEIR ATTENTION SO I COULD SNEAK INTO THE CITY AND THEIR HEADQUAR-TERS UNOB-SERVED...
TUG TUG
HUH ?

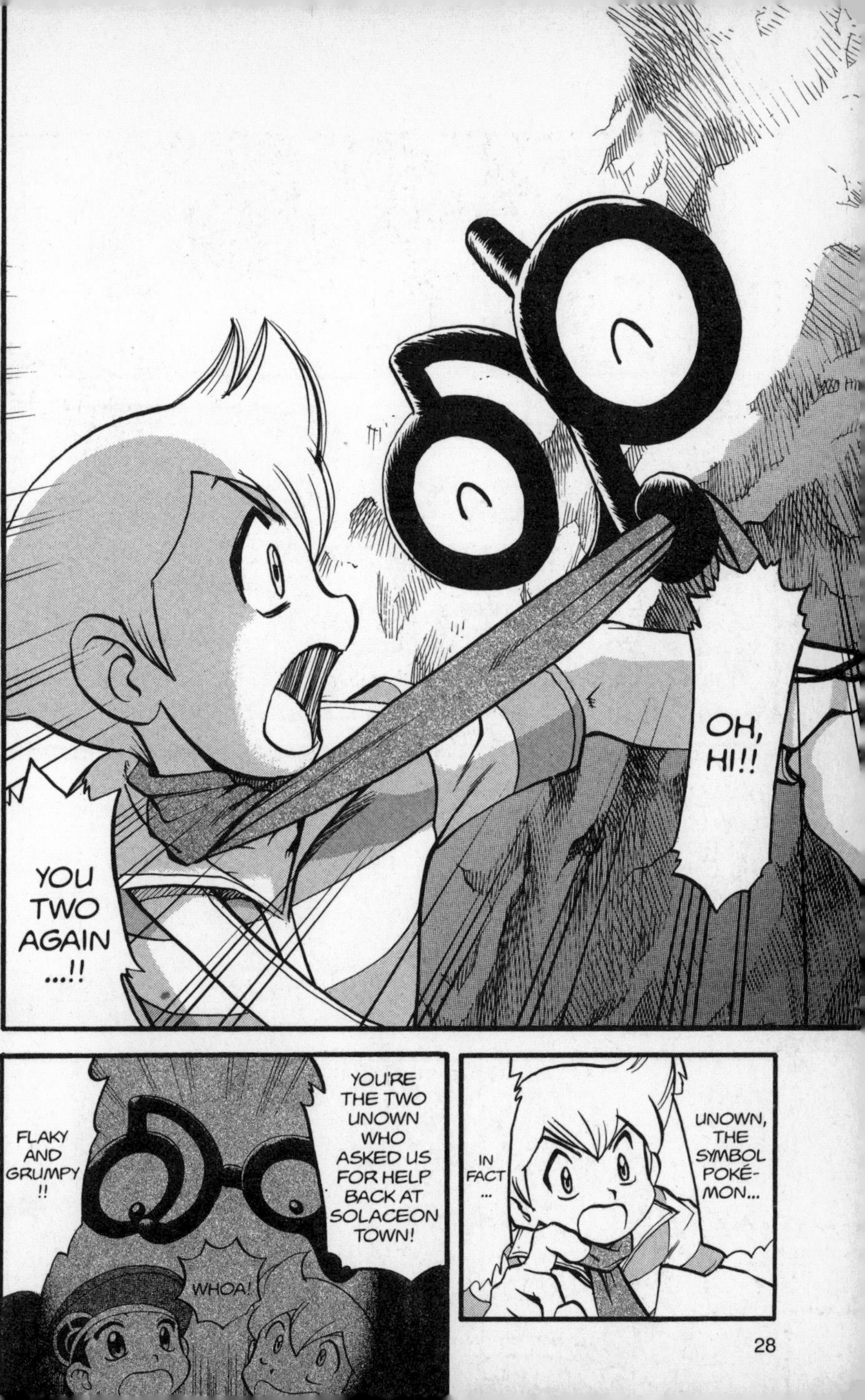
OH, HI!!
YOU TWO AGAIN ...!!
UNOWN, THE SYMBOL POKÉMON...
IN FACT ...
YOU'RE THE TWO UNOWN WHO ASKED US FOR HELP BACK AT SOLACEON TOWN!
WHOA!
FLAKY AND GRUMPY !!

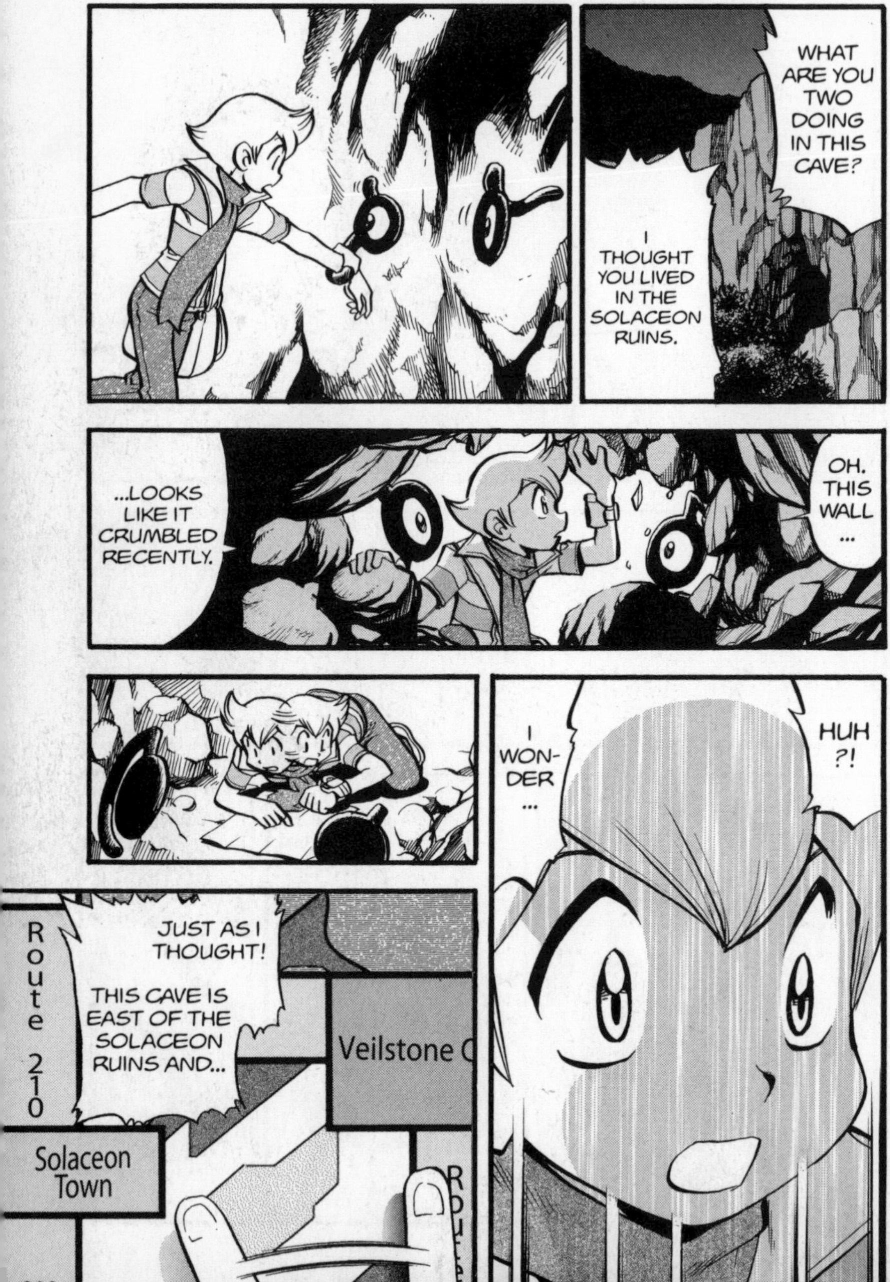
WHAT ARE YOU TWO DOING IN THIS CAVE?
I THOUGHT YOU LIVED IN THE SOLACEON RUINS.
OH. THIS WALL ...
...LOOKS LIKE IT CRUMBLED RECENTLY.
HUH ?!
I WONDER ...
JUST AS I THOUGHT!
THIS CAVE IS EAST OF THE SOLACEON RUINS AND...
Route 210
Veilstone
Solaceon Town

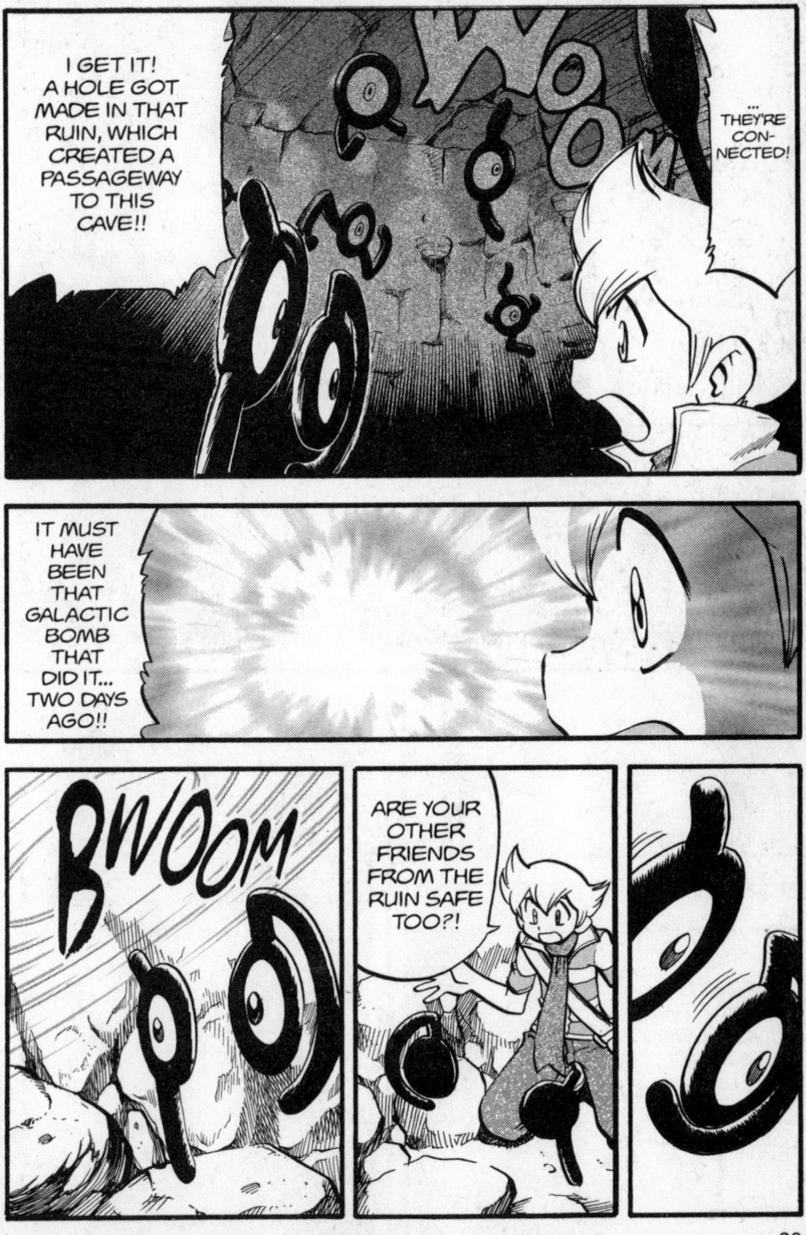
... THEY'RE CON-NECTED!
I GET IT! A HOLE GOT MADE IN THAT RUIN, WHICH CREATED A PASSAGEWAY TO THIS CAVE!!
IT MUST HAVE BEEN THAT GALACTIC BOMB THAT DID IT... TWO DAYS AGO!!
ARE YOUR OTHER FRIENDS FROM THE RUIN SAFE TOO?!
BWOOM

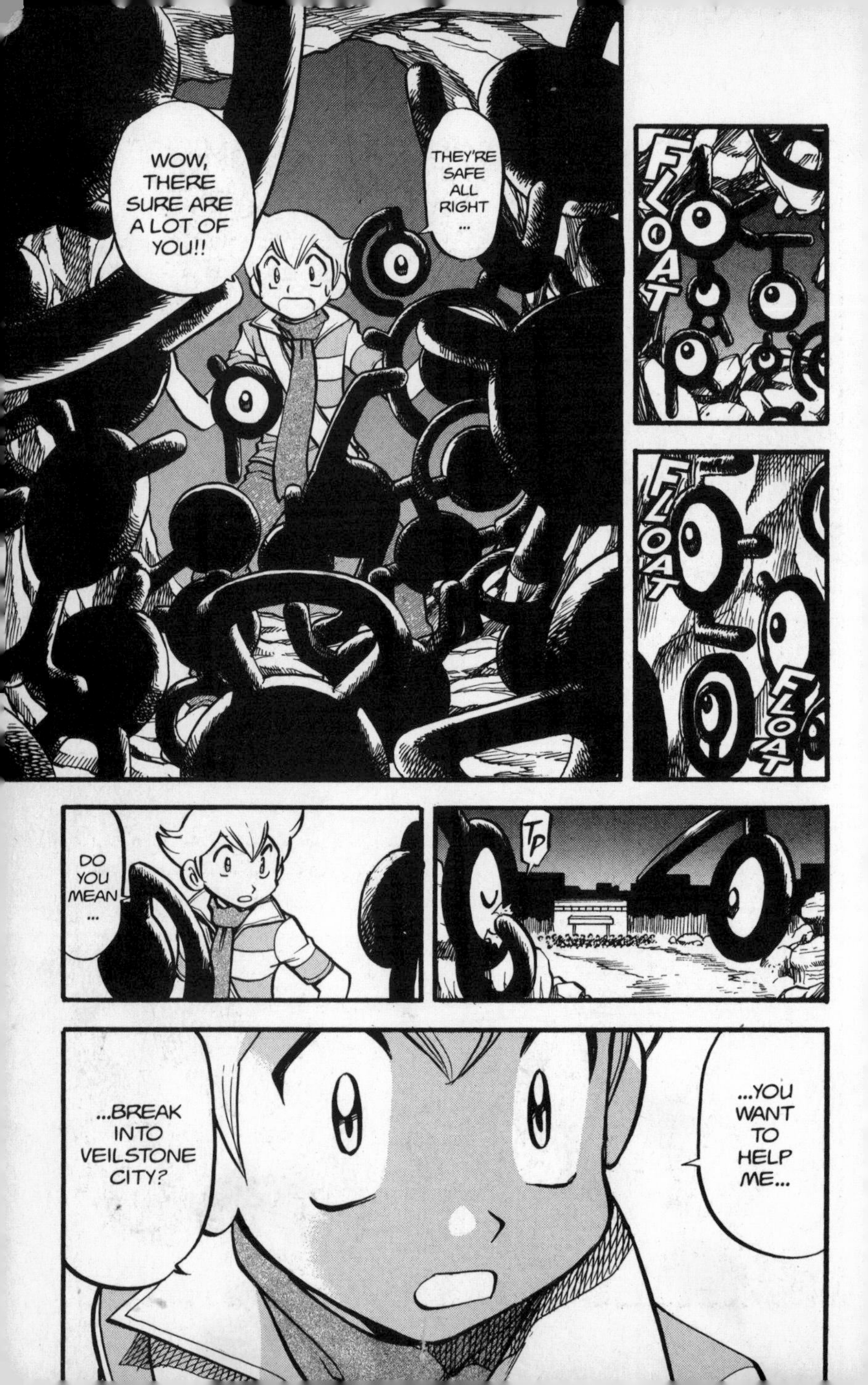
FLOAT
FLOAT
FLOAT
THEY'RE SAFE ALL RIGHT ...
WOW, THERE SURE ARE A LOT OF YOU!!
TP
DO YOU MEAN ...
...YOU WANT TO HELP ME...
...BREAK INTO VEILSTONE CITY?

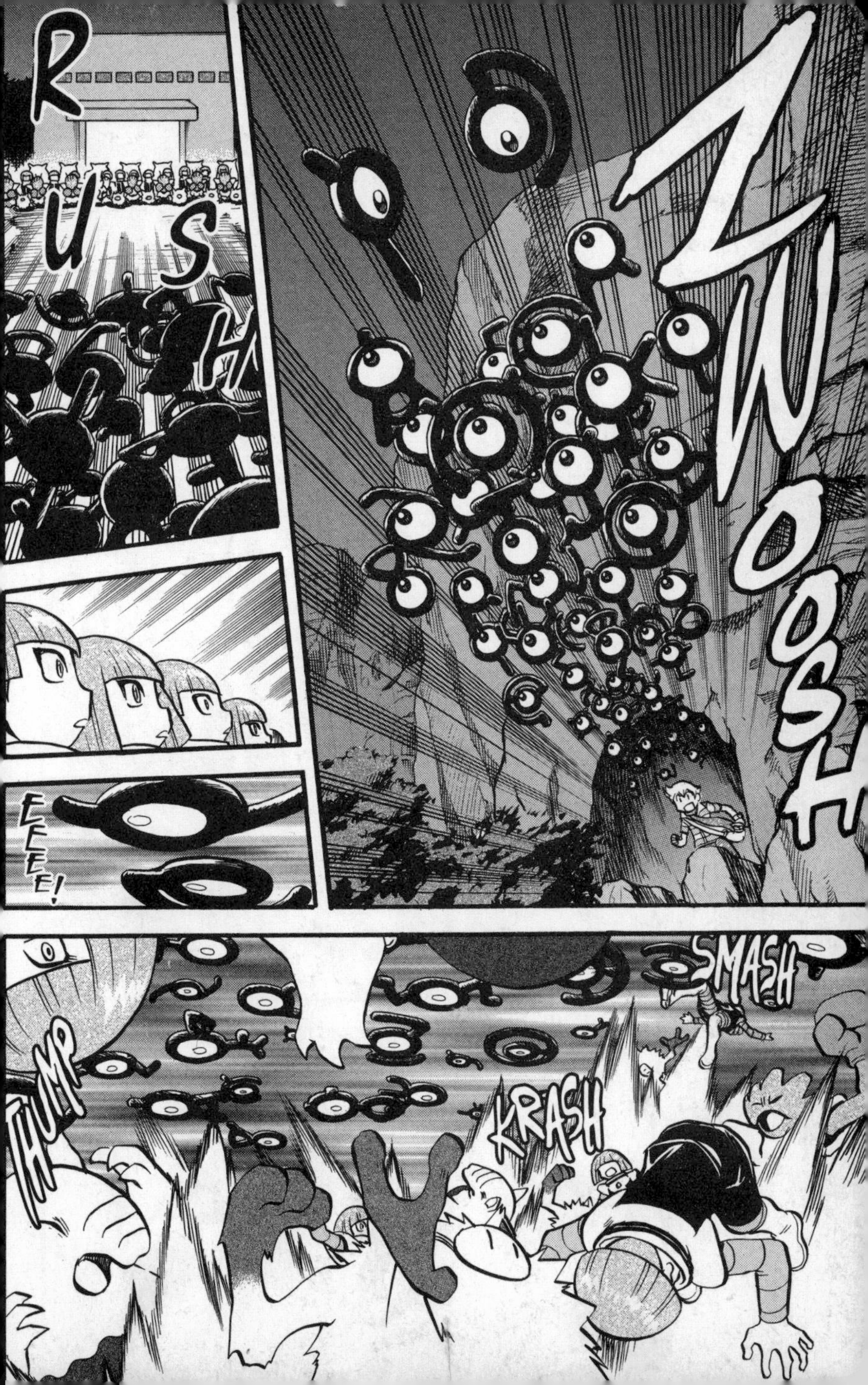
ZWOOSH
RUSH
EEEEE!
SMASH
KRASH
THUMP

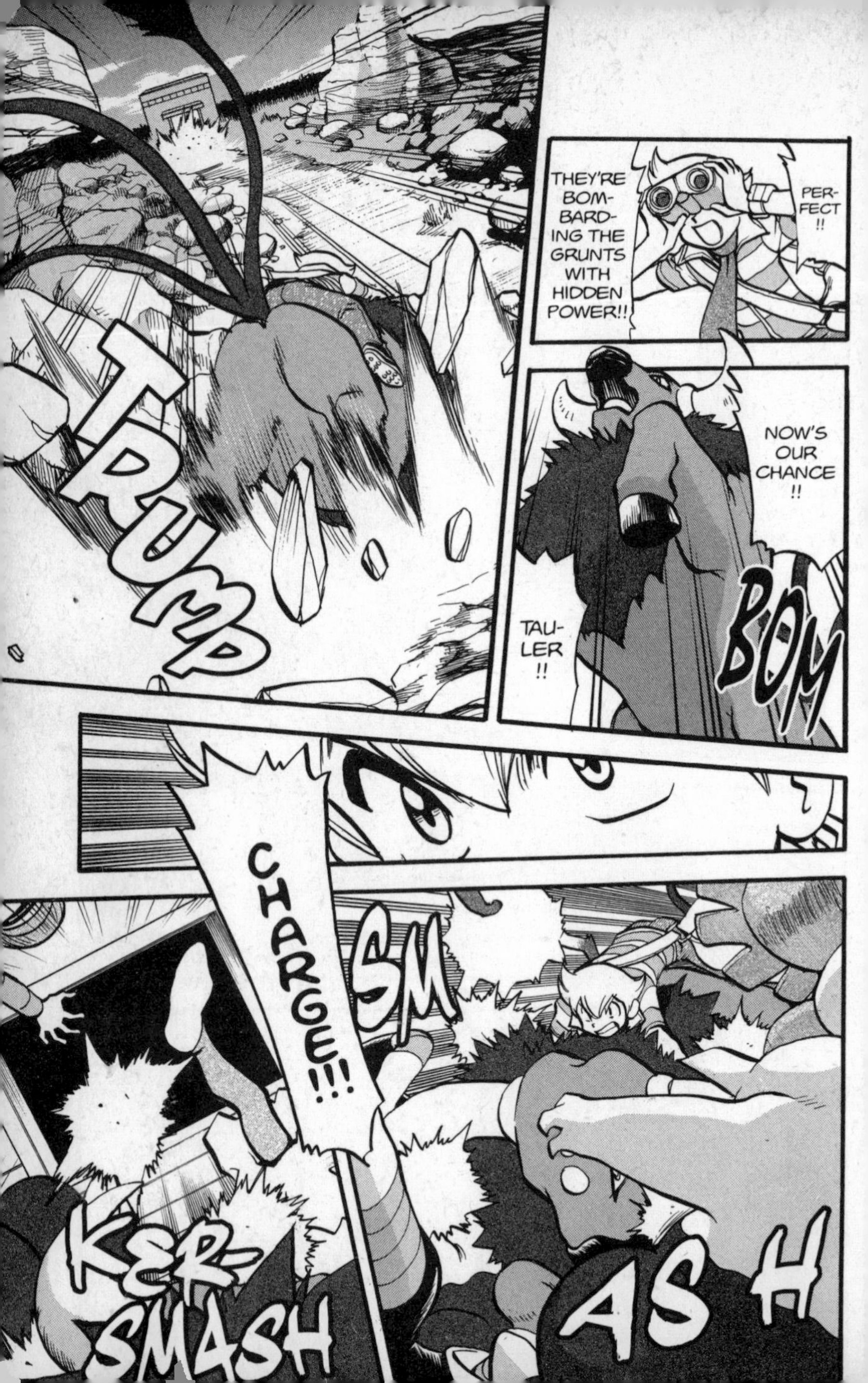
PER-
FECT
!!
THEY'RE BOM-BARD-ING THE GRUNTS WITH HIDDEN POWER!!
NOW'S OUR CHANCE !!
BOM
TAU-
LER
!!
TRUMP
CHARGE!!!
SM
AS H
KER-
SMASH

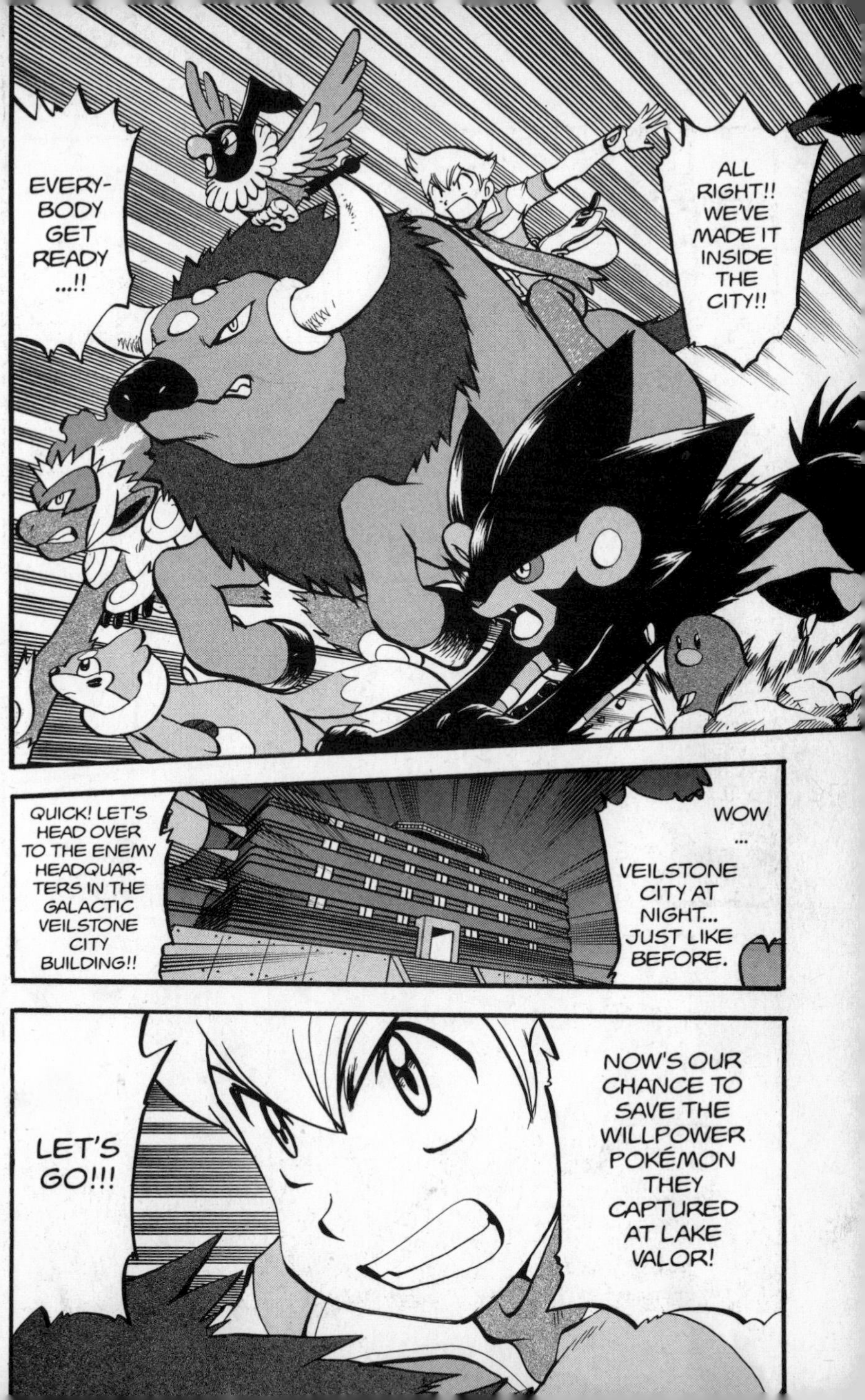
ALL RIGHT!! WE'VE MADE IT INSIDE THE CITY!!
EVERY-BODY GET READY ...!!
WOW ... VEILSTONE CITY AT NIGHT... JUST LIKE BEFORE.
QUICK! LET'S HEAD OVER TO THE ENEMY HEADQUAR-TERS IN THE GALACTIC VEILSTONE CITY BUILDING!!
NOW'S OUR CHANCE TO SAVE THE WILLPOWER POKÉMON THEY CAPTURED AT LAKE VALOR!
LET'S GO!!!

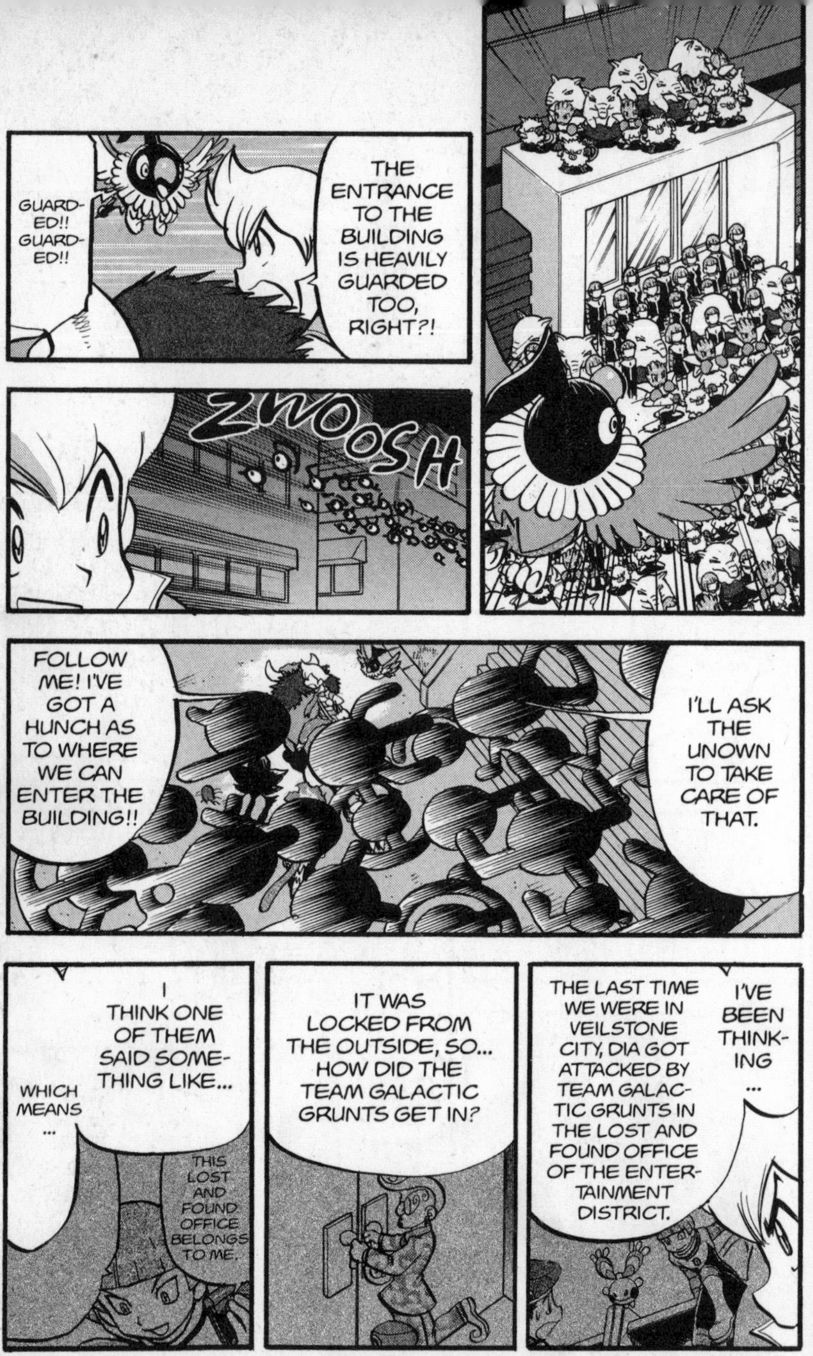
THE ENTRANCE TO THE BUILDING IS HEAVILY GUARDED TOO, RIGHT?!
GUARD-ED!! GUARD-ED!!
ZWOOSH
I'LL ASK THE UNOWN TO TAKE CARE OF THAT.
FOLLOW ME! I'VE GOT A HUNCH AS TO WHERE WE CAN ENTER THE BUILDING!!
I'VE BEEN THINKING...
THE LAST TIME WE WERE IN VEILSTONE CITY, DIA GOT ATTACKED BY TEAM GALACTIC GRUNTS IN THE LOST AND FOUND OFFICE OF THE ENTERTAINMENT DISTRICT.
IT WAS LOCKED FROM THE OUTSIDE, SO... HOW DID THE TEAM GALACTIC GRUNTS GET IN?
I THINK ONE OF THEM SAID SOMETHING LIKE...
THIS LOST AND FOUND OFFICE BELONGS TO ME.
WHICH MEANS...

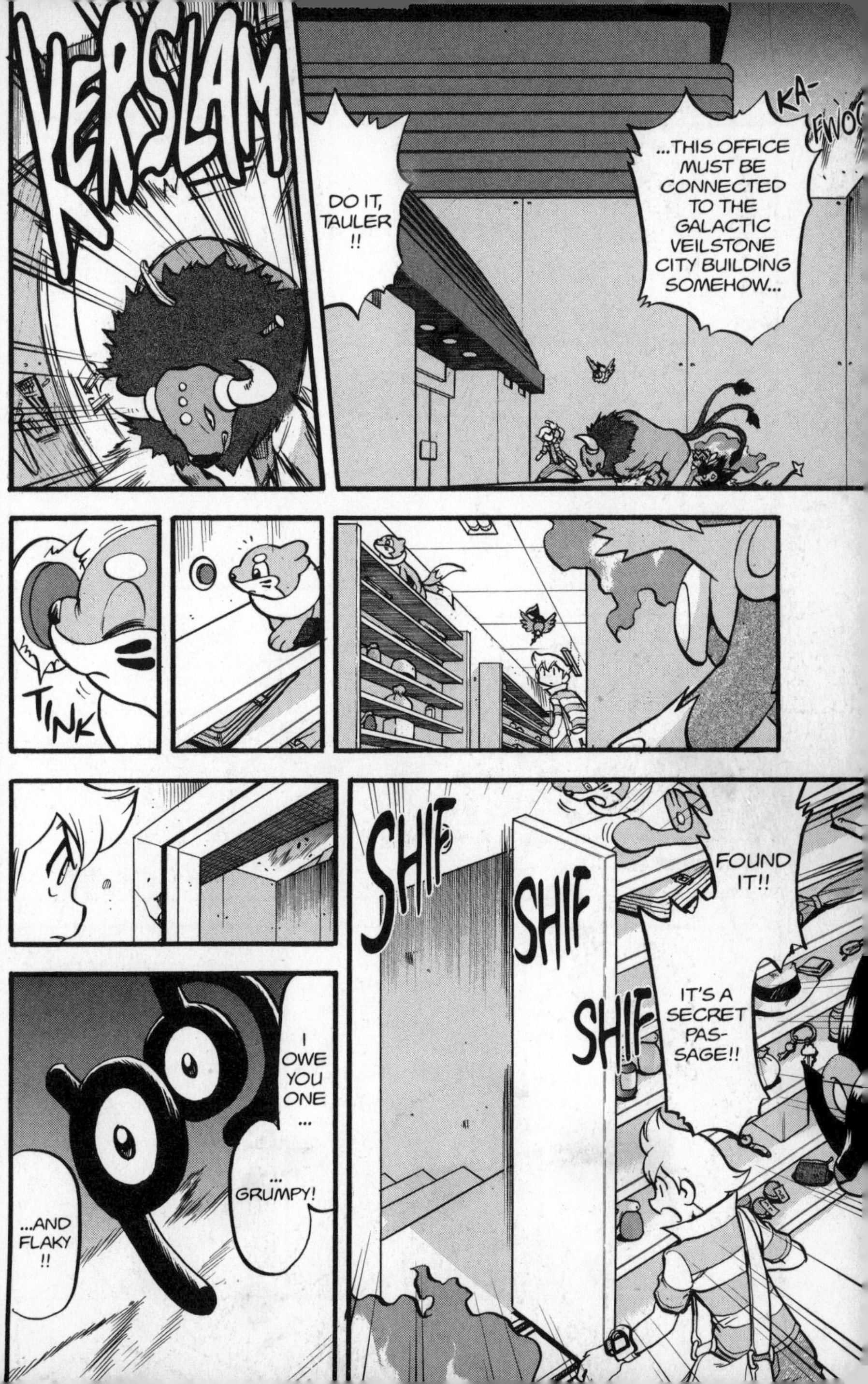
KA-
FWOO
...THIS OFFICE MUST BE CONNECTED TO THE GALACTIC VEILSTONE CITY BUILDING SOMEHOW...
DO IT, TAULER!!
KERSLAM
TINK
SHIF
FOUND IT!!
SHIF
IT'S A SECRET PAS-SAGE!!
SHIF
I OWE YOU ONE...
...GRUMPY!
...AND FLAKY!!

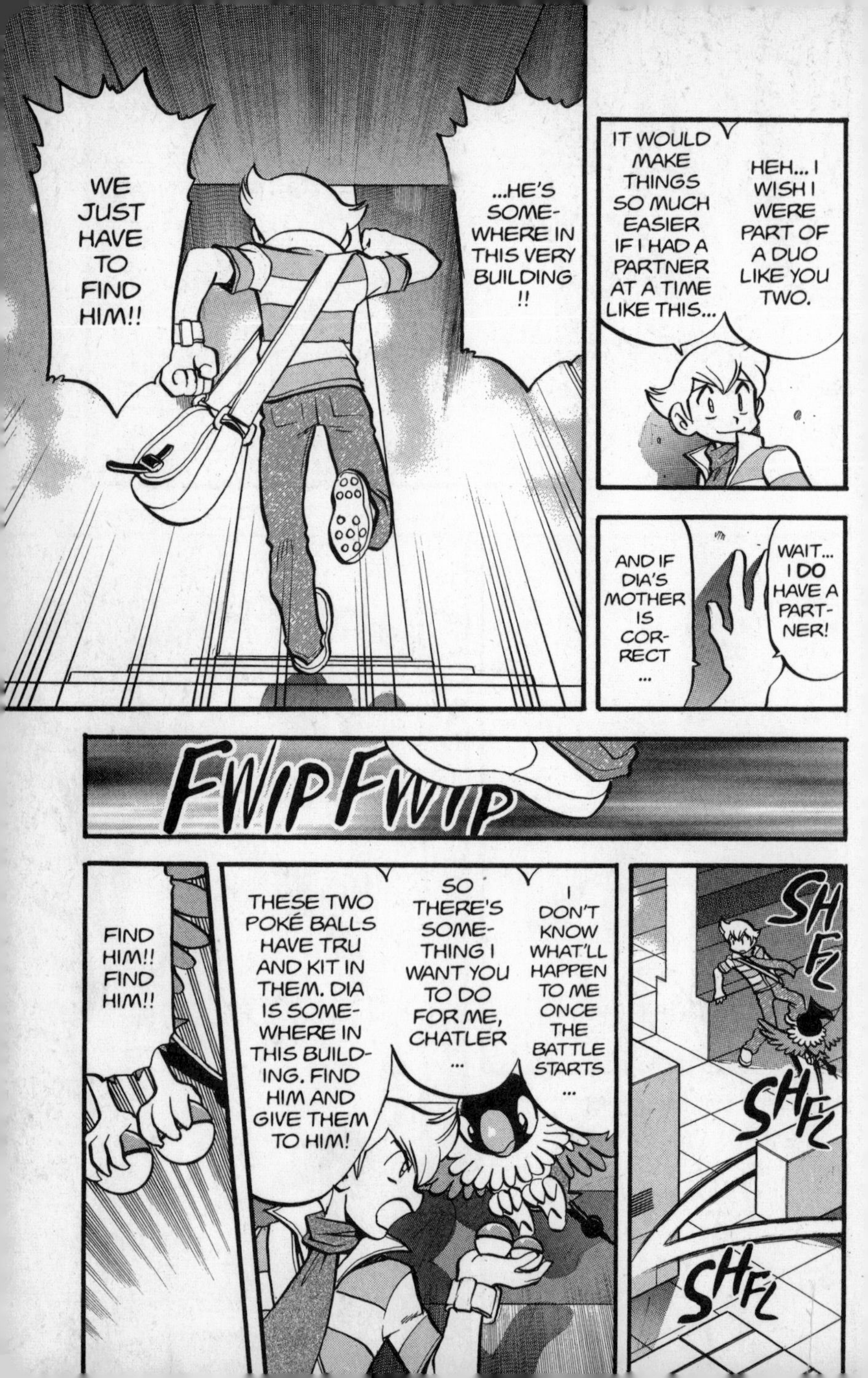
HEH... I WISH I WERE PART OF A DUO LIKE YOU TWO.
IT WOULD MAKE THINGS SO MUCH EASIER IF I HAD A PARTNER AT A TIME LIKE THIS...
WAIT... I DO HAVE A PART-NER!
AND IF DIA'S MOTHER IS COR-RECT...
...HE'S SOME-WHERE IN THIS VERY BUILDING!!
WE JUST HAVE TO FIND HIM!!
FWIP FWIP
SHFL
SHFL
SHFL
I DON'T KNOW WHAT'LL HAPPEN TO ME ONCE THE BATTLE STARTS...
SO THERE'S SOME-THING I WANT YOU TO DO FOR ME, CHATLER...
THESE TWO POKÉ BALLS HAVE TRU AND KIT IN THEM. DIA IS SOME-WHERE IN THIS BUILD-ING. FIND HIM AND GIVE THEM TO HIM!
FIND HIM!! FIND HIM!!

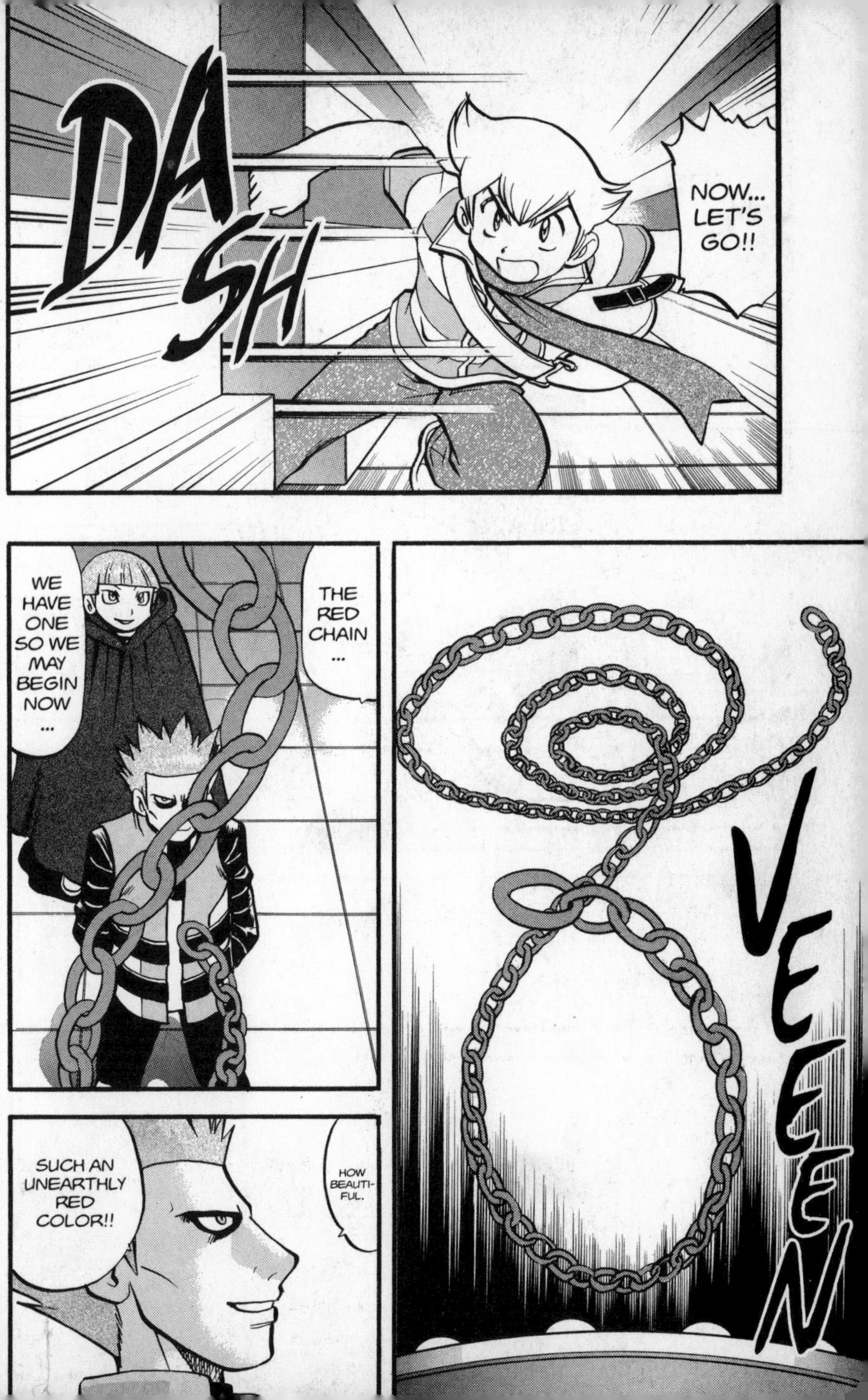
NOW... LET'S GO!!
DASH
VEEEEN
THE RED CHAIN...
WE HAVE ONE SO WE MAY BEGIN NOW...
HOW BEAUTIFUL.
SUCH AN UNEARTHLY RED COLOR!!

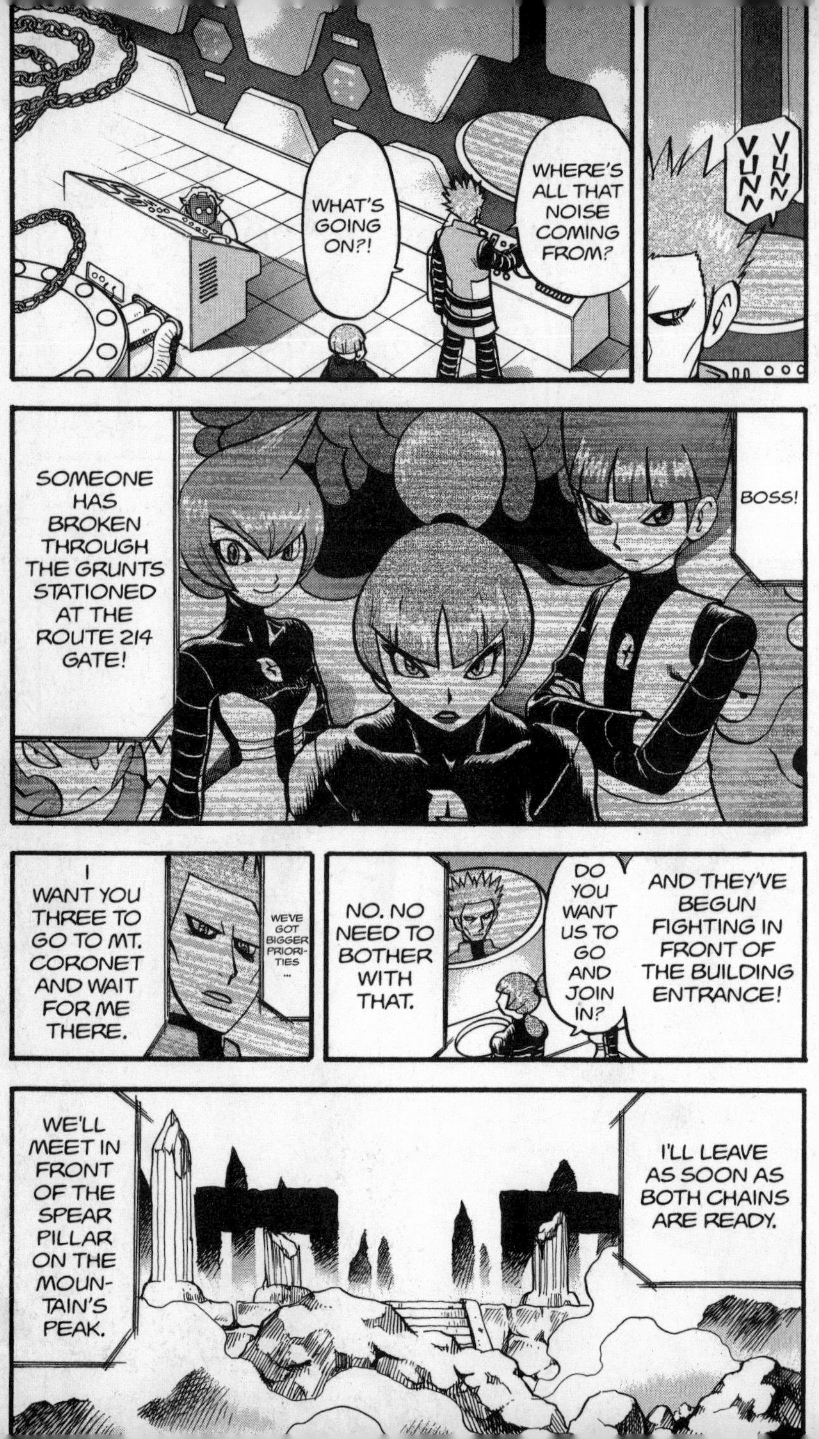
VUNN
VUNN
WHERE'S ALL THAT NOISE COMING FROM?
WHAT'S GOING ON?!
BOSS!
SOMEONE HAS BROKEN THROUGH THE GRUNTS STATIONED AT THE ROUTE 214 GATE!
AND THEY'VE BEGUN FIGHTING IN FRONT OF THE BUILDING ENTRANCE!
DO YOU WANT US TO GO AND JOIN IN?
NO. NO NEED TO BOTHER WITH THAT.
WE'VE GOT BIGGER PRIORITIES...
I WANT YOU THREE TO GO TO MT. CORONET AND WAIT FOR ME THERE.
I'LL LEAVE AS SOON AS BOTH CHAINS ARE READY.
WE'LL MEET IN FRONT OF THE SPEAR PILLAR ON THE MOUNTAIN'S PEAK.

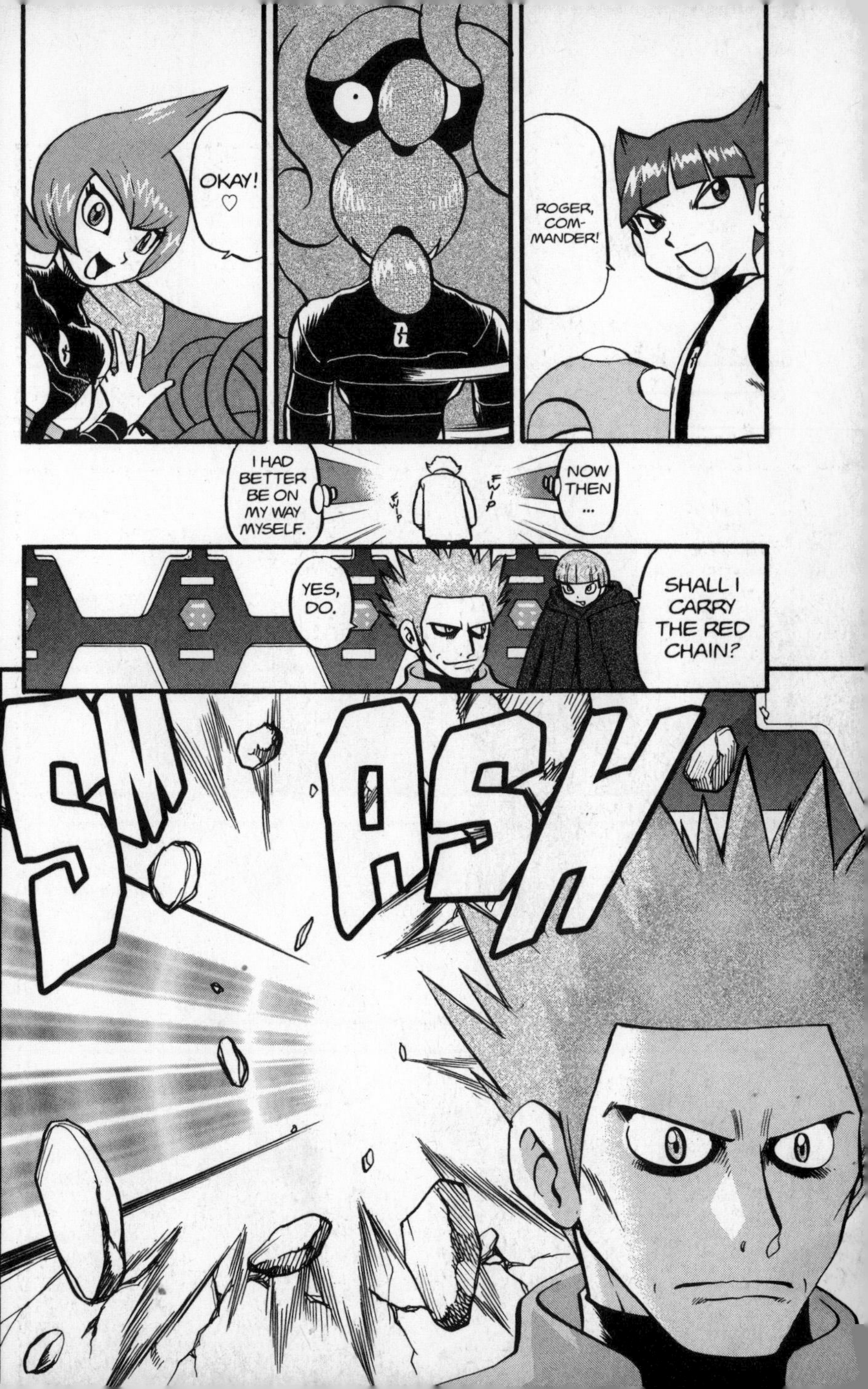
ROGER, COM-MANDER!
OKAY! ♡
NOW THEN ...
FWIP
FWIP
I HAD BETTER BE ON MY WAY MYSELF.
SHALL I CARRY THE RED CHAIN?
YES, DO.
SMASH

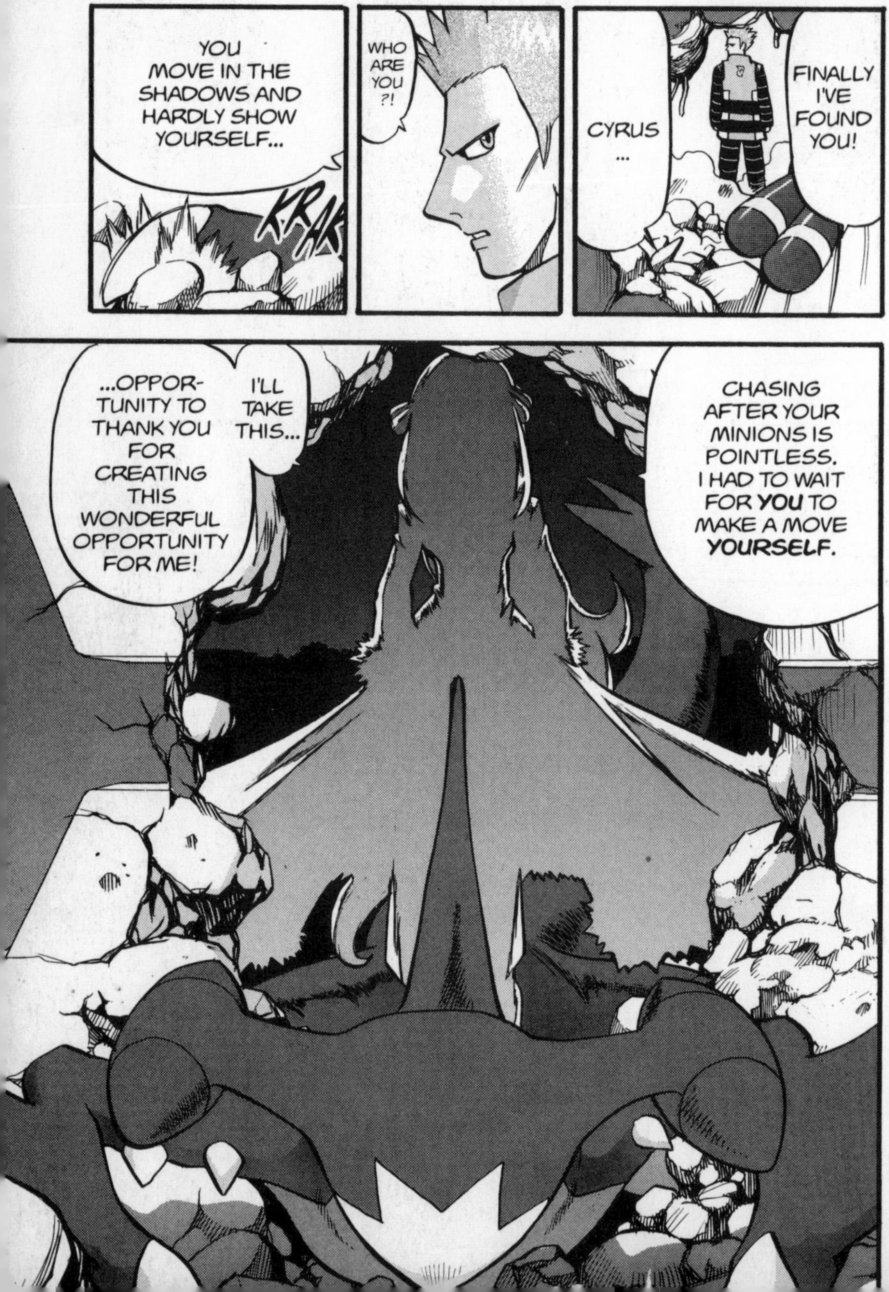
FINALLY I'VE FOUND YOU!
CYRUS ...
WHO ARE YOU ?!
YOU MOVE IN THE SHADOWS AND HARDLY SHOW YOURSELF...
KRAK
CHASING AFTER YOUR MINIONS IS POINTLESS. I HAD TO WAIT FOR YOU TO MAKE A MOVE YOURSELF.
I'LL TAKE THIS...
...OPPOR-TUNITY TO THANK YOU FOR CREATING THIS WONDERFUL OPPORTUNITY FOR ME!

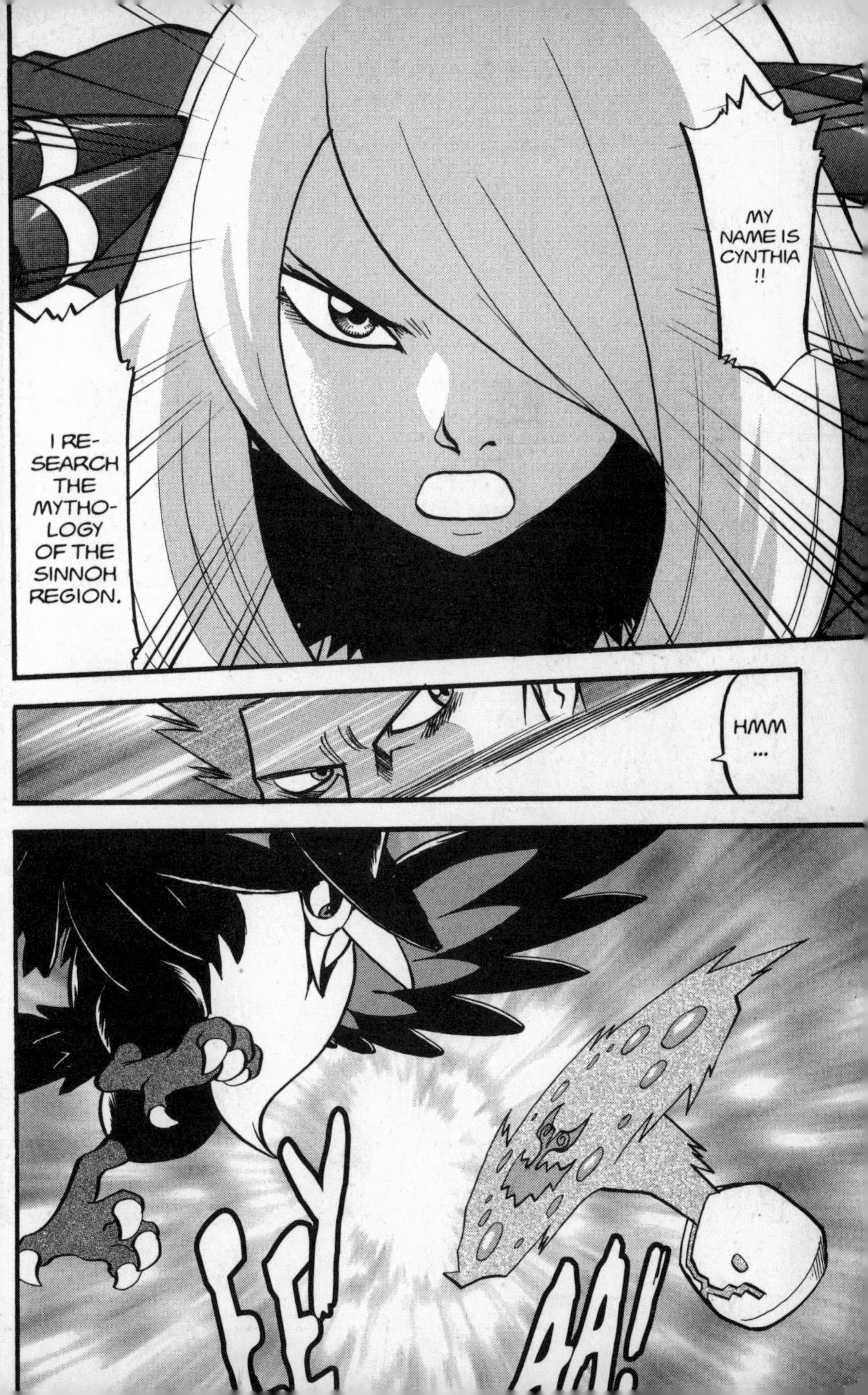
MY NAME IS CYNTHIA !!
I RE-SEARCH THE MYTHOLOGY OF THE SINNOH REGION.
HMM ...

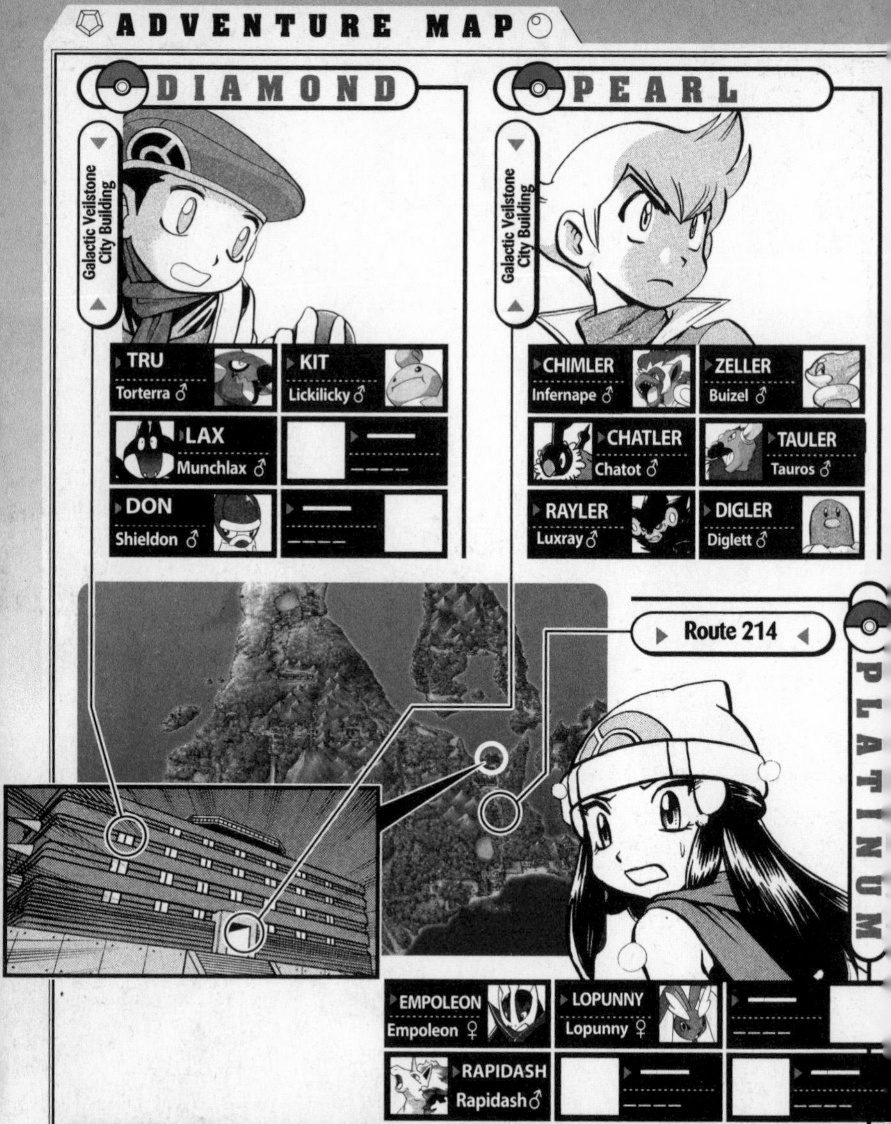
ADVENTURE MAP
DIAMOND
Galactic Veilstone City Building
TRU
Torterra ♂
KIT
Lickilicky ♂
LAX
Munchlax ♂
DON
Shieldon ♂
PEARL
Galactic Veilstone City Building
CHIMLER
Infernape ♂
ZELLER
Buizel ♂
CHATLER
Chatot ♂
TAULER
Tauros ♂
RAYLER
Luxray ♂
DIGLER
Diglett ♂
Route 214
PLATINUM
EMPOLEON
Empoleon ♀
LOPUNNY
Lopunny ♀
RAPIDASH
Rapidash ♂

Oreburgh	Eterna	Veilstone	Pastoria	Hearthome	Canalave	Snowpoint City	Sunyshore Cit
VS Roark	VS Gardenia	VS Maylene	VS Wake	VS Fantina	VS Byron	VS Candice	VS Volker
Coal Badge	Forest Badge	Cobble Badge	Fen Badge	Relic Badge	Mine Badge	Icicle Badge	Beacon Badge

70

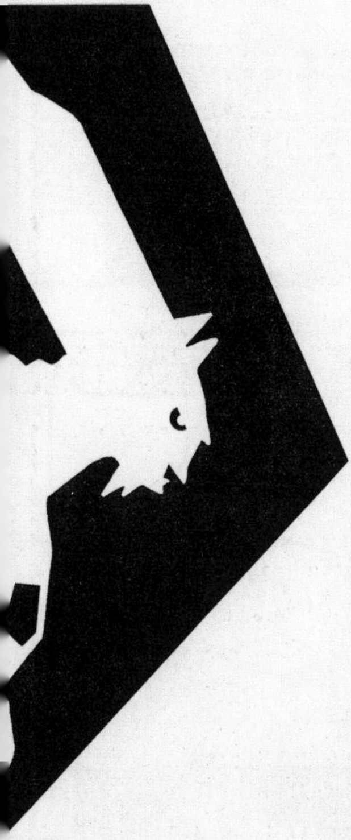

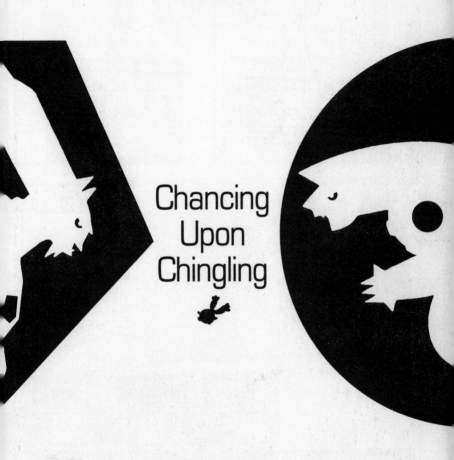

Chancing Upon Chingling

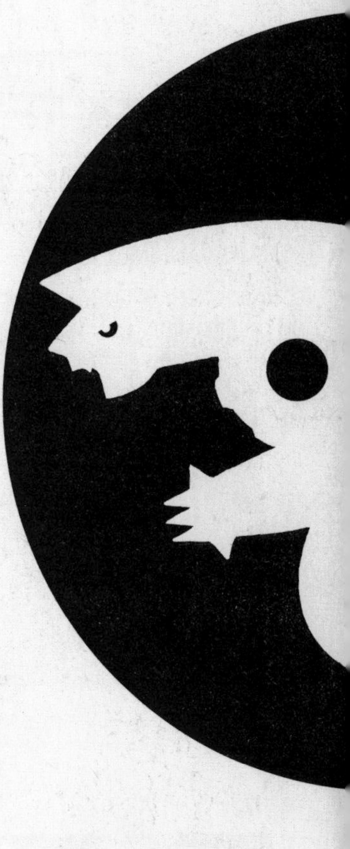

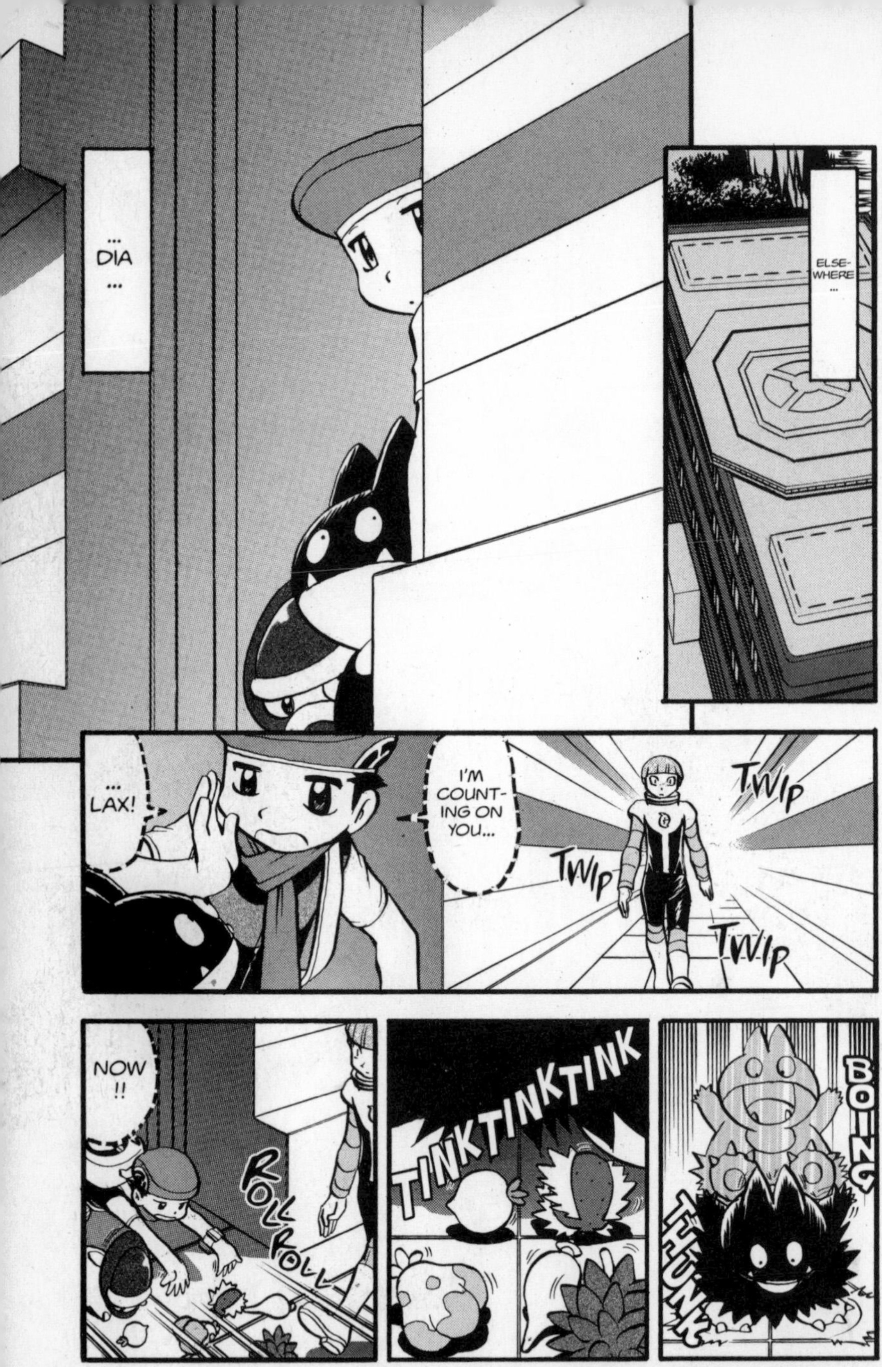
ELSE-WHERE ...
... DIA ...
TWIP
TWIP
TWIP
I'M COUNTING ON YOU...
... LAX!
BOING
THUNK
TINKTINKTINK
NOW !!
ROLL ROLL

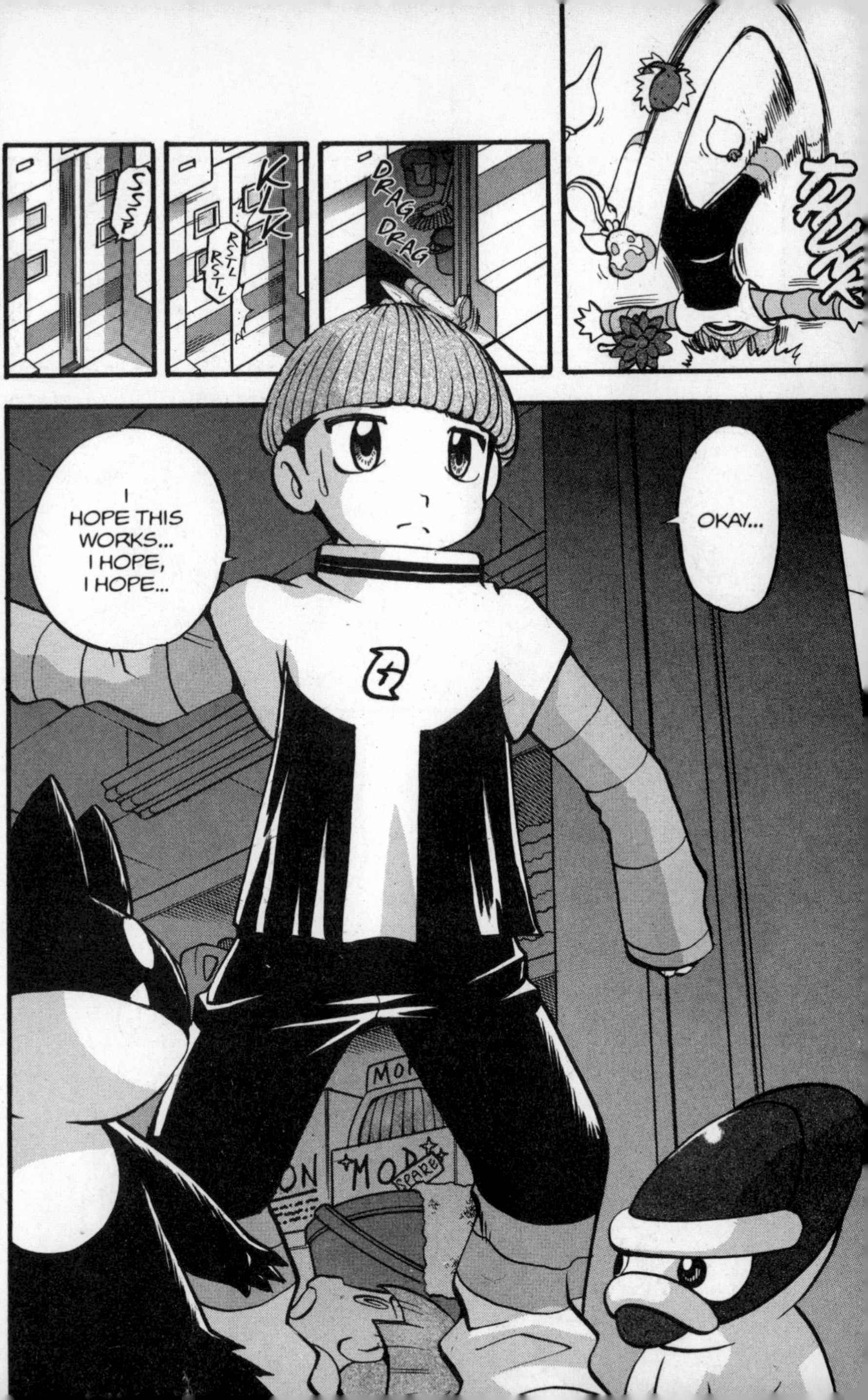
THUNK
DRAG DRAG
KLK
RSTL RSTL
SSSP
OKAY...
I HOPE THIS WORKS... I HOPE, I HOPE...
MOD
SPARE

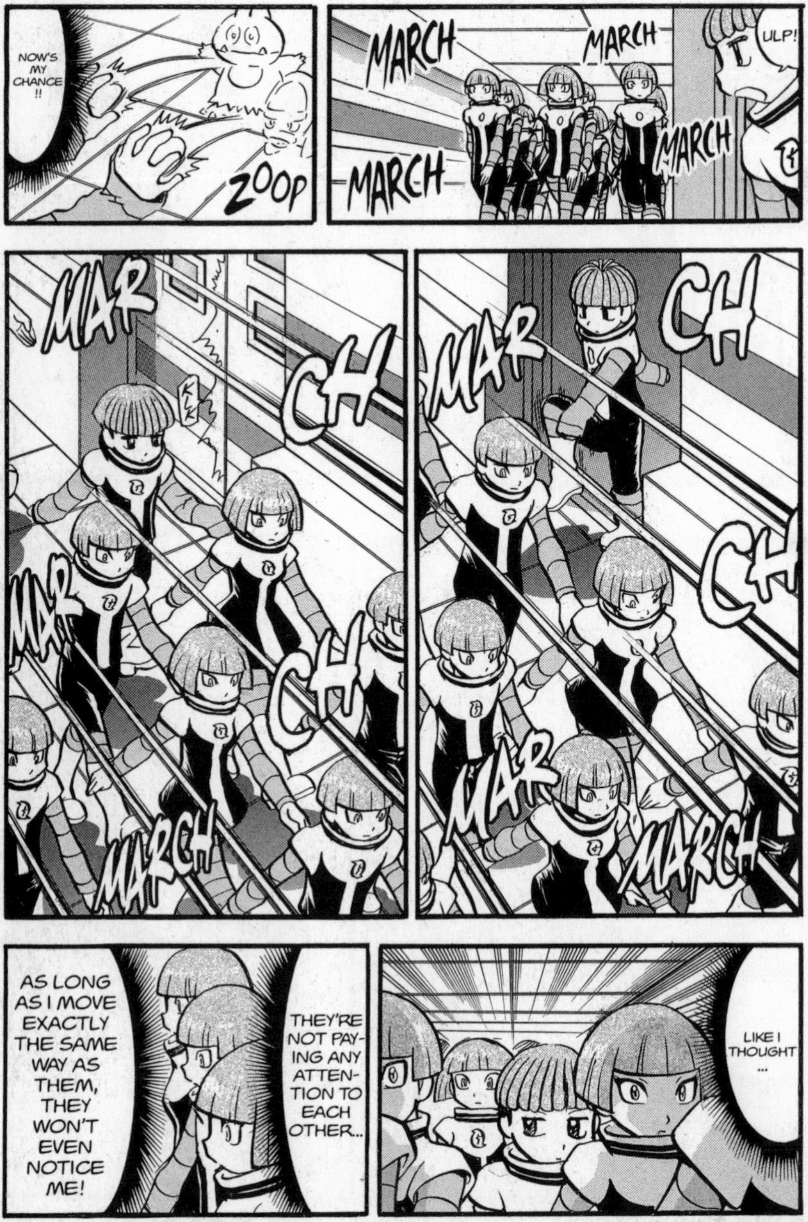
ULP!
MARCH
MARCH
MARCH
MARCH
NOW'S MY CHANCE!!
ZOOP
MAR CH
CH
MAR MARCH
MAR CH
MAR CH
MARCH
LIKE I THOUGHT...
THEY'RE NOT PAYING ANY ATTENTION TO EACH OTHER...
AS LONG AS I MOVE EXACTLY THE SAME WAY AS THEM, THEY WON'T EVEN NOTICE ME!

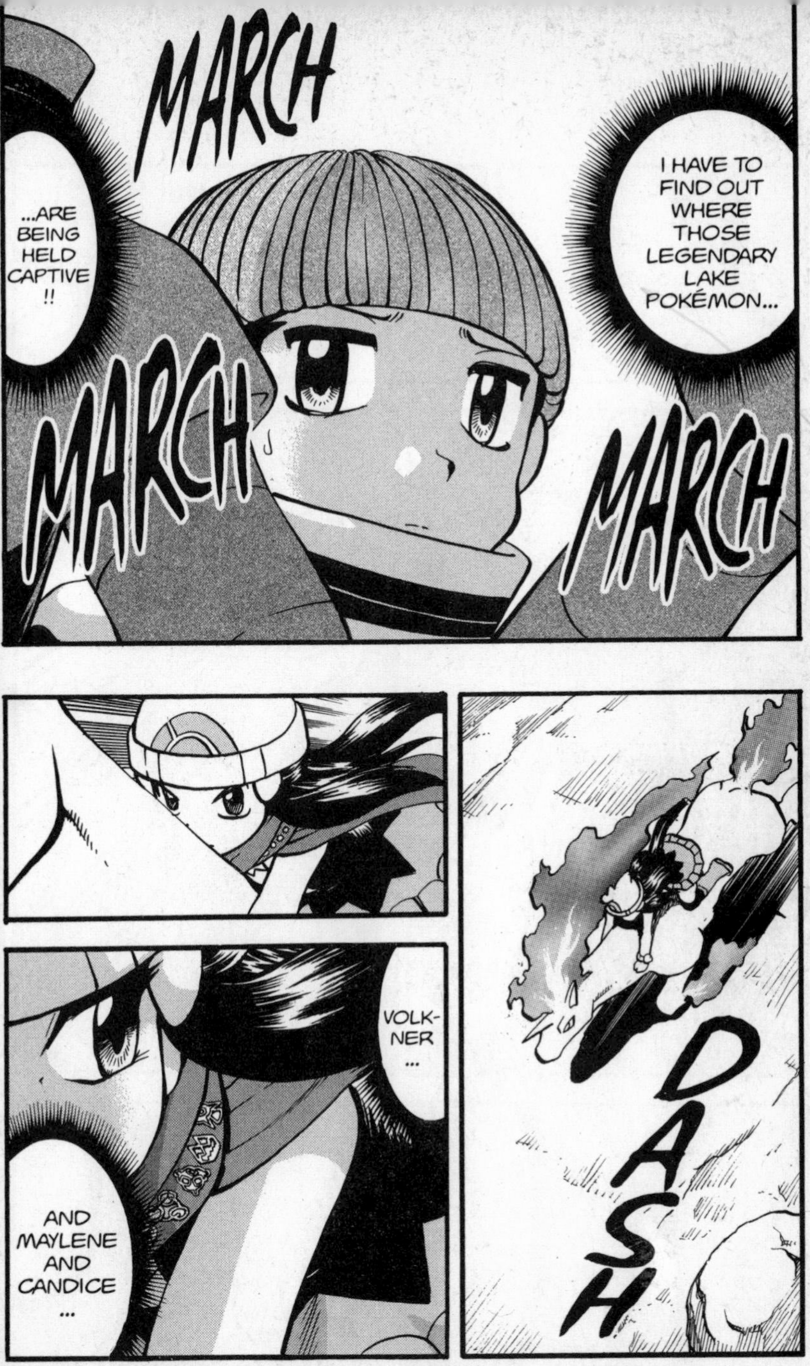
I HAVE TO FIND OUT WHERE THOSE LEGENDARY LAKE POKÉMON...
MARCH
...ARE BEING HELD CAPTIVE !!
MARCH
MARCH
DASH
VOLKNER...
AND MAYLENE AND CANDICE...

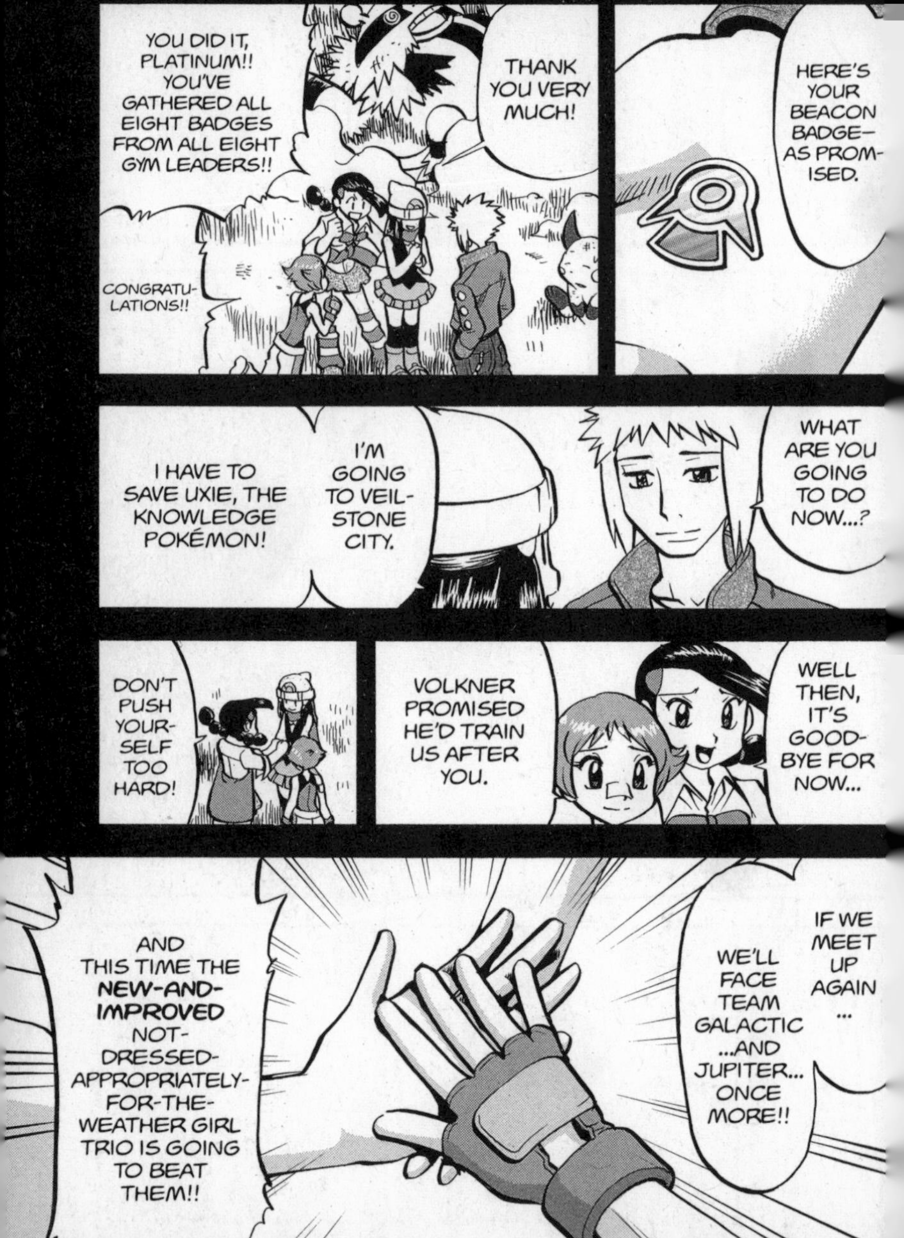
HERE'S YOUR BEACON BADGE—AS PROMISED.
THANK YOU VERY MUCH!
YOU DID IT, PLATINUM!! YOU'VE GATHERED ALL EIGHT BADGES FROM ALL EIGHT GYM LEADERS!!
CONGRATULATIONS!!
WHAT ARE YOU GOING TO DO NOW...?
I'M GOING TO VEILSTONE CITY.
I HAVE TO SAVE UXIE, THE KNOWLEDGE POKÉMON!
WELL THEN, IT'S GOOD-BYE FOR NOW...
VOLKNER PROMISED HE'D TRAIN US AFTER YOU.
DON'T PUSH YOURSELF TOO HARD!
IF WE MEET UP AGAIN...
WE'LL FACE TEAM GALACTIC ...AND JUPITER... ONCE MORE!!
AND THIS TIME THE **NEW-AND-IMPROVED** NOT-DRESSED-APPROPRIATELY-FOR-THE-WEATHER GIRL TRIO IS GOING TO BEAT THEM!!

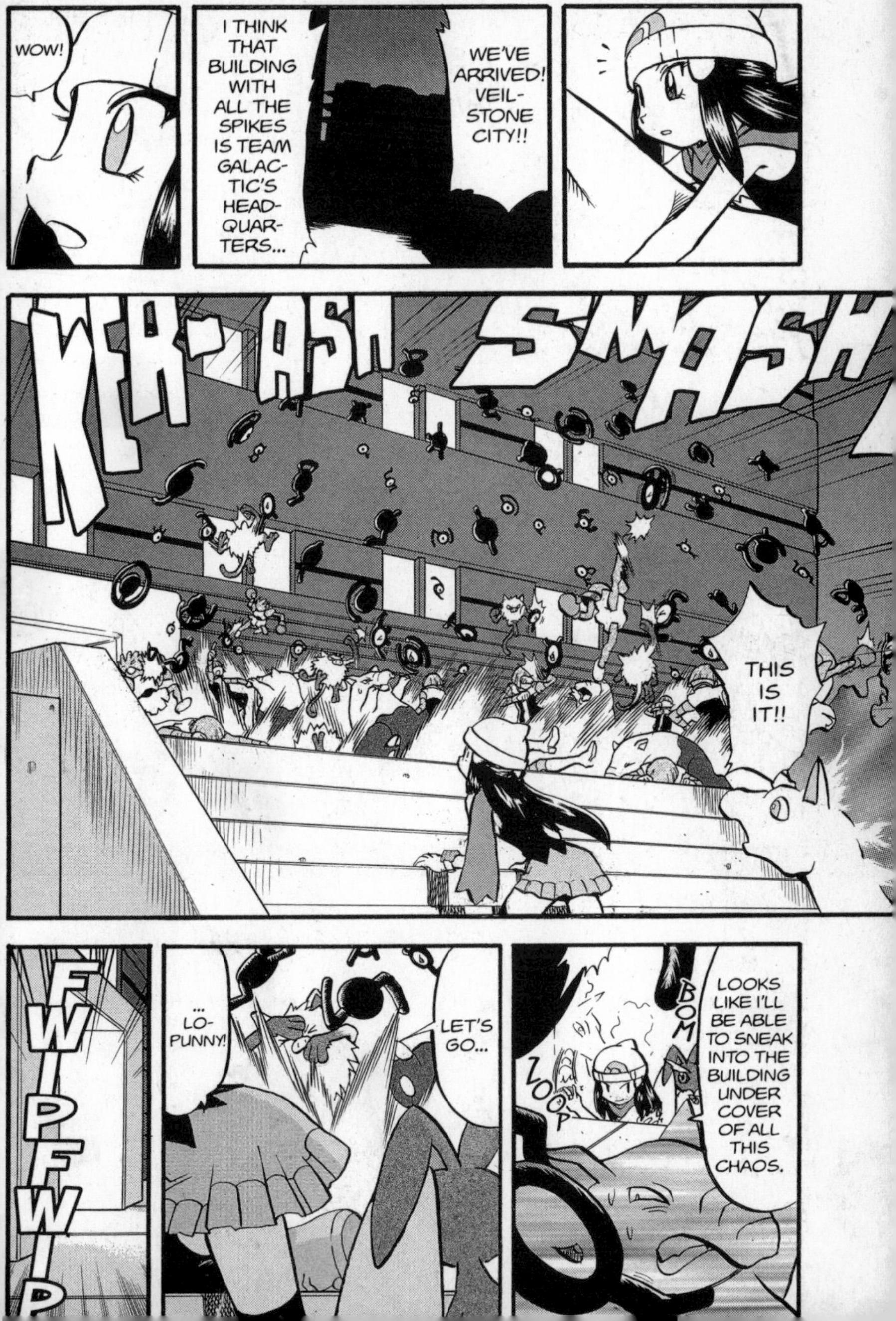
WE'VE ARRIVED! VEIL-STONE CITY!!
I THINK THAT BUILDING WITH ALL THE SPIKES IS TEAM GALAC-TIC'S HEAD-QUAR-TERS...
WOW!
SMASH
KER-ASH
THIS IS IT!!
BOM
LOOKS LIKE I'LL BE ABLE TO SNEAK INTO THE BUILDING UNDER COVER OF ALL THIS CHAOS.
ZOOP
LET'S GO...
... LO-PUNNY!
FWIPFWIP

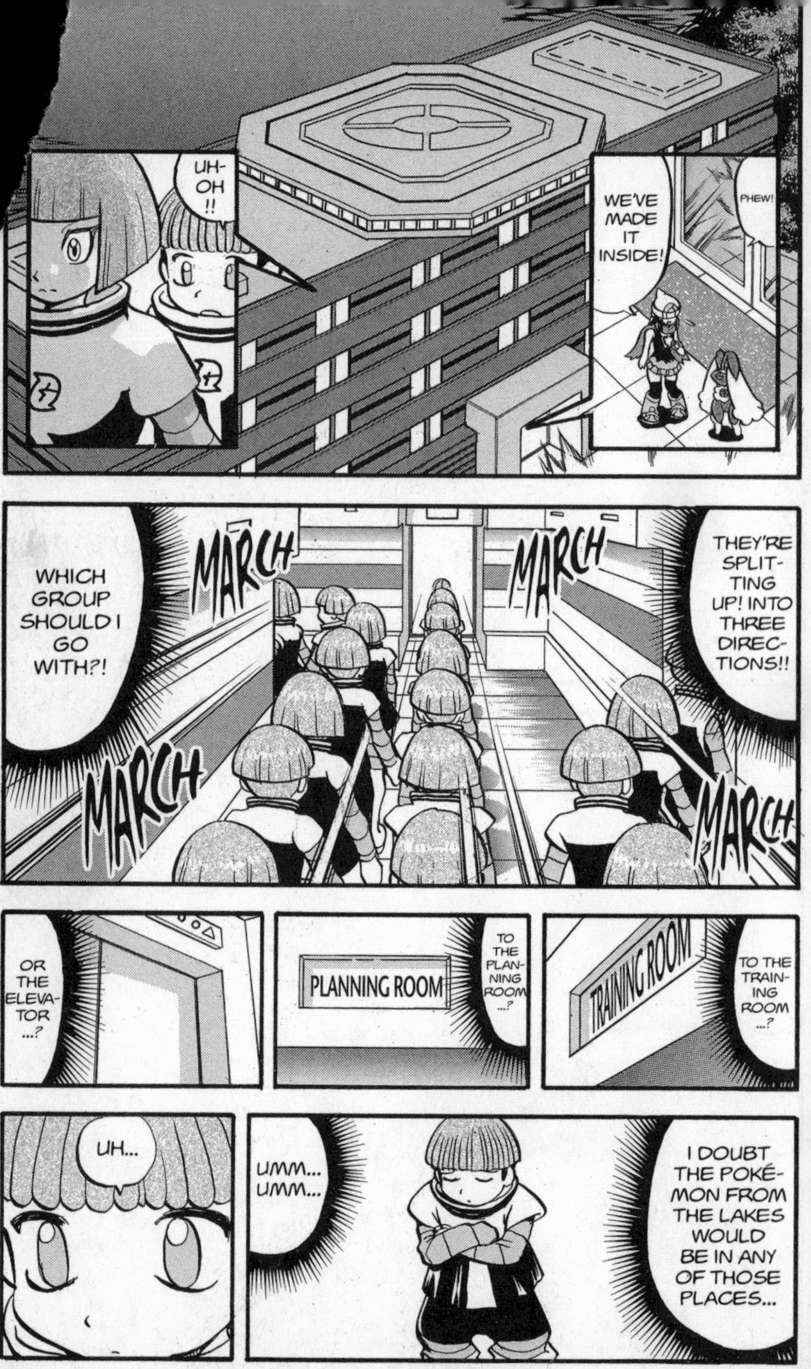
PHEW!
WE'VE MADE IT INSIDE!
UH-OH !!
THEY'RE SPLITTING UP! INTO THREE DIRECTIONS!!
MARCH
MARCH
WHICH GROUP SHOULD I GO WITH?!
MARCH
MARCH
TRAINING ROOM
TO THE TRAINING ROOM ...?
TO THE PLANNING ROOM ...?
PLANNING ROOM
OR THE ELEVATOR ...?
I DOUBT THE POKÉMON FROM THE LAKES WOULD BE IN ANY OF THOSE PLACES...
UMM... UMM...
UH...

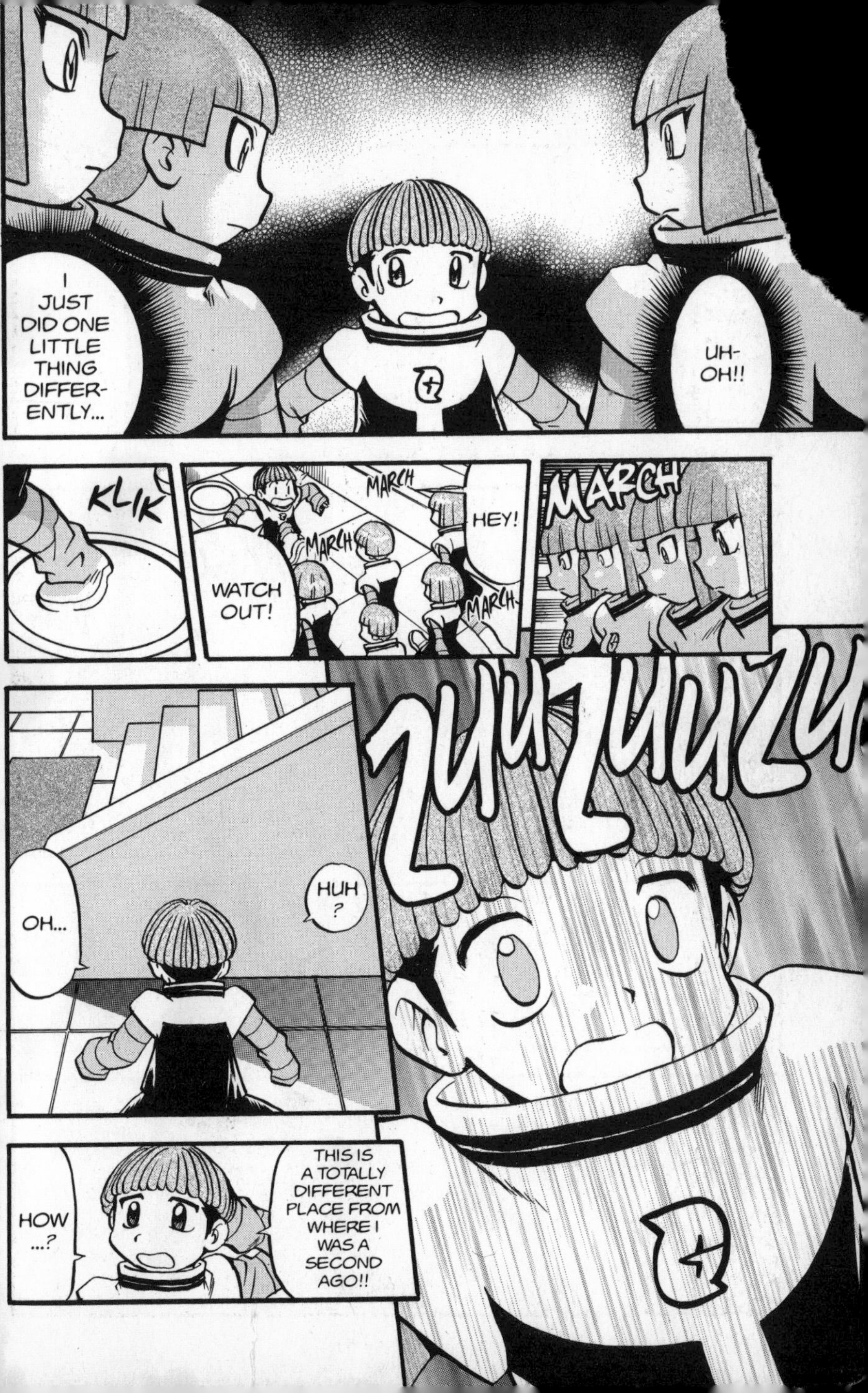
UH-OH!!
I JUST DID ONE LITTLE THING DIFFERENTLY...
MARCH
HEY!
MARCH
MARCH
WATCH OUT!
MARCH
KLIK
ZUUZUUZU
HUH?
OH...
THIS IS A TOTALLY DIFFERENT PLACE FROM WHERE I WAS A SECOND AGO!!
HOW...?

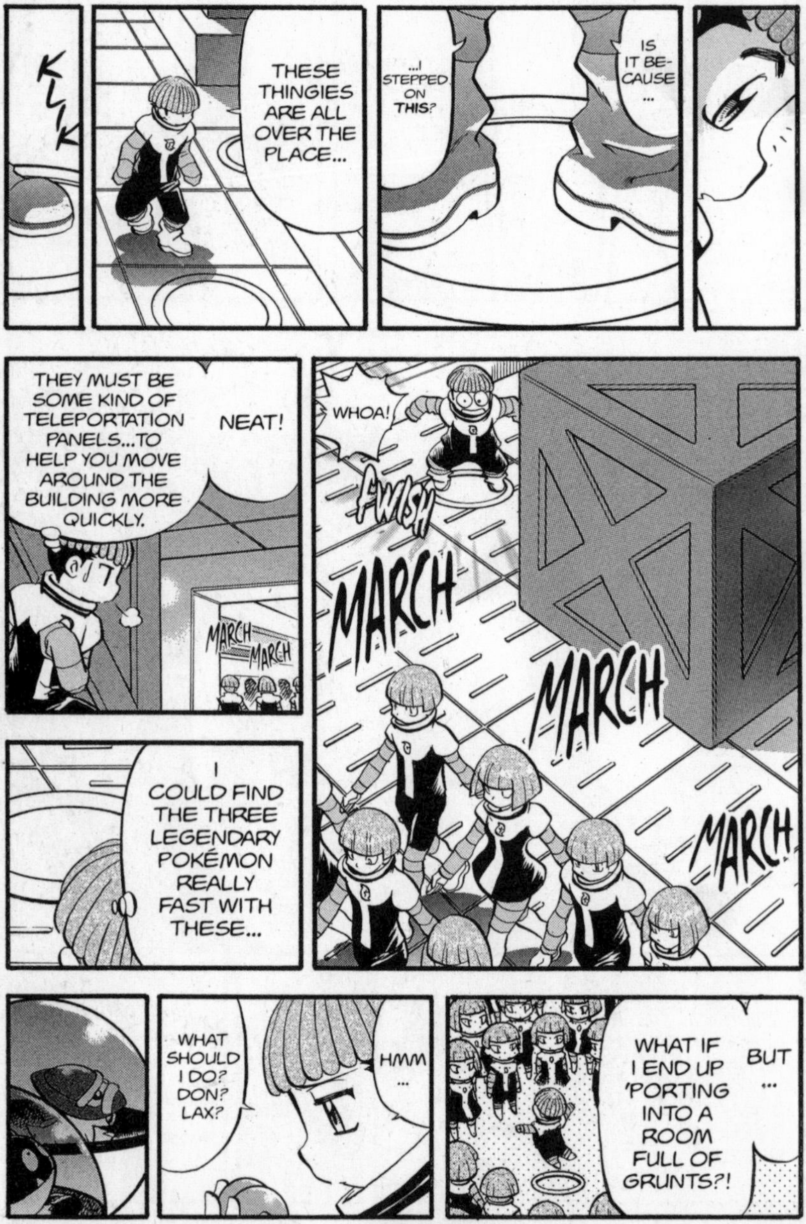
IS IT BE-CAUSE ...
...I STEPPED ON THIS?
THESE THINGIES ARE ALL OVER THE PLACE...
KLIK
WHOA!
FWISH
MARCH
MARCH
MARCH
NEAT!
THEY MUST BE SOME KIND OF TELEPORTATION PANELS...TO HELP YOU MOVE AROUND THE BUILDING MORE QUICKLY.
MARCH MARCH
I COULD FIND THE THREE LEGENDARY POKÉMON REALLY FAST WITH THESE...
BUT ...
WHAT IF I END UP 'PORTING INTO A ROOM FULL OF GRUNTS?!
HMM ...
WHAT SHOULD I DO? DON? LAX?

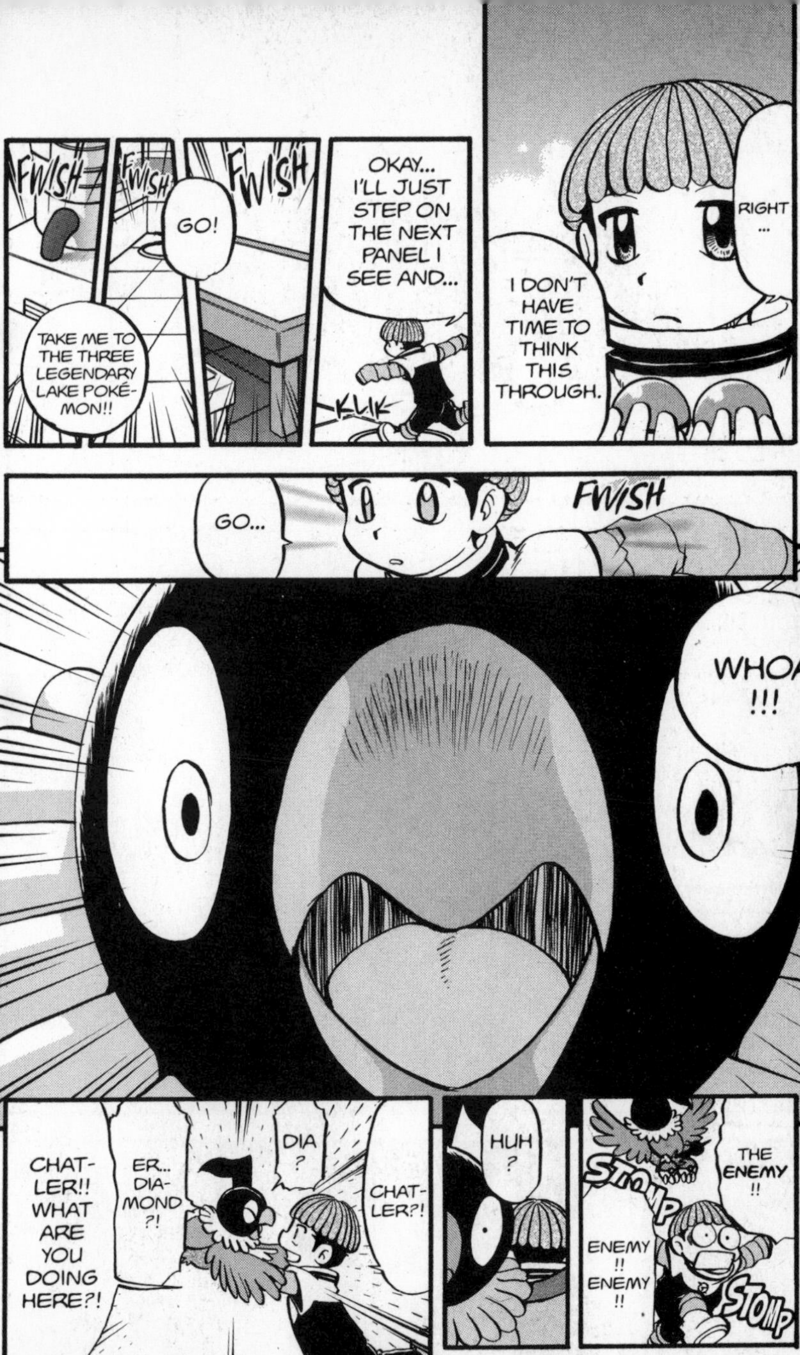
RIGHT ...
I DON'T HAVE TIME TO THINK THIS THROUGH.
OKAY... I'LL JUST STEP ON THE NEXT PANEL I SEE AND...
KLIK
FWISH
GO!
TAKE ME TO THE THREE LEGENDARY LAKE POKÉMON!!
FWISH
FWISH
FWISH
GO...
WHOA !!!
THE ENEMY !!
STOMP
ENEMY !! ENEMY !!
STOMP
HUH ?
CHAT-LER?!
DIA ?
ER... DIA-MOND ?!
CHAT-LER!! WHAT ARE YOU DOING HERE?!

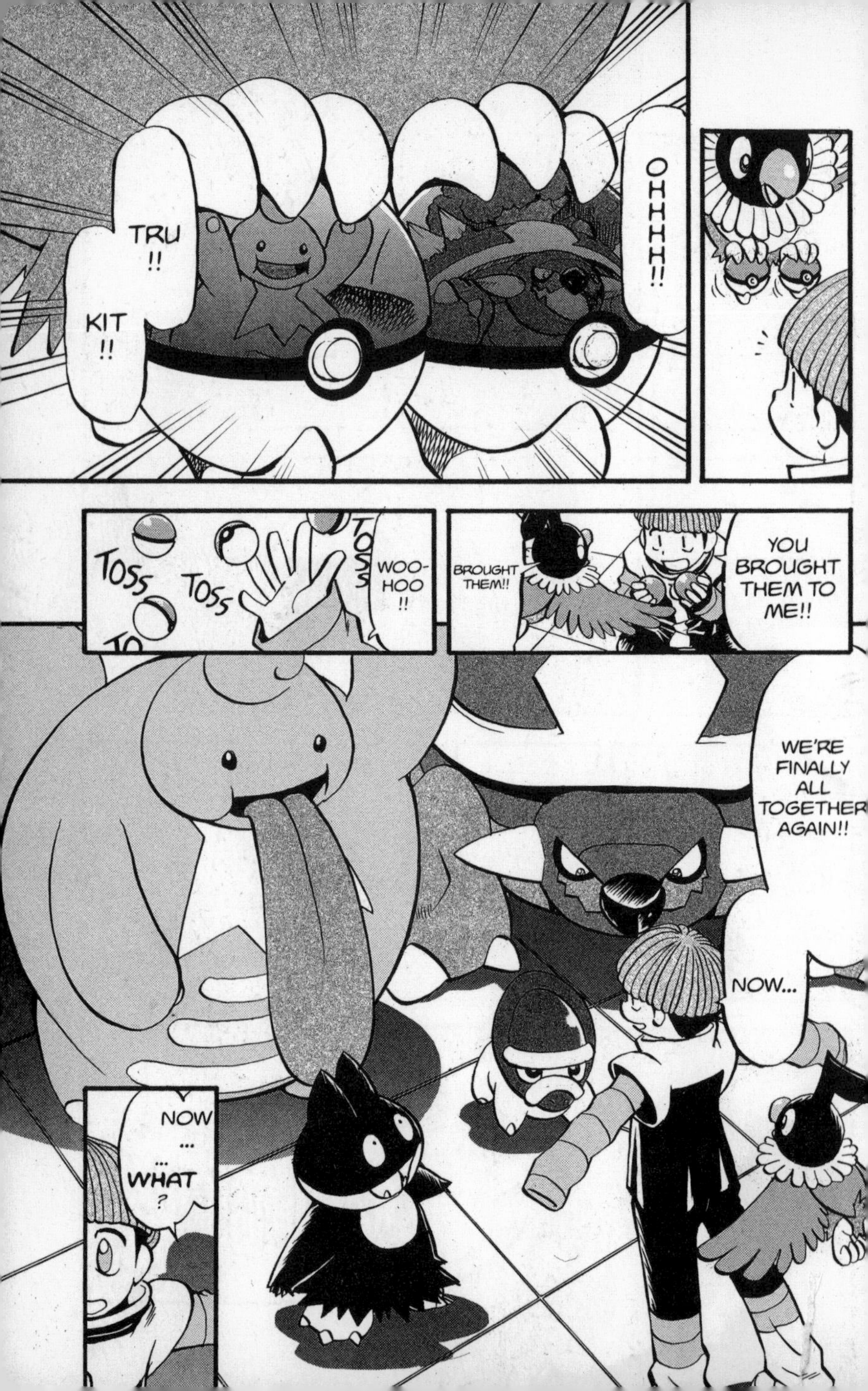
OHHHH!!
TRU!! KIT!!
YOU BROUGHT THEM TO ME!!
BROUGHT THEM!!
WOO-HOO!!
TOSS
TOSS
TOSS
WE'RE FINALLY ALL TOGETHER AGAIN!!
NOW...
NOW... ...WHAT?

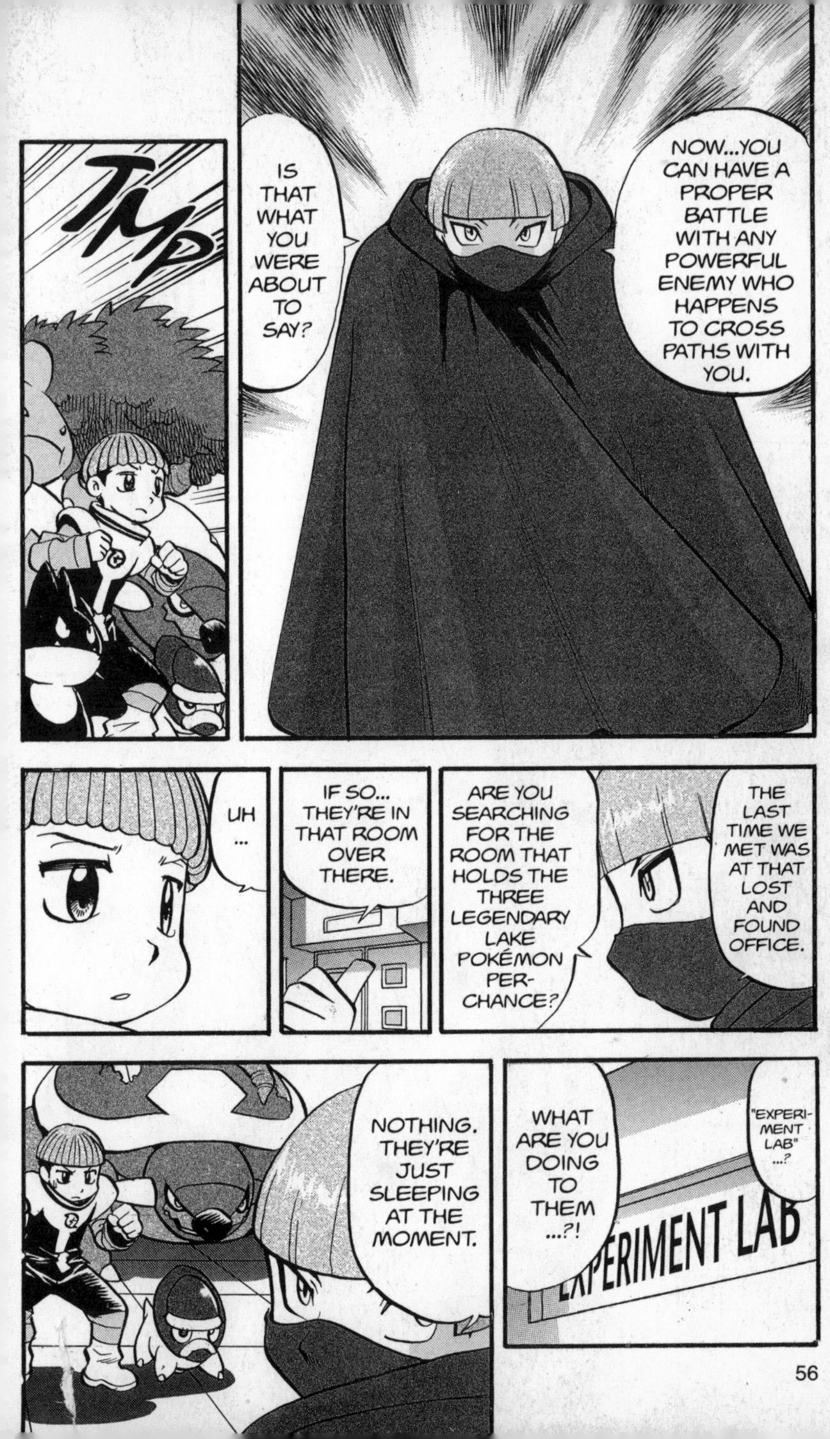
NOW...YOU CAN HAVE A PROPER BATTLE WITH ANY POWERFUL ENEMY WHO HAPPENS TO CROSS PATHS WITH YOU.
IS THAT WHAT YOU WERE ABOUT TO SAY?
TMP
THE LAST TIME WE MET WAS AT THAT LOST AND FOUND OFFICE.
ARE YOU SEARCHING FOR THE ROOM THAT HOLDS THE THREE LEGENDARY LAKE POKÉMON PER-CHANCE?
IF SO... THEY'RE IN THAT ROOM OVER THERE.
UH ...
"EXPERI-MENT LAB" ...?
WHAT ARE YOU DOING TO THEM ...?!
EXPERIMENT LAB
NOTHING. THEY'RE JUST SLEEPING AT THE MOMENT.

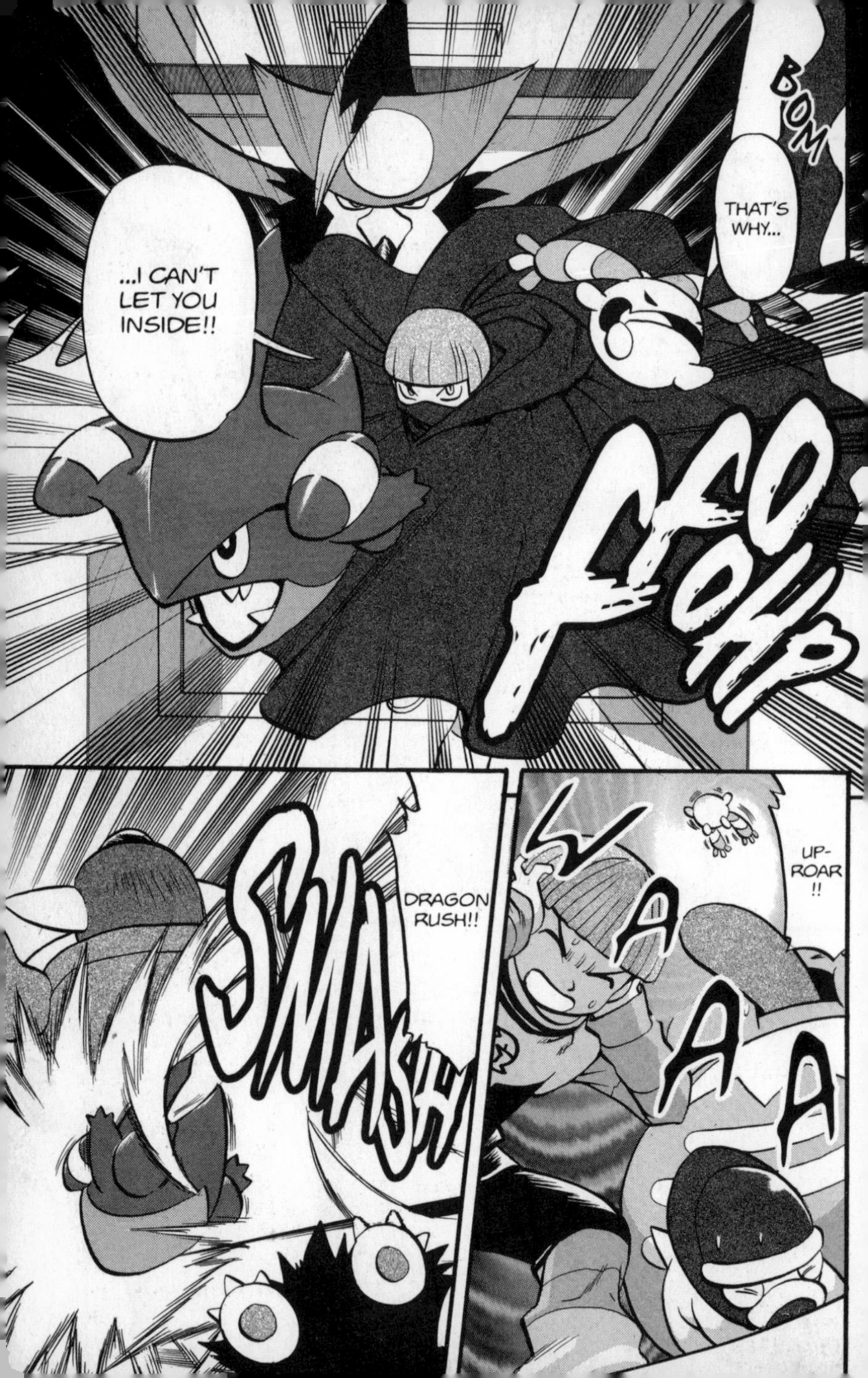
BOM
THAT'S WHY...
...I CAN'T LET YOU INSIDE!!
WAAAA
UP-ROAR!!
DRAGON RUSH!!
SMASH

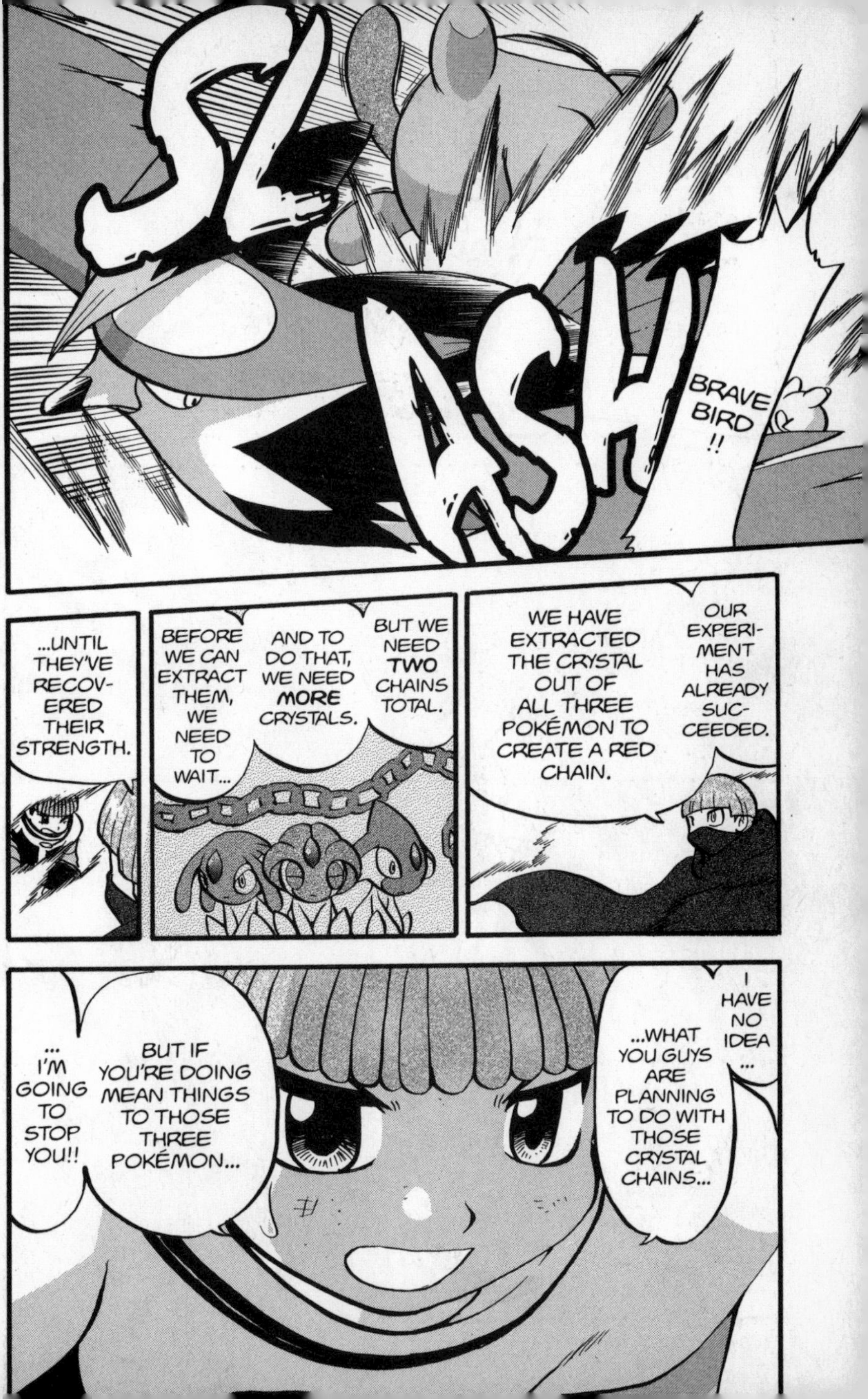
BRAVE BIRD !!
SLASH
OUR EXPERIMENT HAS ALREADY SUCCEEDED.
WE HAVE EXTRACTED THE CRYSTAL OUT OF ALL THREE POKÉMON TO CREATE A RED CHAIN.
BUT WE NEED **TWO** CHAINS TOTAL.
AND TO DO THAT, WE NEED **MORE** CRYSTALS.
BEFORE WE CAN EXTRACT THEM, WE NEED TO WAIT...
...UNTIL THEY'VE RECOVERED THEIR STRENGTH.
I HAVE NO IDEA ...
...WHAT YOU GUYS ARE PLANNING TO DO WITH THOSE CRYSTAL CHAINS...
BUT IF YOU'RE DOING MEAN THINGS TO THOSE THREE POKÉMON...
... I'M GOING TO STOP YOU!!

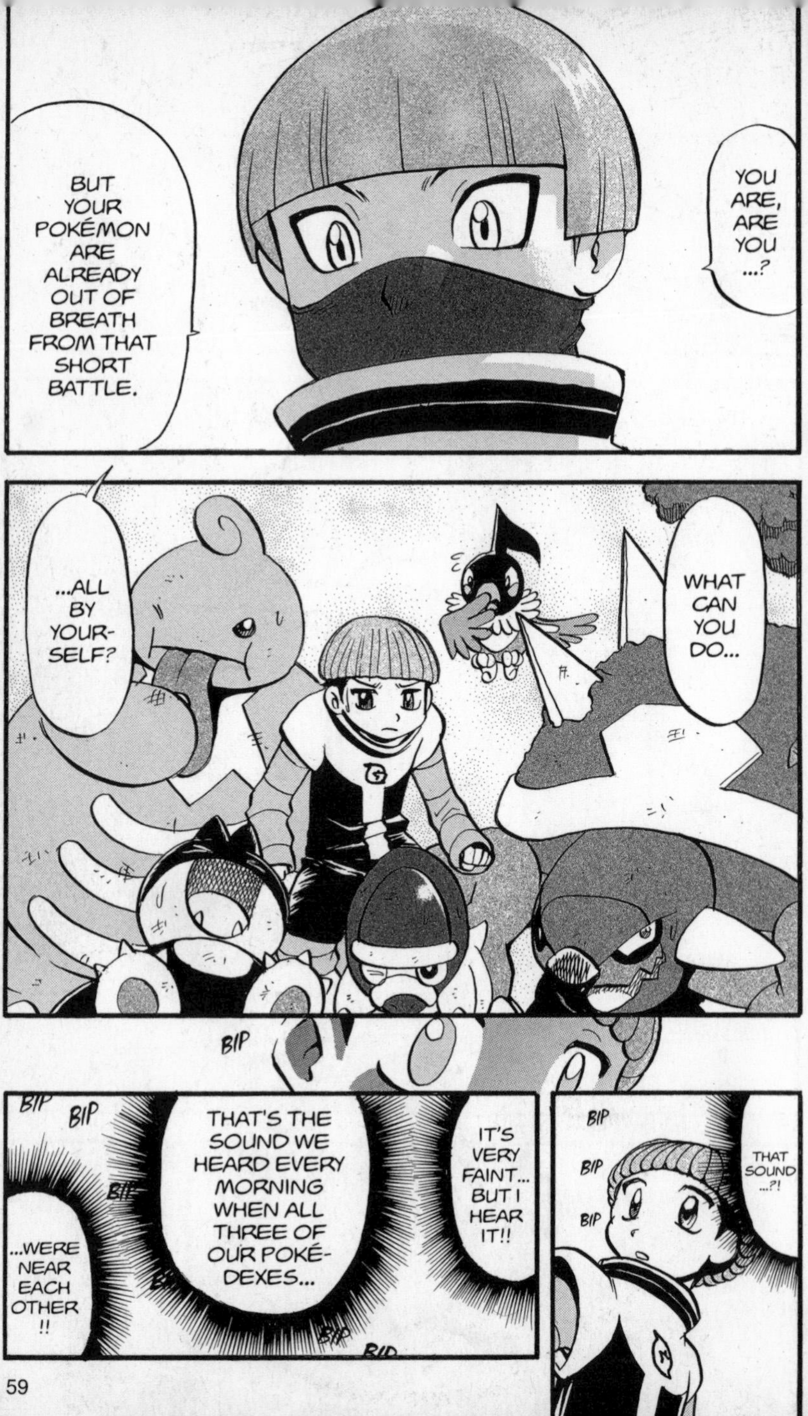
YOU ARE, ARE YOU ...?
BUT YOUR POKÉMON ARE ALREADY OUT OF BREATH FROM THAT SHORT BATTLE.
WHAT CAN YOU DO...
...ALL BY YOURSELF?
BIP
BIP
BIP
BIP
THAT SOUND ...?!
IT'S VERY FAINT... BUT I HEAR IT!!
THAT'S THE SOUND WE HEARD EVERY MORNING WHEN ALL THREE OF OUR POKÉDEXES...
...WERE NEAR EACH OTHER !!
BIP
BIP

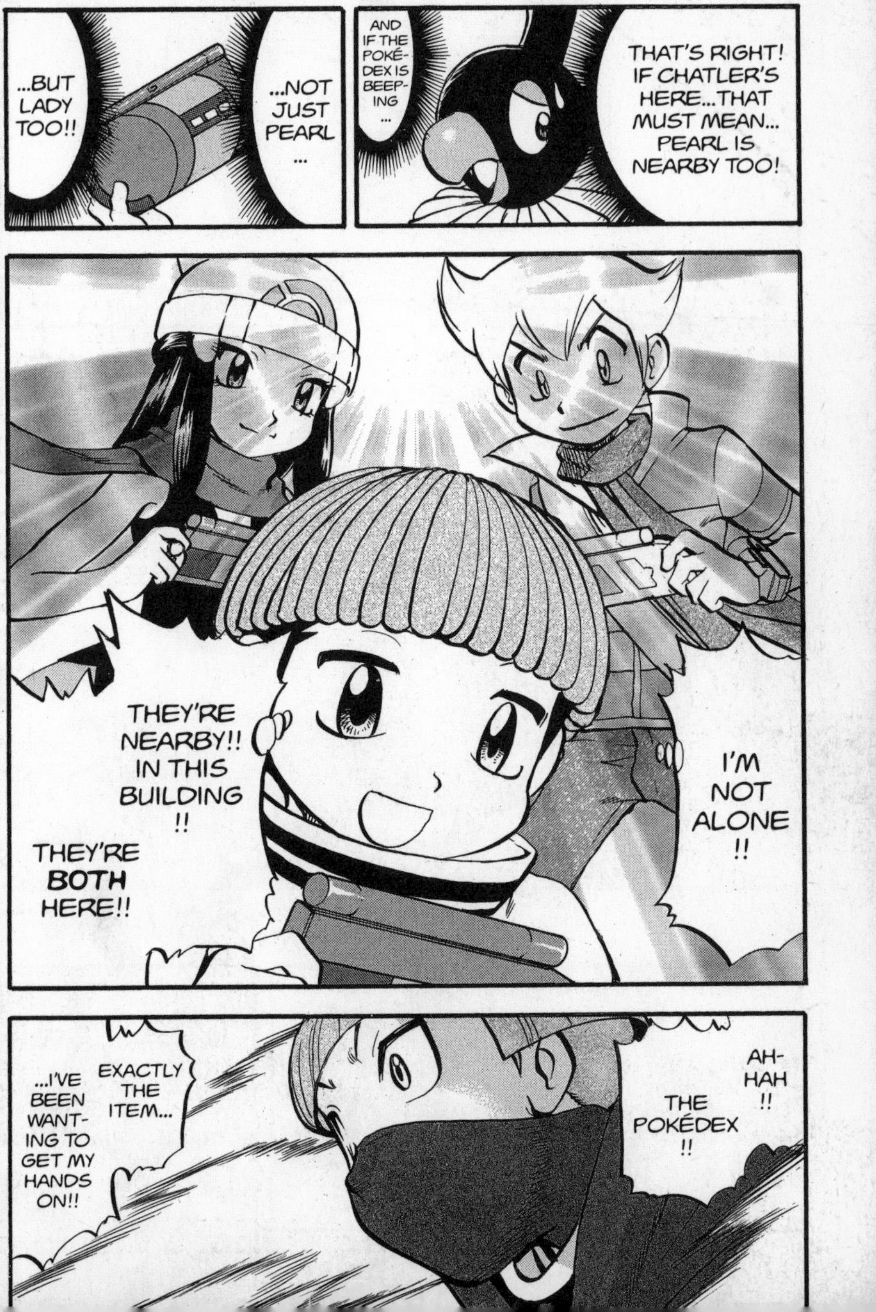
THAT'S RIGHT! IF CHATLER'S HERE...THAT MUST MEAN... PEARL IS NEARBY TOO!
AND IF THE POKÉ-DEX IS BEEP-ING ...
...NOT JUST PEARL ...
...BUT LADY TOO!!
THEY'RE NEARBY!! IN THIS BUILDING !!
THEY'RE **BOTH** HERE!!
I'M NOT ALONE !!
AH-HAH !!
THE POKÉDEX !!
EXACTLY THE ITEM...
...I'VE BEEN WANT-ING TO GET MY HANDS ON!!

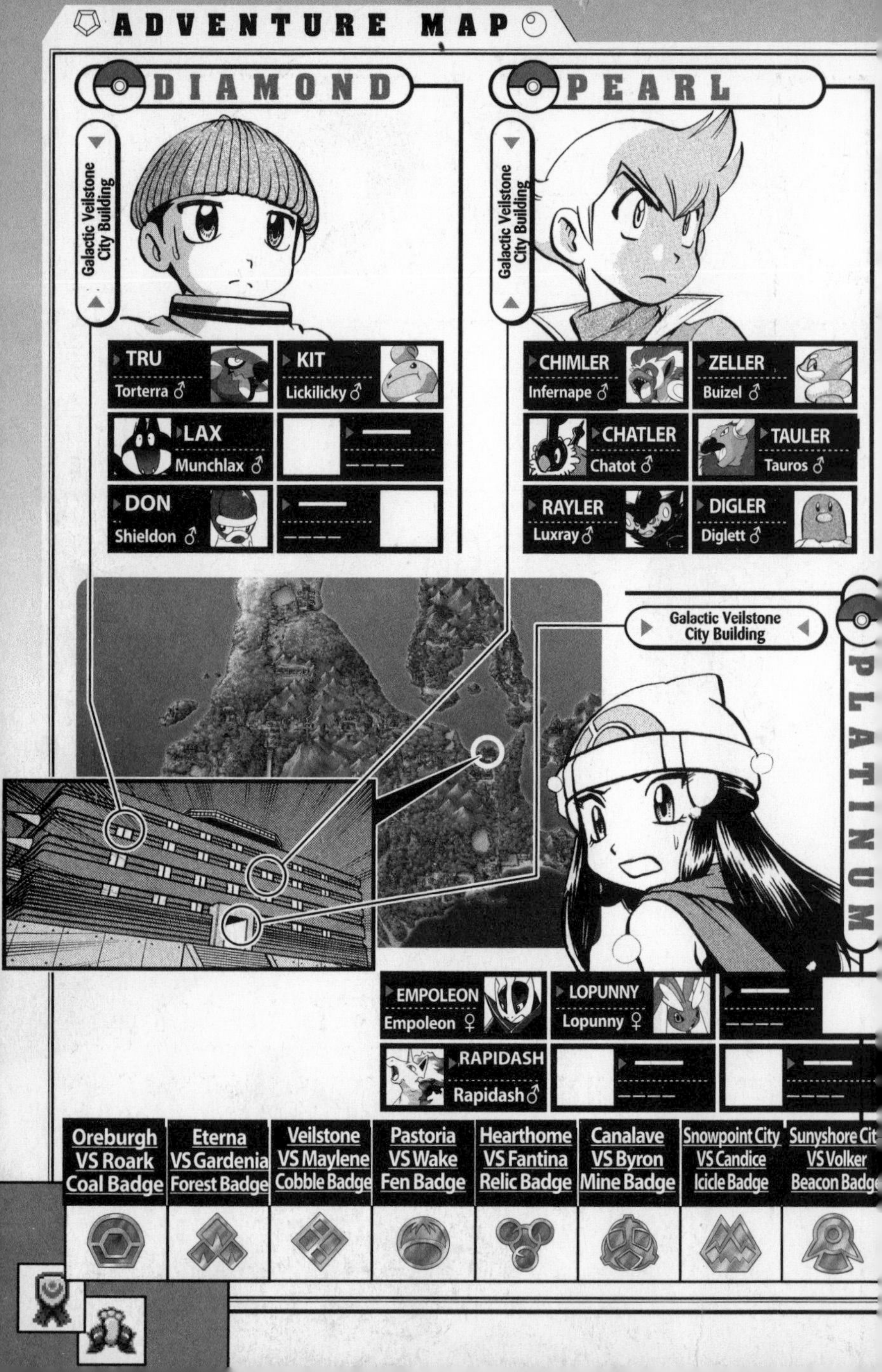
ADVENTURE MAP
DIAMOND
Galactic Veilstone City Building
TRU
Torterra ♂
KIT
Lickilicky ♂
LAX
Munchlax ♂
DON
Shieldon ♂
PEARL
Galactic Veilstone City Building
CHIMLER
Infernape ♂
ZELLER
Buizel ♂
CHATLER
Chatot ♂
TAULER
Tauros ♂
RAYLER
Luxray ♂
DIGLER
Diglett ♂
PLATINUM
Galactic Veilstone City Building
EMPOLEON
Empoleon ♀
LOPUNNY
Lopunny ♀
RAPIDASH
Rapidash ♂
Oreburgh VS Roark Coal Badge
Eterna VS Gardenia Forest Badge
Veilstone VS Maylene Cobble Badge
Pastoria VS Wake Fen Badge
Hearthome VS Fantina Relic Badge
Canalave VS Byron Mine Badge
Snowpoint City VS Candice Icicle Badge
Sunyshore Cit VS Volker Beacon Badge

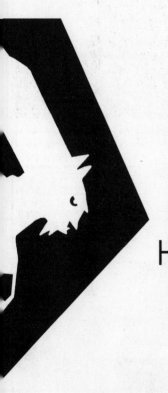

71

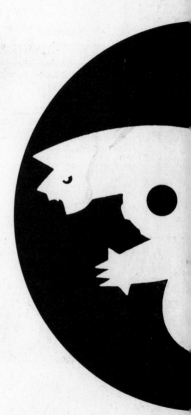

High-
Tailing
It from
Haunter

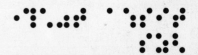

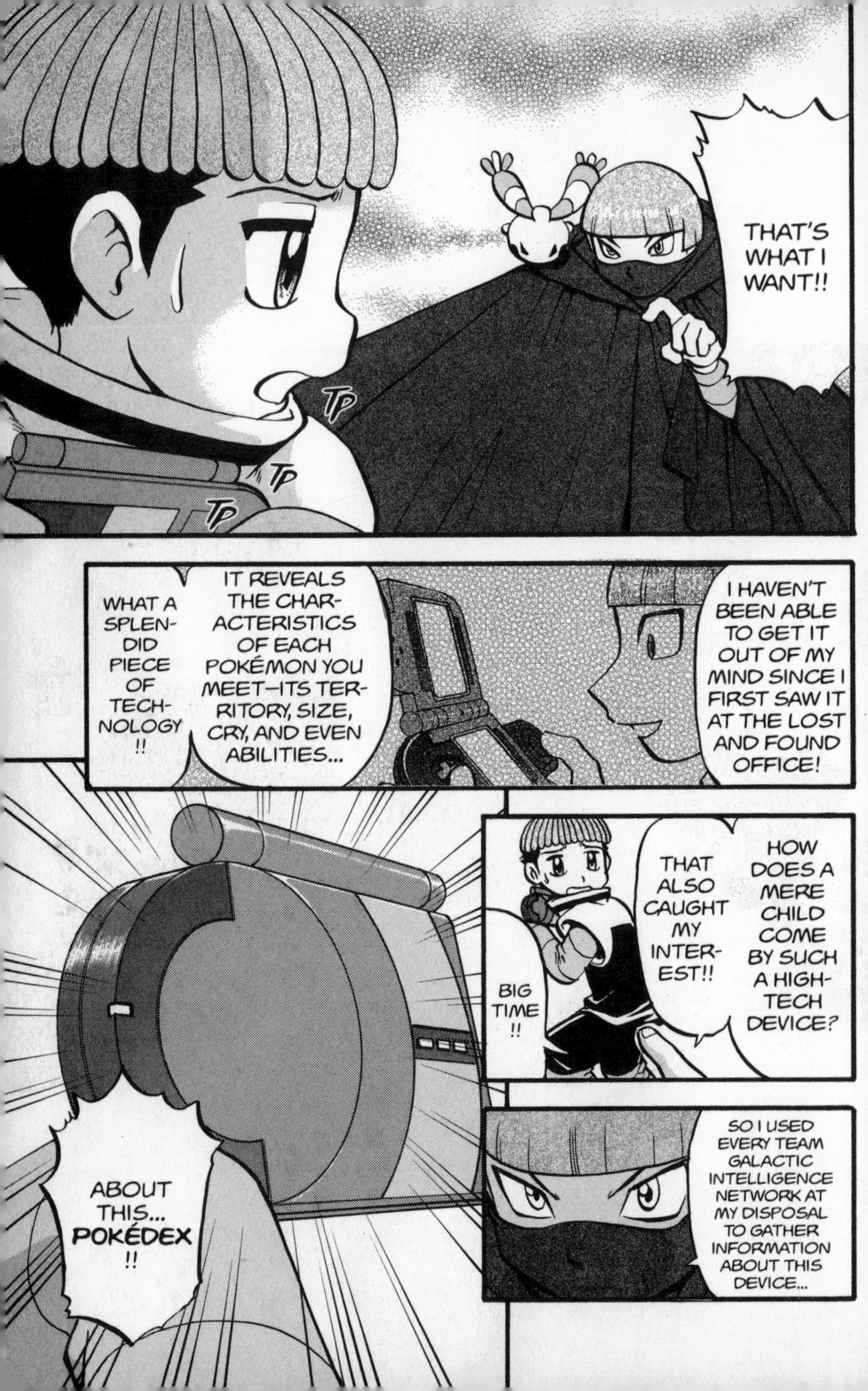
THAT'S WHAT I WANT!!
TP
TP
TP
I HAVEN'T BEEN ABLE TO GET IT OUT OF MY MIND SINCE I FIRST SAW IT AT THE LOST AND FOUND OFFICE!
IT REVEALS THE CHAR-ACTERISTICS OF EACH POKÉMON YOU MEET—ITS TER-RITORY, SIZE, CRY, AND EVEN ABILITIES...
WHAT A SPLEN-DID PIECE OF TECH-NOLOGY!!
HOW DOES A MERE CHILD COME BY SUCH A HIGH-TECH DEVICE?
THAT ALSO CAUGHT MY INTER-EST!!
BIG TIME!!
SO I USED EVERY TEAM GALACTIC INTELLIGENCE NETWORK AT MY DISPOSAL TO GATHER INFORMATION ABOUT THIS DEVICE...
ABOUT THIS... **POKÉDEX**!!

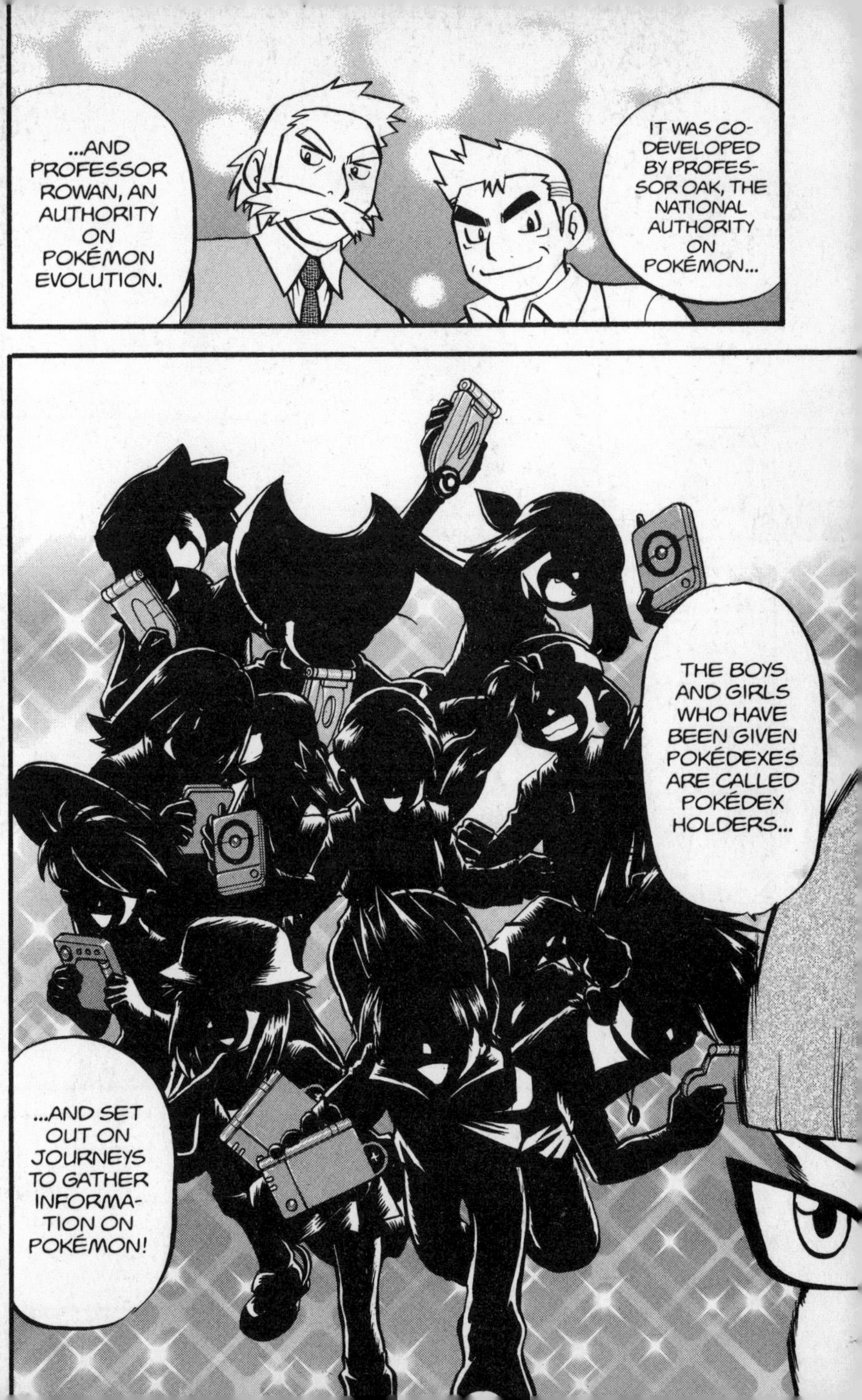
IT WAS CO-DEVELOPED BY PROFESSOR OAK, THE NATIONAL AUTHORITY ON POKÉMON...
...AND PROFESSOR ROWAN, AN AUTHORITY ON POKÉMON EVOLUTION.
THE BOYS AND GIRLS WHO HAVE BEEN GIVEN POKÉDEXES ARE CALLED POKÉDEX HOLDERS...
...AND SET OUT ON JOURNEYS TO GATHER INFORMATION ON POKÉMON!

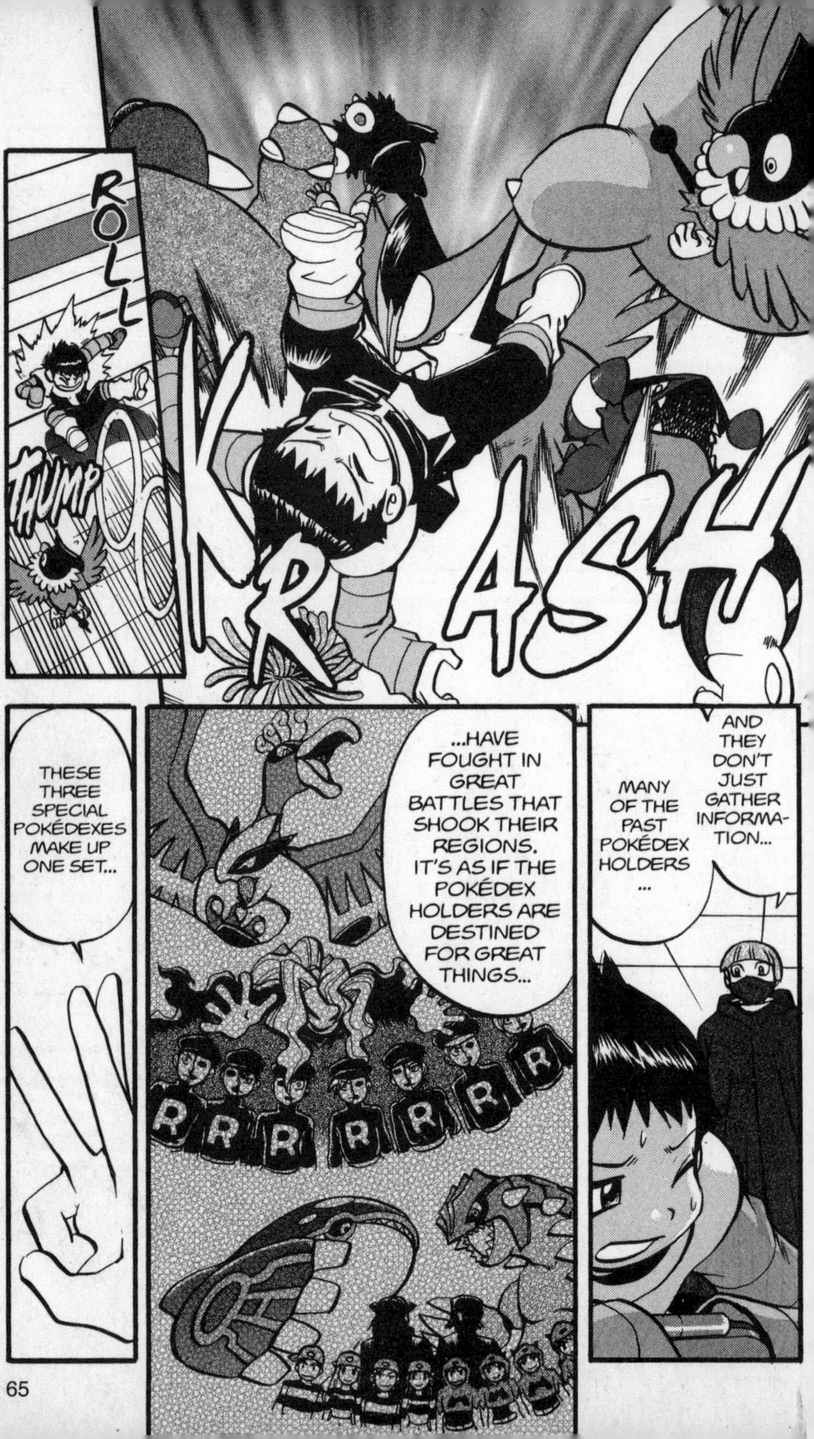
KRASH
ROLL
THUMP
AND THEY DON'T JUST GATHER INFORMATION...
MANY OF THE PAST POKÉDEX HOLDERS ...
...HAVE FOUGHT IN GREAT BATTLES THAT SHOOK THEIR REGIONS. IT'S AS IF THE POKÉDEX HOLDERS ARE DESTINED FOR GREAT THINGS...
THESE THREE SPECIAL POKÉDEXES MAKE UP ONE SET...

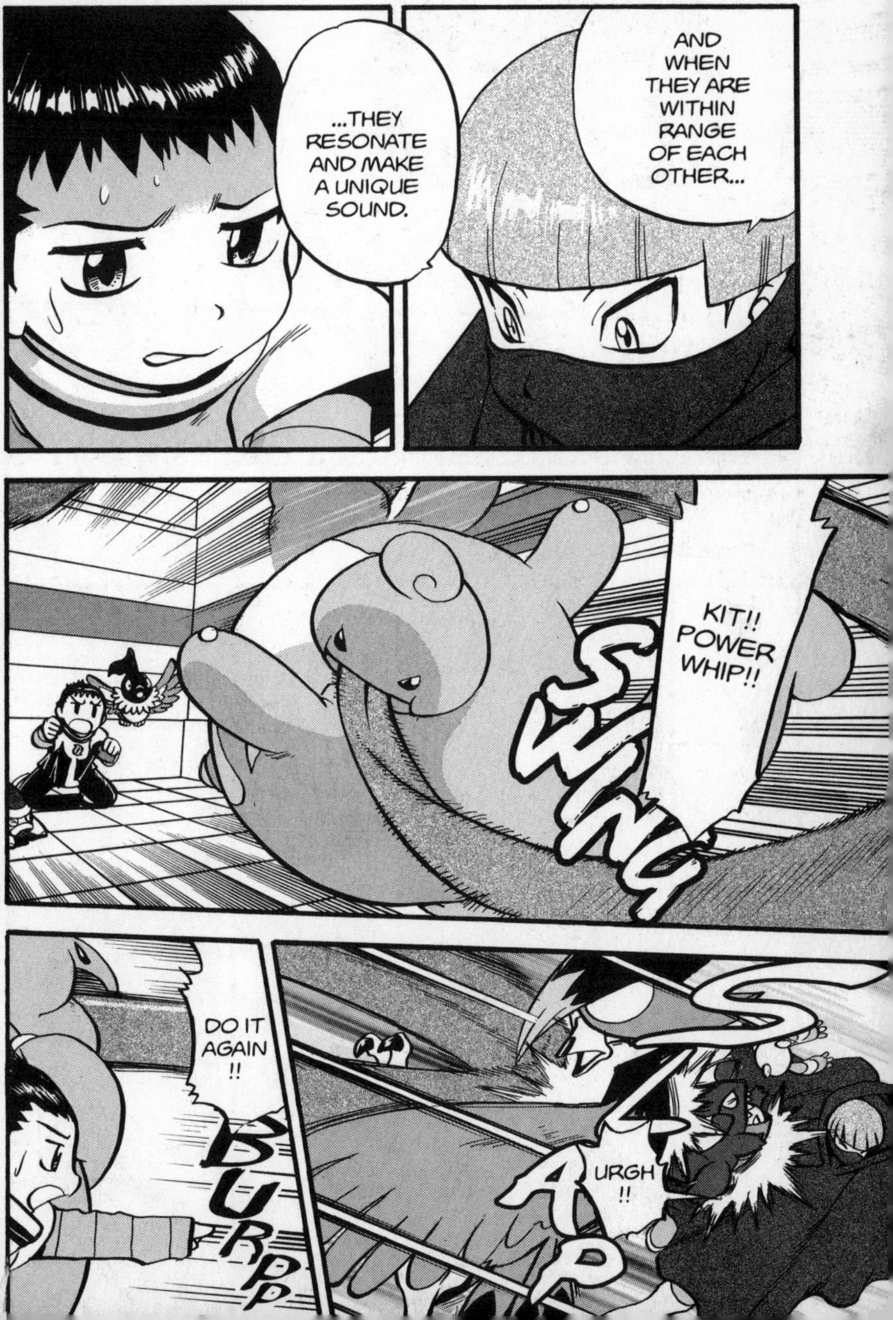
AND WHEN THEY ARE WITHIN RANGE OF EACH OTHER...
...THEY RESONATE AND MAKE A UNIQUE SOUND.
KIT!! POWER WHIP!!
SWING
URGH!!
DO IT AGAIN!!
BURPP

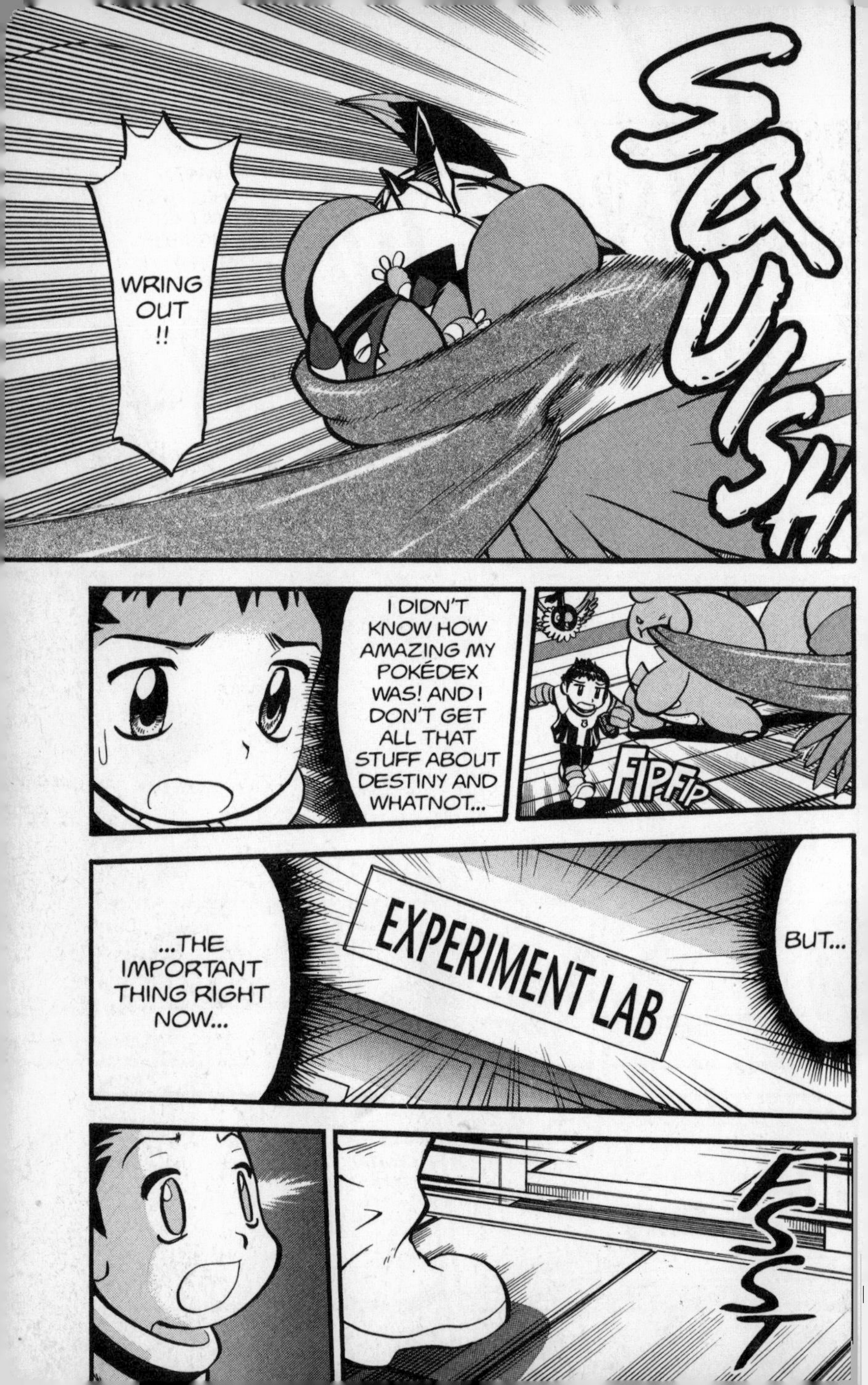
SQUISH
WRING OUT!!
FIP FIP
I DIDN'T KNOW HOW AMAZING MY POKÉDEX WAS! AND I DON'T GET ALL THAT STUFF ABOUT DESTINY AND WHATNOT...
BUT...
EXPERIMENT LAB
...THE IMPORTANT THING RIGHT NOW...
FSST

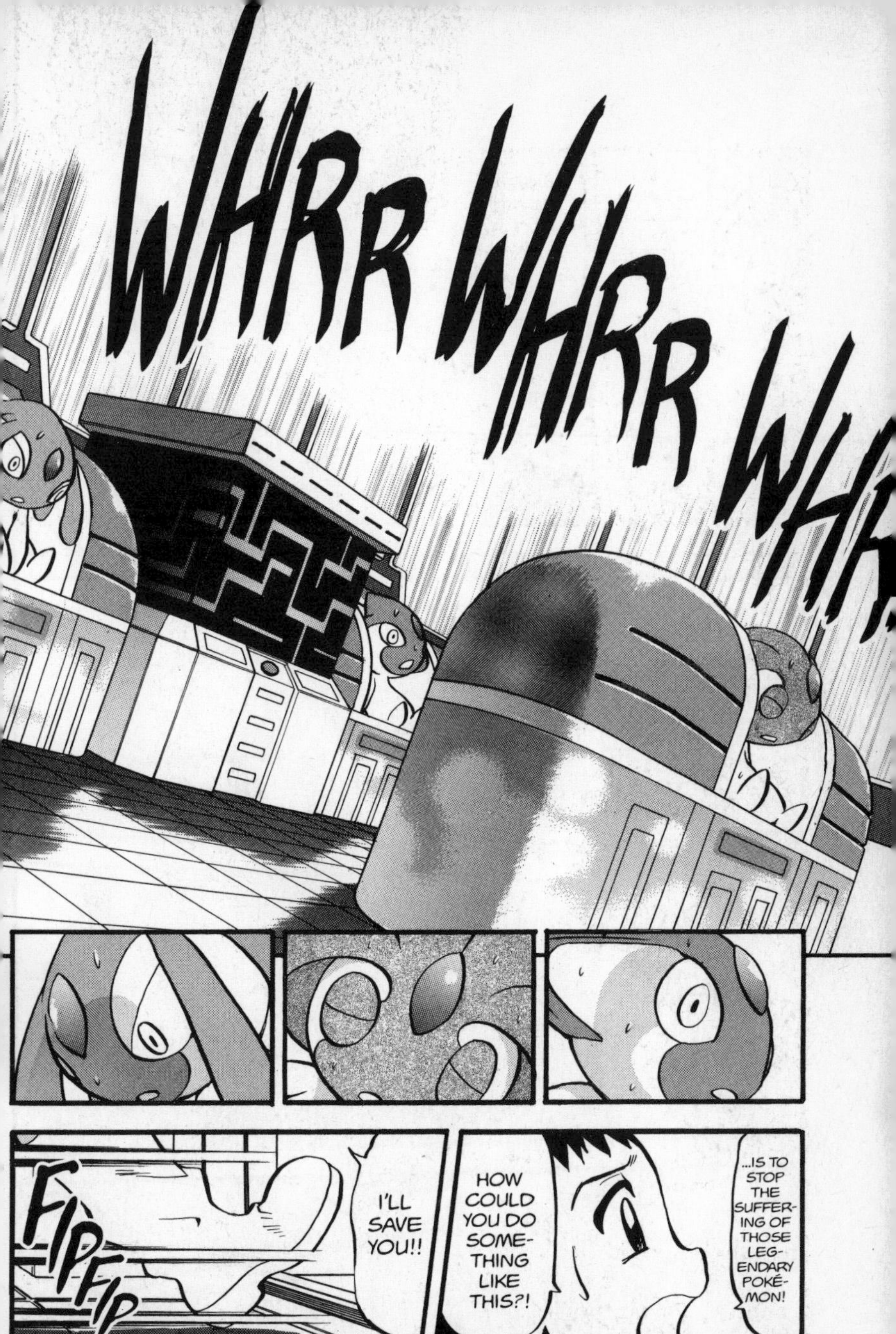
WHRR WHRR WHR...
...IS TO STOP THE SUFFERING OF THOSE LEGENDARY POKÉMON!
HOW COULD YOU DO SOMETHING LIKE THIS?!
I'LL SAVE YOU!!
FIP FIP

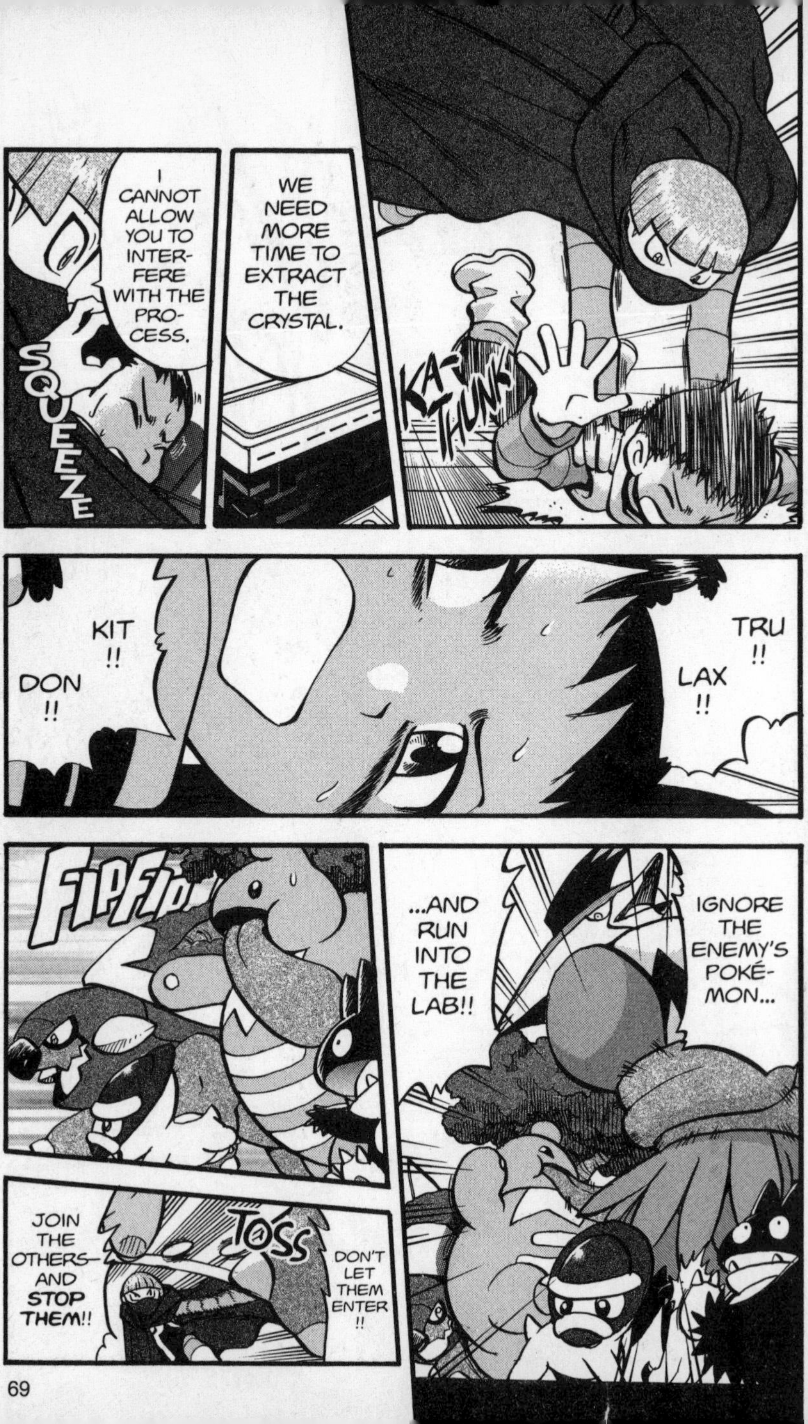
KA-THUNK
WE NEED MORE TIME TO EXTRACT THE CRYSTAL.
I CANNOT ALLOW YOU TO INTERFERE WITH THE PROCESS.
SQUEEZE
TRU!!
LAX!!
KIT!!
DON!!
IGNORE THE ENEMY'S POKÉMON...
...AND RUN INTO THE LAB!!
FLIPFLIP
DON'T LET THEM ENTER!!
TOSS
JOIN THE OTHERS—AND **STOP THEM!!**

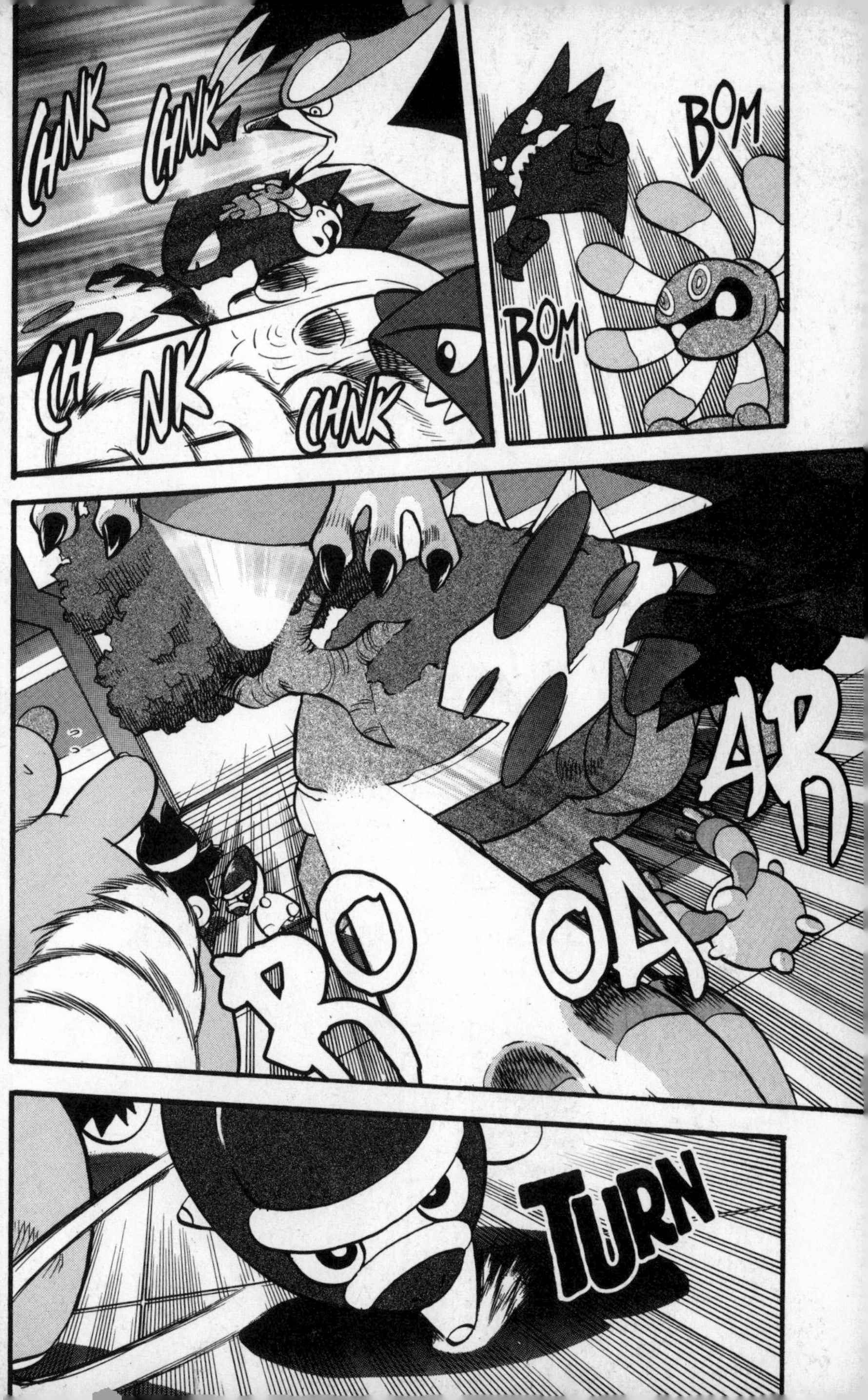
BOM
BOM
CHNK
CHNK
CH NK
CHNK
ROOAAR
TURN

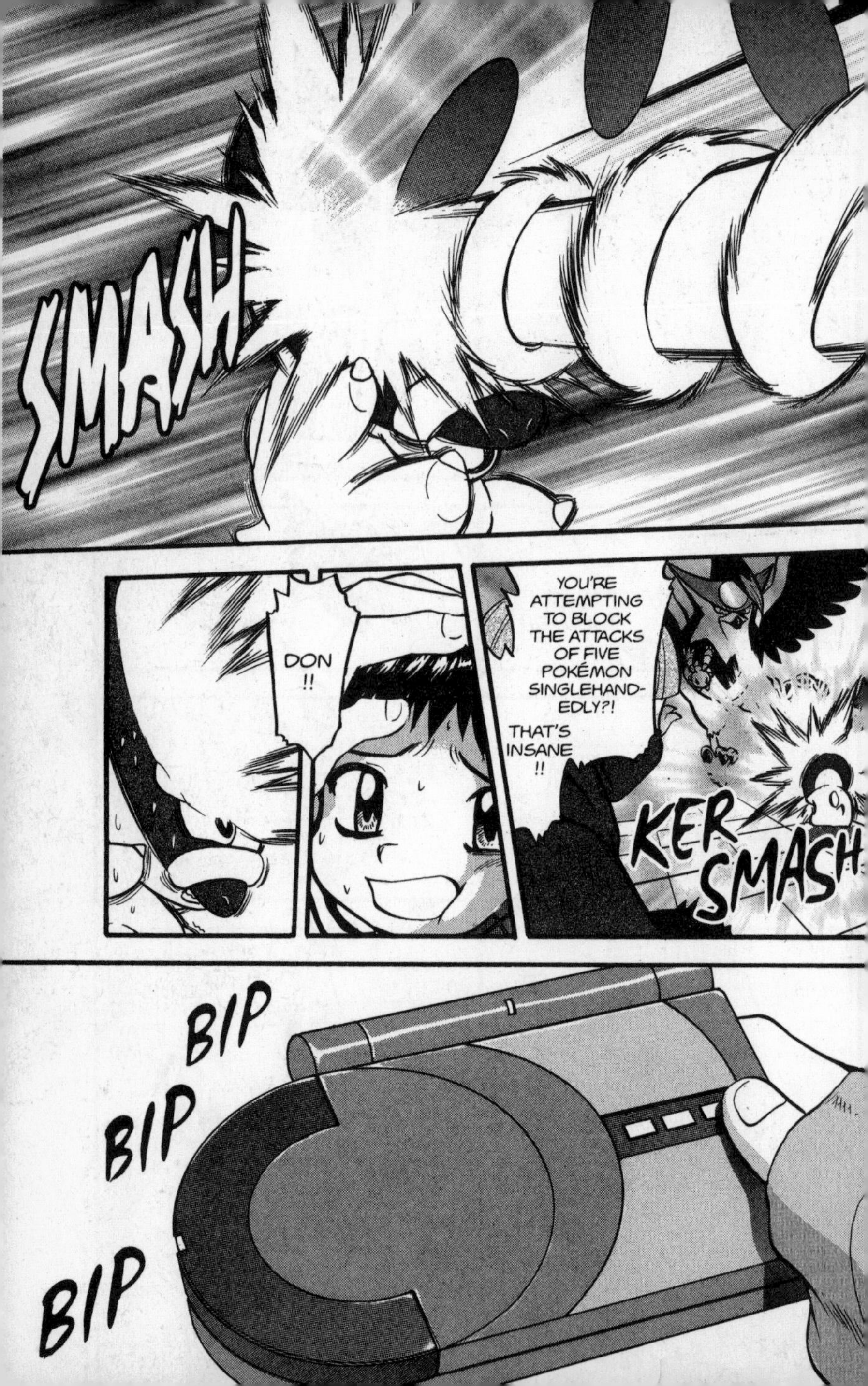
SMASH
YOU'RE ATTEMPTING TO BLOCK THE ATTACKS OF FIVE POKéMON SINGLEHAND-EDLY?!
THAT'S INSANE !!
KER SMASH
DON !!
BIP BIP
BIP
BIP

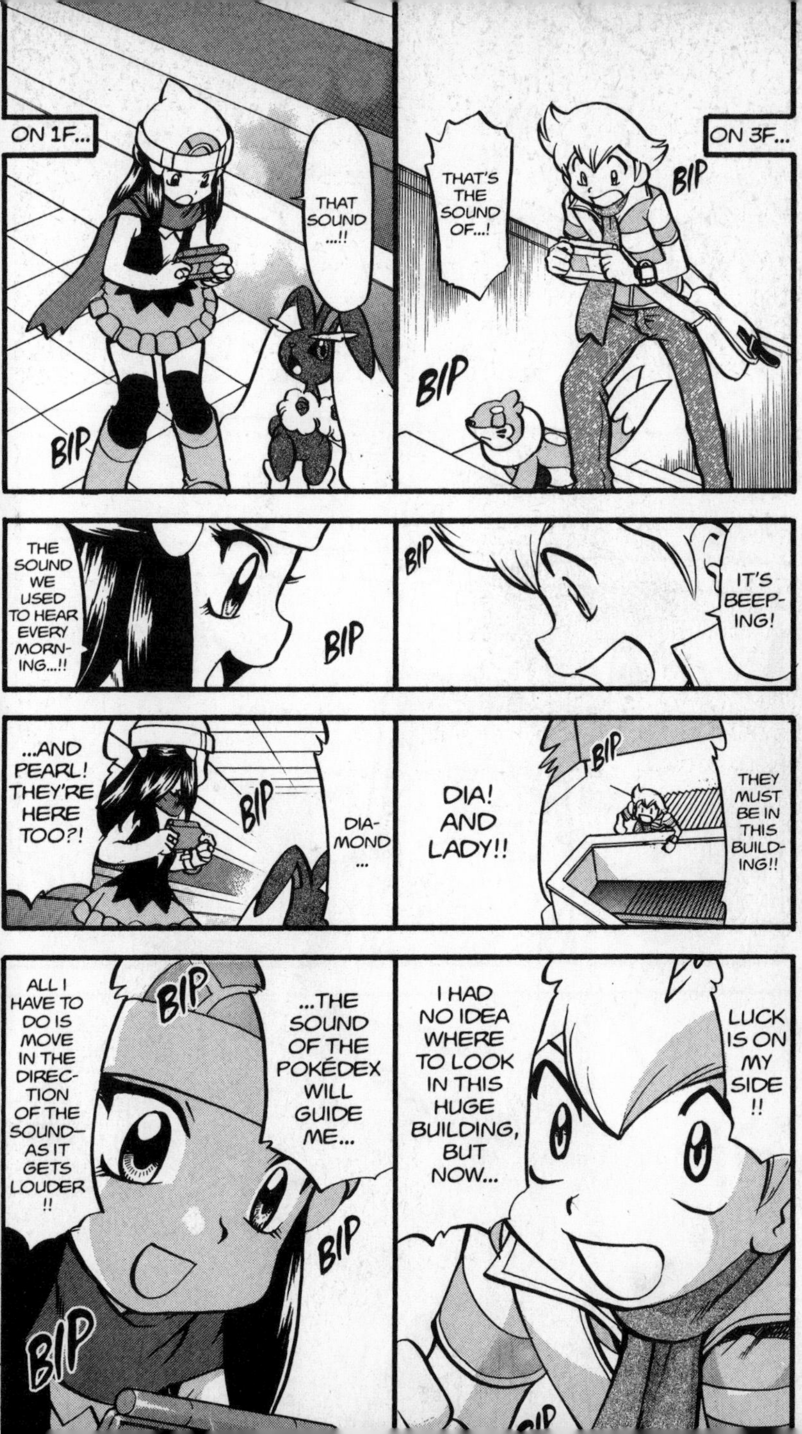
ON 3F...
BIP
THAT'S THE SOUND OF...!
BIP
THAT SOUND ...!!
ON 1F...
BIP
IT'S BEEPING!
BIP
BIP
THE SOUND WE USED TO HEAR EVERY MORNING...!!
THEY MUST BE IN THIS BUILDING!!
BIP
DIA! AND LADY!!
DIAMOND ...
BIP
...AND PEARL! THEY'RE HERE TOO?!
LUCK IS ON MY SIDE!!
I HAD NO IDEA WHERE TO LOOK IN THIS HUGE BUILDING, BUT NOW...
...THE SOUND OF THE POKÉDEX WILL GUIDE ME...
BIP
ALL I HAVE TO DO IS MOVE IN THE DIRECTION OF THE SOUND—AS IT GETS LOUDER!!
BIP
BIP

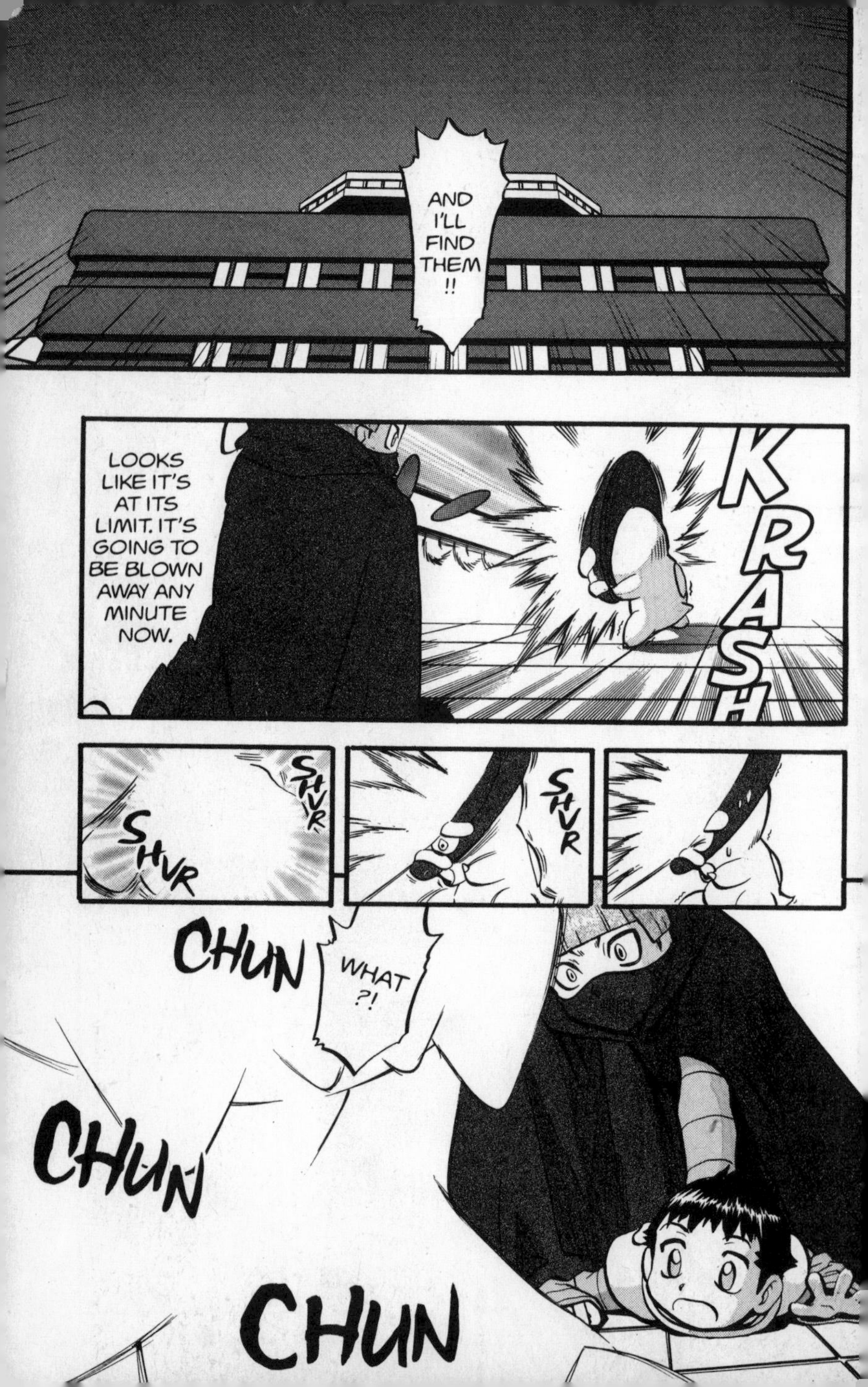
AND I'LL FIND THEM!!
KRASH
LOOKS LIKE IT'S AT ITS LIMIT. IT'S GOING TO BE BLOWN AWAY ANY MINUTE NOW.
SHVR
SHVR
SHVR
SHVR
WHAT?!
CHUN
CHUN
CHUN

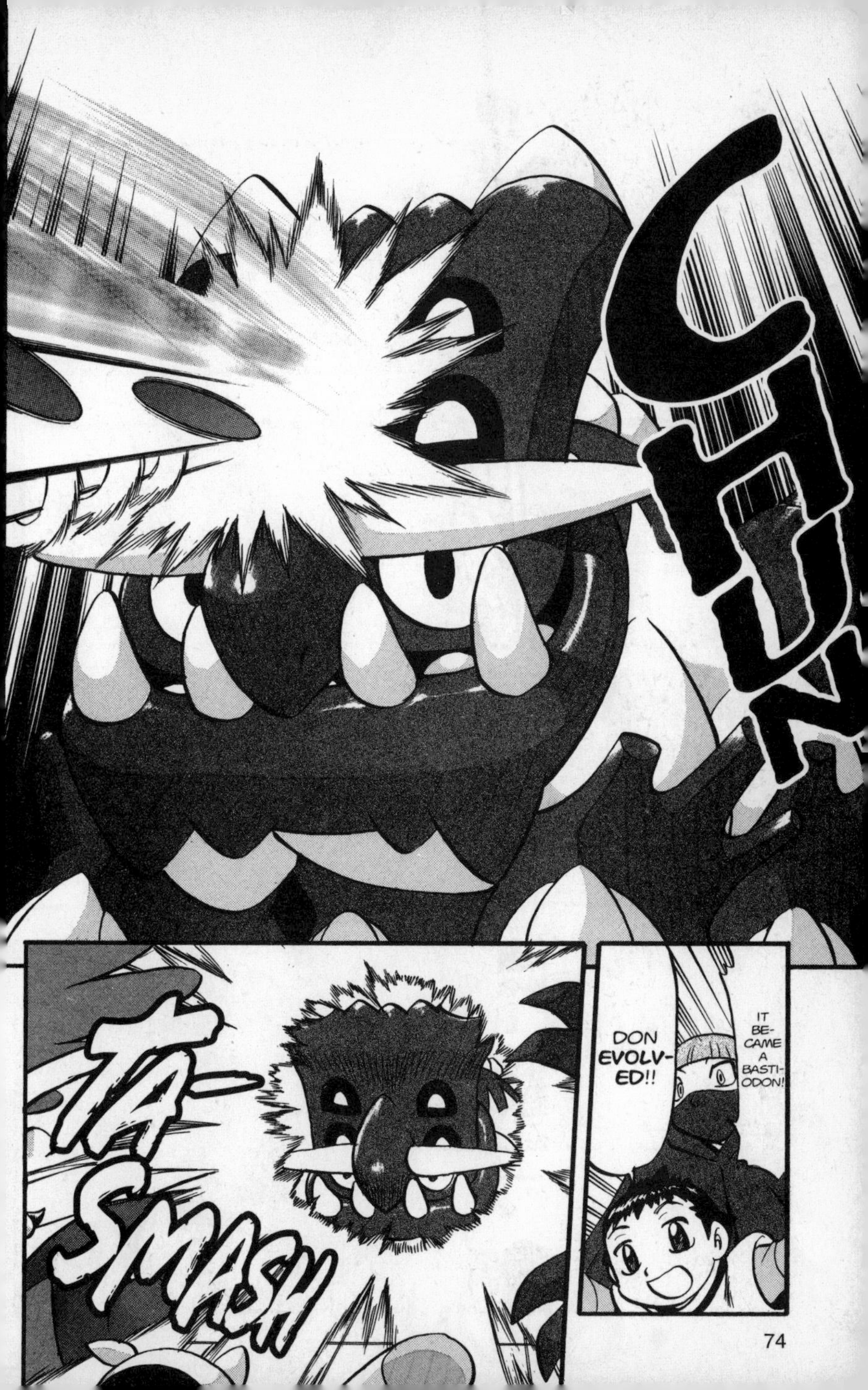
CHUNK
IT BE-CAME A BASTI-ODON!
DON EVOLV-ED!!
TA
SMASH

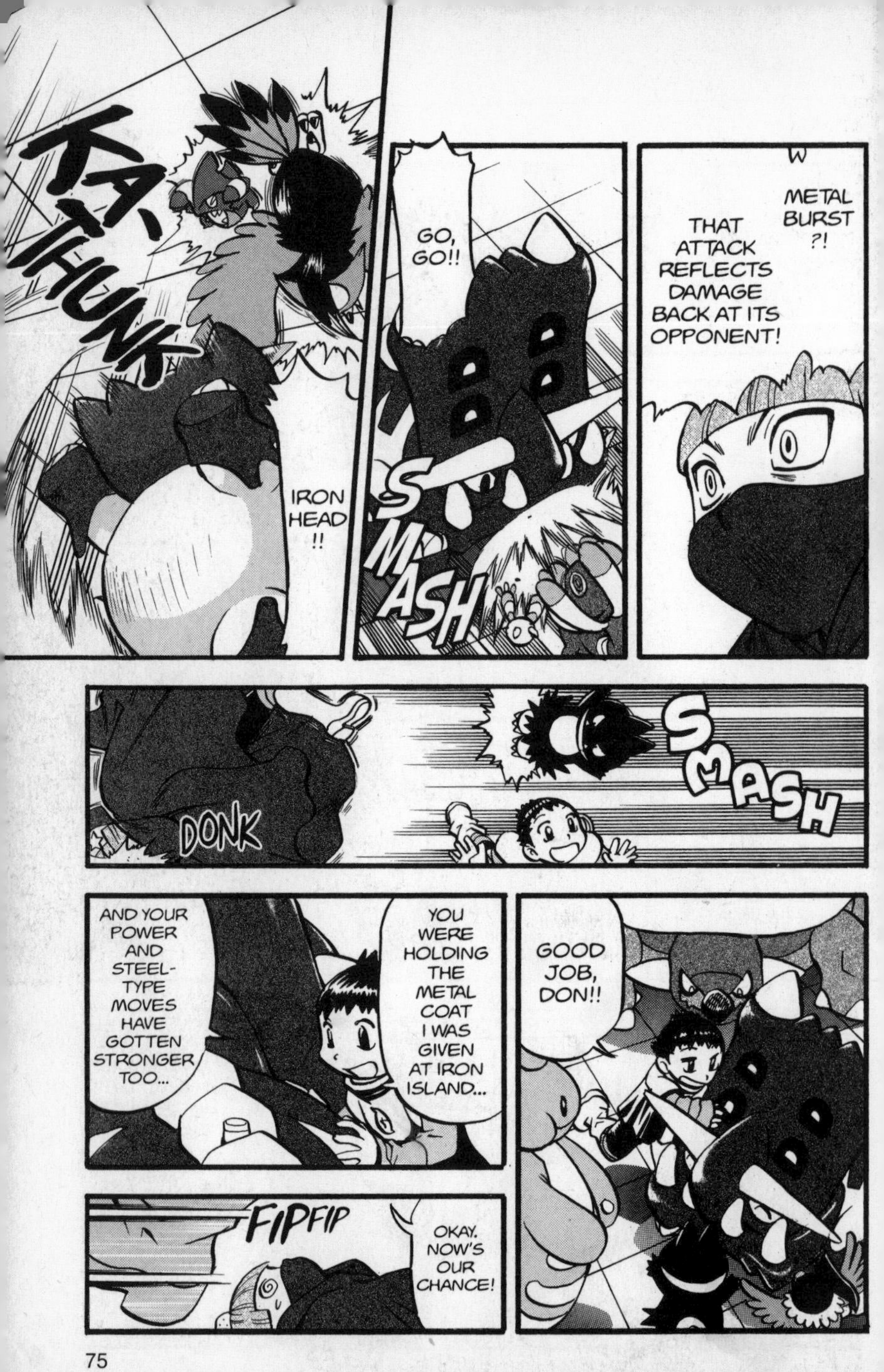
W
METAL BURST ?!
THAT ATTACK REFLECTS DAMAGE BACK AT ITS OPPONENT!
GO, GO!!
SMASH
IRON HEAD !!
KA-THUNK
SMASH
DONK
GOOD JOB, DON!!
YOU WERE HOLDING THE METAL COAT I WAS GIVEN AT IRON ISLAND...
AND YOUR POWER AND STEEL-TYPE MOVES HAVE GOTTEN STRONGER TOO...
OKAY. NOW'S OUR CHANCE!
FIPFIP

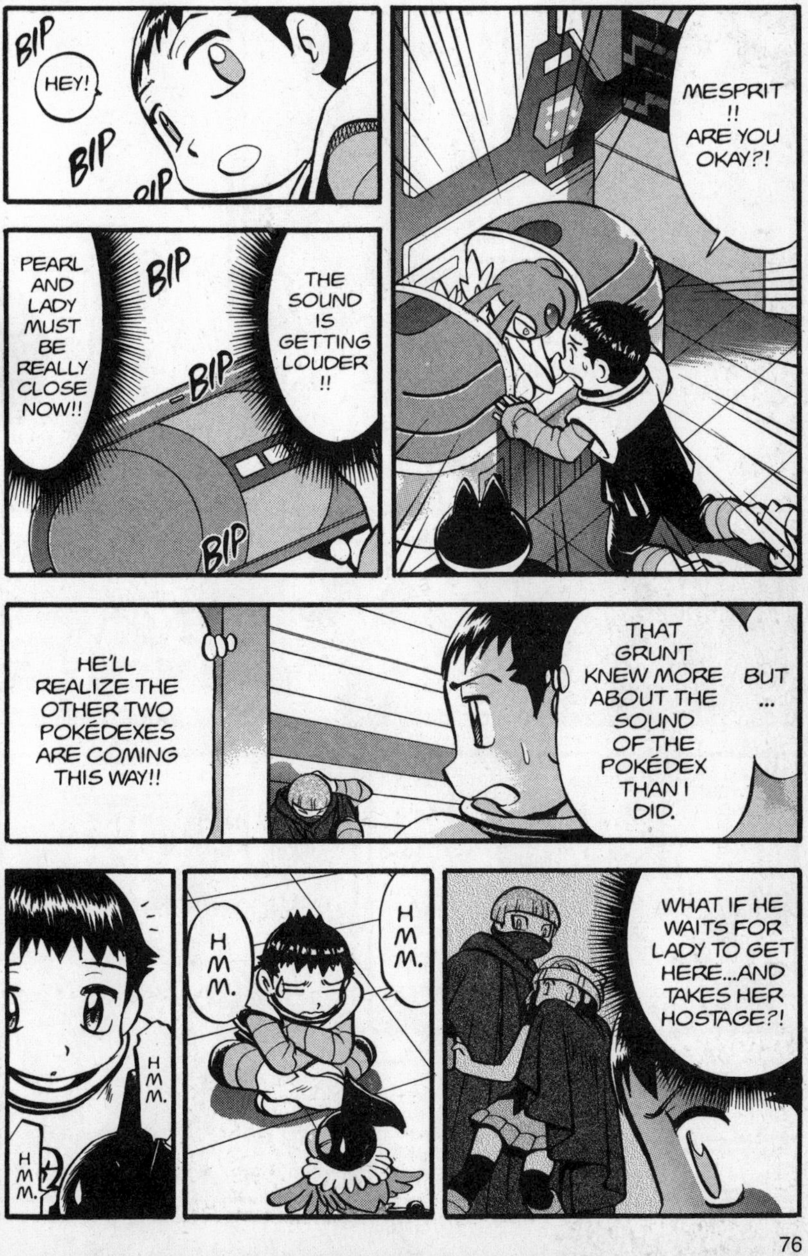
MESPRIT !! ARE YOU OKAY?!
BIP
HEY!
BIP
BIP
THE SOUND IS GETTING LOUDER !!
BIP
PEARL AND LADY MUST BE REALLY CLOSE NOW!!
BIP
BIP
BUT ...
THAT GRUNT KNEW MORE ABOUT THE SOUND OF THE POKÉDEX THAN I DID.
HE'LL REALIZE THE OTHER TWO POKÉDEXES ARE COMING THIS WAY!!
WHAT IF HE WAITS FOR LADY TO GET HERE...AND TAKES HER HOSTAGE?!
HMM.
HMM.
HMM.
HMM.

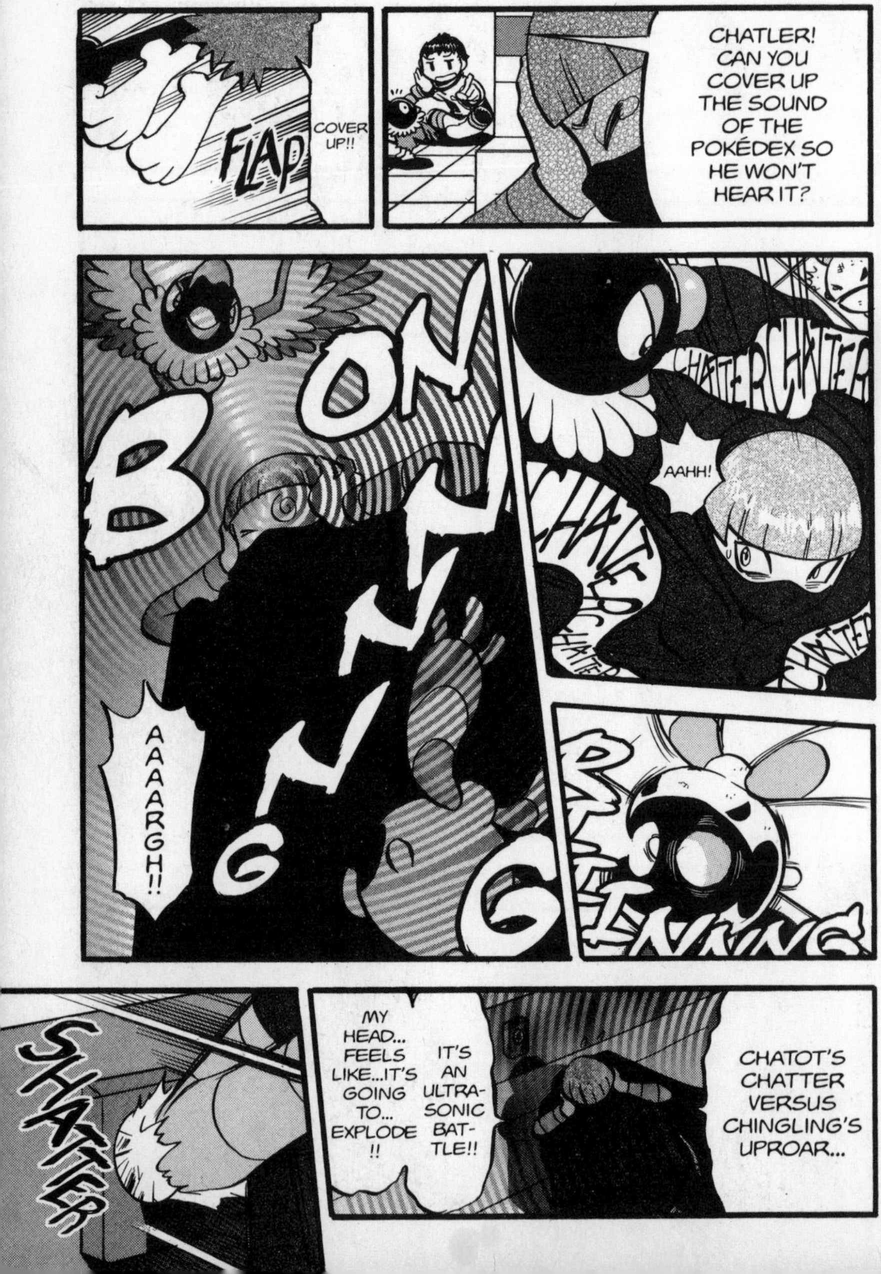
CHATLER! CAN YOU COVER UP THE SOUND OF THE POKÉDEX SO HE WON'T HEAR IT?
COVER UP!!
FLAP
CHATTERCHATTER
AAHH!
CHATTERCHATTER
CHATTER
BONG
AAAARGH!!
CHATOT'S CHATTER VERSUS CHINGLING'S UPROAR...
IT'S AN ULTRASONIC BATTLE!!
MY HEAD... FEELS LIKE...IT'S GOING TO... EXPLODE!!
SHATTER

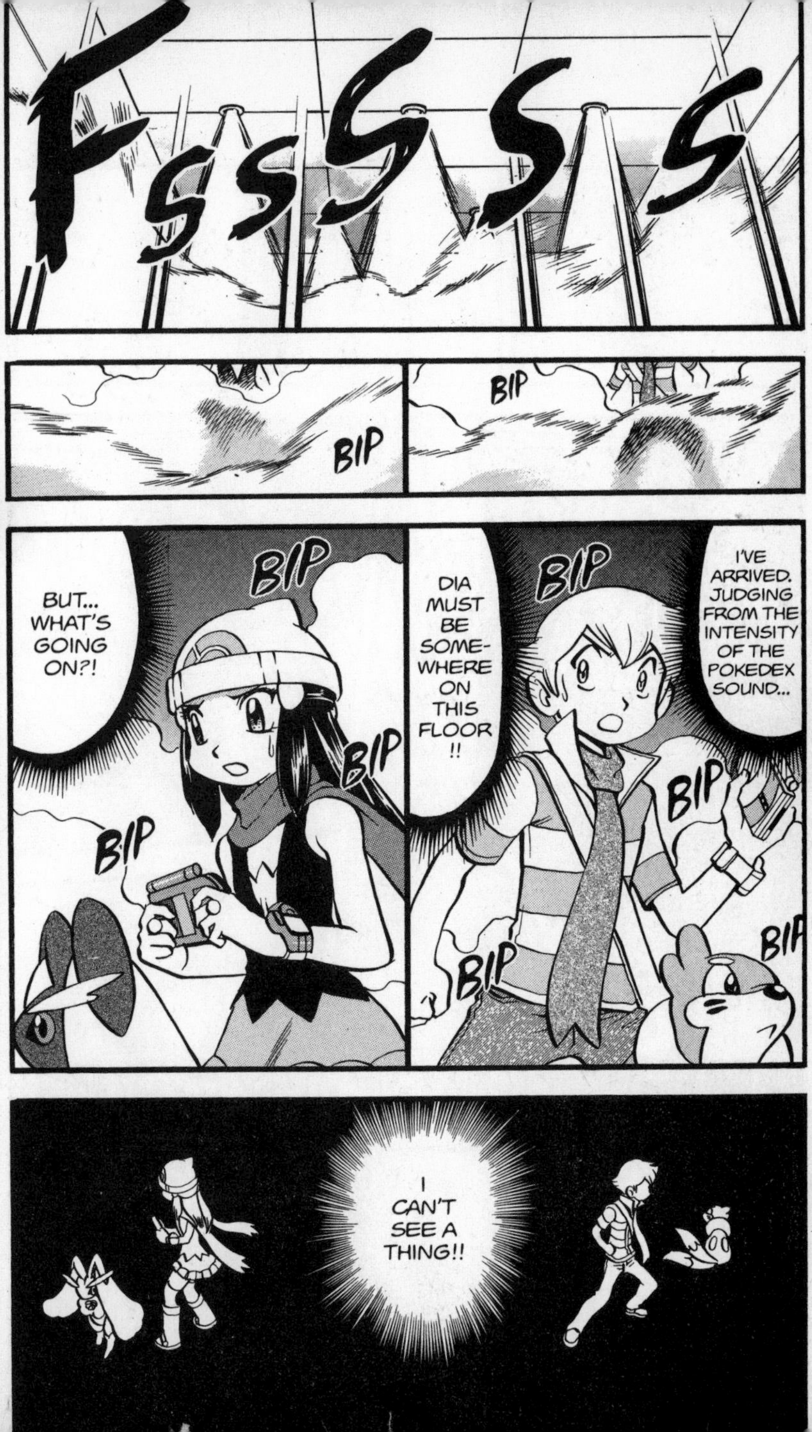
FSSSSS
BIP
BIP
I'VE ARRIVED. JUDGING FROM THE INTENSITY OF THE POKEDEX SOUND...
BIP
DIA MUST BE SOMEWHERE ON THIS FLOOR!!
BIP
BIP
BIP
BIP
BUT... WHAT'S GOING ON?!
BIP
BIP
I CAN'T SEE A THING!!

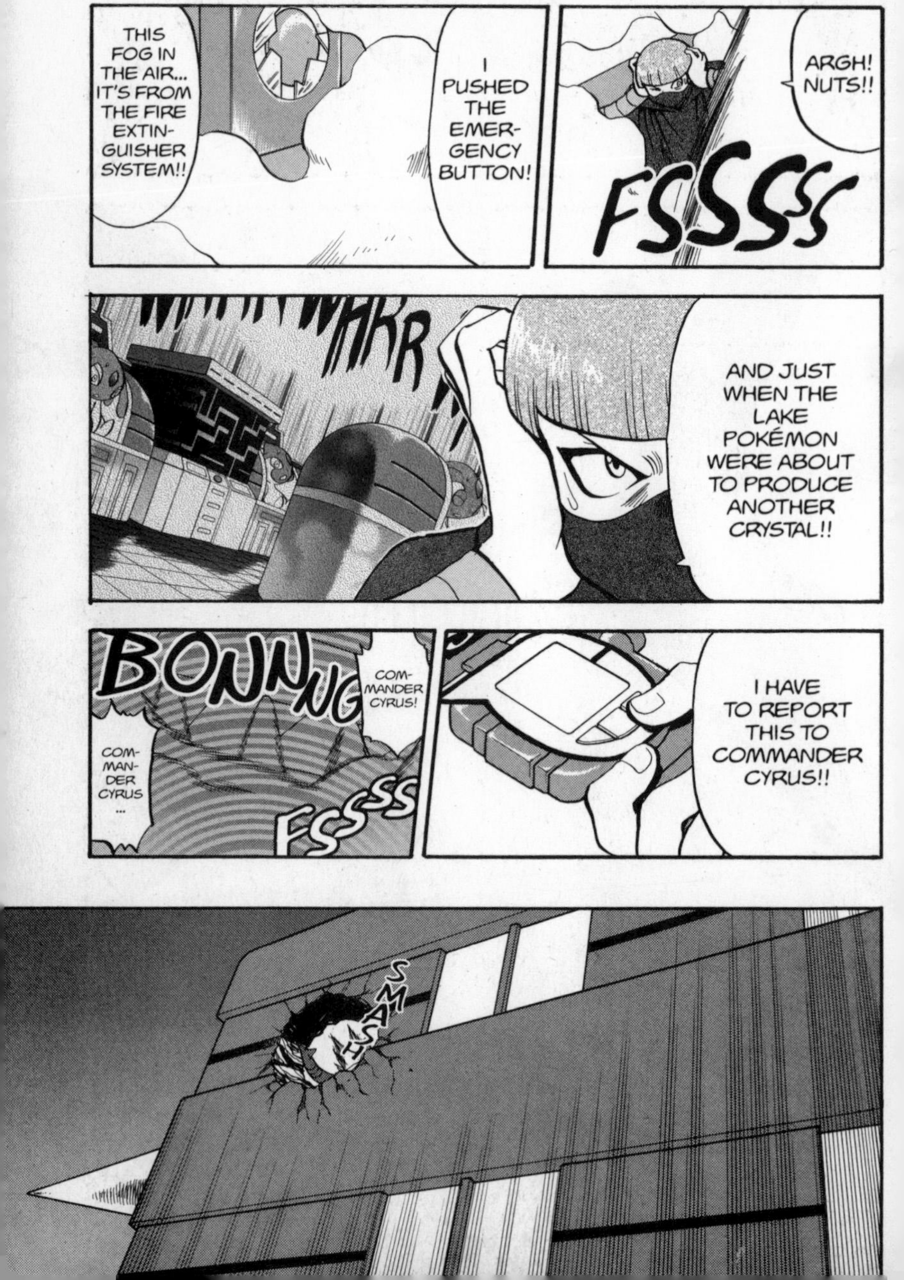
ARGH! NUTS!!
FSSSSS
I PUSHED THE EMERGENCY BUTTON!
THIS FOG IN THE AIR... IT'S FROM THE FIRE EXTINGUISHER SYSTEM!!
AND JUST WHEN THE LAKE POKÉMON WERE ABOUT TO PRODUCE ANOTHER CRYSTAL!!
I HAVE TO REPORT THIS TO COMMANDER CYRUS!!
BONNNG
COMMANDER CYRUS!
FSSSS
COMMANDER CYRUS...
SMASH

72

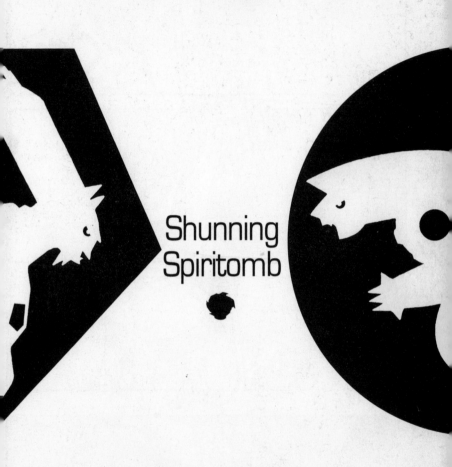

Shunning
Spiritomb

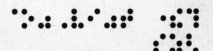

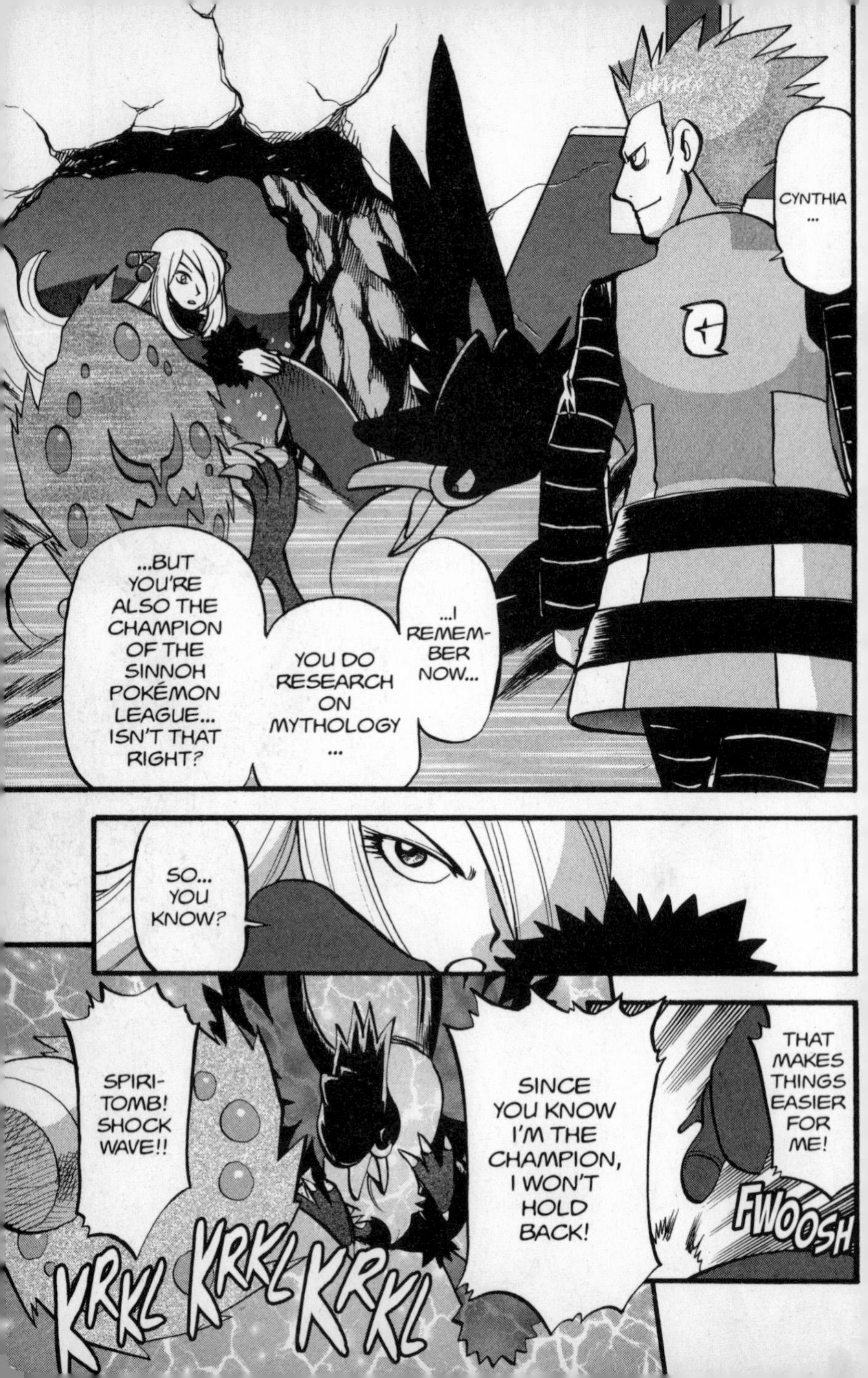
CYNTHIA ...
...I REMEMBER NOW...
YOU DO RESEARCH ON MYTHOLOGY ...
...BUT YOU'RE ALSO THE CHAMPION OF THE SINNOH POKÉMON LEAGUE... ISN'T THAT RIGHT?
SO... YOU KNOW?
THAT MAKES THINGS EASIER FOR ME!
FWOOSH
SINCE YOU KNOW I'M THE CHAMPION, I WON'T HOLD BACK!
SPIRITOMB! SHOCK WAVE!!
KRKL KRKL KRKL

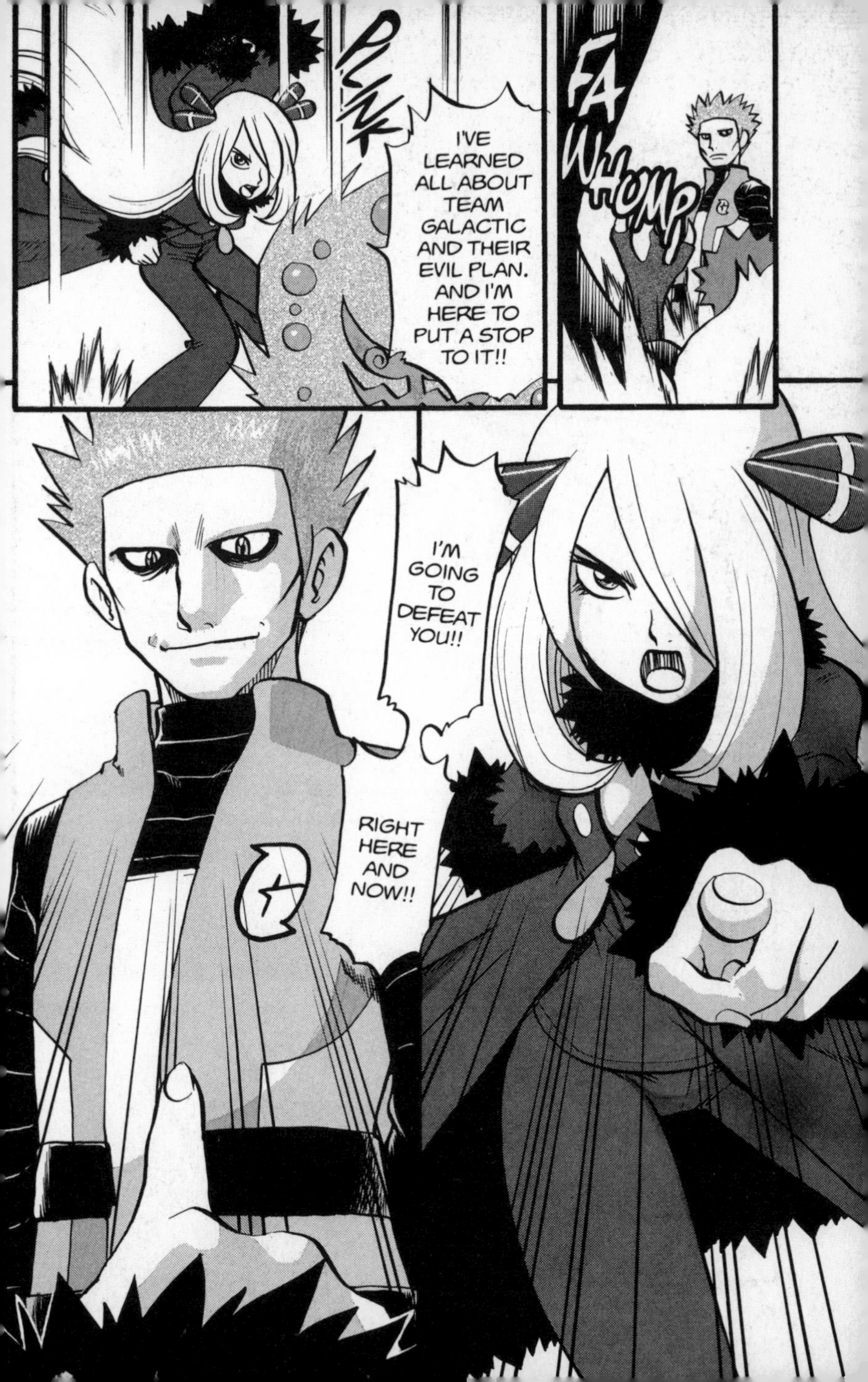

FA WHOMP
PLINK
I'VE LEARNED ALL ABOUT TEAM GALACTIC AND THEIR EVIL PLAN. AND I'M HERE TO PUT A STOP TO IT!!
I'M GOING TO DEFEAT YOU!!
RIGHT HERE AND NOW!!

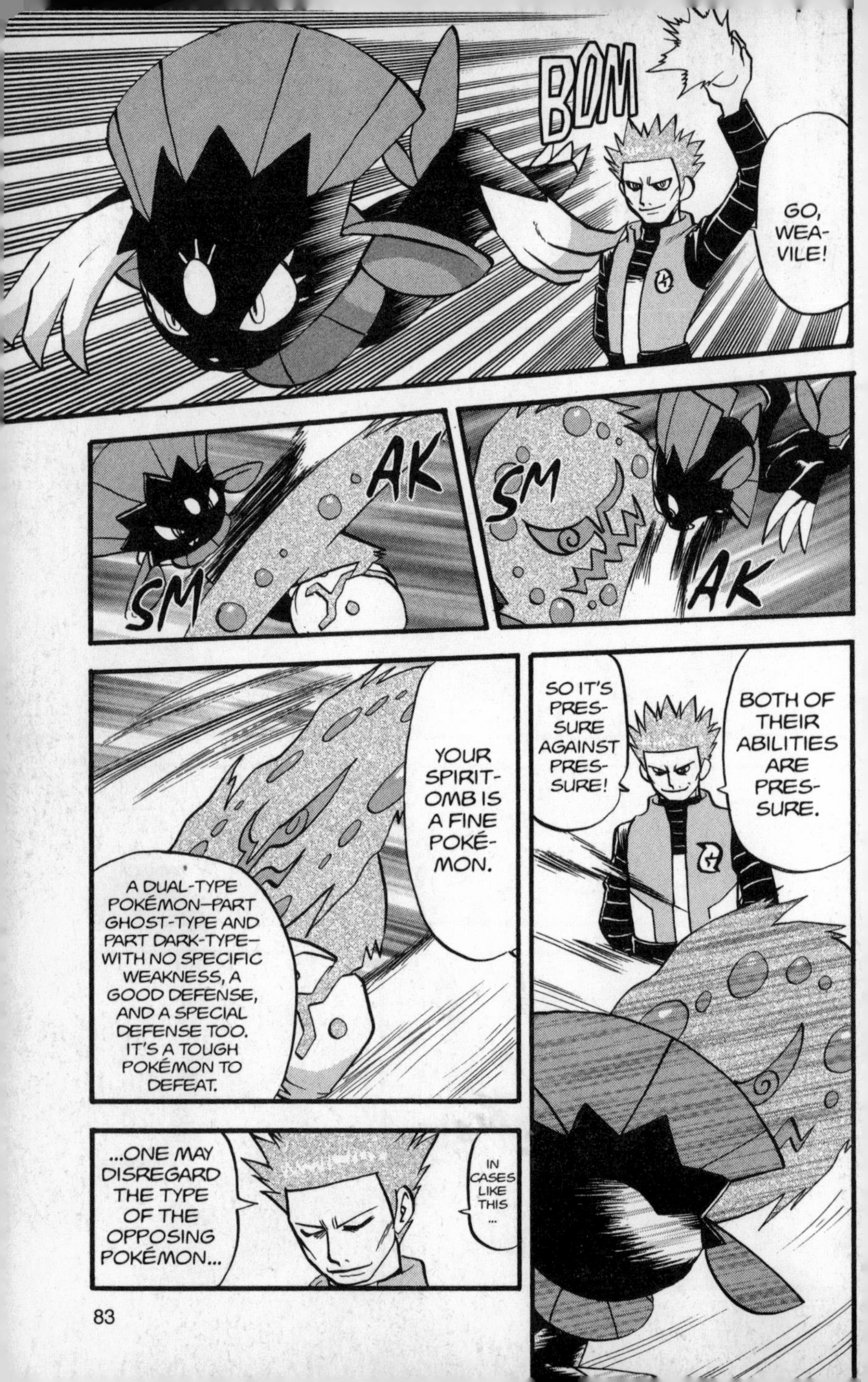
BOM
GO, WEA-VILE!
SM
AK
AK
SM
BOTH OF THEIR ABILITIES ARE PRES-SURE.
SO IT'S PRES-SURE AGAINST PRES-SURE!
YOUR SPIRIT-OMB IS A FINE POKÉ-MON.
A DUAL-TYPE POKÉMON—PART GHOST-TYPE AND PART DARK-TYPE—WITH NO SPECIFIC WEAKNESS, A GOOD DEFENSE, AND A SPECIAL DEFENSE TOO. IT'S A TOUGH POKÉMON TO DEFEAT.
IN CASES LIKE THIS ...
...ONE MAY DISREGARD THE TYPE OF THE OPPOSING POKÉMON...

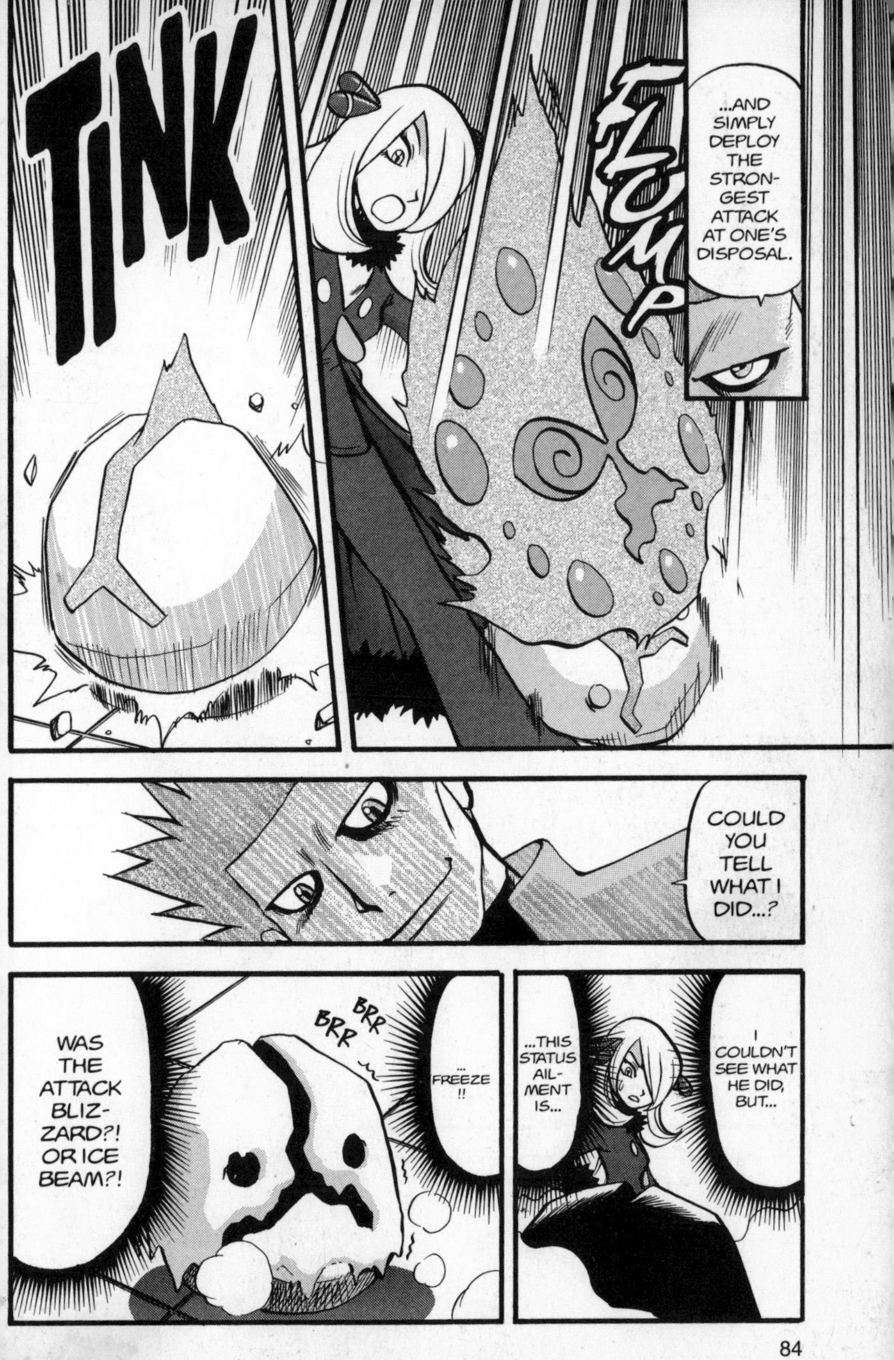
...AND SIMPLY DEPLOY THE STRON-GEST ATTACK AT ONE'S DISPOSAL.
FLUMP
TINK
COULD YOU TELL WHAT I DID...?
I COULDN'T SEE WHAT HE DID, BUT...
...THIS STATUS AIL-MENT IS...
...FREEZE!!
BRR
BRR
WAS THE ATTACK BLIZ-ZARD?! OR ICE BEAM?!

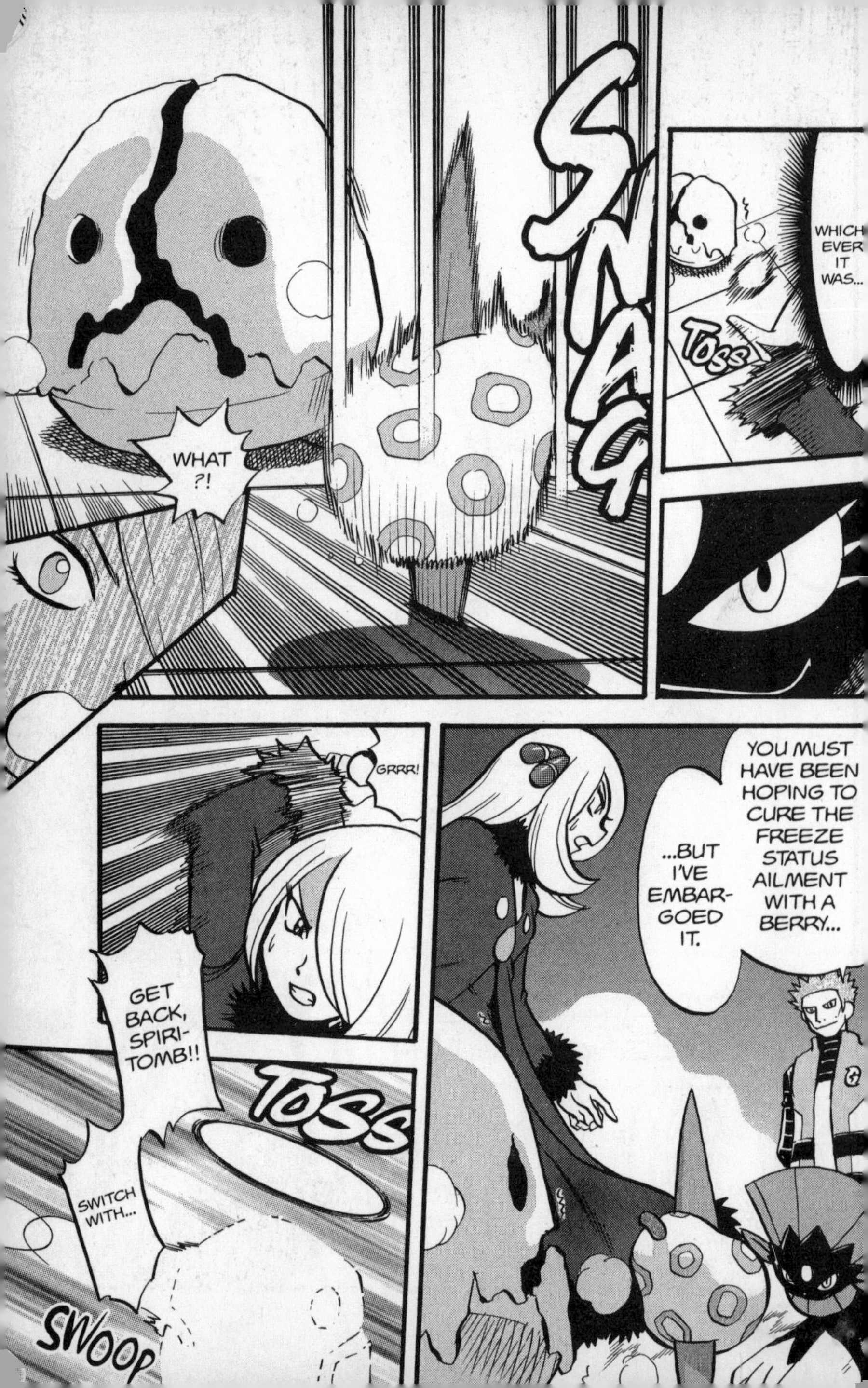

WHICH EVER IT WAS...
TOSS
SNAG
WHAT ?!
YOU MUST HAVE BEEN HOPING TO CURE THE FREEZE STATUS AILMENT WITH A BERRY...
...BUT I'VE EMBAR-GOED IT.
GRRR!
GET BACK, SPIRI-TOMB!!
TOSS
SWITCH WITH...
SWOOP

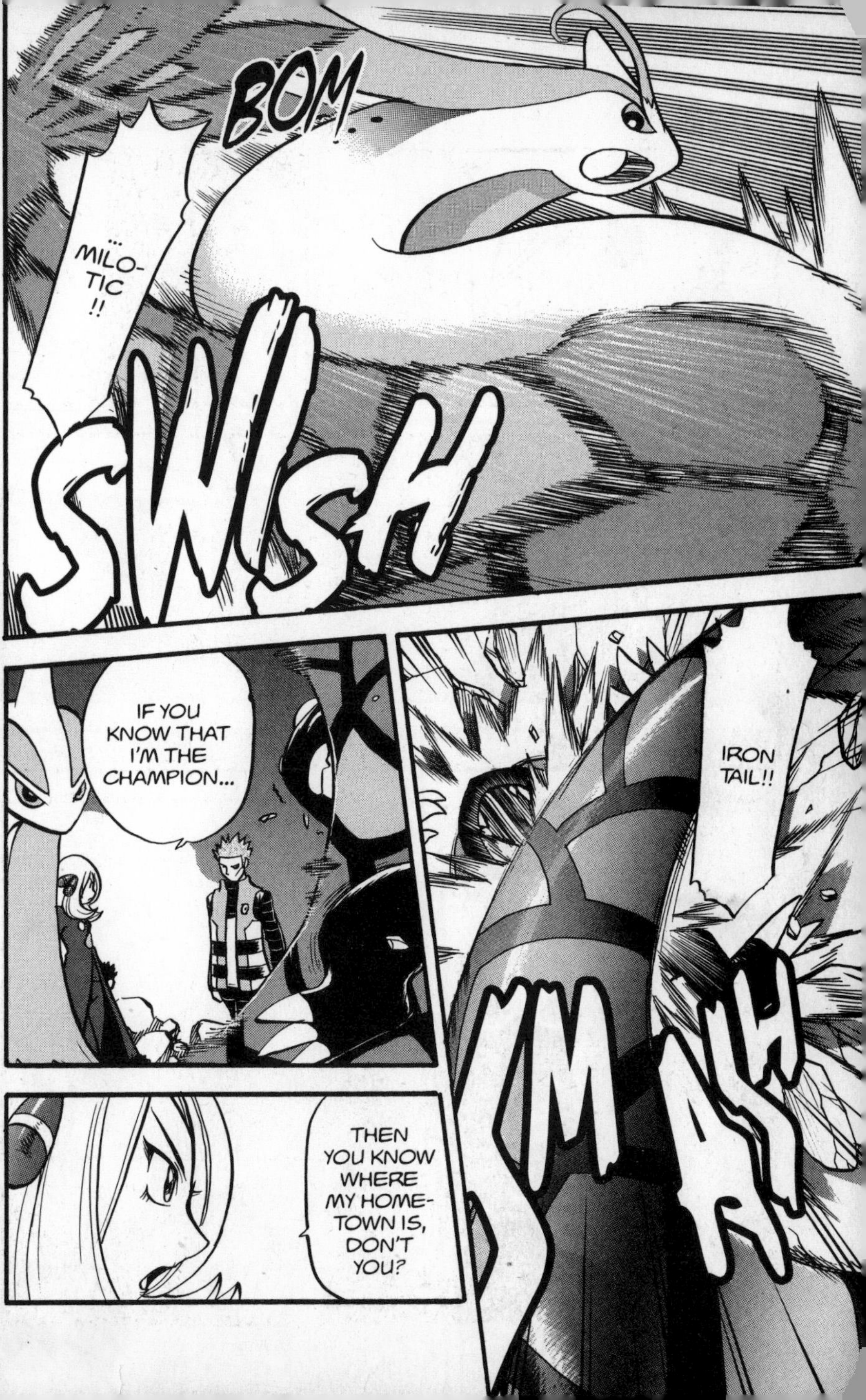
BOM
... MILO-TIC!!
SWISH
IRON TAIL!!
IF YOU KNOW THAT I'M THE CHAMPION...
THEN YOU KNOW WHERE MY HOME-TOWN IS, DON'T YOU?

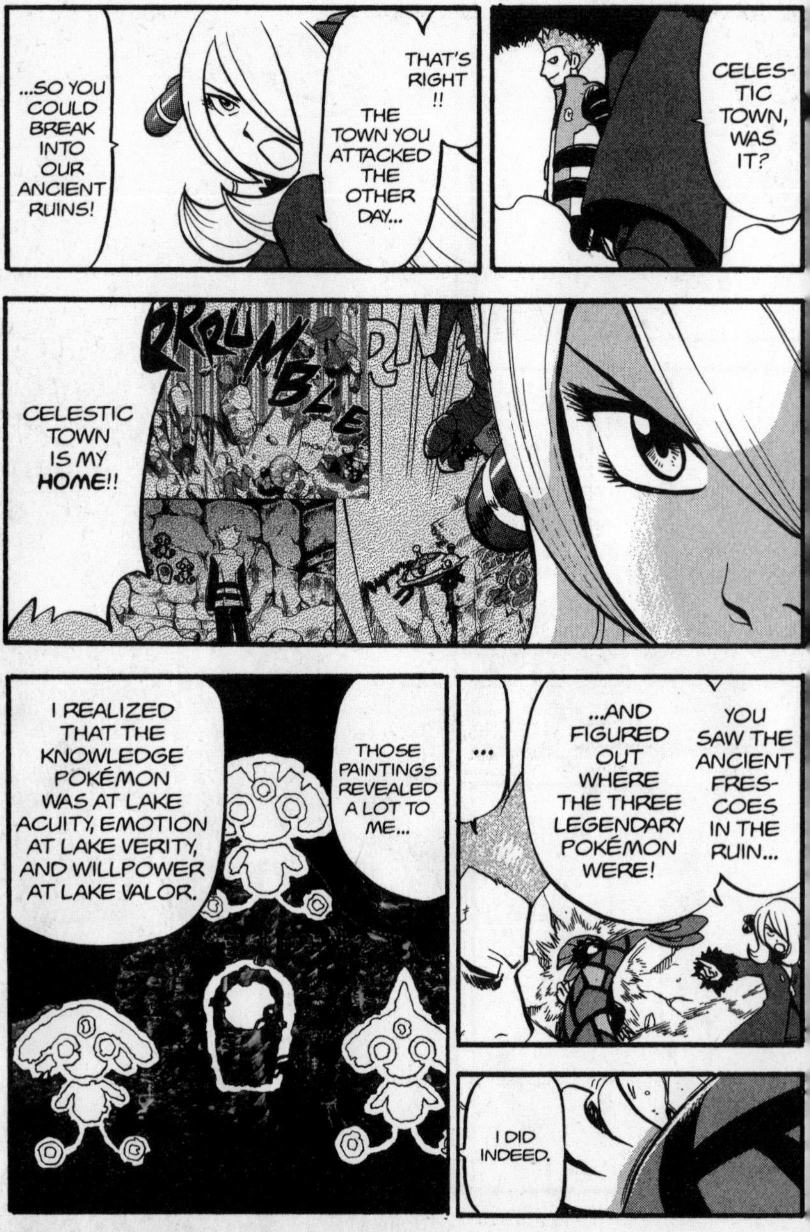

CELESTIC TOWN, WAS IT?
THAT'S RIGHT!! THE TOWN YOU ATTACKED THE OTHER DAY...
...SO YOU COULD BREAK INTO OUR ANCIENT RUINS!
CELESTIC TOWN IS MY **HOME**!!
YOU SAW THE ANCIENT FRESCOES IN THE RUIN...
...AND FIGURED OUT WHERE THE THREE LEGENDARY POKÉMON WERE!
...
I DID INDEED.
THOSE PAINTINGS REVEALED A LOT TO ME...
I REALIZED THAT THE KNOWLEDGE POKÉMON WAS AT LAKE ACUITY, EMOTION AT LAKE VERITY, AND WILLPOWER AT LAKE VALOR.

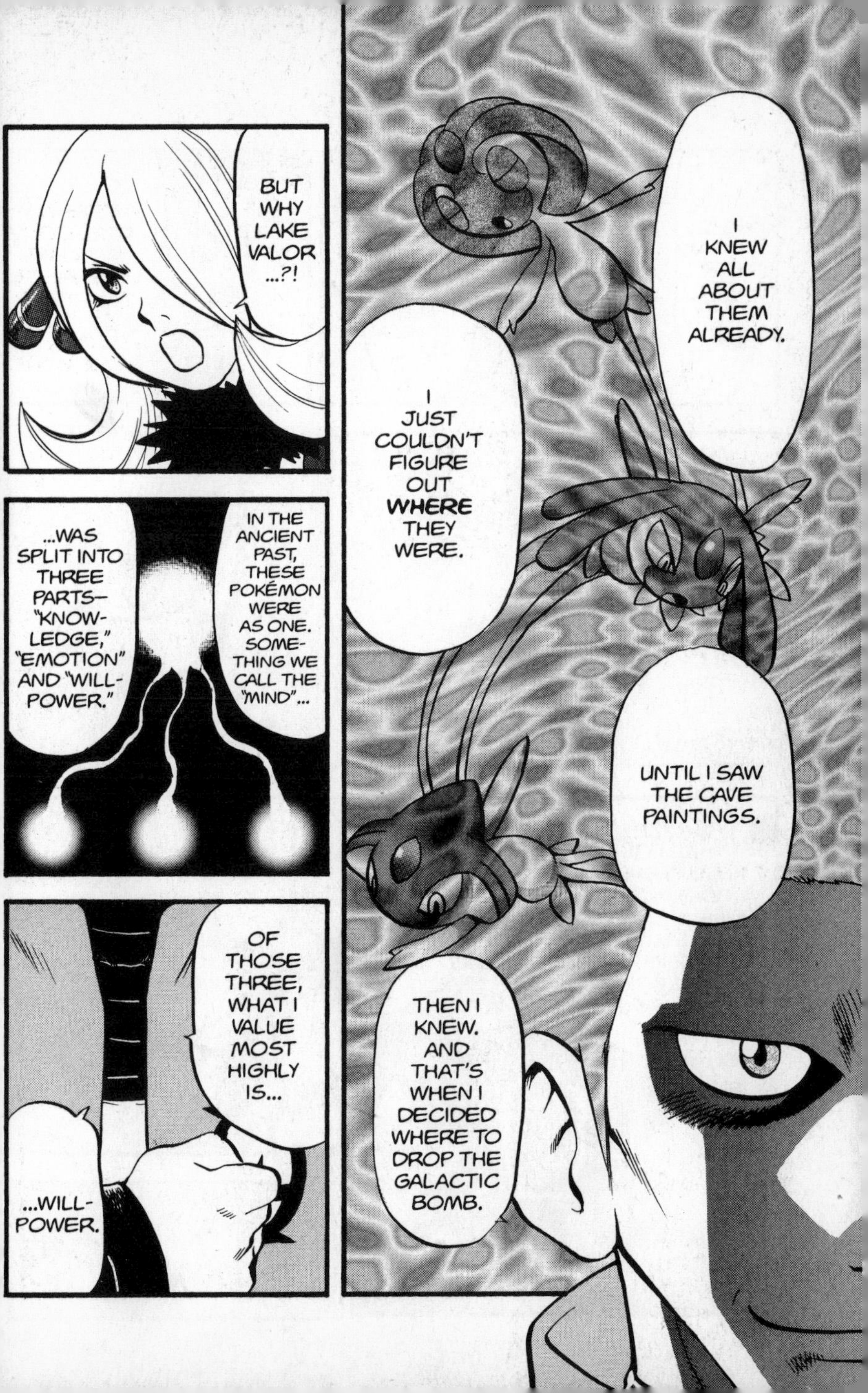
I KNEW ALL ABOUT THEM ALREADY.
I JUST COULDN'T FIGURE OUT **WHERE** THEY WERE.
UNTIL I SAW THE CAVE PAINTINGS.
THEN I KNEW. AND THAT'S WHEN I DECIDED WHERE TO DROP THE GALACTIC BOMB.
BUT WHY LAKE VALOR ...?!
IN THE ANCIENT PAST, THESE POKÉMON WERE AS ONE. SOME-THING WE CALL THE "MIND"...
...WAS SPLIT INTO THREE PARTS— "KNOW-LEDGE," "EMOTION" AND "WILL-POWER."
OF THOSE THREE, WHAT I VALUE MOST HIGHLY IS...
...WILL-POWER.

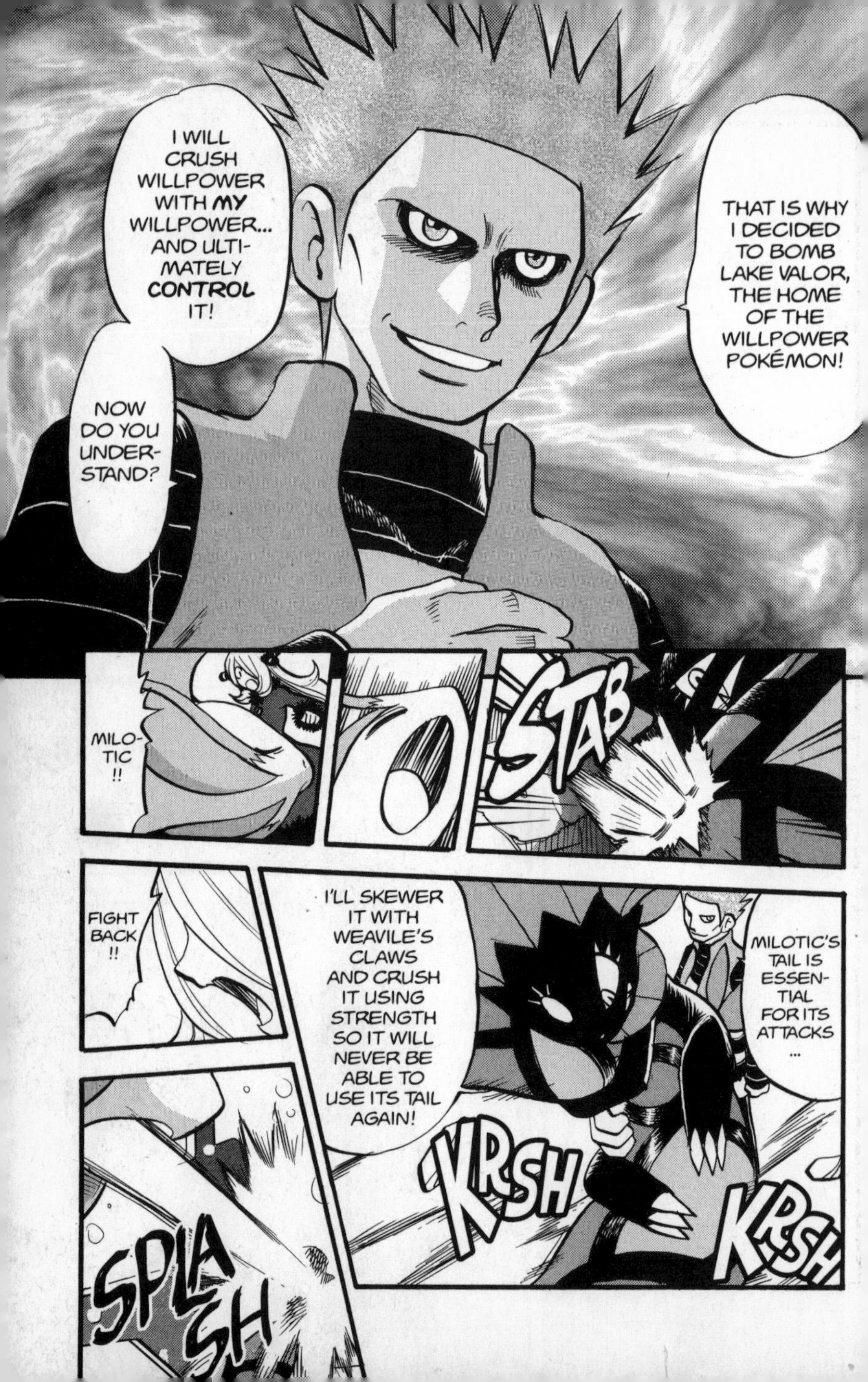
THAT IS WHY I DECIDED TO BOMB LAKE VALOR, THE HOME OF THE WILLPOWER POKÉMON!
I WILL CRUSH WILLPOWER WITH **MY** WILLPOWER... AND ULTI-MATELY **CONTROL** IT!
NOW DO YOU UNDER-STAND?
STAB
MILO-TIC !!
MILOTIC'S TAIL IS ESSEN-TIAL FOR ITS ATTACKS ...
I'LL SKEWER IT WITH WEAVILE'S CLAWS AND CRUSH IT USING STRENGTH SO IT WILL NEVER BE ABLE TO USE ITS TAIL AGAIN!
KRSH
KRSH
FIGHT BACK !!
SPLASH

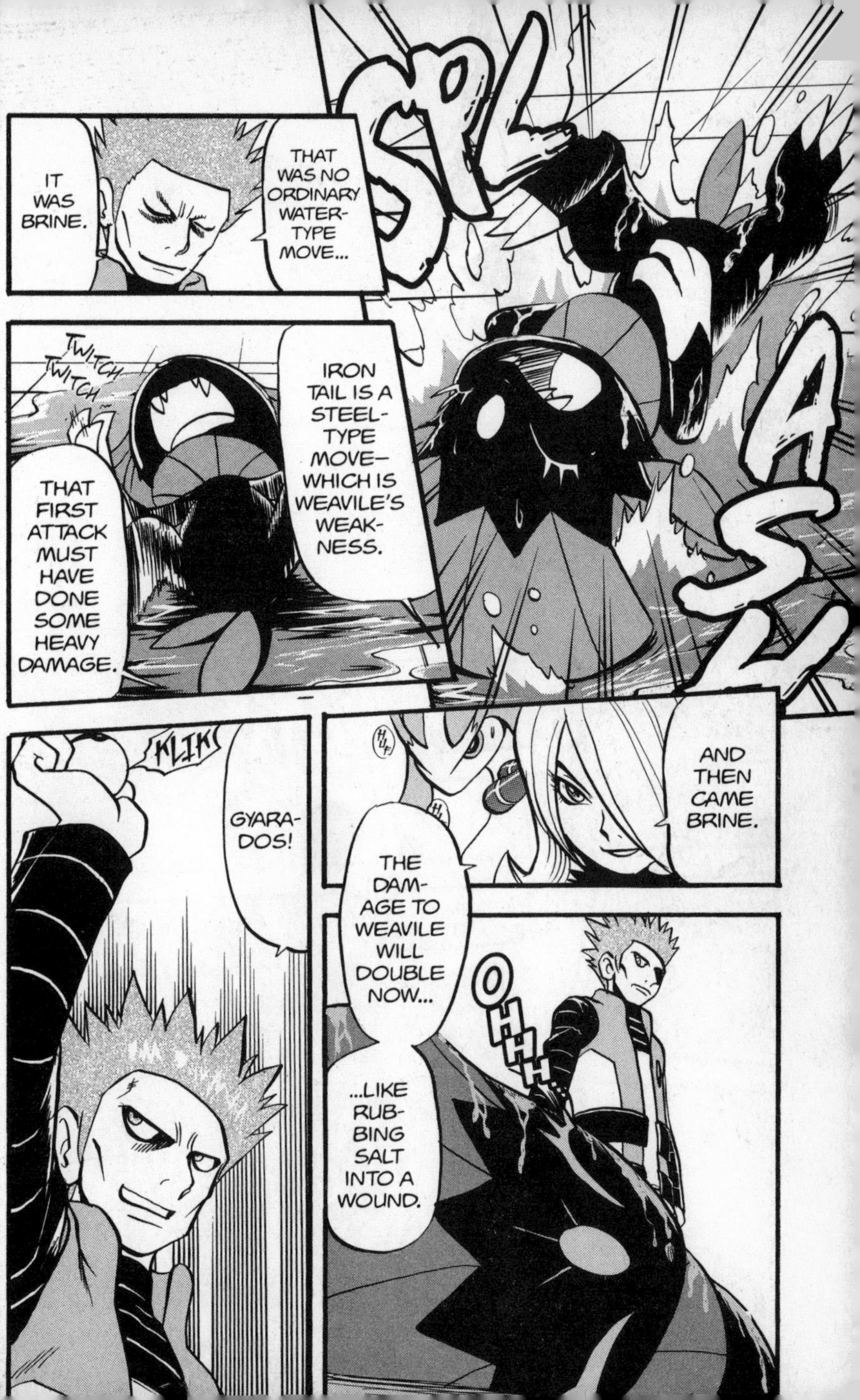
SPLASH
THAT WAS NO ORDINARY WATER-TYPE MOVE...
IT WAS BRINE.
IRON TAIL IS A STEEL-TYPE MOVE—WHICH IS WEAVILE'S WEAKNESS.
TWITCH TWITCH
THAT FIRST ATTACK MUST HAVE DONE SOME HEAVY DAMAGE.
AND THEN CAME BRINE.
HUF HUF
THE DAMAGE TO WEAVILE WILL DOUBLE NOW...
OHHHH
...LIKE RUBBING SALT INTO A WOUND.
KLIK
GYARADOS!

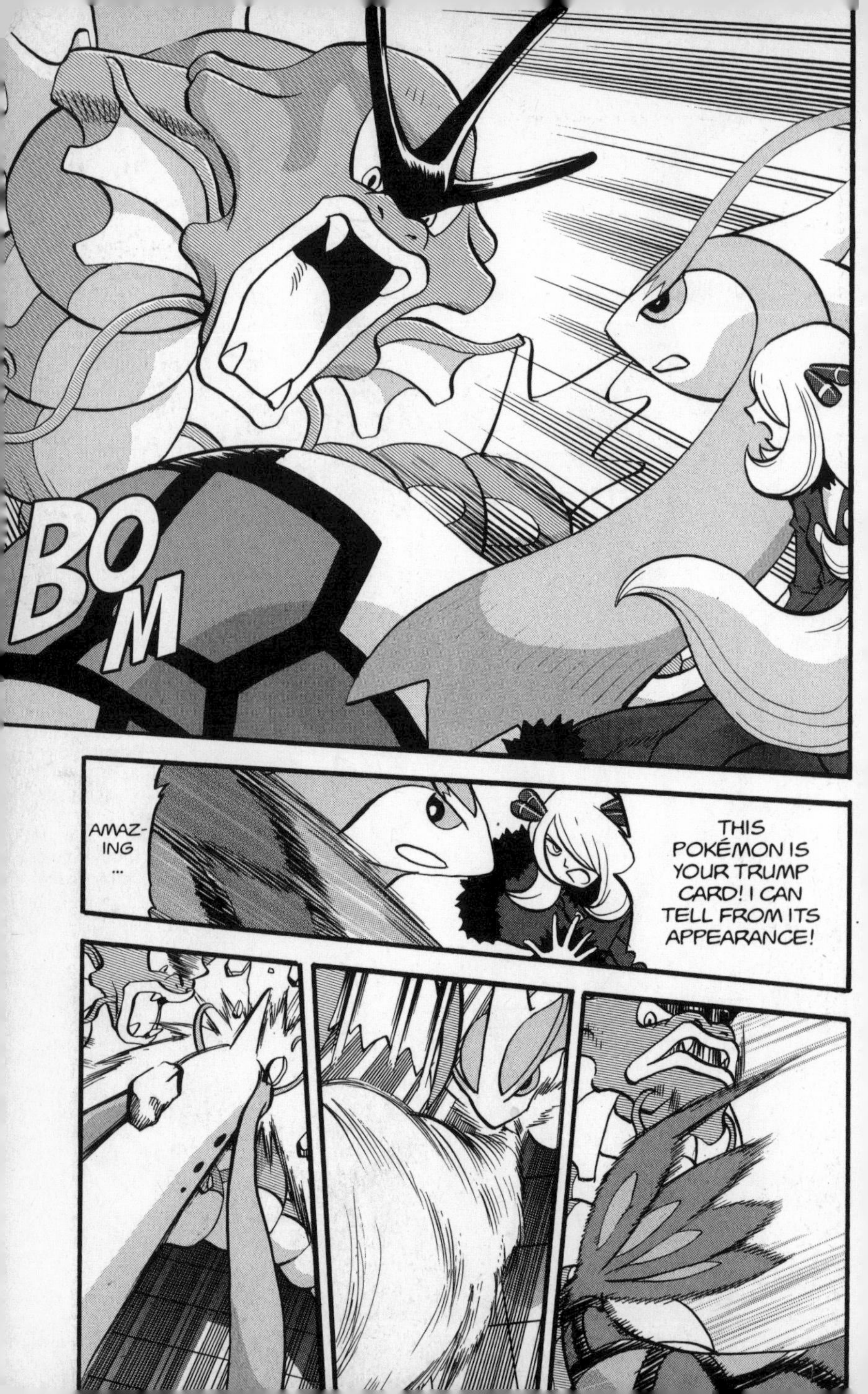
BOM
THIS POKÉMON IS YOUR TRUMP CARD! I CAN TELL FROM ITS APPEARANCE!
AMAZ-ING ...

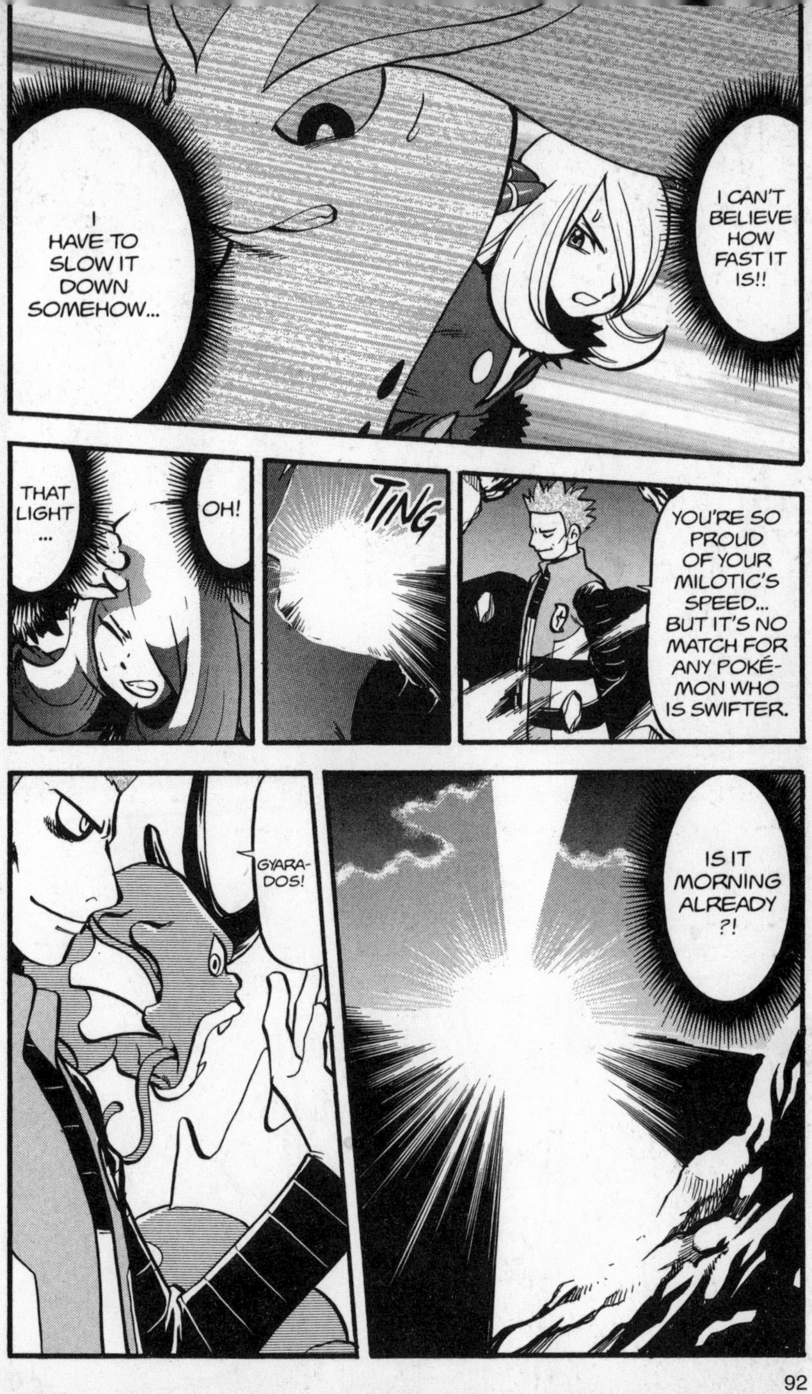
I CAN'T BELIEVE HOW FAST IT IS!!
I HAVE TO SLOW IT DOWN SOMEHOW...
YOU'RE SO PROUD OF YOUR MILOTIC'S SPEED... BUT IT'S NO MATCH FOR ANY POKÉ-MON WHO IS SWIFTER.
TING
OH!
THAT LIGHT ...
IS IT MORNING ALREADY ?!
GYARA-DOS!

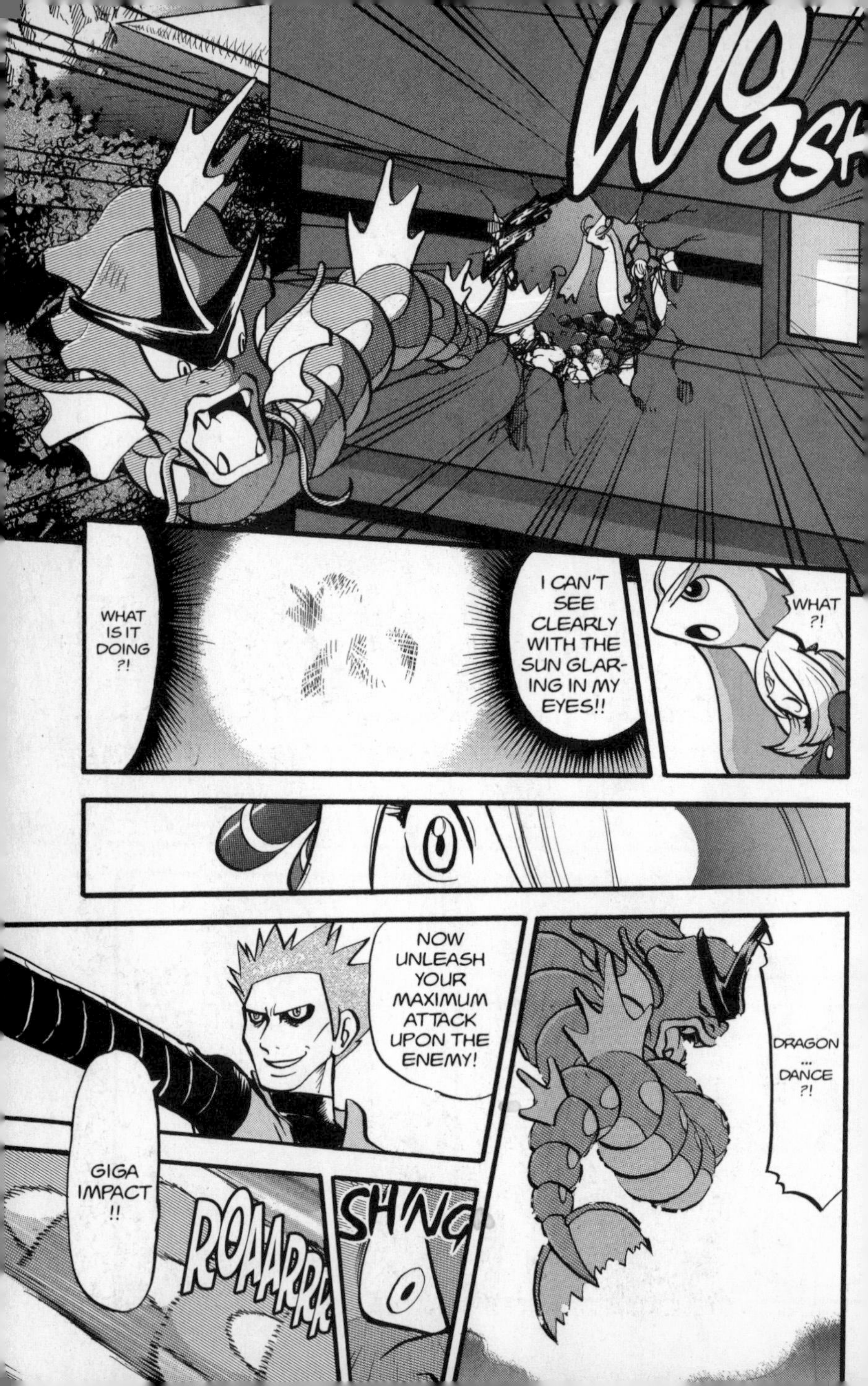
WOOSH
WHAT ?!
I CAN'T SEE CLEARLY WITH THE SUN GLARING IN MY EYES!!
WHAT IS IT DOING ?!
DRAGON ... DANCE ?!
NOW UNLEASH YOUR MAXIMUM ATTACK UPON THE ENEMY!
GIGA IMPACT !!
SHING
ROAARRRK

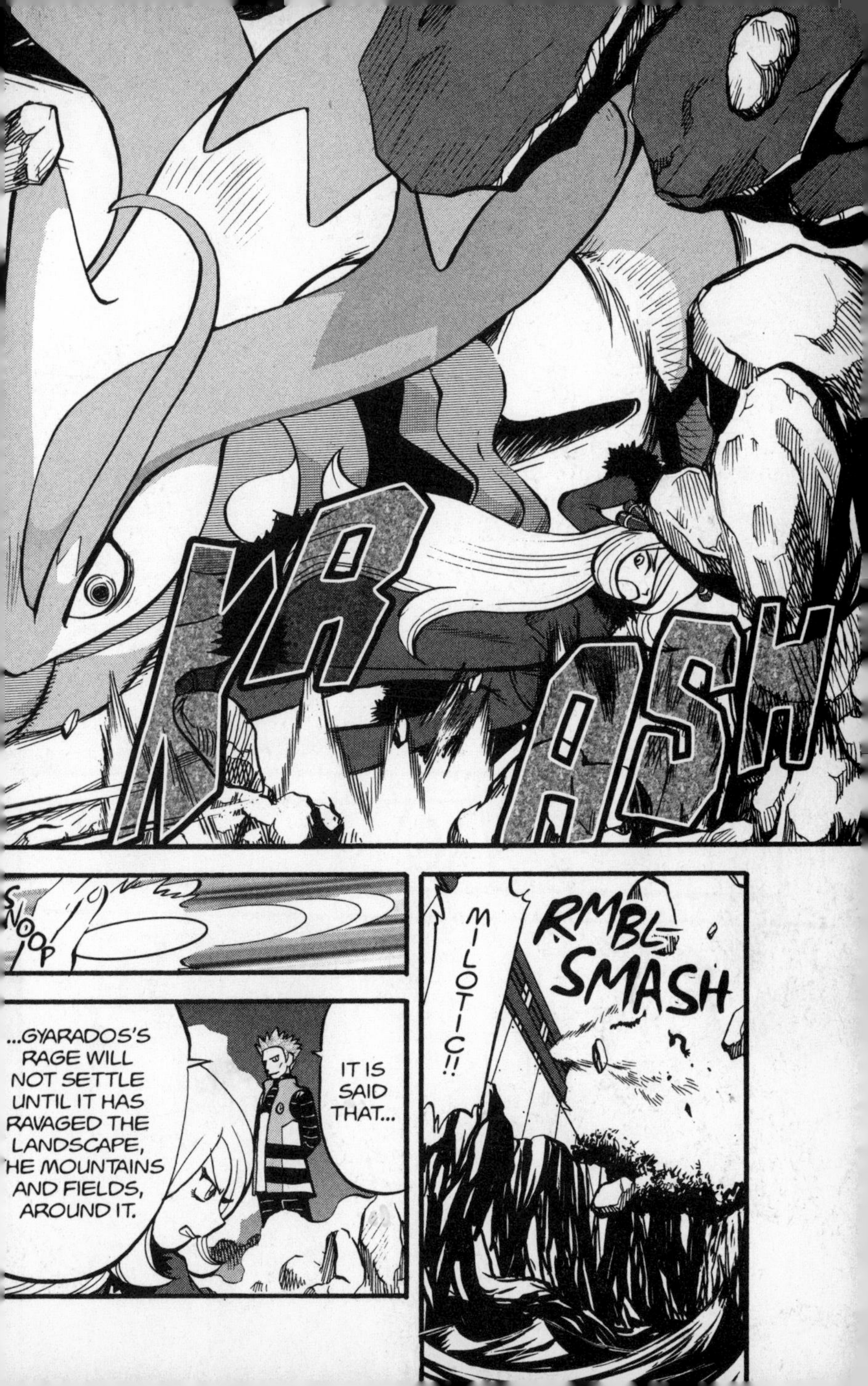
KRASH
MILOTIC!!
RMBL-
SMASH
SWOOP
IT IS SAID THAT...
...GYARADOS'S RAGE WILL NOT SETTLE UNTIL IT HAS RAVAGED THE LANDSCAPE, HE MOUNTAINS AND FIELDS, AROUND IT.

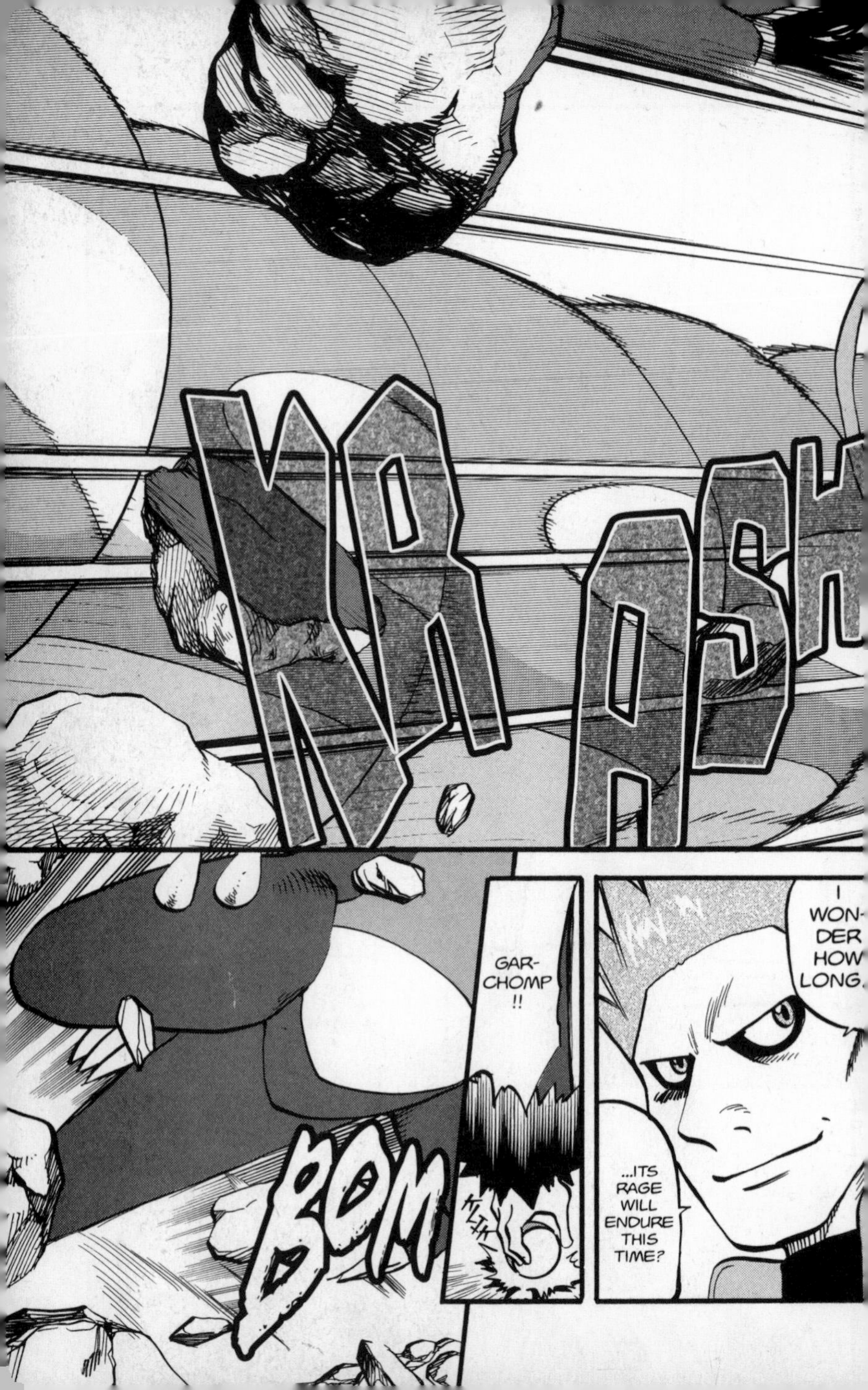
KRASH
I WONDER HOW LONG...
...ITS RAGE WILL ENDURE THIS TIME?
GARCHOMP!!
KLIK
BOM

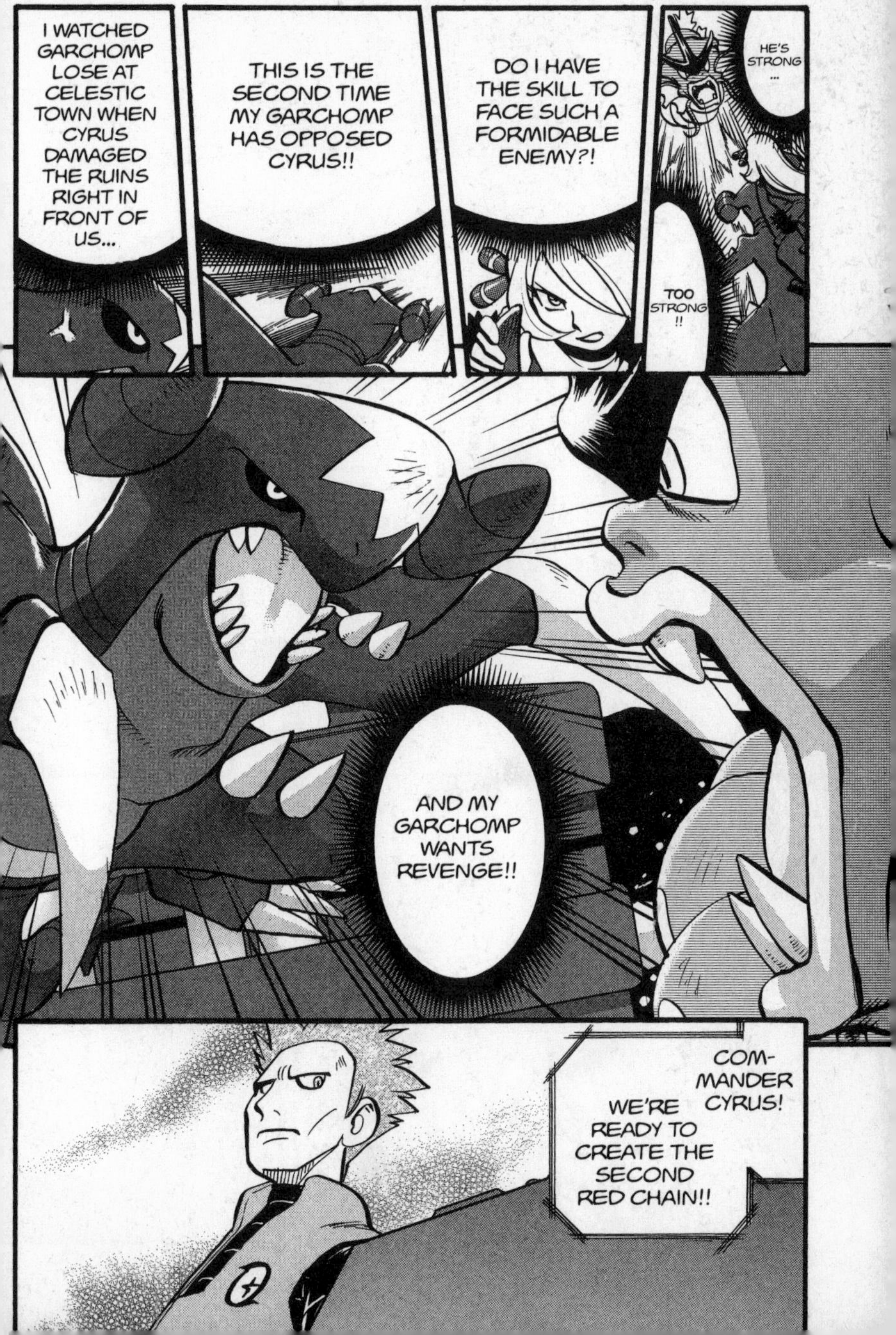
HE'S STRONG ...
TOO STRONG !!
DO I HAVE THE SKILL TO FACE SUCH A FORMIDABLE ENEMY?!
THIS IS THE SECOND TIME MY GARCHOMP HAS OPPOSED CYRUS!!
I WATCHED GARCHOMP LOSE AT CELESTIC TOWN WHEN CYRUS DAMAGED THE RUINS RIGHT IN FRONT OF US...
AND MY GARCHOMP WANTS REVENGE!!
COM-MANDER CYRUS!
WE'RE READY TO CREATE THE SECOND RED CHAIN!!

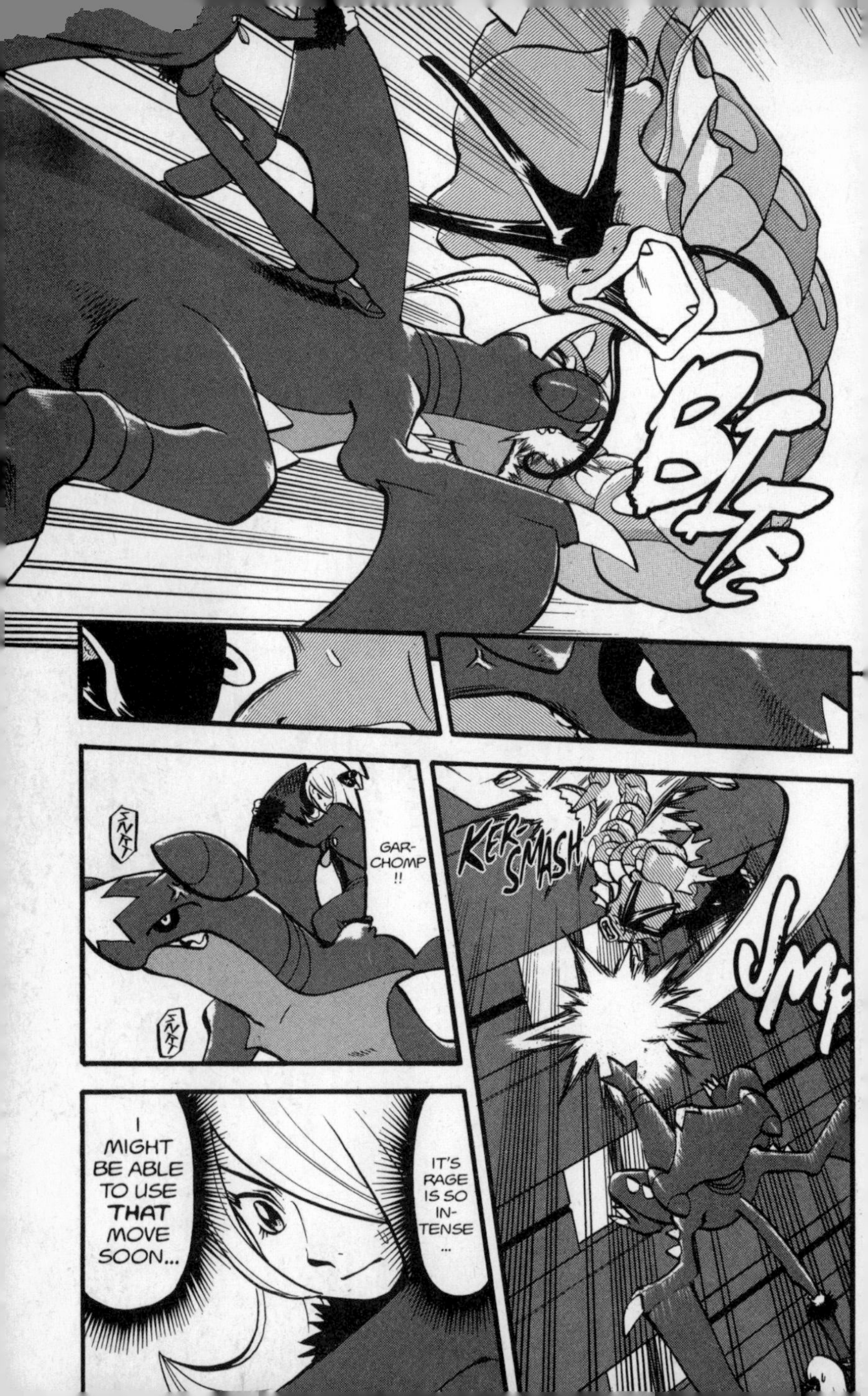
BITE
KER-SMASH
GAR-CHOMP!!
SNRT
SNRT
IT'S RAGE IS SO IN-TENSE...
I MIGHT BE ABLE TO USE THAT MOVE SOON...

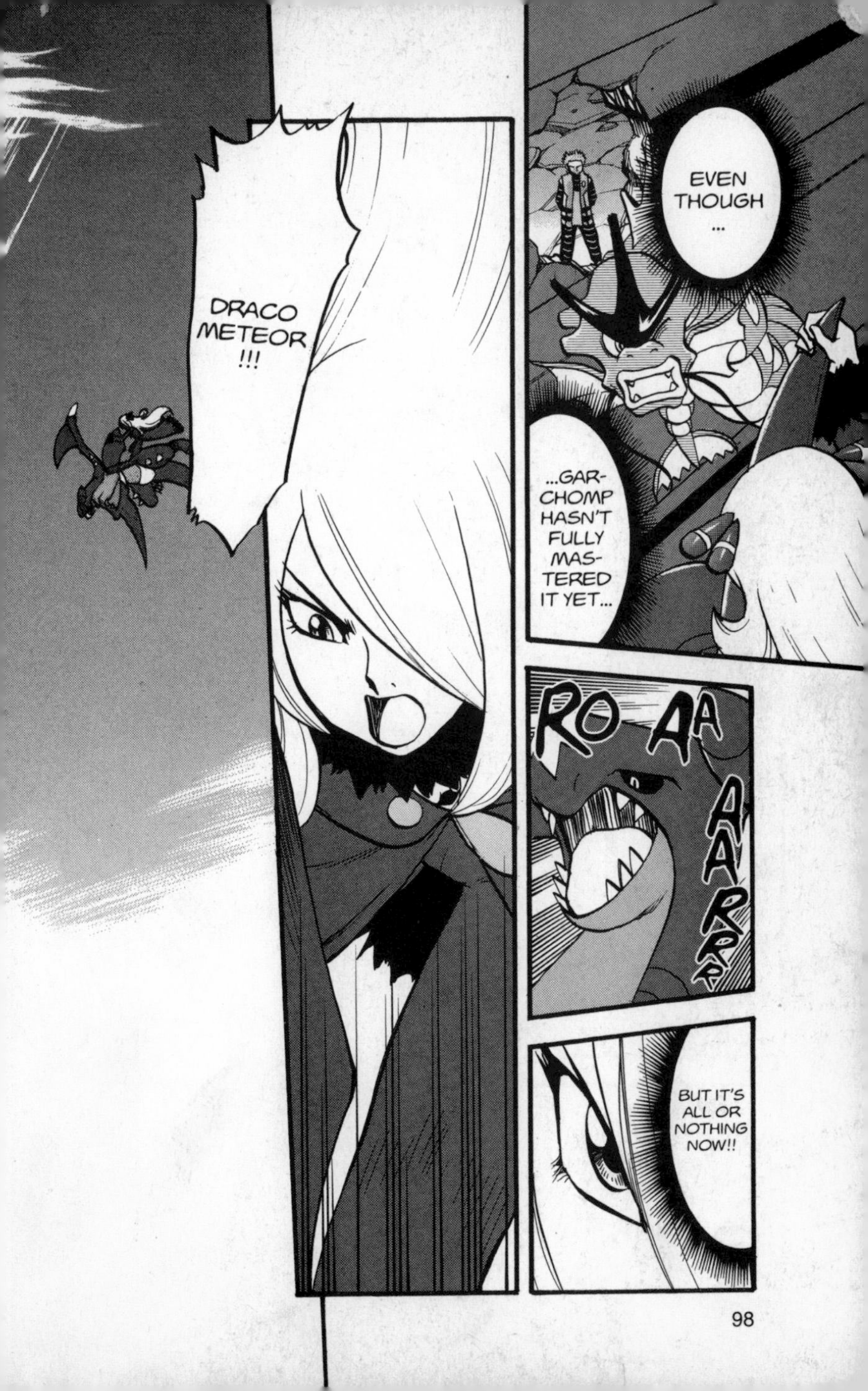
EVEN THOUGH ...
...GAR-CHOMP HASN'T FULLY MAS-TERED IT YET...
ROAAAARRR
BUT IT'S ALL OR NOTHING NOW!!
DRACO METEOR !!!

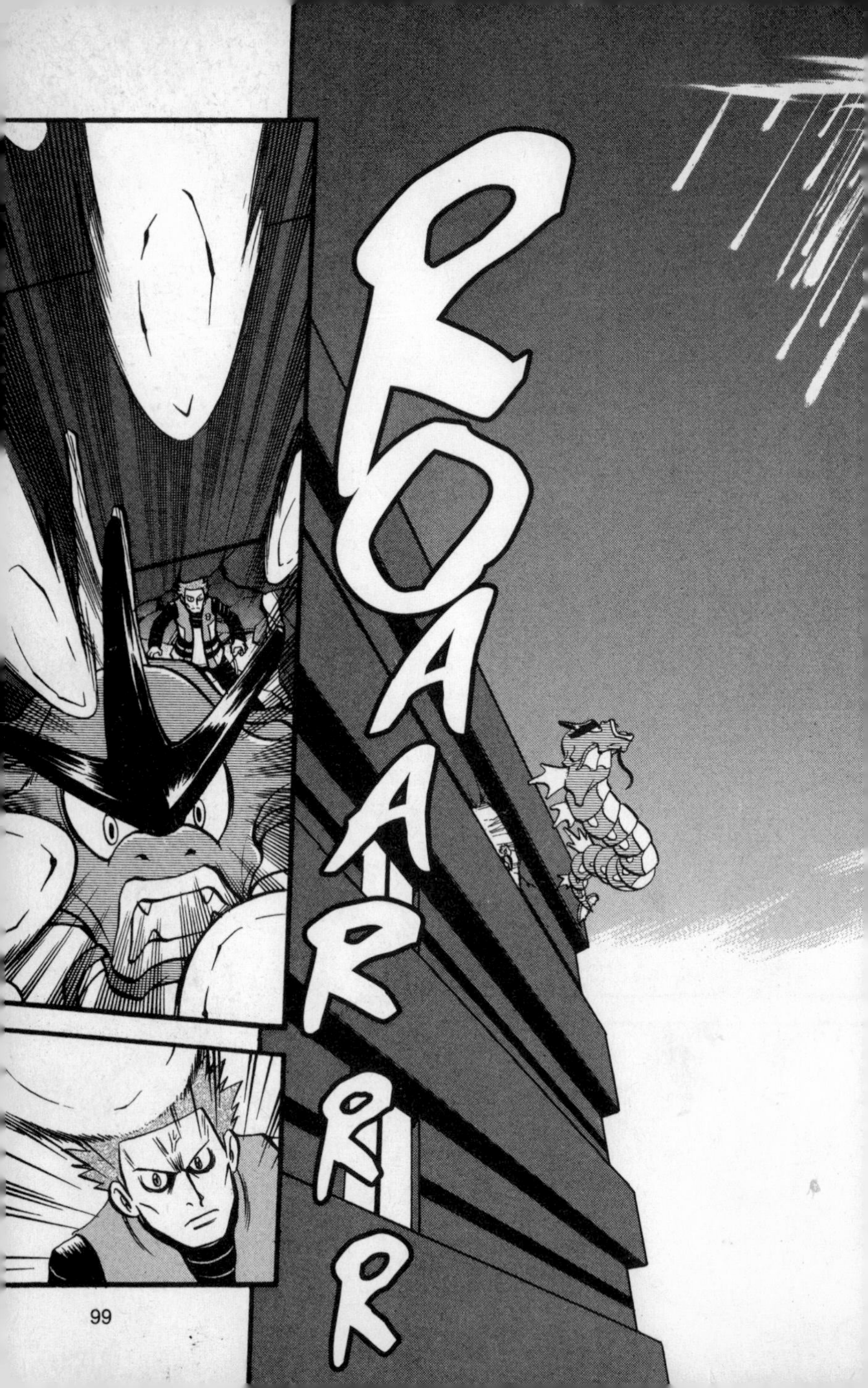
ROOAARRRR

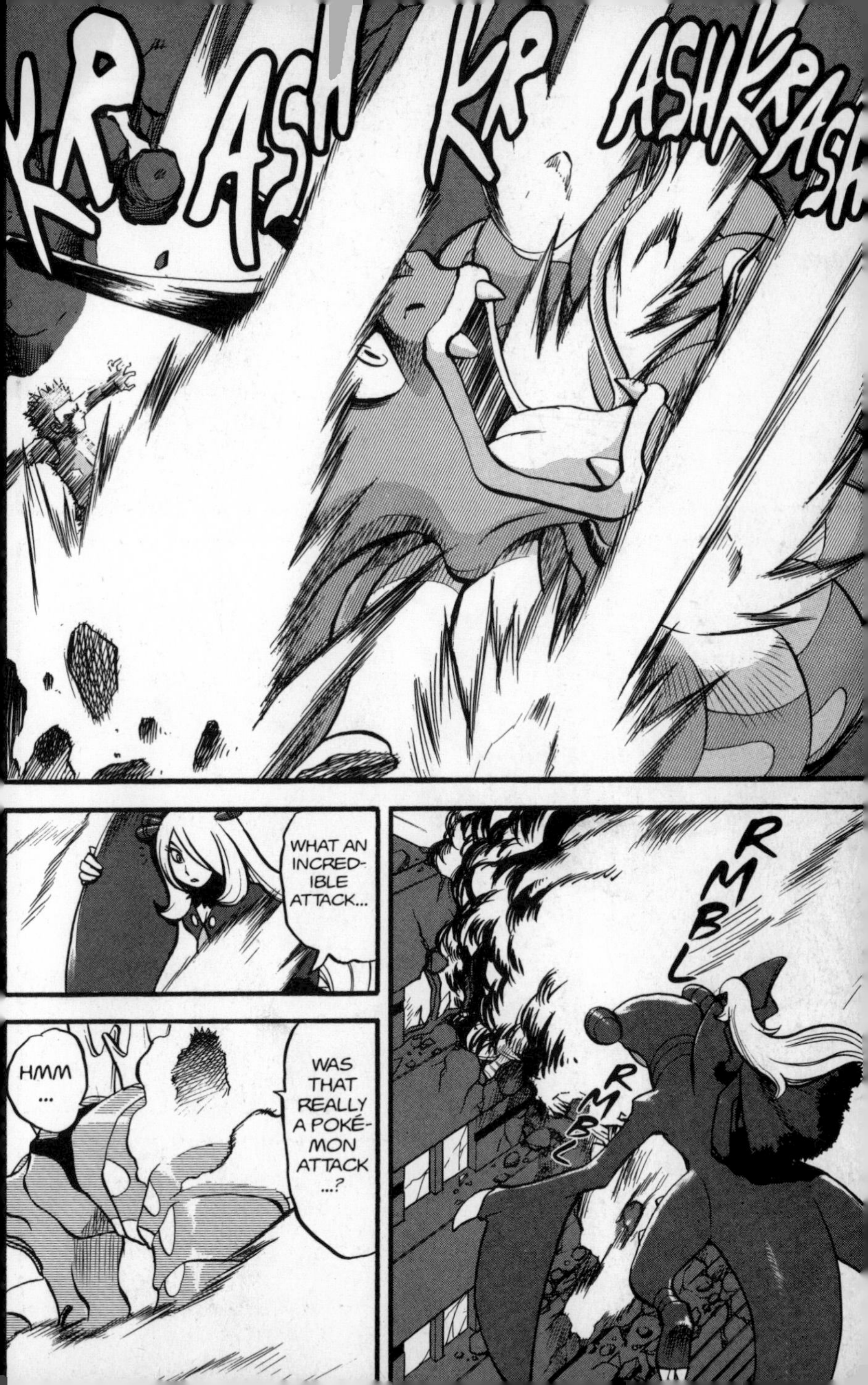
KRASH KRASHKRASH
RMBL
RMBL
WHAT AN INCREDIBLE ATTACK...
WAS THAT REALLY A POKÉMON ATTACK ...?
HMM ...

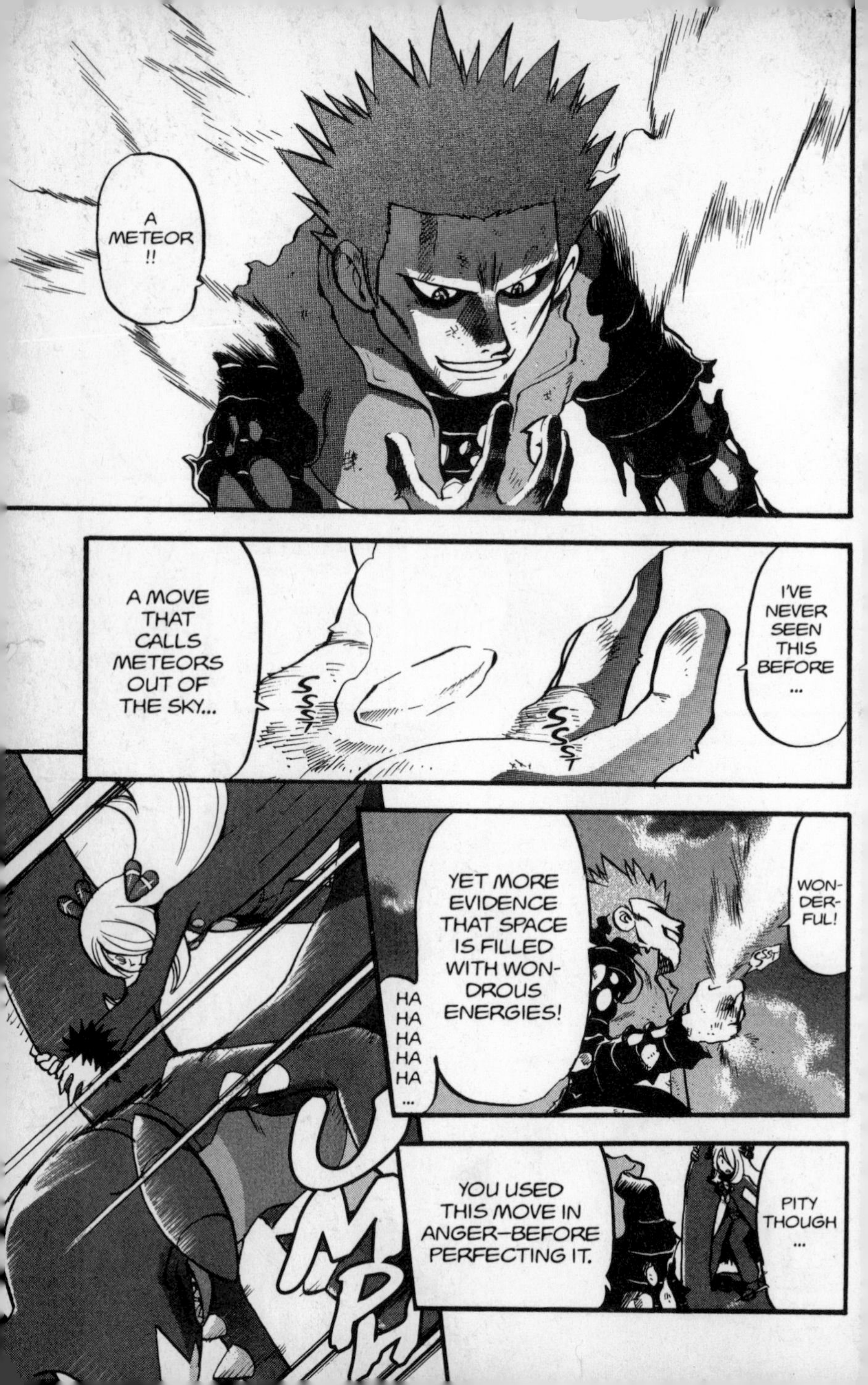
A METEOR !!
I'VE NEVER SEEN THIS BEFORE ...
A MOVE THAT CALLS METEORS OUT OF THE SKY...
SSST
SSST
WON-DER-FUL!
YET MORE EVIDENCE THAT SPACE IS FILLED WITH WON-DROUS ENERGIES!
SSST
HA HA HA HA HA ...
PITY THOUGH ...
YOU USED THIS MOVE IN ANGER—BEFORE PERFECTING IT.

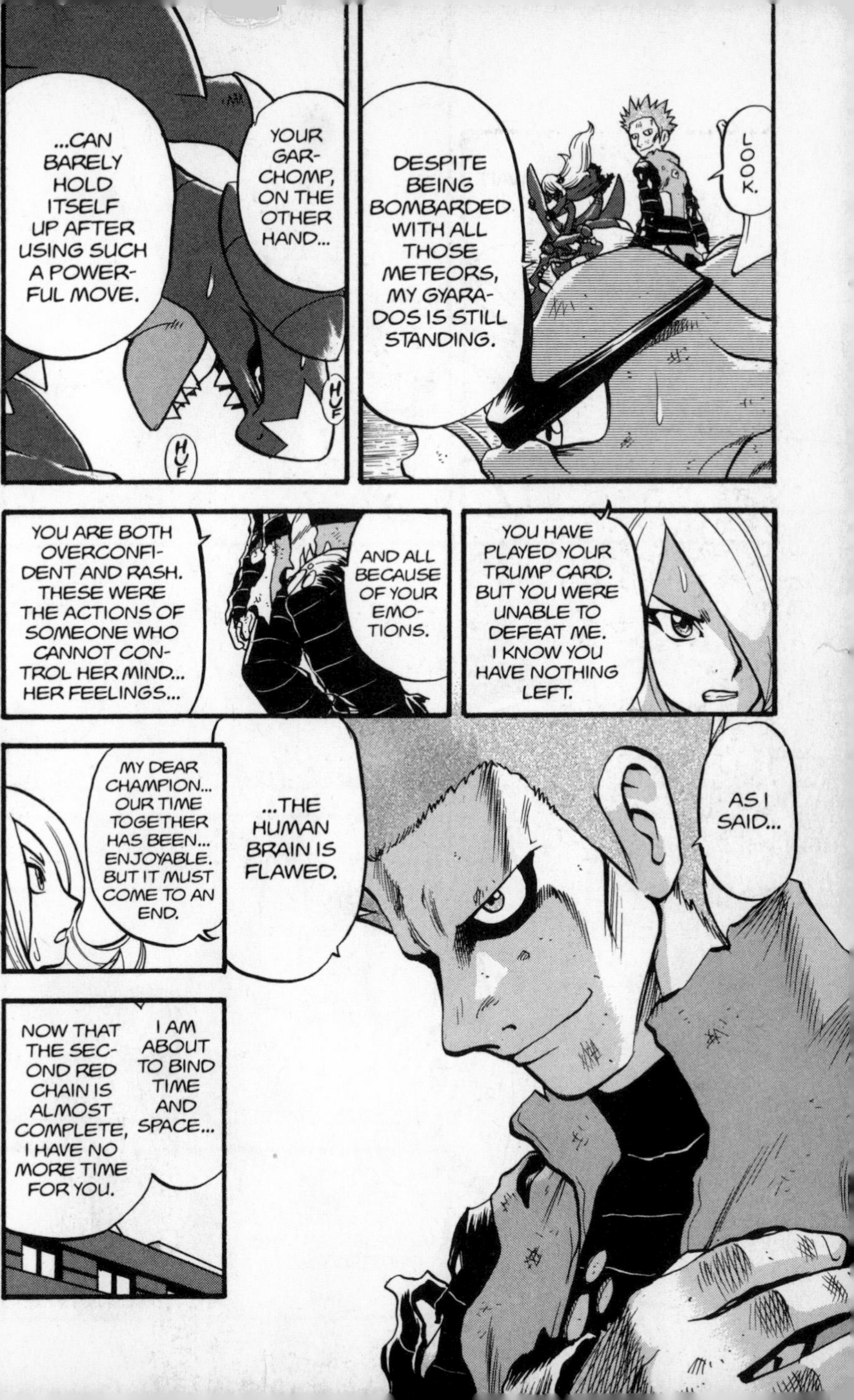
LOOK.
DESPITE BEING BOMBARDED WITH ALL THOSE METEORS, MY GYARADOS IS STILL STANDING.
YOUR GARCHOMP, ON THE OTHER HAND...
...CAN BARELY HOLD ITSELF UP AFTER USING SUCH A POWERFUL MOVE.
HUF
HUF
YOU HAVE PLAYED YOUR TRUMP CARD. BUT YOU WERE UNABLE TO DEFEAT ME. I KNOW YOU HAVE NOTHING LEFT.
AND ALL BECAUSE OF YOUR EMOTIONS.
YOU ARE BOTH OVERCONFIDENT AND RASH. THESE WERE THE ACTIONS OF SOMEONE WHO CANNOT CONTROL HER MIND... HER FEELINGS...
AS I SAID...
...THE HUMAN BRAIN IS FLAWED.
MY DEAR CHAMPION... OUR TIME TOGETHER HAS BEEN... ENJOYABLE. BUT IT MUST COME TO AN END.
I AM ABOUT TO BIND TIME AND SPACE...
NOW THAT THE SECOND RED CHAIN IS ALMOST COMPLETE, I HAVE NO MORE TIME FOR YOU.

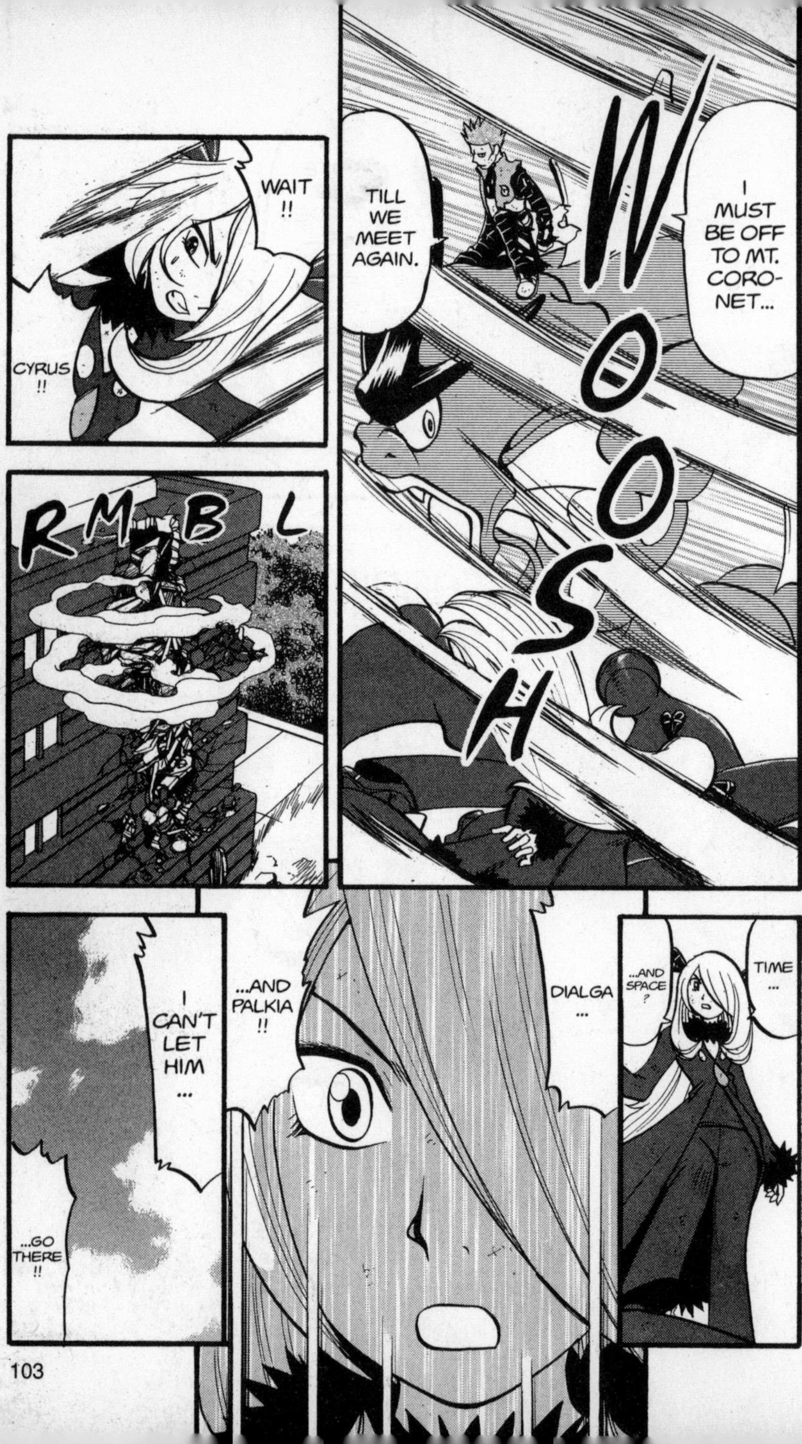

I MUST BE OFF TO MT. CORONET...
WOOSH
TILL WE MEET AGAIN.
WAIT!!
CYRUS!!
RMBL
TIME...
...AND SPACE?
DIALGA...
...AND PALKIA!!
I CAN'T LET HIM...
...GO THERE!!

73

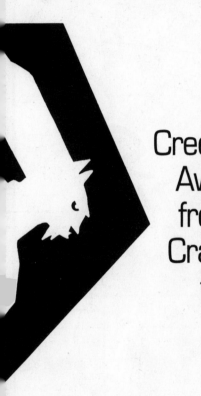

Creeping
Away
from
Cradily

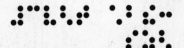

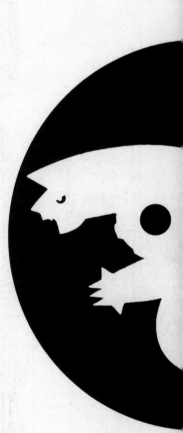

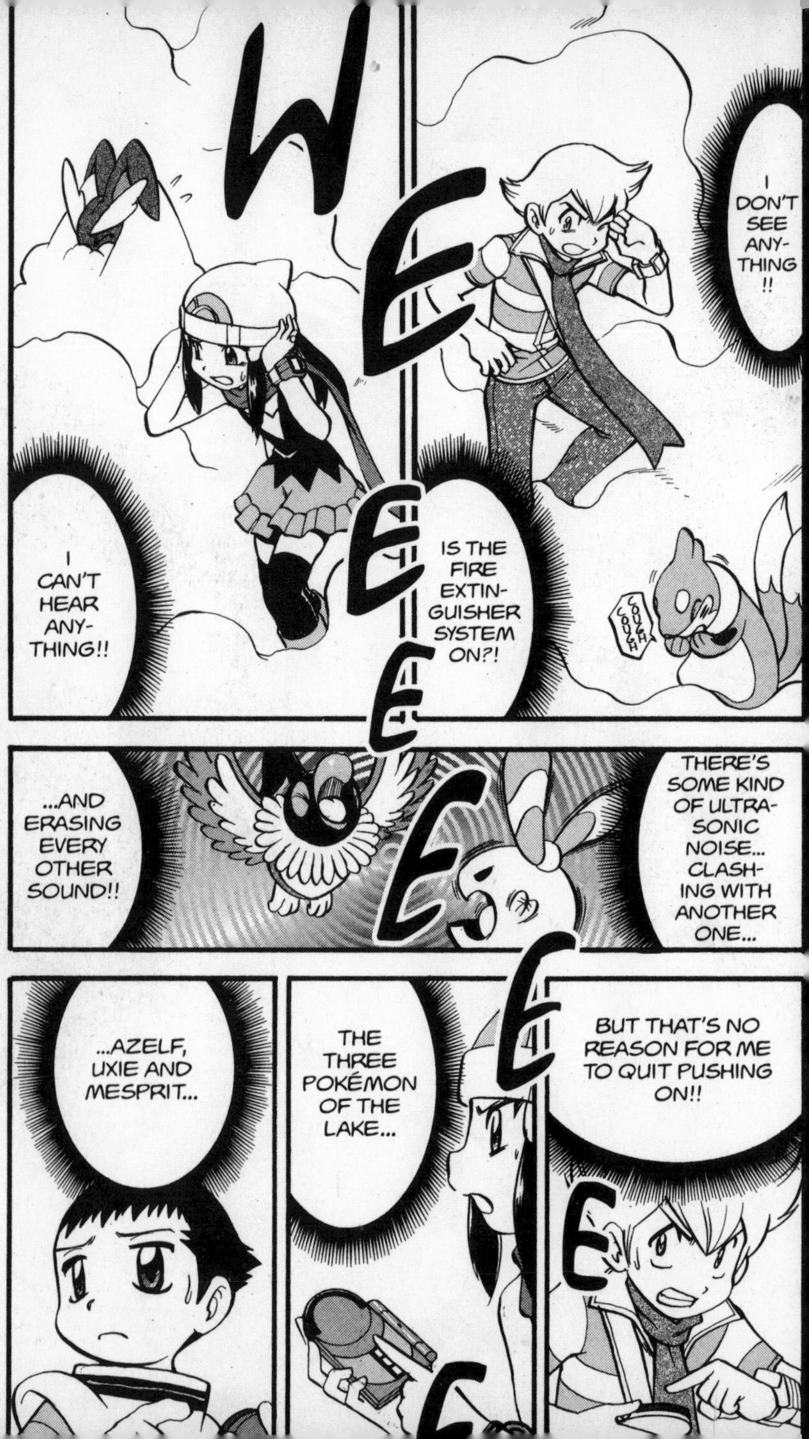
WEEEEEEEEE
I DON'T SEE ANYTHING!!
IS THE FIRE EXTINGUISHER SYSTEM ON?!
COUGH COUGH
I CAN'T HEAR ANYTHING!!
THERE'S SOME KIND OF ULTRASONIC NOISE... CLASHING WITH ANOTHER ONE...
...AND ERASING EVERY OTHER SOUND!!
BUT THAT'S NO REASON FOR ME TO QUIT PUSHING ON!!
THE THREE POKÉMON OF THE LAKE...
...AZELF, UXIE AND MESPRIT...

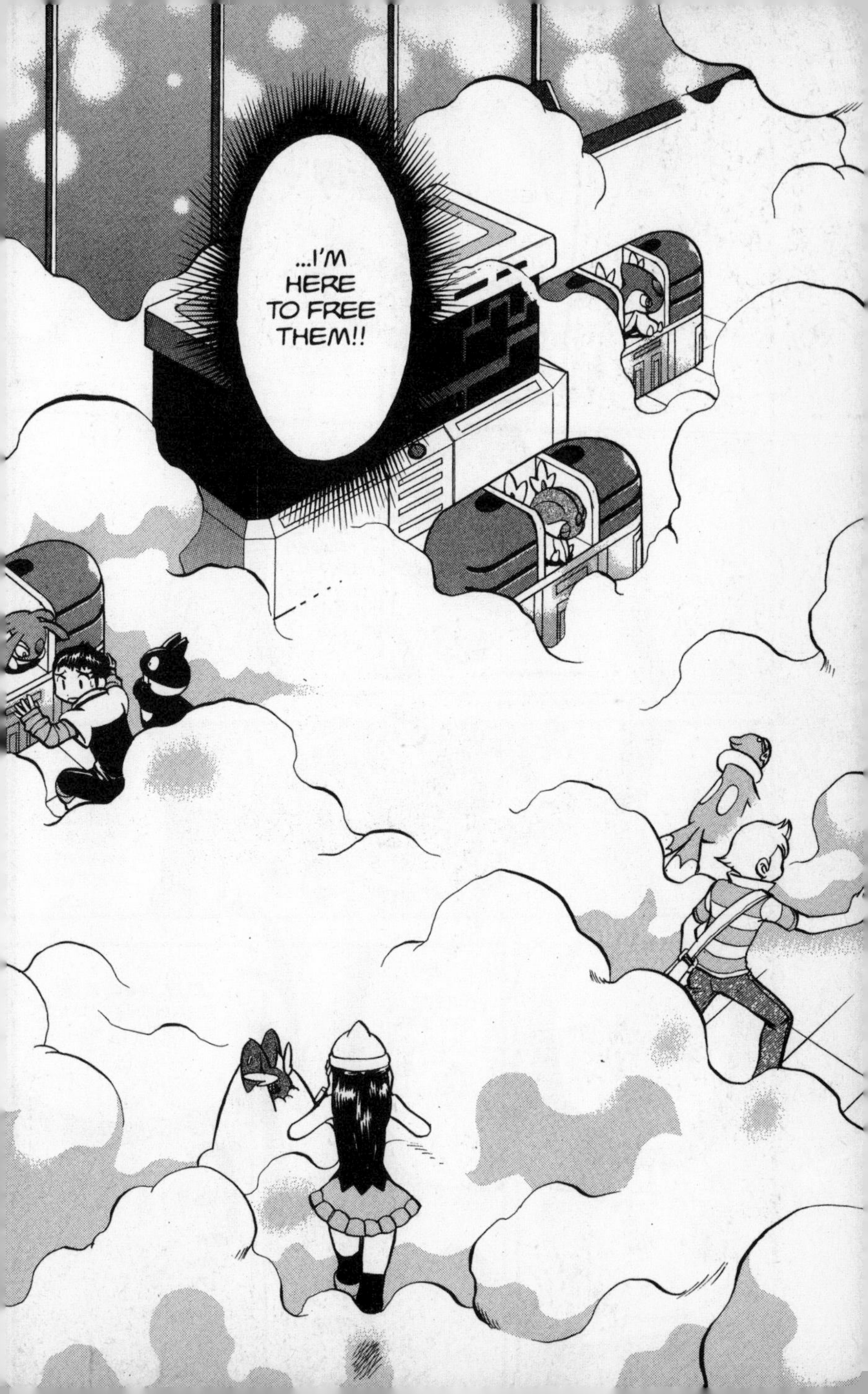
...I'M HERE TO FREE THEM!!

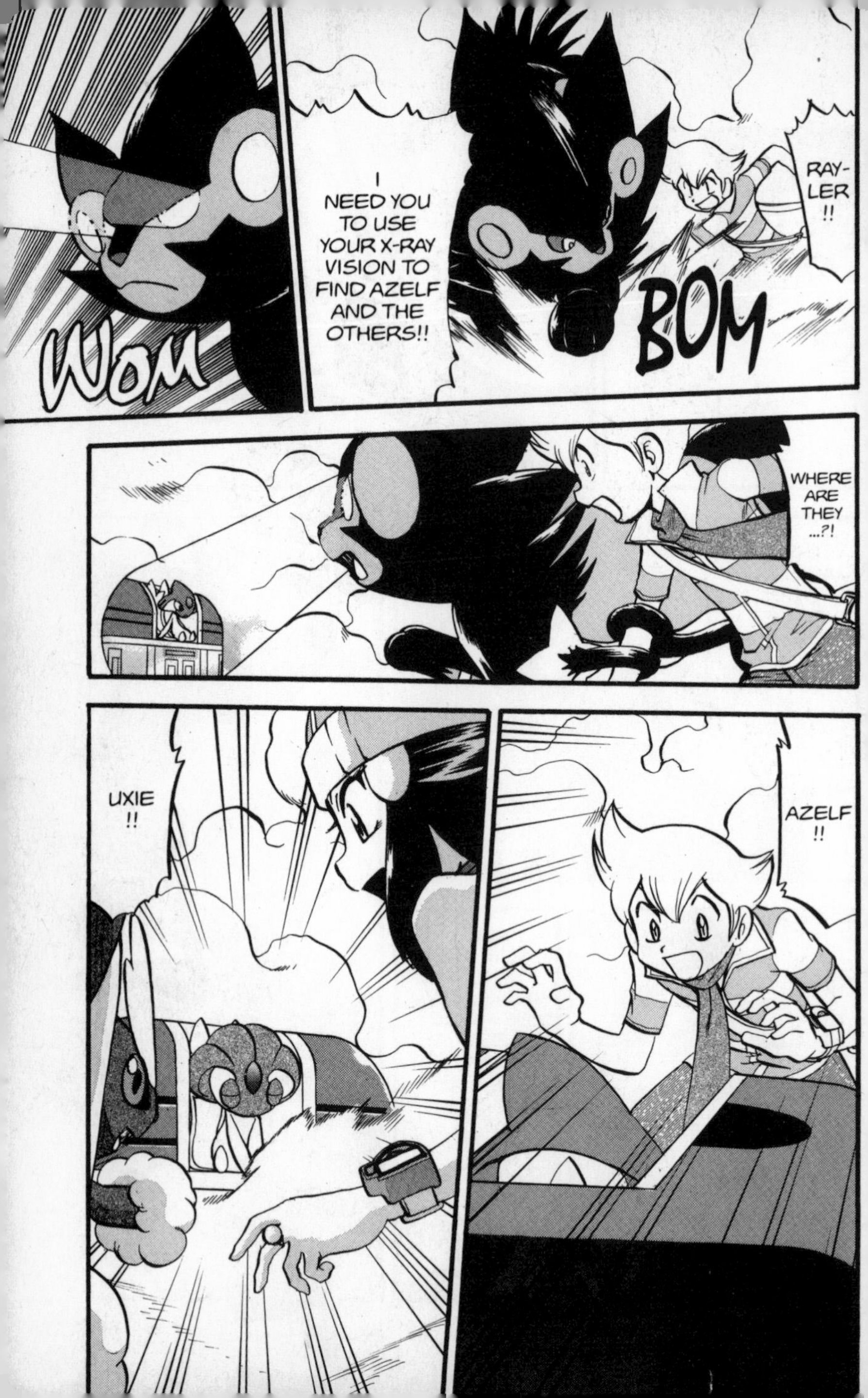
RAY-LER!!
I NEED YOU TO USE YOUR X-RAY VISION TO FIND AZELF AND THE OTHERS!!
BOM
WOM
WHERE ARE THEY ...?!
AZELF!!
UXIE!!

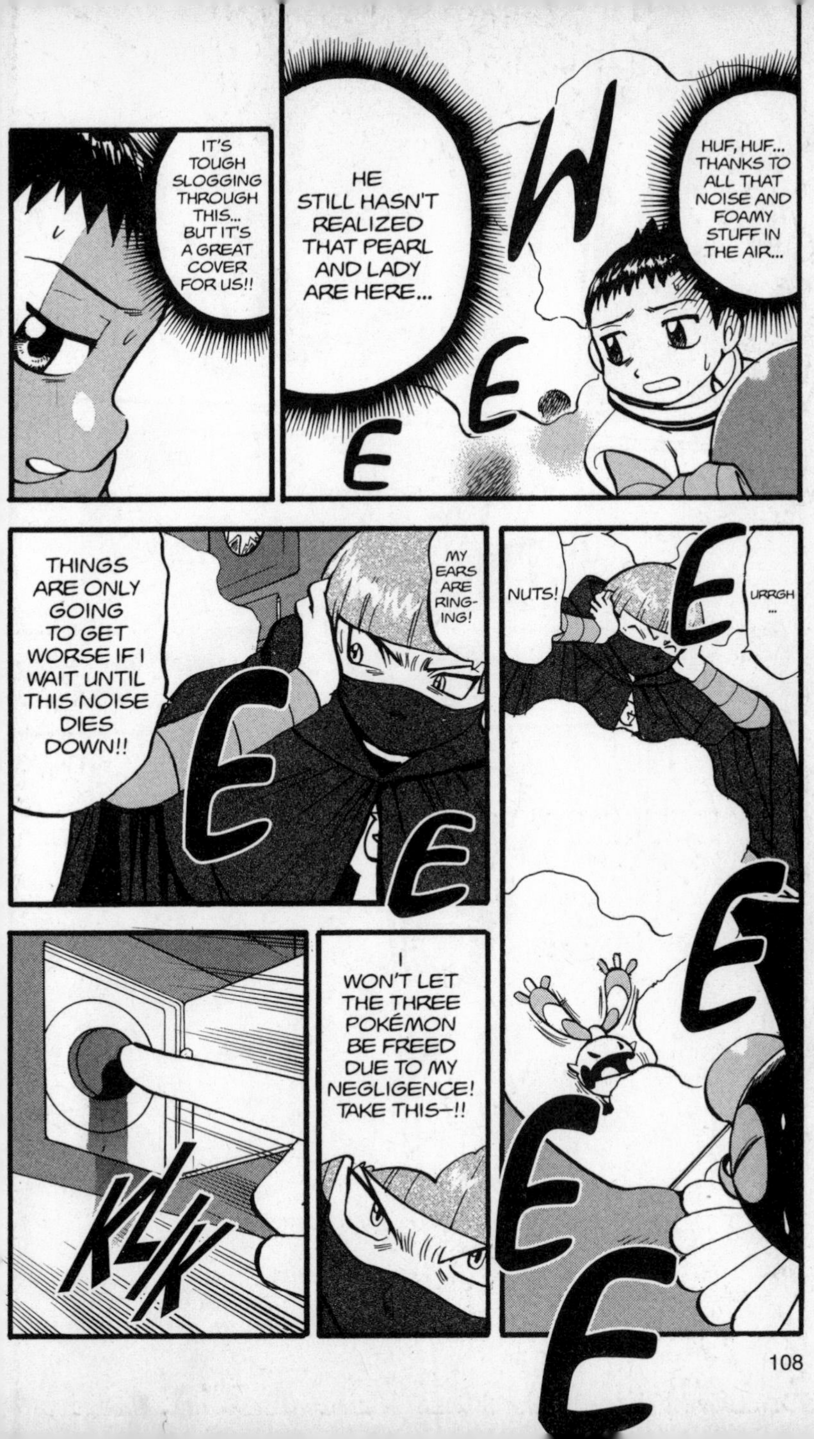
HUF, HUF... THANKS TO ALL THAT NOISE AND FOAMY STUFF IN THE AIR...
HE STILL HASN'T REALIZED THAT PEARL AND LADY ARE HERE...
IT'S TOUGH SLOGGING THROUGH THIS... BUT IT'S A GREAT COVER FOR US!!
URRGH ...
NUTS!
MY EARS ARE RING-ING!
THINGS ARE ONLY GOING TO GET WORSE IF I WAIT UNTIL THIS NOISE DIES DOWN!!
I WON'T LET THE THREE POKÉMON BE FREED DUE TO MY NEGLIGENCE! TAKE THIS—!!
KLIK

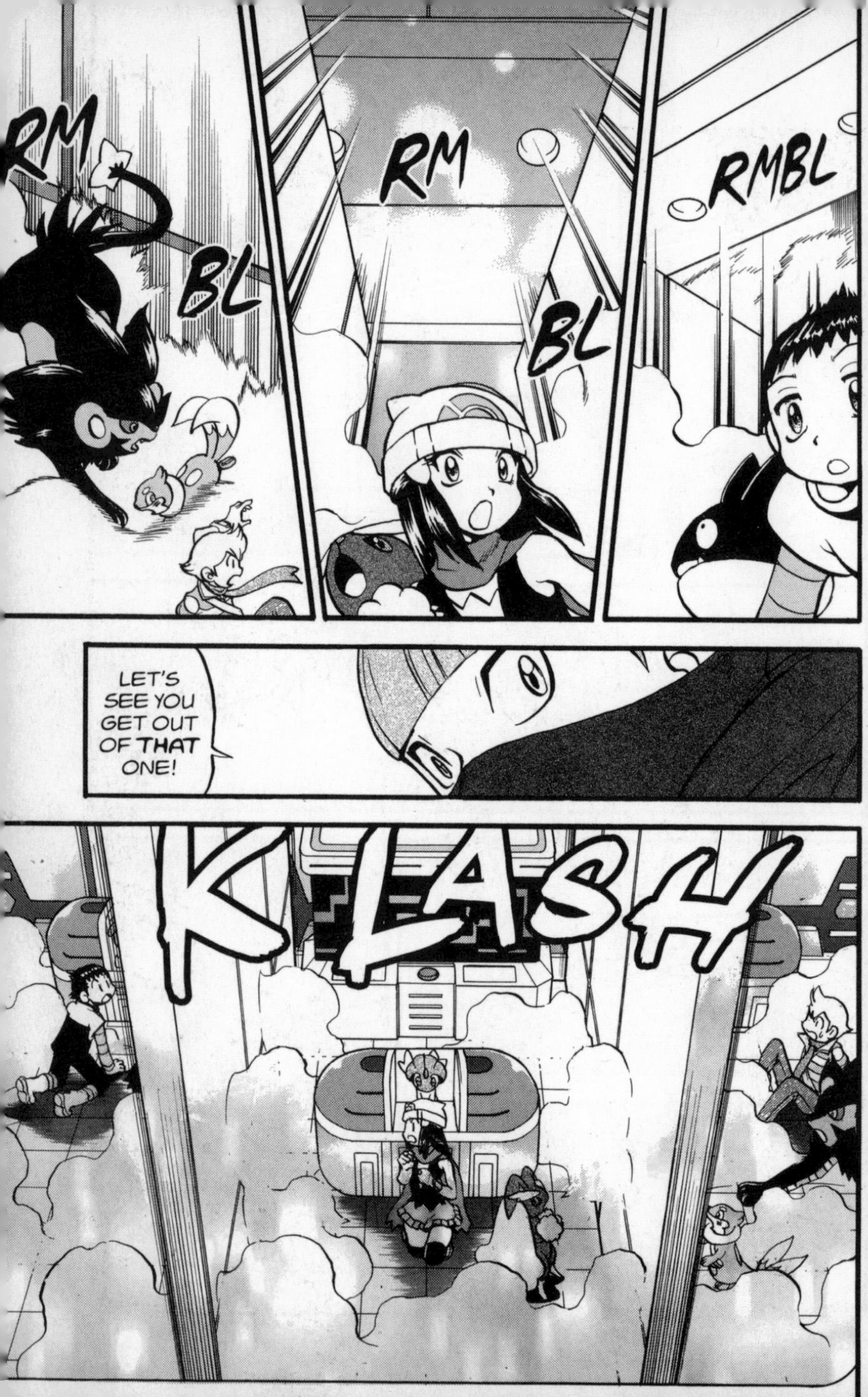
RMBL
RM
BL
RM
BL
LET'S SEE YOU GET OUT OF THAT ONE!
KLASH

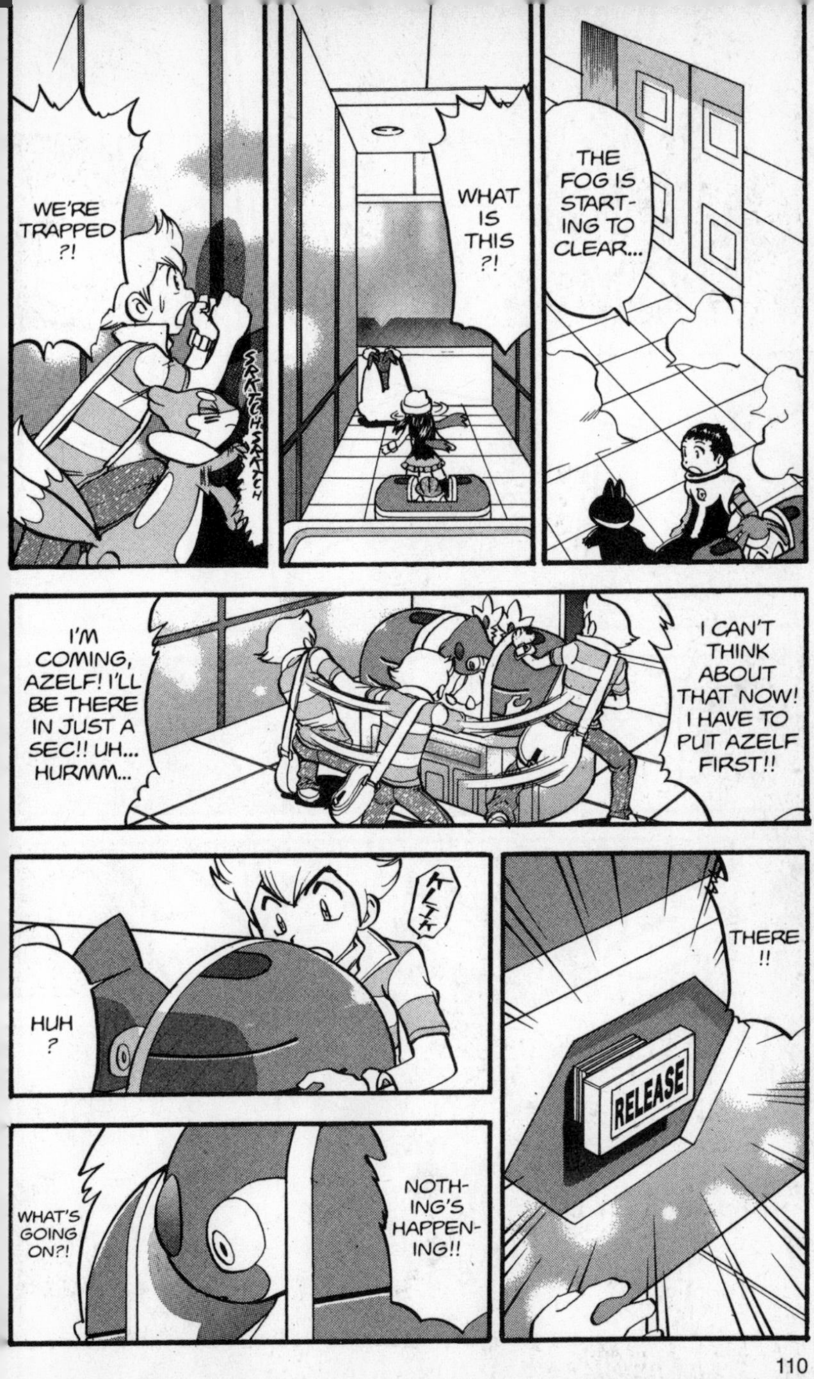
THE FOG IS STARTING TO CLEAR...
WHAT IS THIS ?!
WE'RE TRAPPED ?!
SRKATCH SRKATCH
I CAN'T THINK ABOUT THAT NOW! I HAVE TO PUT AZELF FIRST!!
I'M COMING, AZELF! I'LL BE THERE IN JUST A SEC!! UH... HURMM...
THERE !!
RELEASE
KLIK
HUH ?
NOTHING'S HAPPENING!!
WHAT'S GOING ON?!

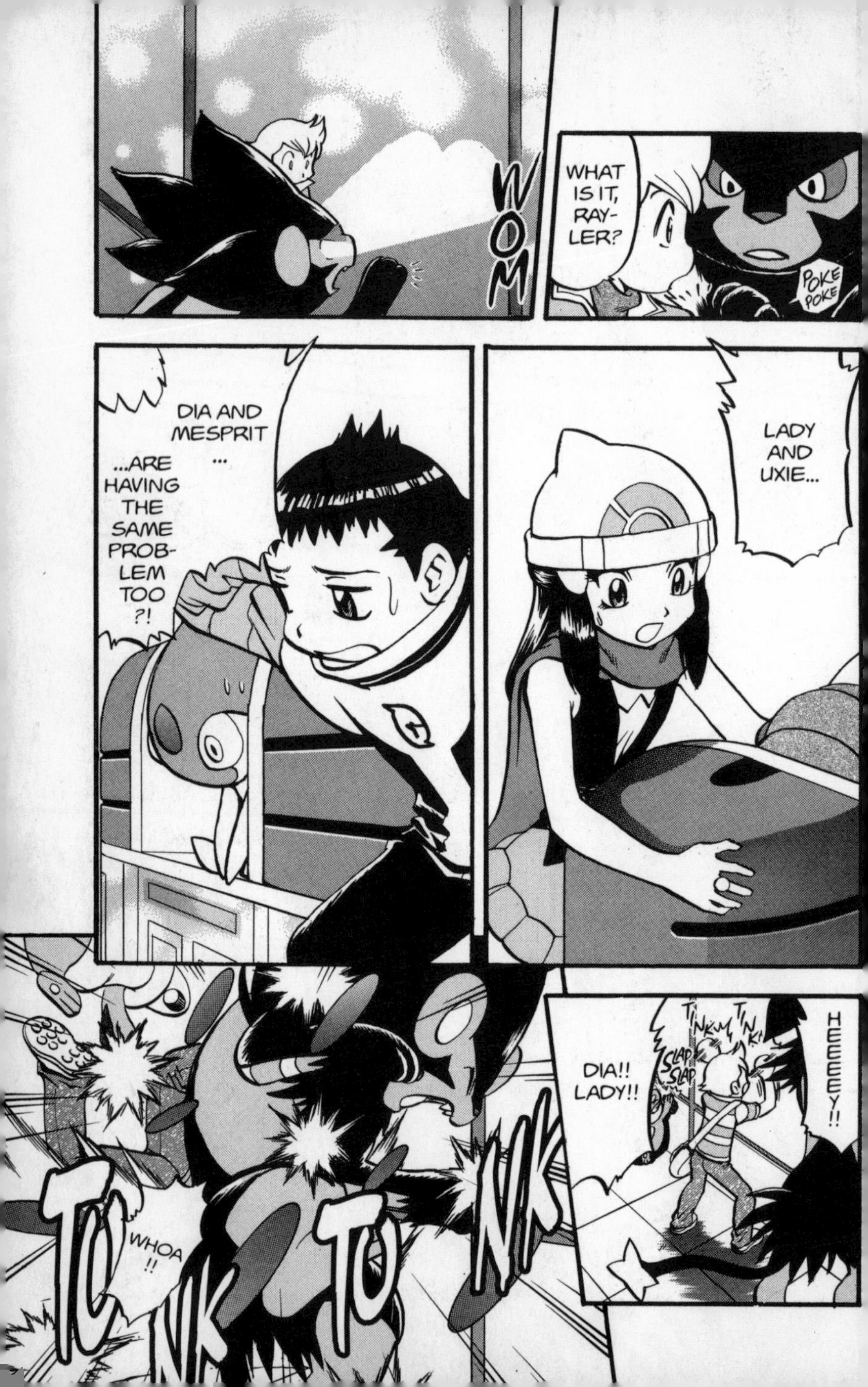
WHAT IS IT, RAYLER?
POKE POKE
WOM
LADY AND UXIE...
DIA AND MESPRIT ...
...ARE HAVING THE SAME PROBLEM TOO?!
HEEEEEY!!
TINK! TINK!
SLAP SLAP
DIA!! LADY!!
TONK
TONK
WHOA!!

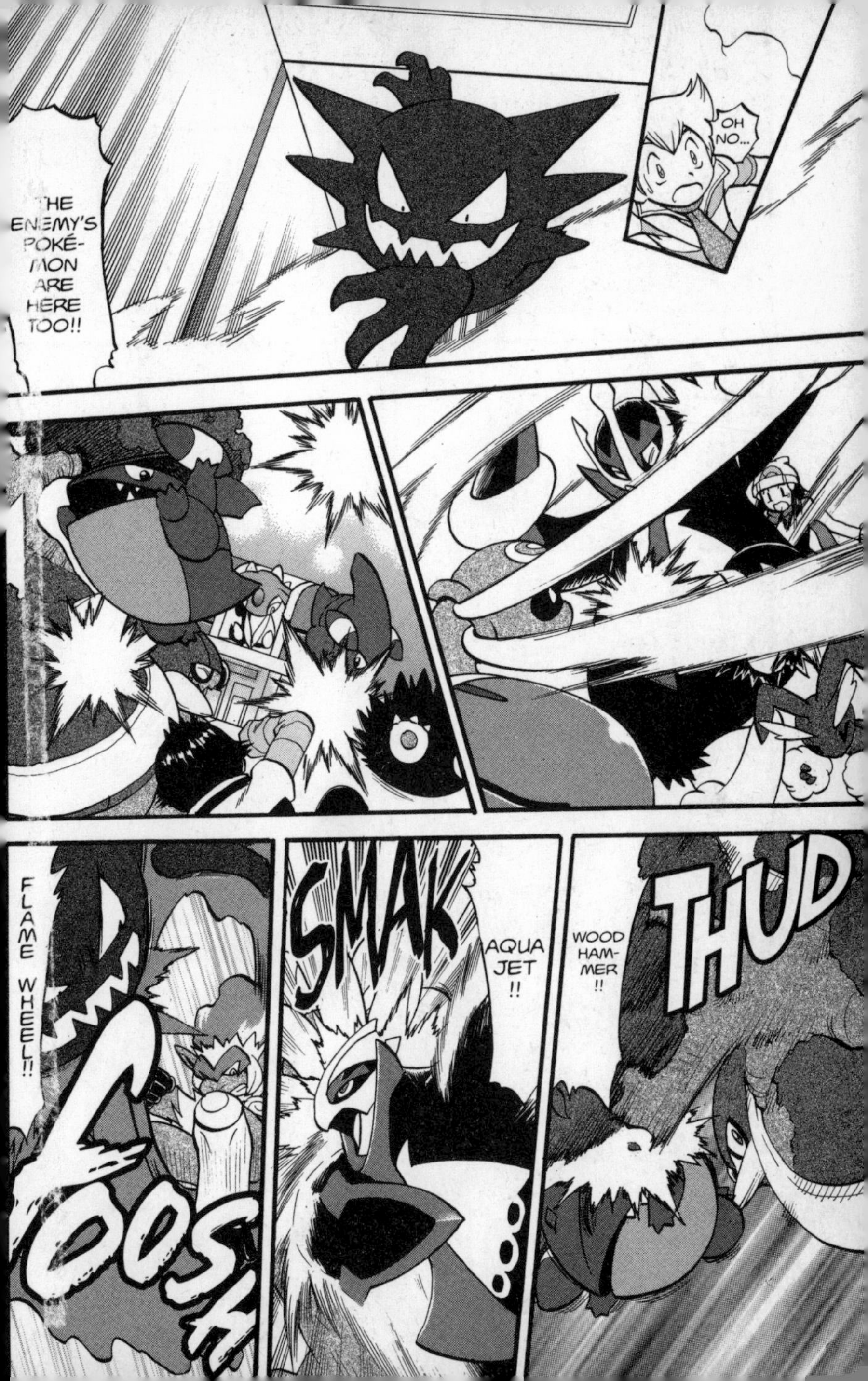
OH NO...
THE ENEMY'S POKÉ-MON ARE HERE TOO!!
THUD
WOOD HAM-MER !!
AQUA JET !!
SMAK
FLAME WHEEL!!
WOOSH

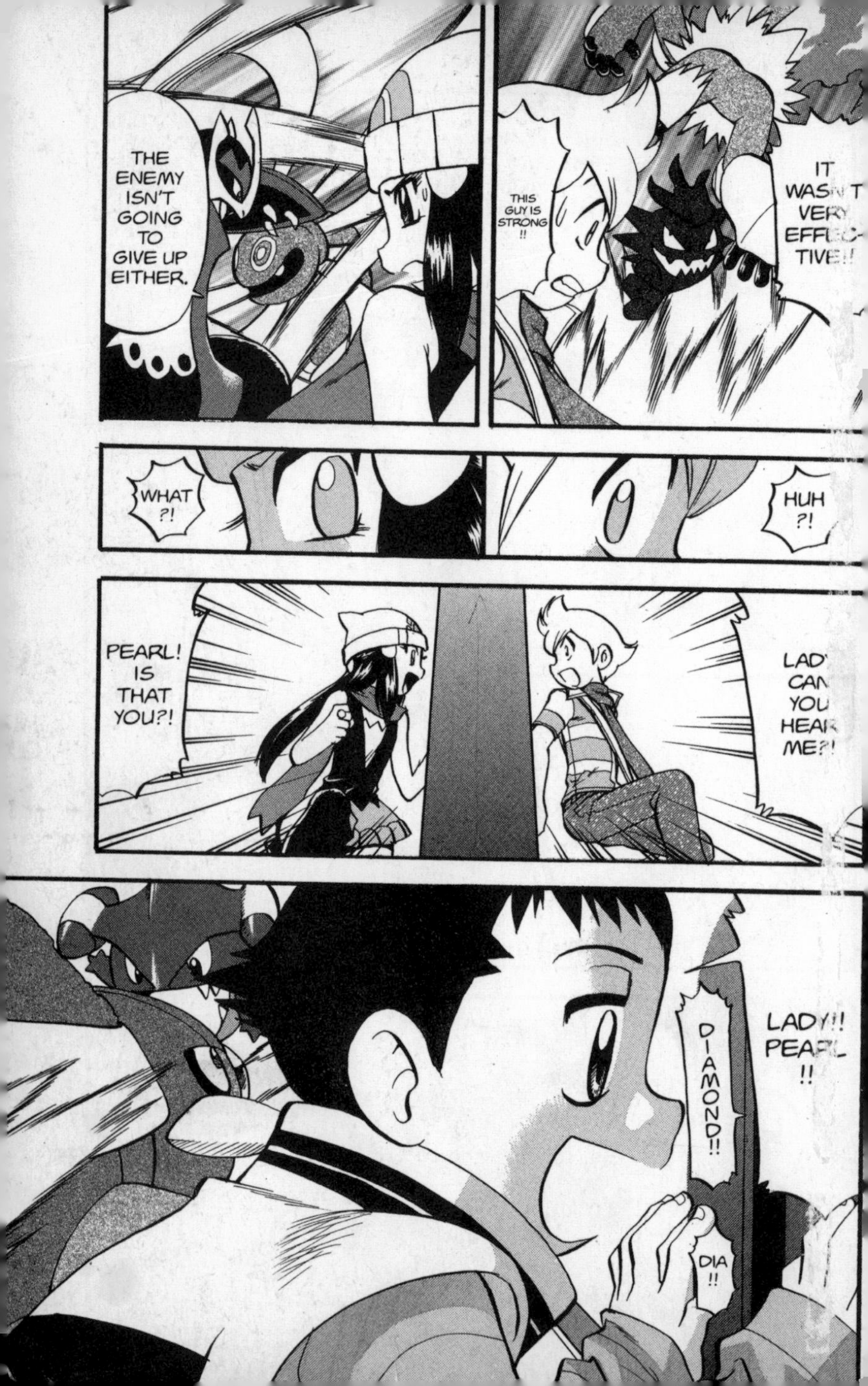
IT WASN'T VERY EFFECTIVE!!
THIS GUY IS STRONG!!
THE ENEMY ISN'T GOING TO GIVE UP EITHER.
HUH?!
WHAT?!
LADY CAN YOU HEAR ME?!
PEARL! IS THAT YOU?!
LADY!! PEARL!!
DIAMOND!!
DIA!!

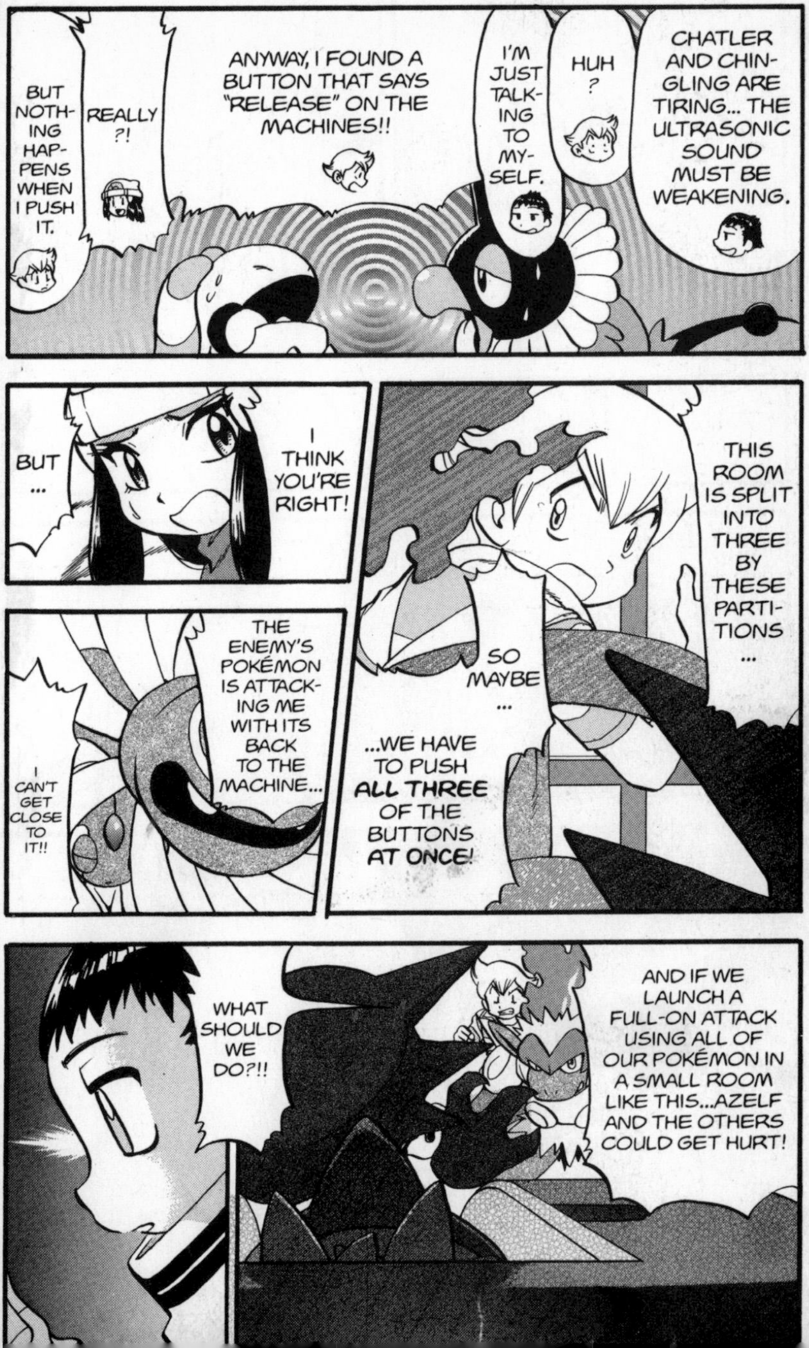
CHATLER AND CHINGLING ARE TIRING... THE ULTRASONIC SOUND MUST BE WEAKENING.
HUH?
I'M JUST TALKING TO MYSELF.
ANYWAY, I FOUND A BUTTON THAT SAYS "RELEASE" ON THE MACHINES!!
REALLY?!
BUT NOTHING HAPPENS WHEN I PUSH IT.
THIS ROOM IS SPLIT INTO THREE BY THESE PARTITIONS...
SO MAYBE...
...WE HAVE TO PUSH **ALL THREE** OF THE BUTTONS **AT ONCE**!
I THINK YOU'RE RIGHT!
BUT...
THE ENEMY'S POKÉMON IS ATTACKING ME WITH ITS BACK TO THE MACHINE...
I CAN'T GET CLOSE TO IT!!
AND IF WE LAUNCH A FULL-ON ATTACK USING ALL OF OUR POKÉMON IN A SMALL ROOM LIKE THIS...AZELF AND THE OTHERS COULD GET HURT!
WHAT SHOULD WE DO?!!

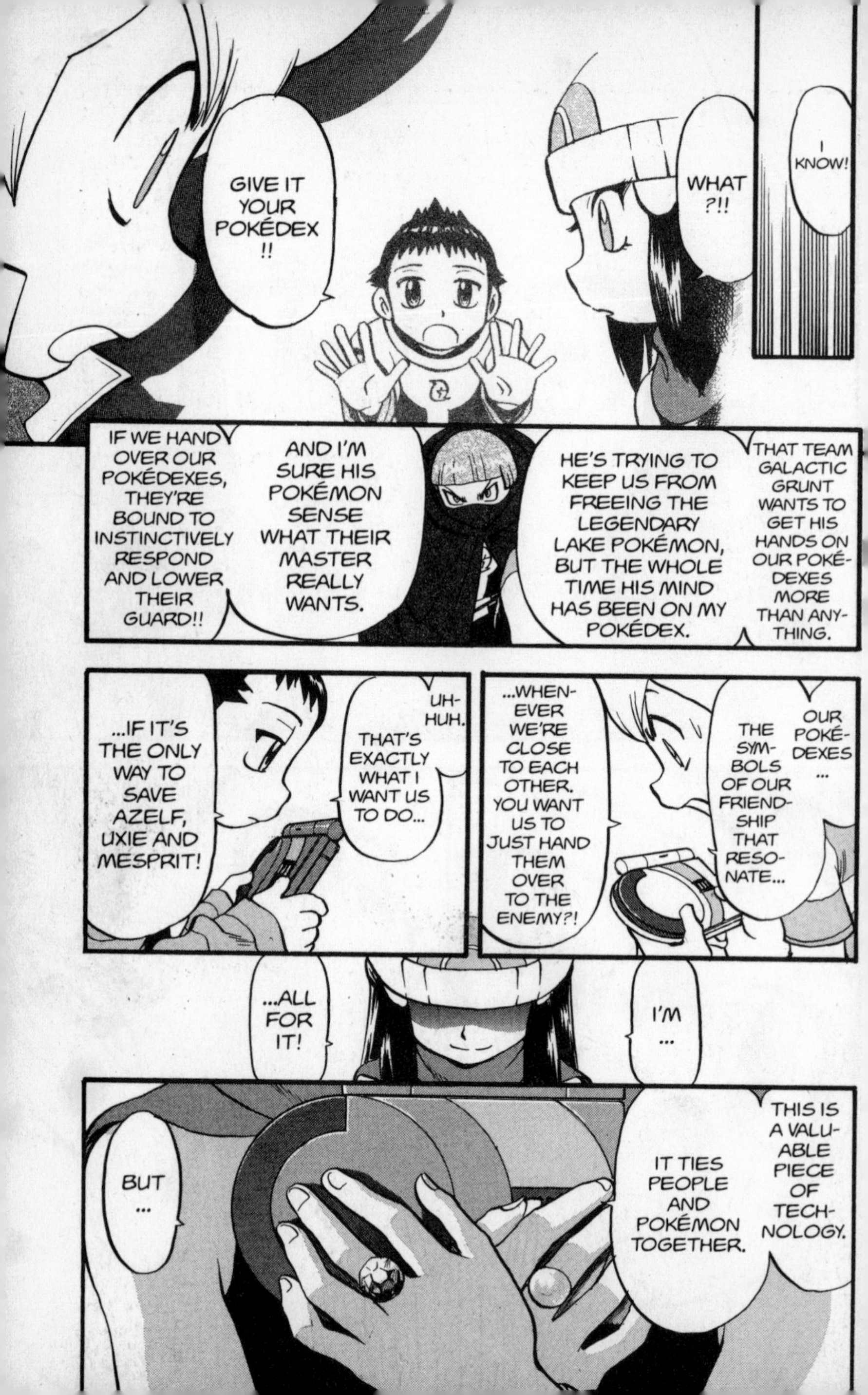
I KNOW!
WHAT?!!
GIVE IT YOUR POKÉDEX!!
THAT TEAM GALACTIC GRUNT WANTS TO GET HIS HANDS ON OUR POKÉDEXES MORE THAN ANYTHING.
HE'S TRYING TO KEEP US FROM FREEING THE LEGENDARY LAKE POKÉMON, BUT THE WHOLE TIME HIS MIND HAS BEEN ON MY POKÉDEX.
AND I'M SURE HIS POKÉMON SENSE WHAT THEIR MASTER REALLY WANTS.
IF WE HAND OVER OUR POKÉDEXES, THEY'RE BOUND TO INSTINCTIVELY RESPOND AND LOWER THEIR GUARD!!
OUR POKÉDEXES...
THE SYMBOLS OF OUR FRIENDSHIP THAT RESONATE...
...WHENEVER WE'RE CLOSE TO EACH OTHER. YOU WANT US TO JUST HAND THEM OVER TO THE ENEMY?!
UH-HUH.
THAT'S EXACTLY WHAT I WANT US TO DO...
...IF IT'S THE ONLY WAY TO SAVE AZELF, UXIE AND MESPRIT!
I'M...
...ALL FOR IT!
THIS IS A VALUABLE PIECE OF TECHNOLOGY.
IT TIES PEOPLE AND POKÉMON TOGETHER.
BUT...

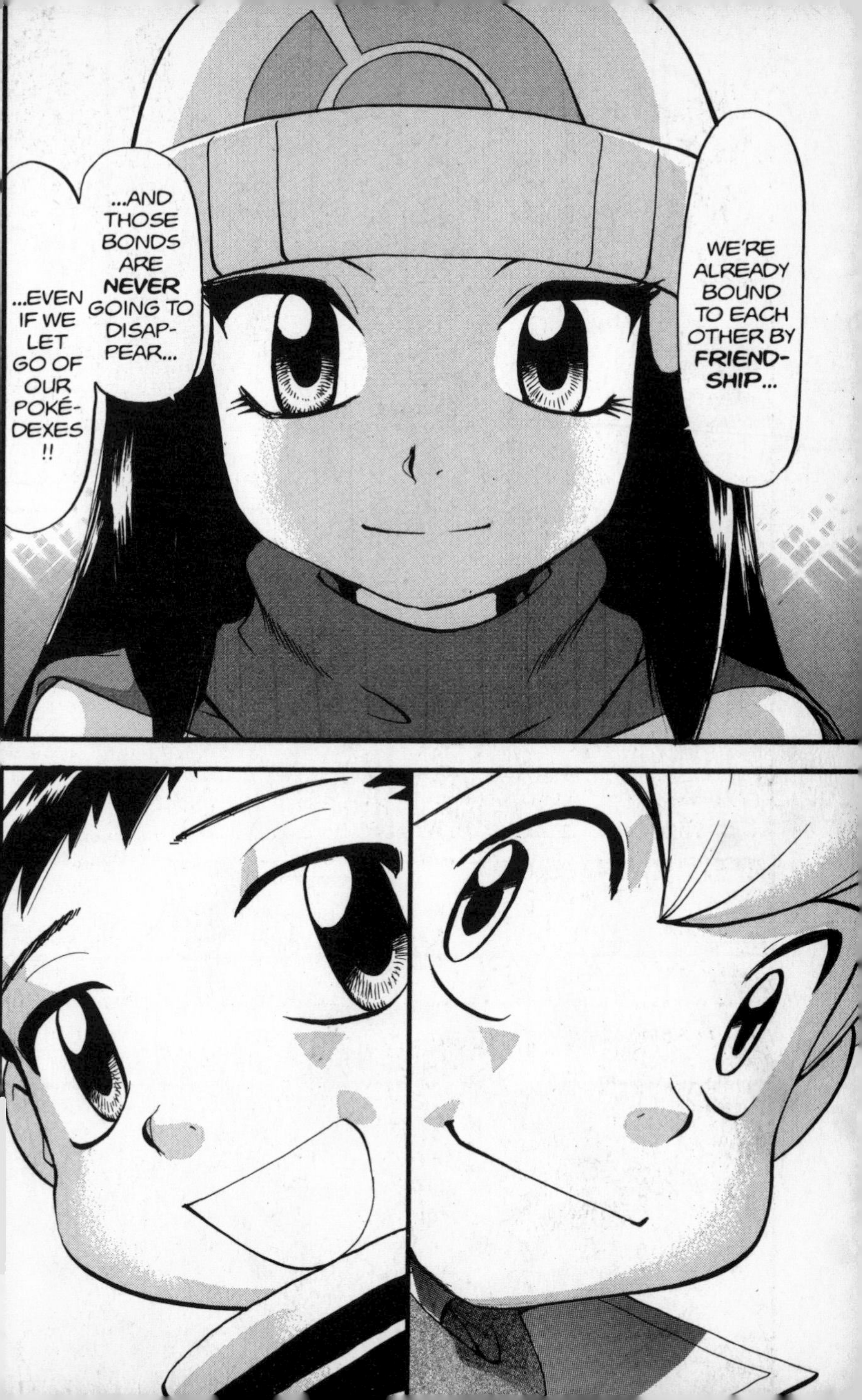
WE'RE ALREADY BOUND TO EACH OTHER BY FRIENDSHIP...
...AND THOSE BONDS ARE NEVER GOING TO DISAPPEAR...
...EVEN IF WE LET GO OF OUR POKÉDEXES!!

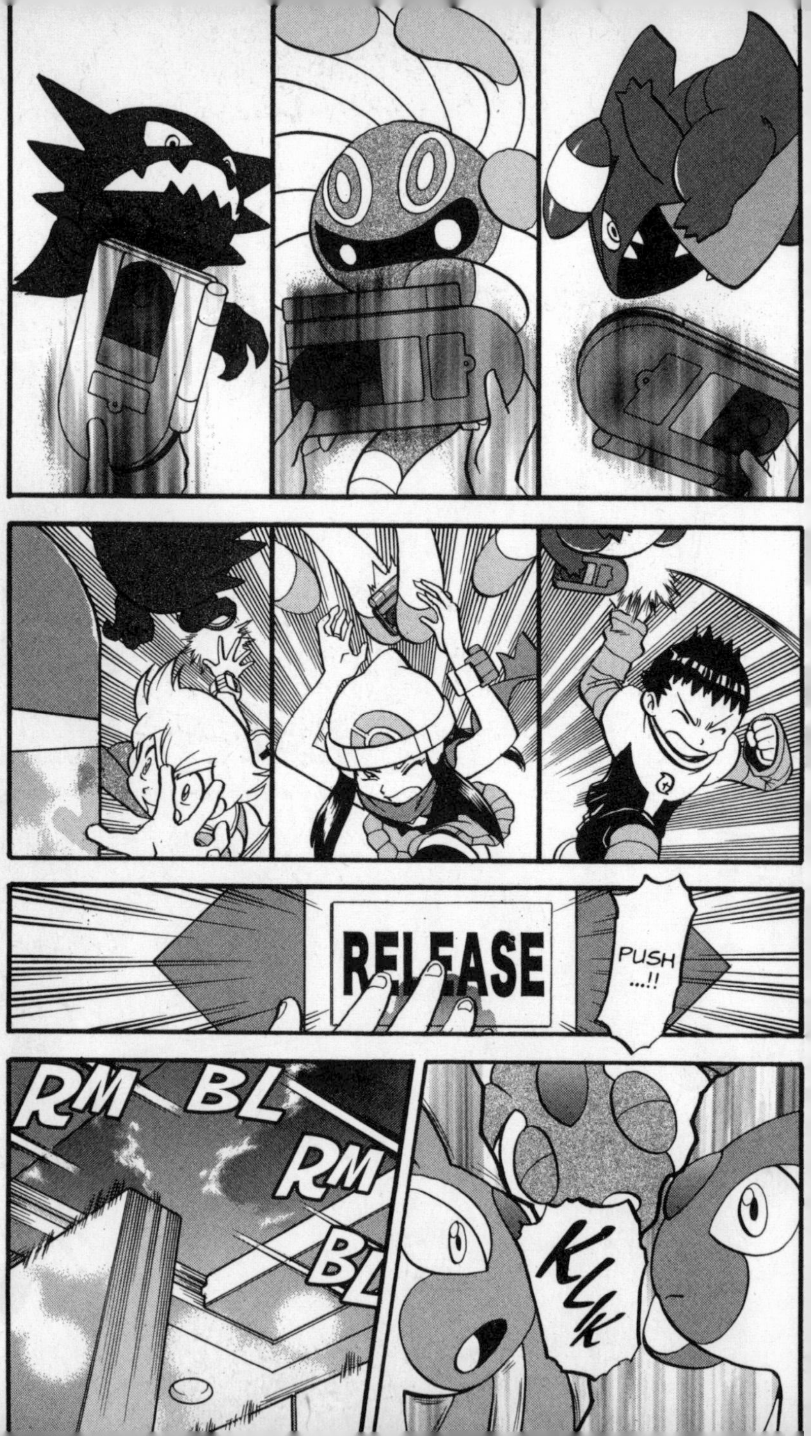
PUSH ...!!
RELEASE
KLIK
RM BL RM BL

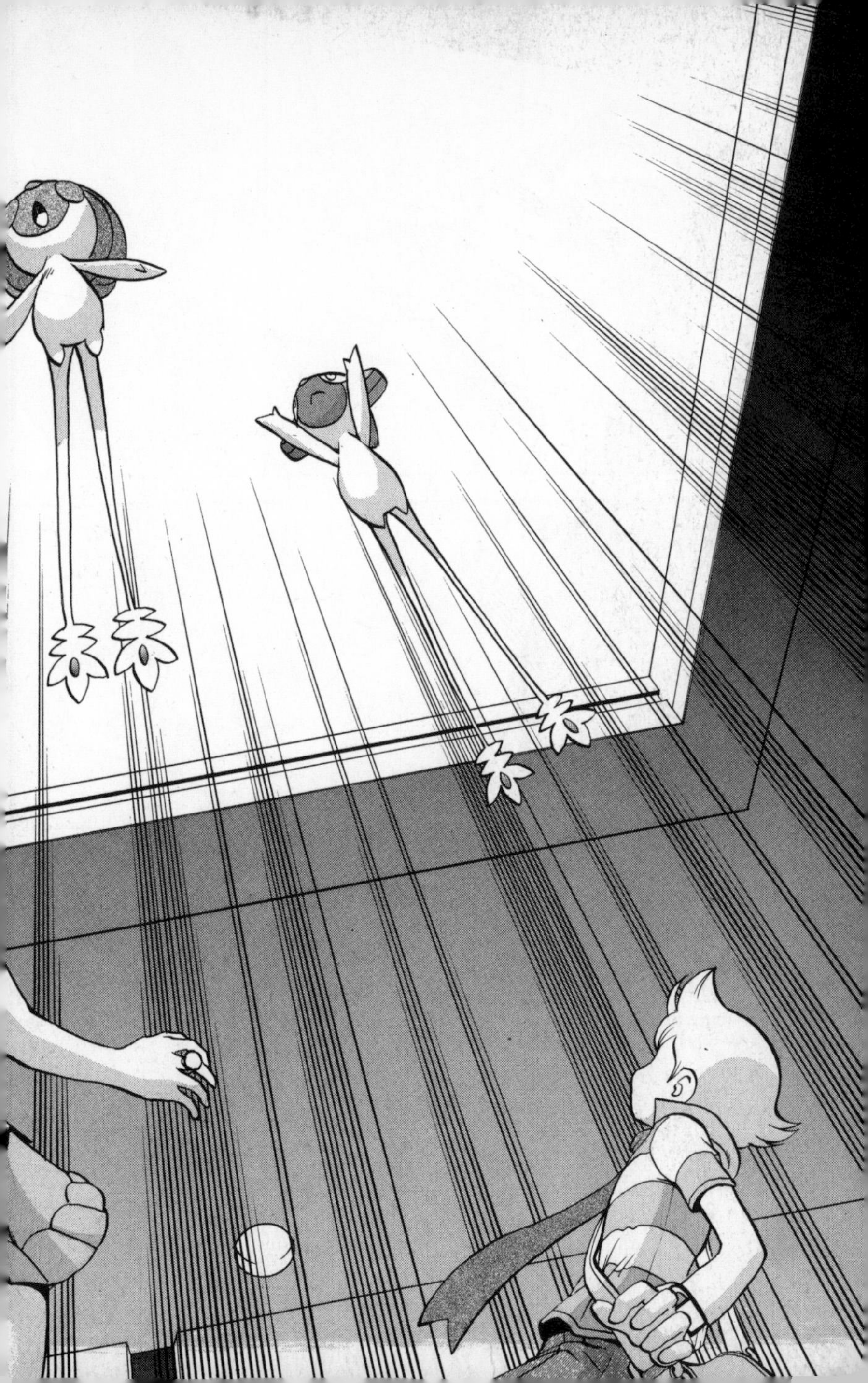

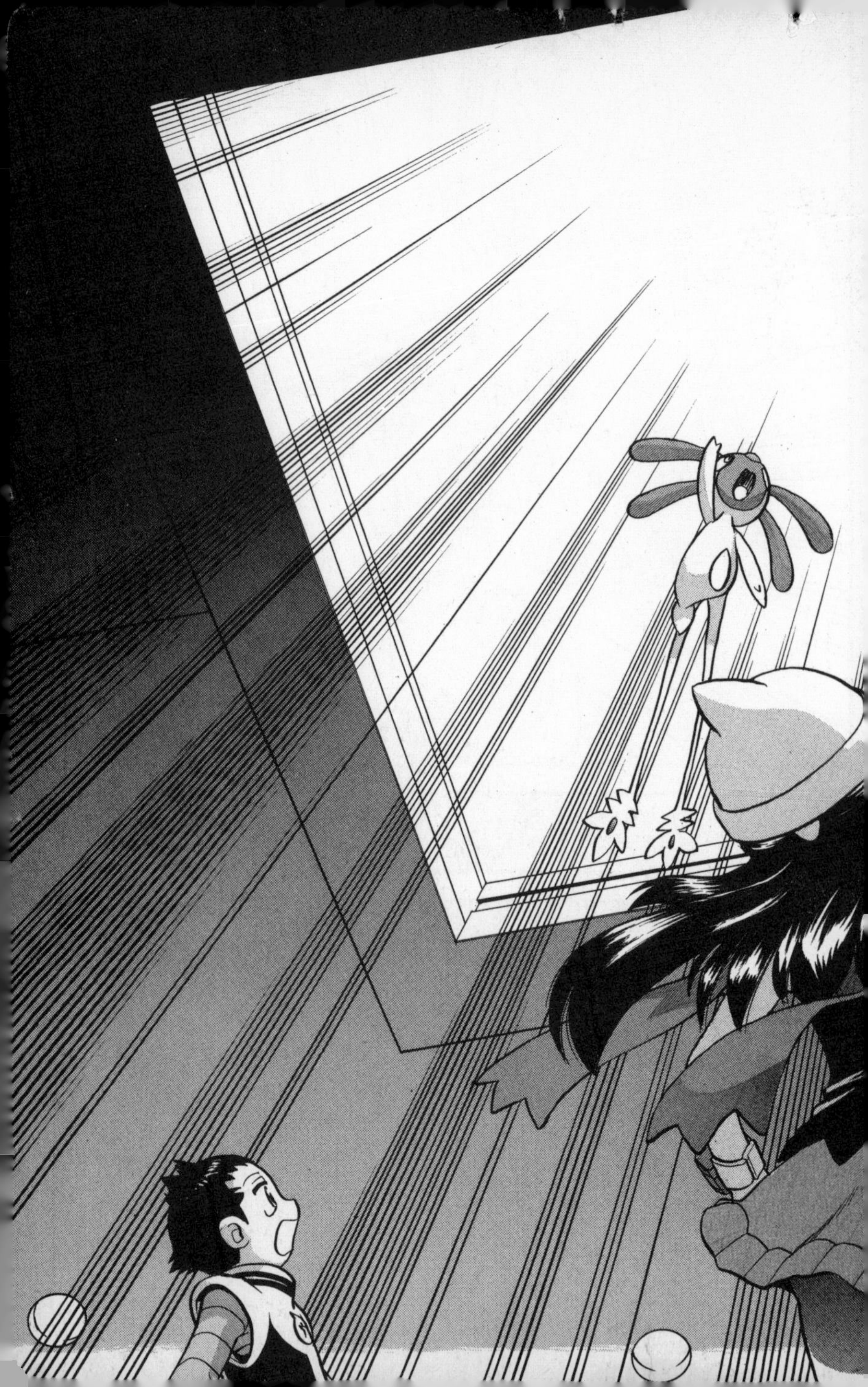

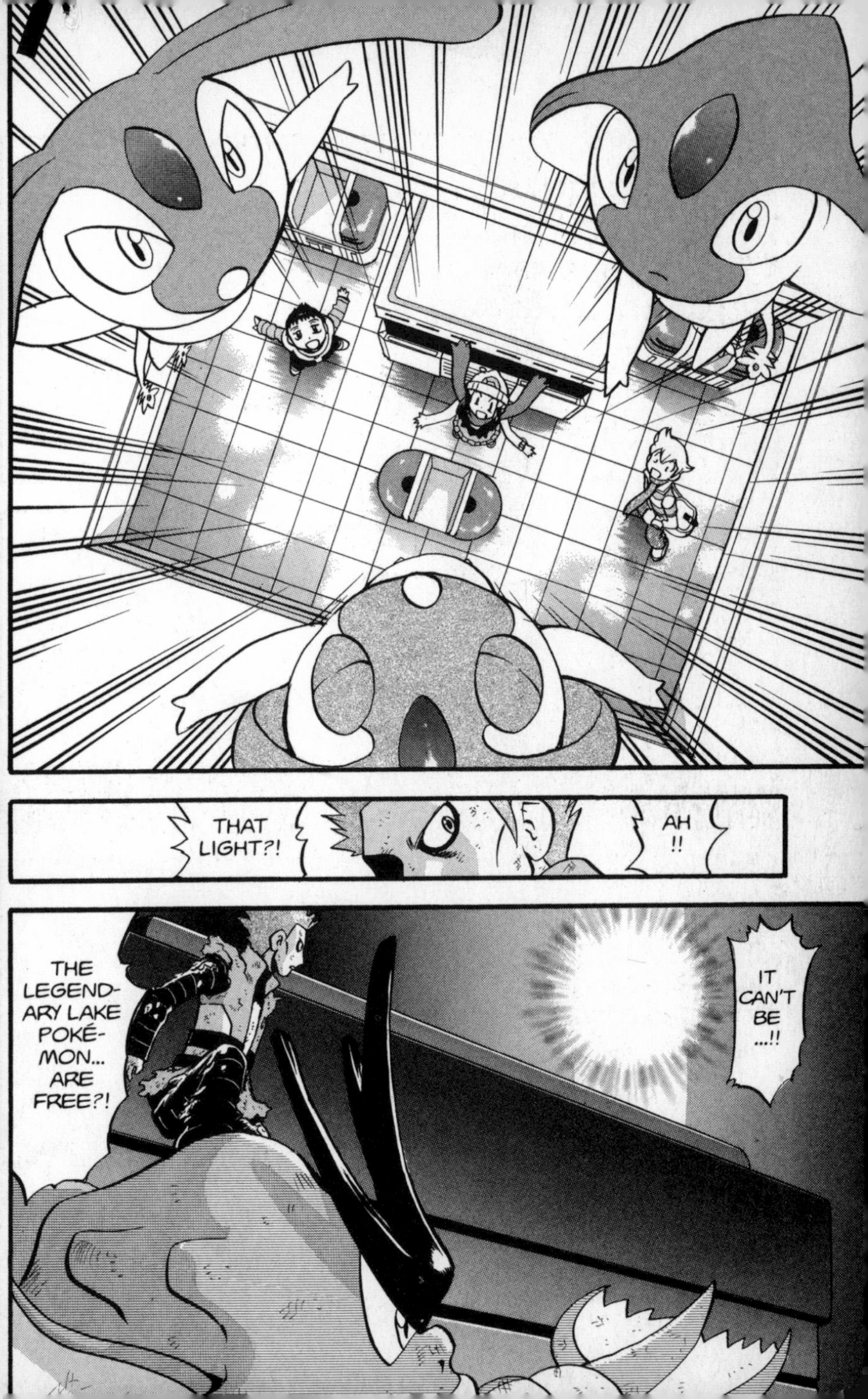
AH !!
THAT LIGHT?!
IT CAN'T BE ...!!
THE LEGENDARY LAKE POKÉMON... ARE FREE?!

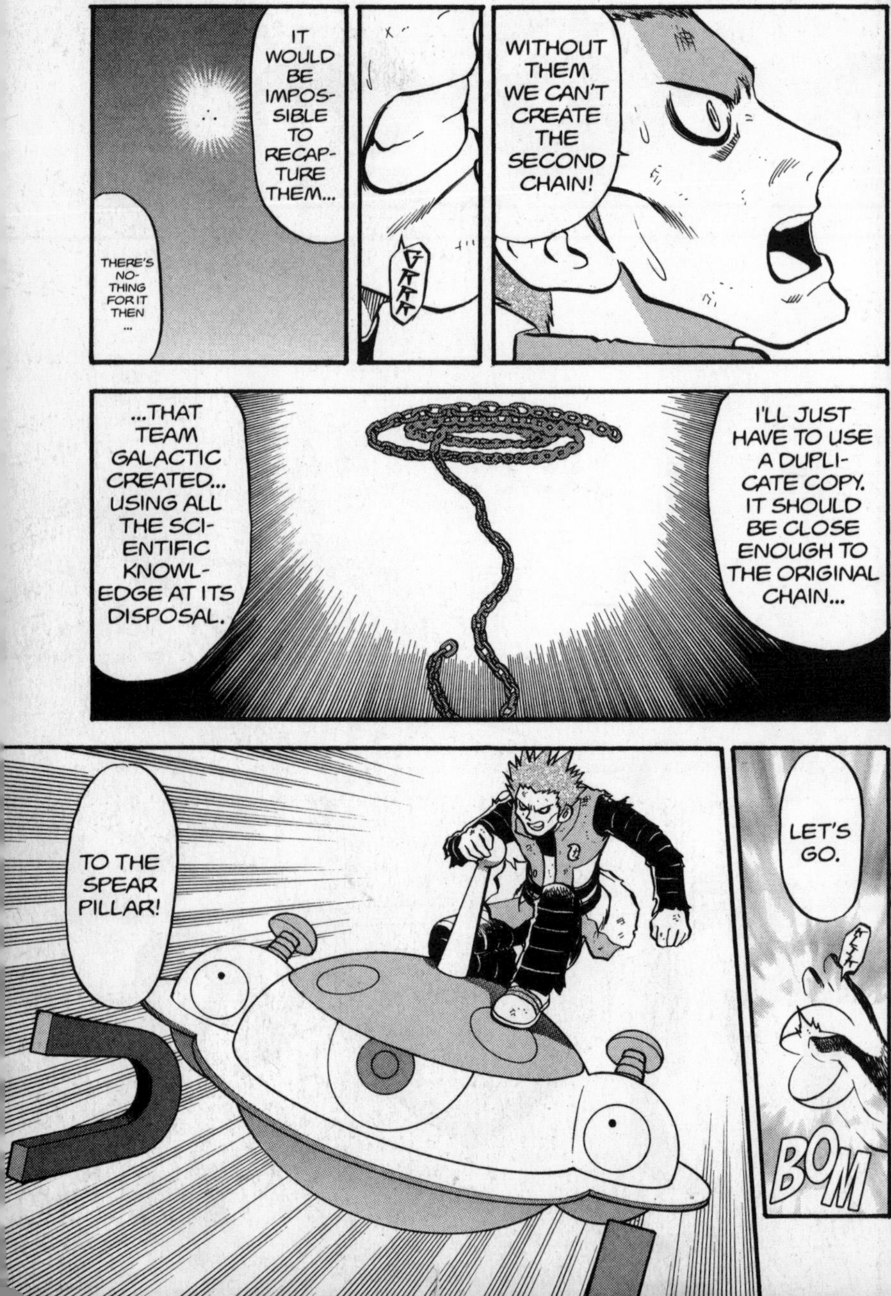
WITHOUT THEM WE CAN'T CREATE THE SECOND CHAIN!
GRRR
IT WOULD BE IMPOSSIBLE TO RECAPTURE THEM...
THERE'S NOTHING FOR IT THEN...
I'LL JUST HAVE TO USE A DUPLICATE COPY. IT SHOULD BE CLOSE ENOUGH TO THE ORIGINAL CHAIN...
...THAT TEAM GALACTIC CREATED... USING ALL THE SCIENTIFIC KNOWLEDGE AT ITS DISPOSAL.
LET'S GO.
BOM
TO THE SPEAR PILLAR!

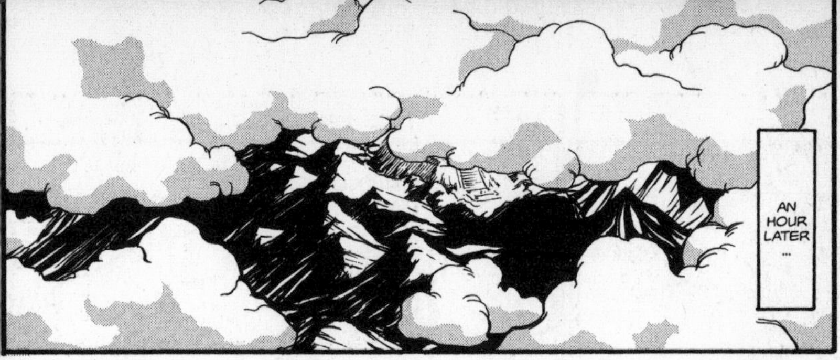
AN HOUR LATER...
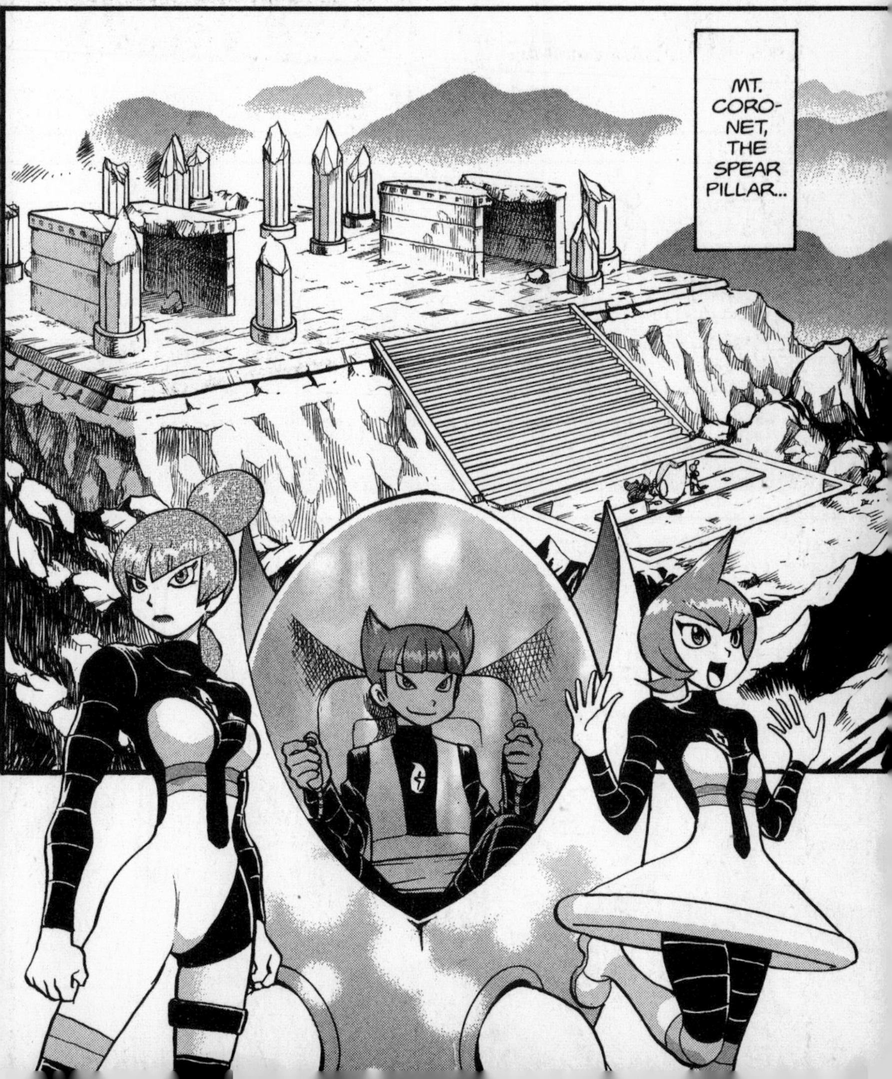
MT. CORONET, THE SPEAR PILLAR...

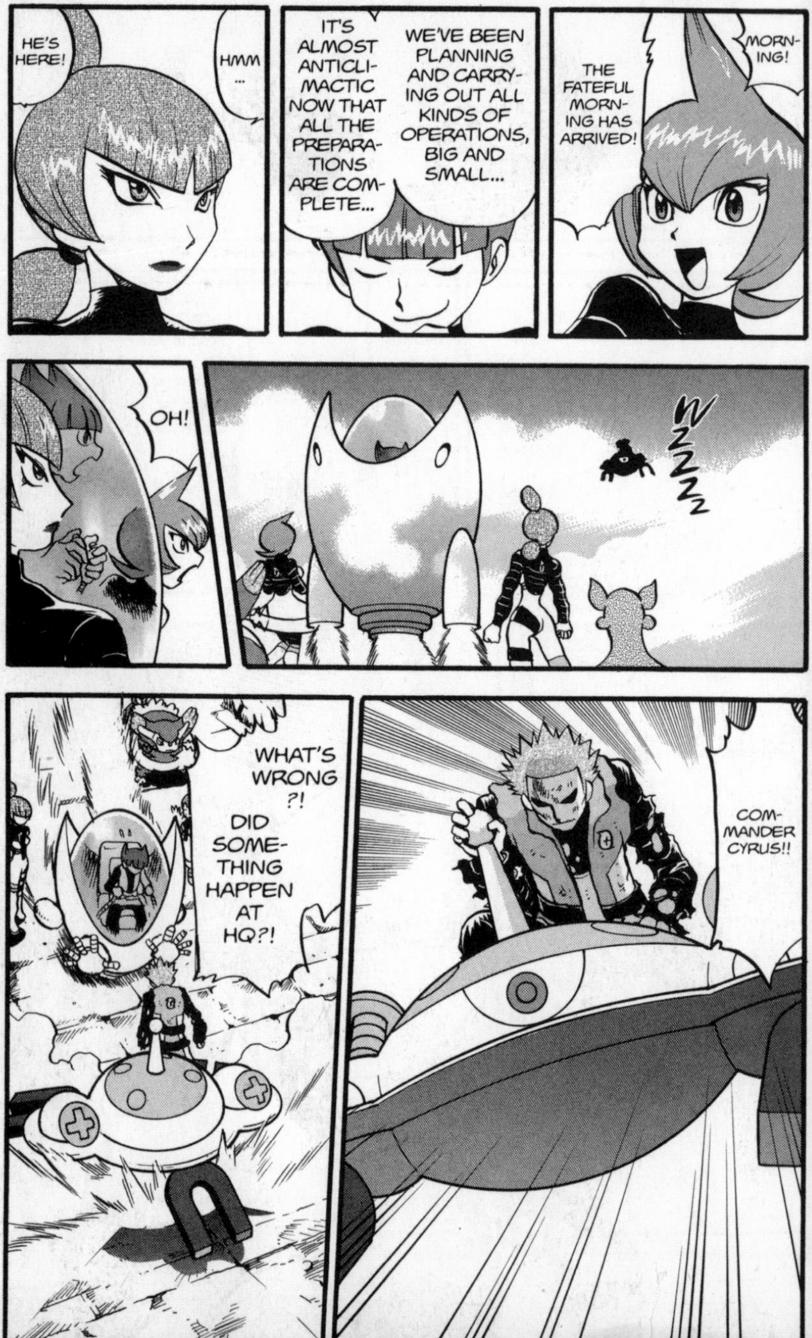
MORNING!
THE FATEFUL MORNING HAS ARRIVED!
WE'VE BEEN PLANNING AND CARRYING OUT ALL KINDS OF OPERATIONS, BIG AND SMALL...
IT'S ALMOST ANTICLIMACTIC NOW THAT ALL THE PREPARATIONS ARE COMPLETE...
HMM...
HE'S HERE!
WZZZZZ
OH!
COMMANDER CYRUS!!
WHAT'S WRONG?!
DID SOMETHING HAPPEN AT HQ?!

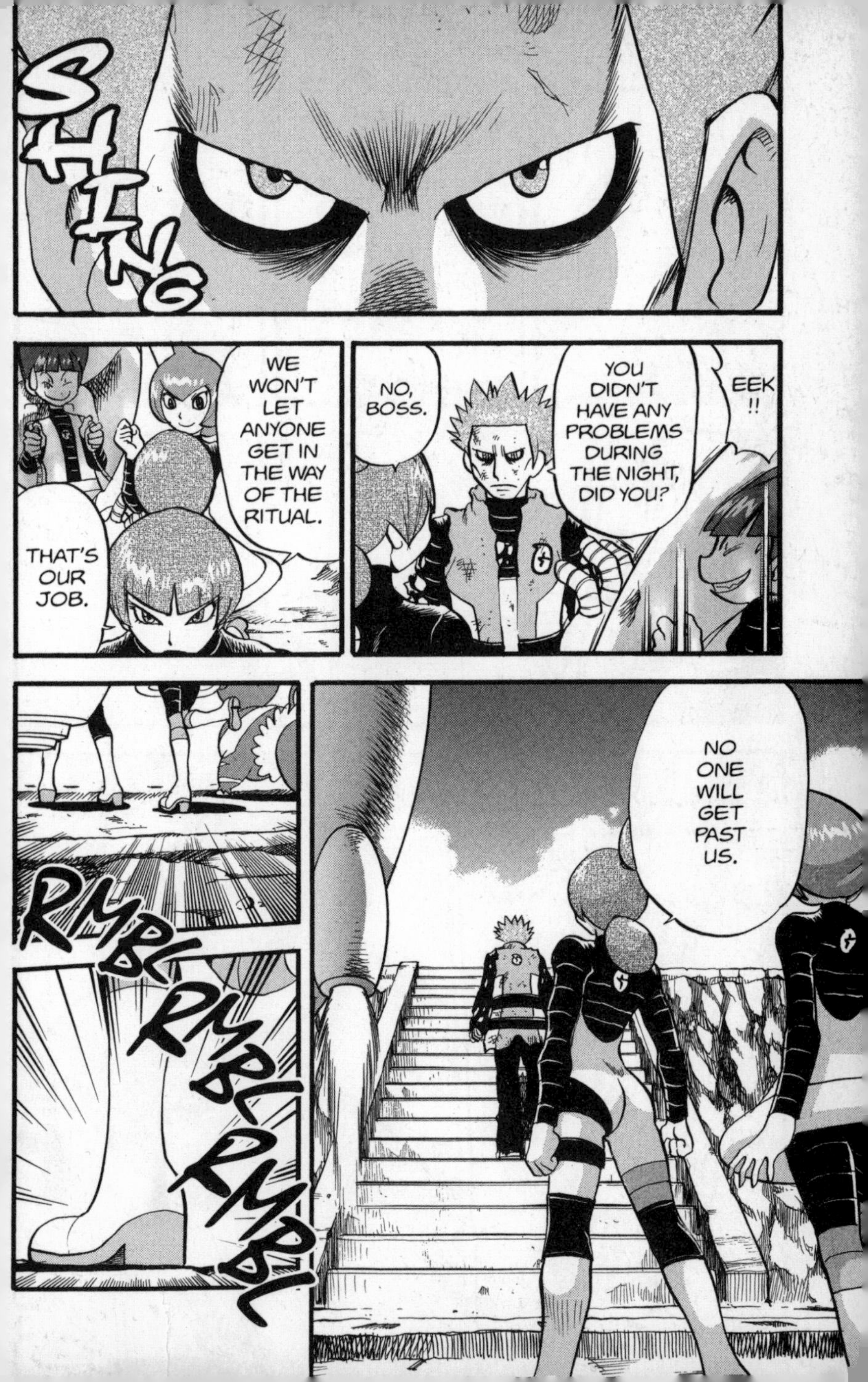
SHING
EEK !!
YOU DIDN'T HAVE ANY PROBLEMS DURING THE NIGHT, DID YOU?
NO, BOSS.
WE WON'T LET ANYONE GET IN THE WAY OF THE RITUAL.
THAT'S OUR JOB.
NO ONE WILL GET PAST US.
RMBL RMBL RMBL RMBL

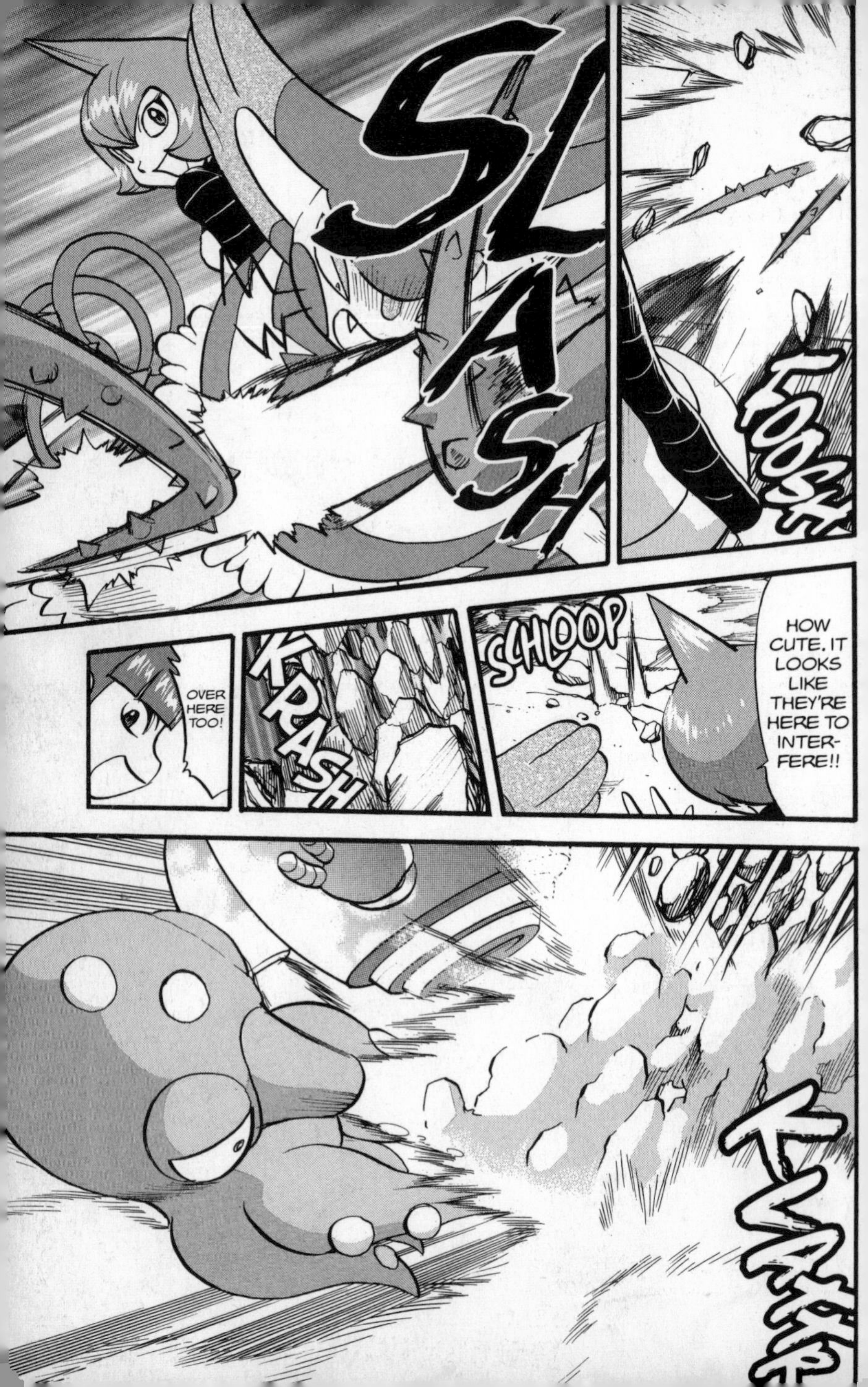
FOOSH
SLASH
HOW CUTE. IT LOOKS LIKE THEY'RE HERE TO INTER-FERE!!
SCHLOOP
KRASH
OVER HERE TOO!

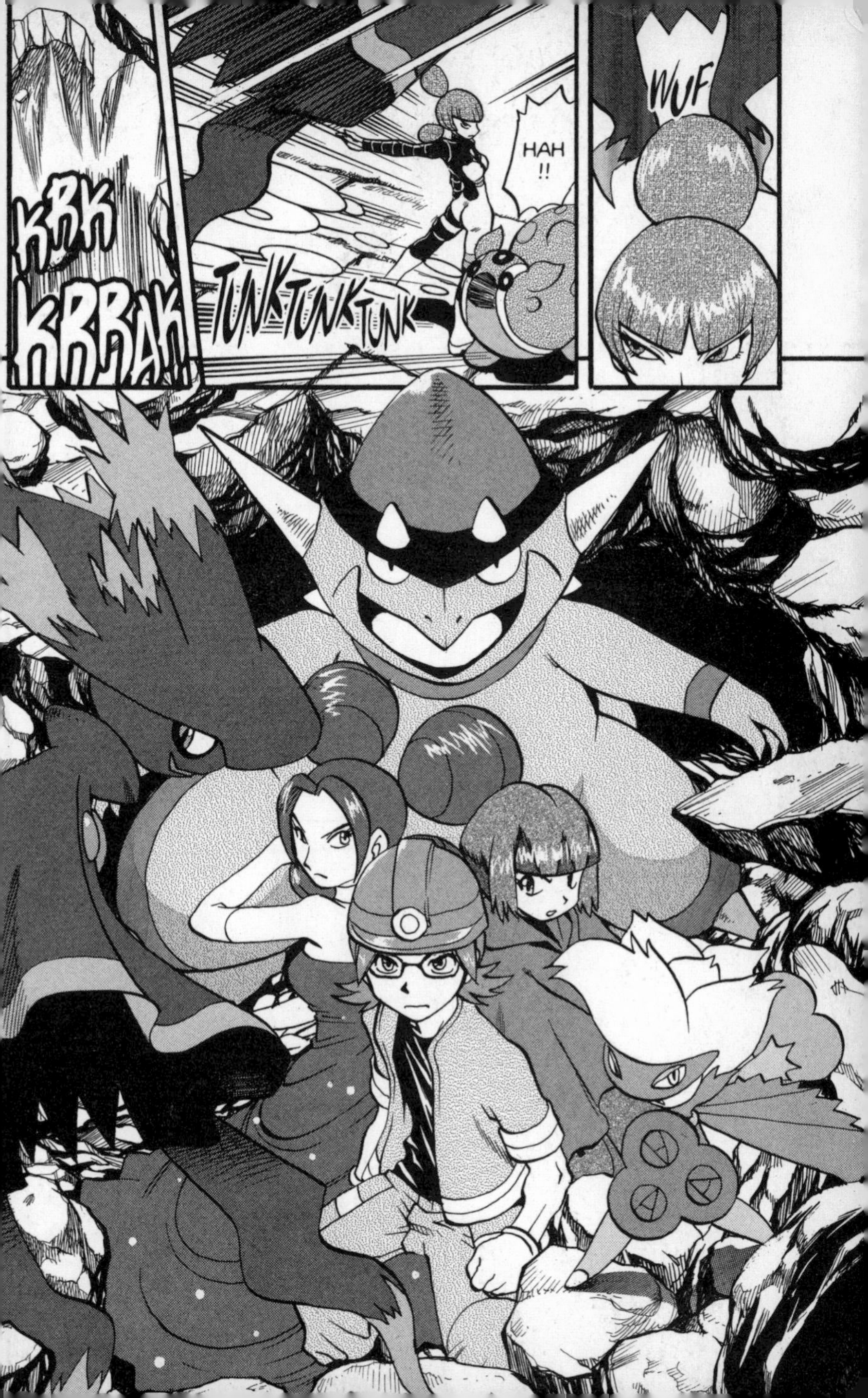
WUF
HAH !!
TUNK TUNK TUNK
KRK KRRAK

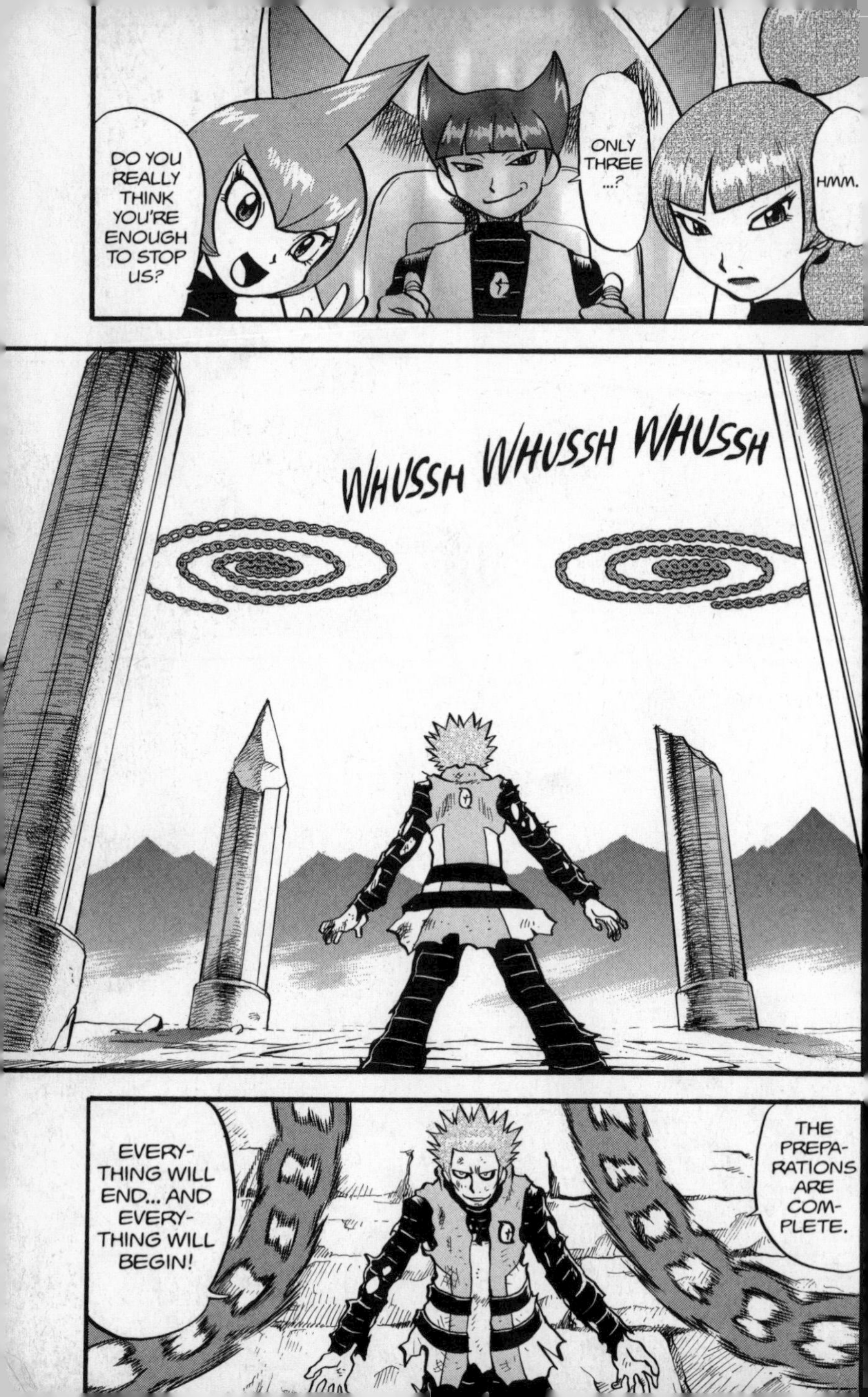
HMM.
ONLY THREE ...?
DO YOU REALLY THINK YOU'RE ENOUGH TO STOP US?
WHUSSH WHUSSH WHUSSH
THE PREPARATIONS ARE COMPLETE.
EVERYTHING WILL END... AND EVERYTHING WILL BEGIN!

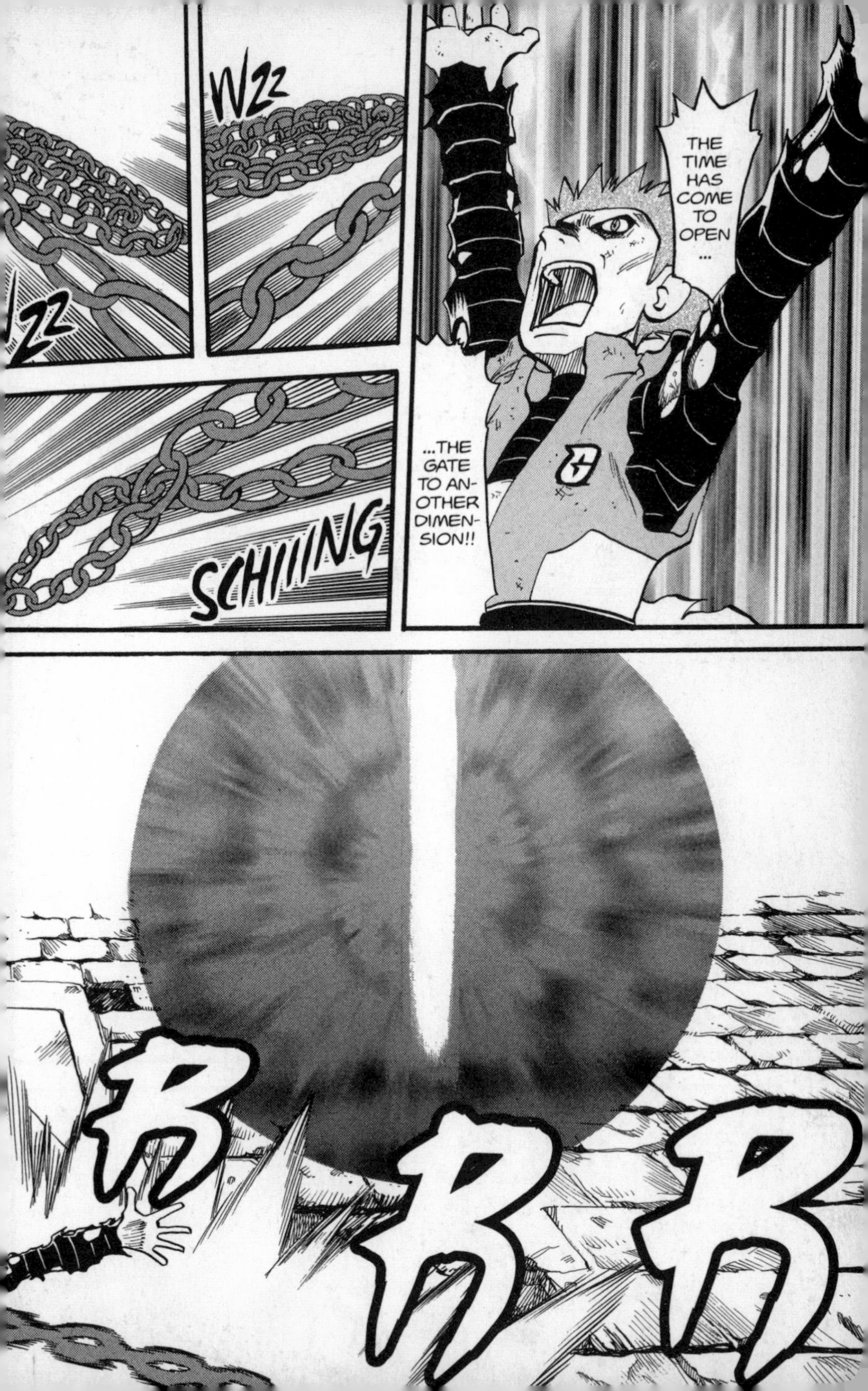
THE TIME HAS COME TO OPEN ...
...THE GATE TO AN-OTHER DIMEN-SION!!
WZZ
ZZ
SCHIIING

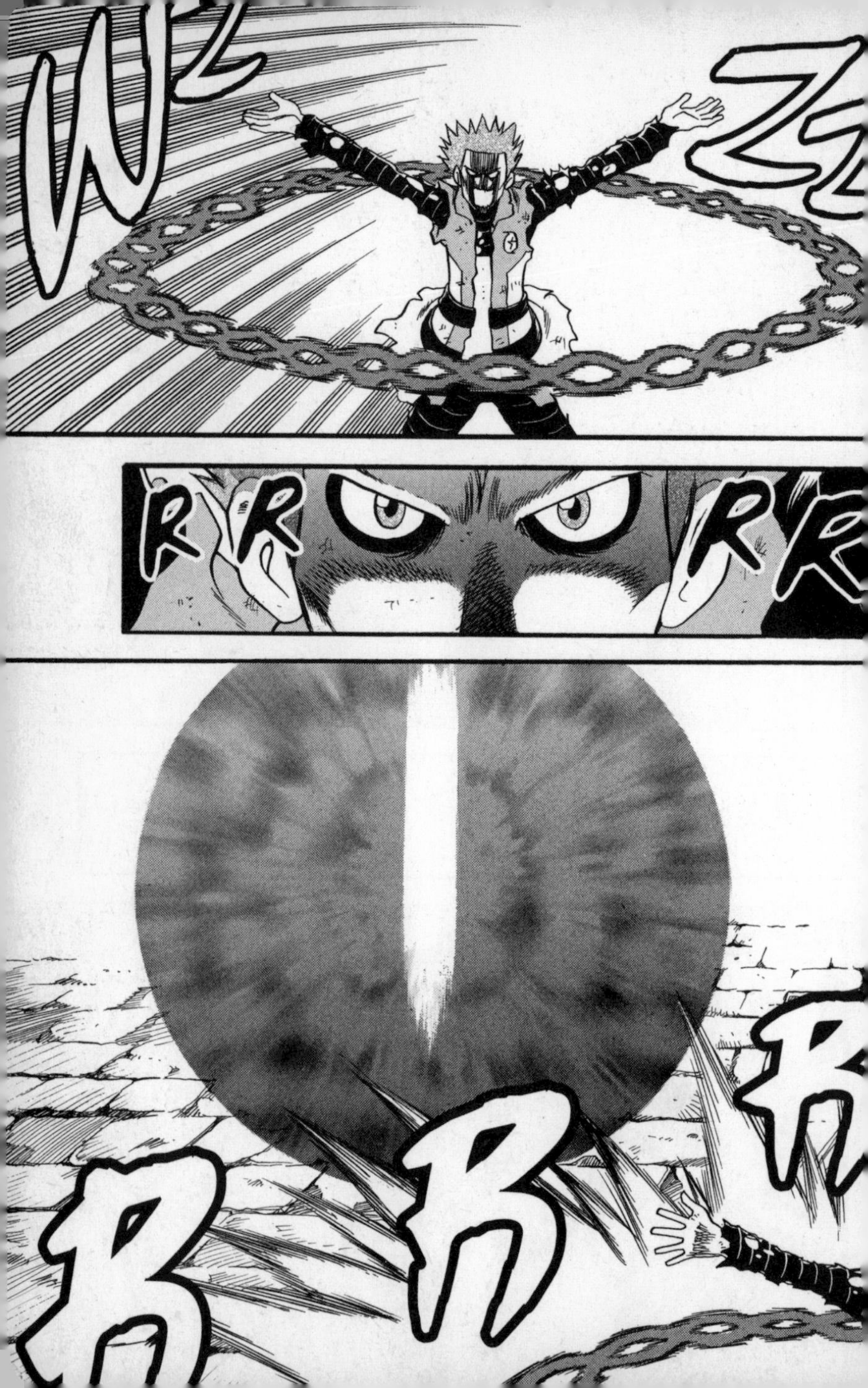
WZ ZZ
RR RR
BRR

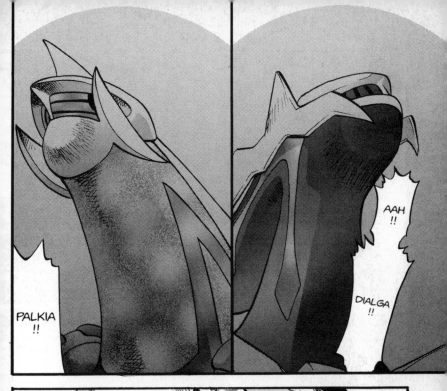

PALKIA
!!

AAH
!!

DIALGA
!!

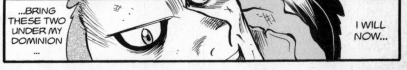

...BRING
THESE TWO
UNDER MY
DOMINION
...

I WILL
NOW...

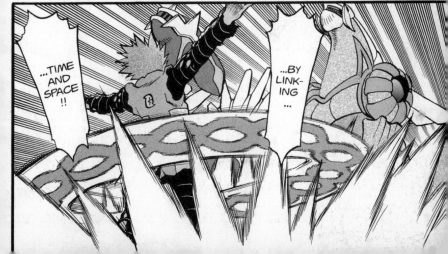

...TIME
AND
SPACE
!!

...BY
LINK-
ING
...

ADVENTURE MAP

DIAMOND

Galactic Veilstone City Building

TRU — Torterra ♂
KIT — Lickilicky ♂
LAX — Munchlax ♂
DON — Shieldon ♂

PEARL

Galactic Veilstone City Building

CHIMLER — Infernape ♂
ZELLER — Buizel ♂
CHATLER — Chatot ♂
TAULER — Tauros ♂
RAYLER — Luxray ♂
DIGLER — Diglett ♂

▶ Galactic Veilstone City Building ◀

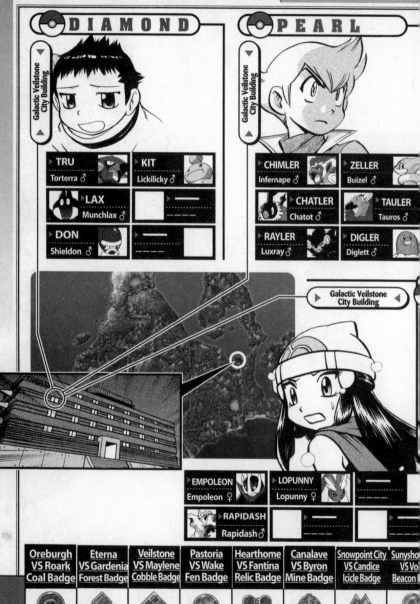

EMPOLEON — Empoleon ♀
LOPUNNY — Lopunny ♀
RAPIDASH — Rapidash ♂

Oreburgh VS Roark Coal Badge	Eterna VS Gardenia Forest Badge	Veilstone VS Maylene Cobble Badge	Pastoria VS Wake Fen Badge	Hearthome VS Fantina Relic Badge	Canalave VS Byron Mine Badge	Snowpoint City VS Candice Icicle Badge	Sunysho VS Vo Beacon

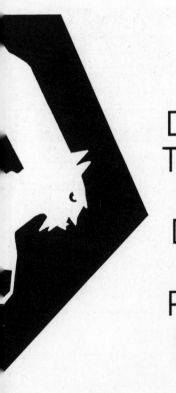

74

Double
Trouble
with
Dialga
and
Palkia I

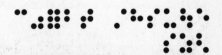

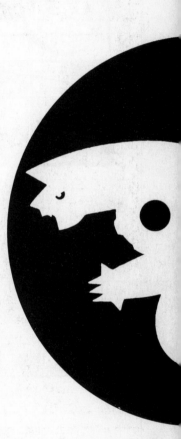

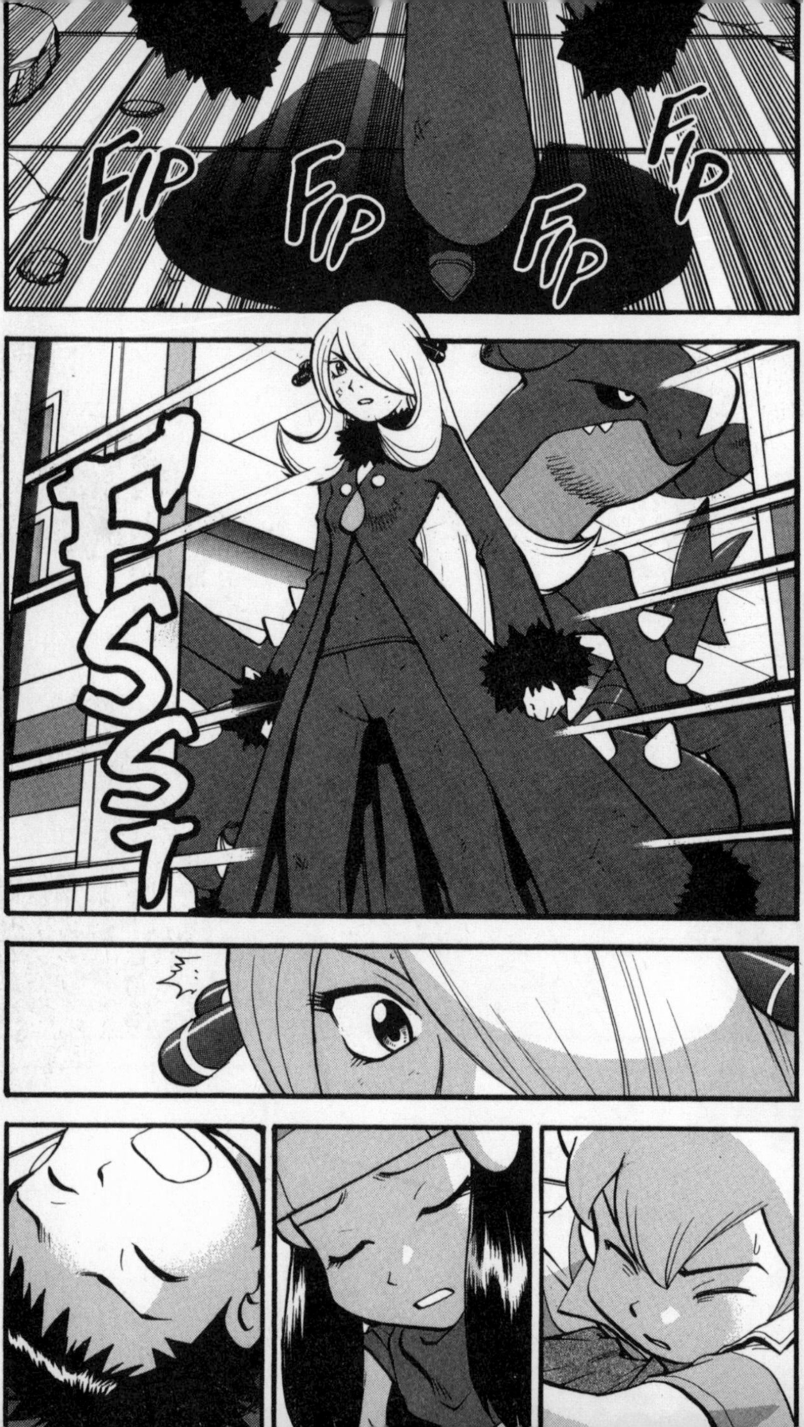
FIP
FIP
FIP
FIP
FSST

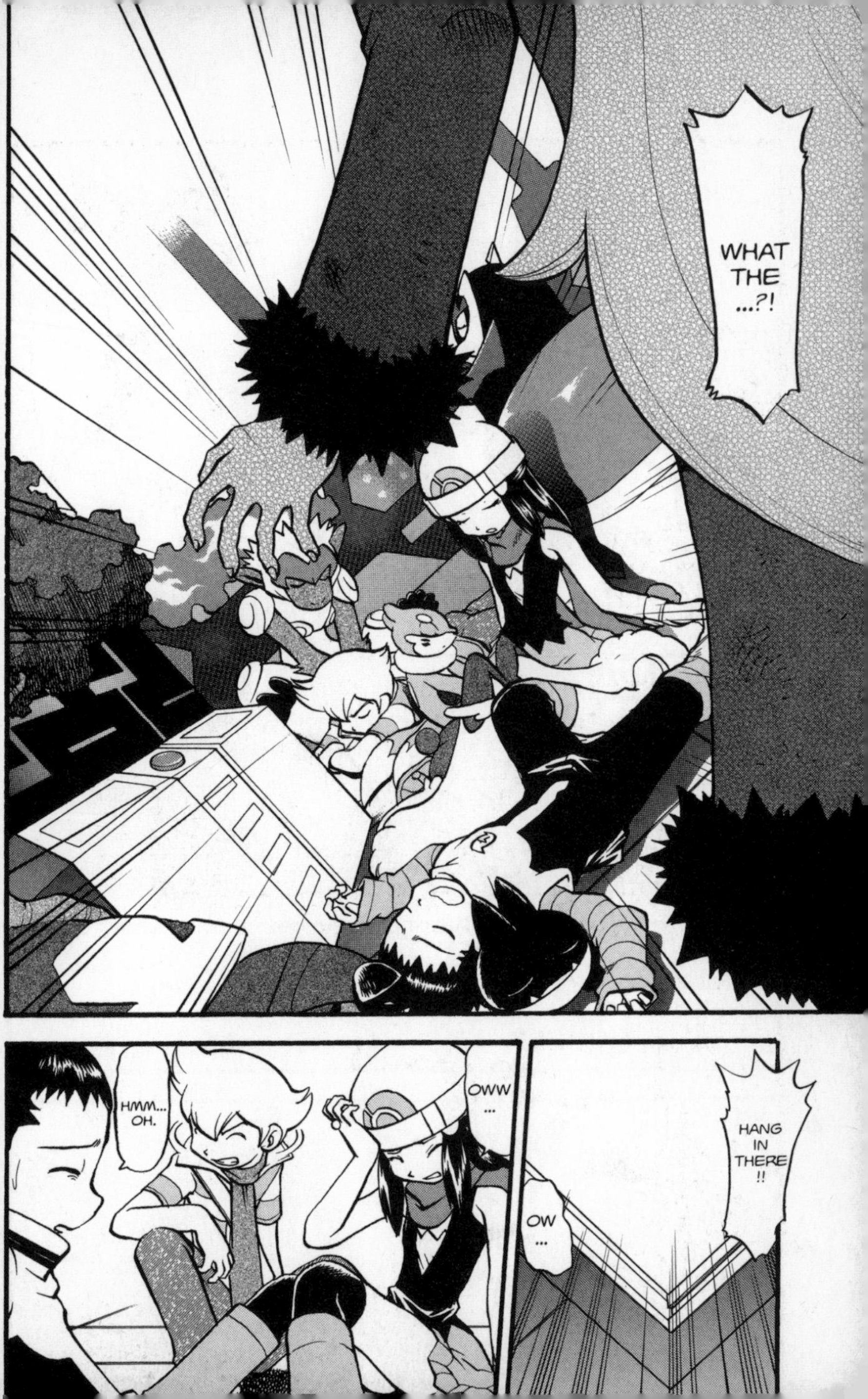
WHAT THE ...?!
HANG IN THERE !!
OWW ...
OW ...
HMM... OH.

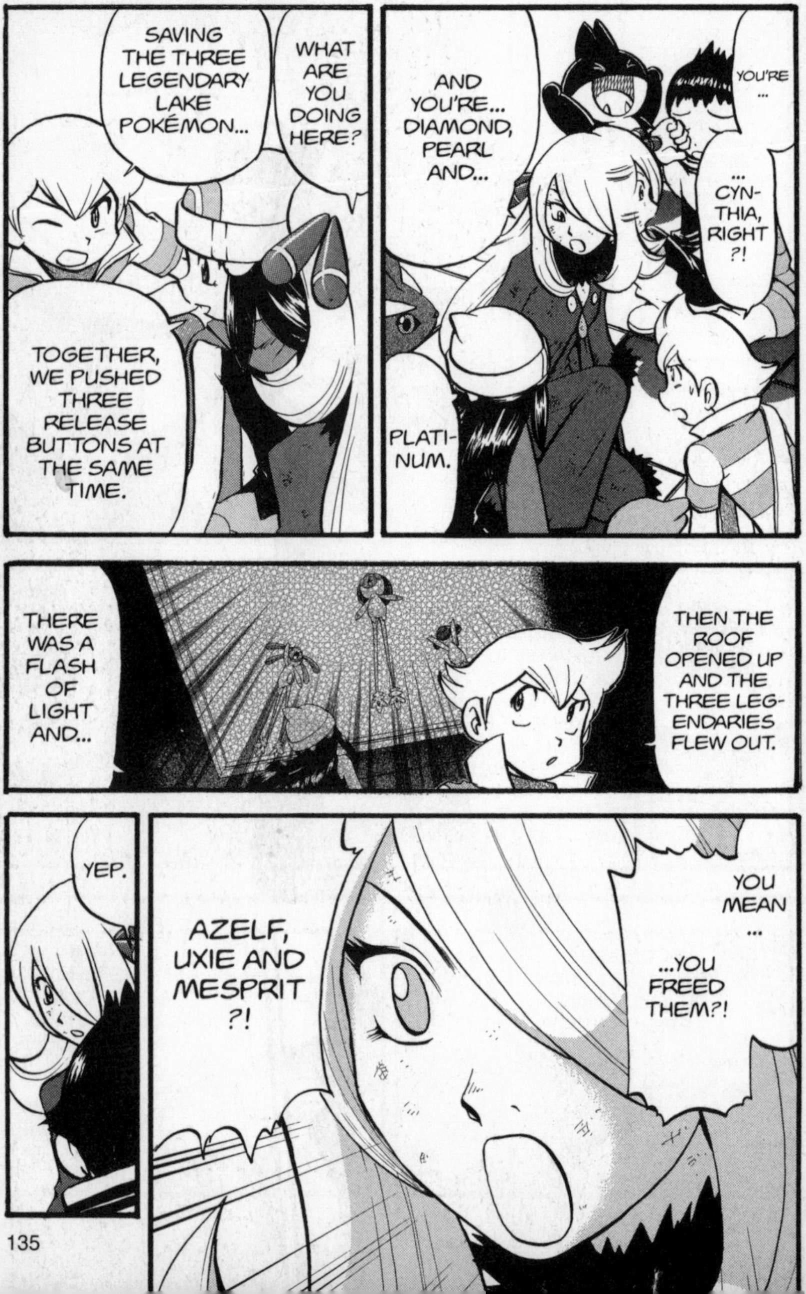
YOU'RE ...
... CYN-THIA, RIGHT ?!
AND YOU'RE... DIAMOND, PEARL AND...
PLATI-NUM.
WHAT ARE YOU DOING HERE?
SAVING THE THREE LEGENDARY LAKE POKÉMON...
TOGETHER, WE PUSHED THREE RELEASE BUTTONS AT THE SAME TIME.
THEN THE ROOF OPENED UP AND THE THREE LEG-ENDARIES FLEW OUT.
THERE WAS A FLASH OF LIGHT AND...
YOU MEAN ...
...YOU FREED THEM?!
AZELF, UXIE AND MESPRIT ?!
YEP.

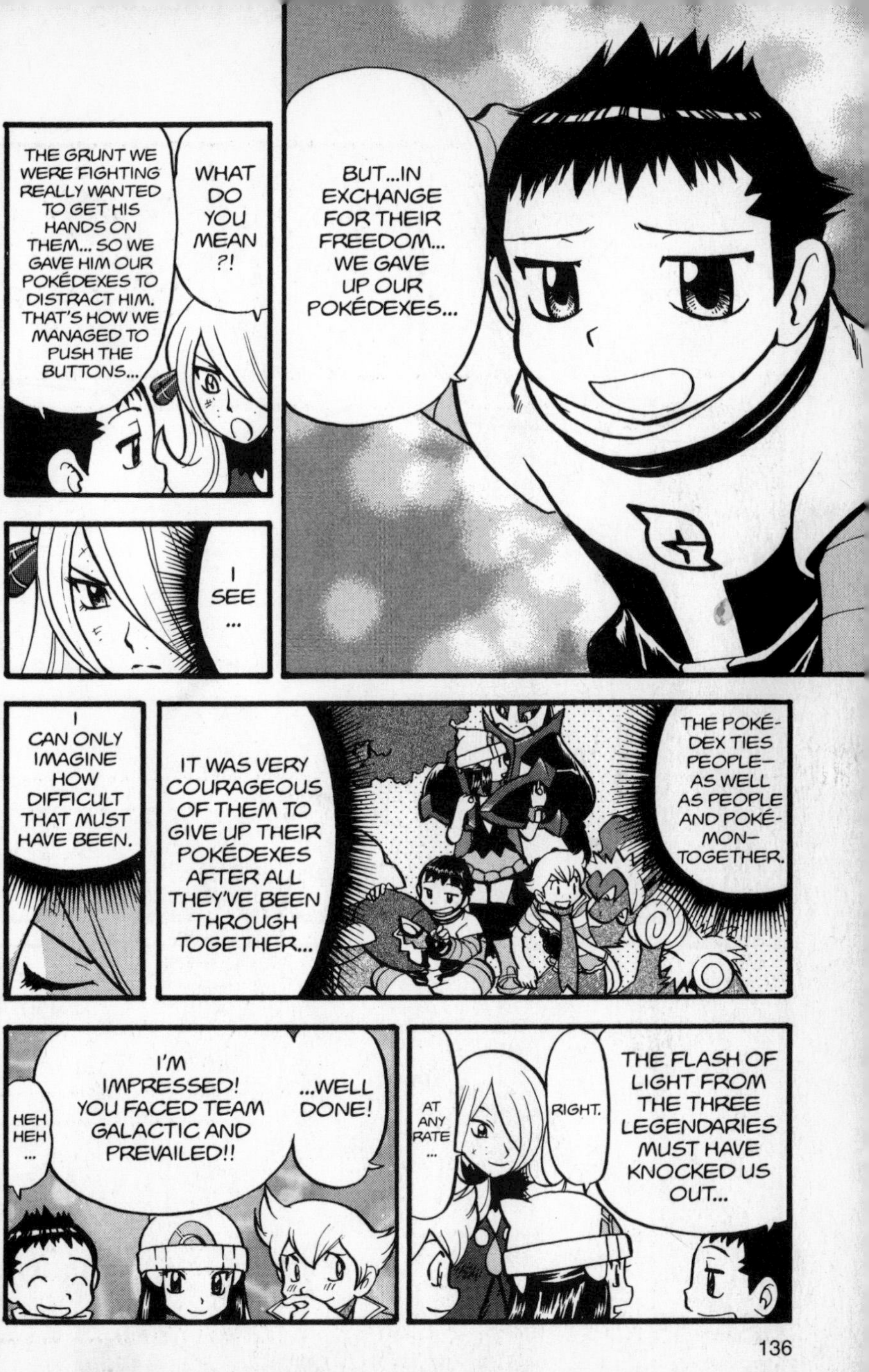
BUT...IN EXCHANGE FOR THEIR FREEDOM... WE GAVE UP OUR POKÉDEXES...
WHAT DO YOU MEAN ?!
THE GRUNT WE WERE FIGHTING REALLY WANTED TO GET HIS HANDS ON THEM... SO WE GAVE HIM OUR POKÉDEXES TO DISTRACT HIM. THAT'S HOW WE MANAGED TO PUSH THE BUTTONS...
I SEE ...
THE POKÉ-DEX TIES PEOPLE—AS WELL AS PEOPLE AND POKÉ-MON—TOGETHER.
IT WAS VERY COURAGEOUS OF THEM TO GIVE UP THEIR POKÉDEXES AFTER ALL THEY'VE BEEN THROUGH TOGETHER...
I CAN ONLY IMAGINE HOW DIFFICULT THAT MUST HAVE BEEN.
THE FLASH OF LIGHT FROM THE THREE LEGENDARIES MUST HAVE KNOCKED US OUT...
RIGHT.
AT ANY RATE ...
...WELL DONE!
I'M IMPRESSED! YOU FACED TEAM GALACTIC AND PREVAILED!!
HEH HEH ...

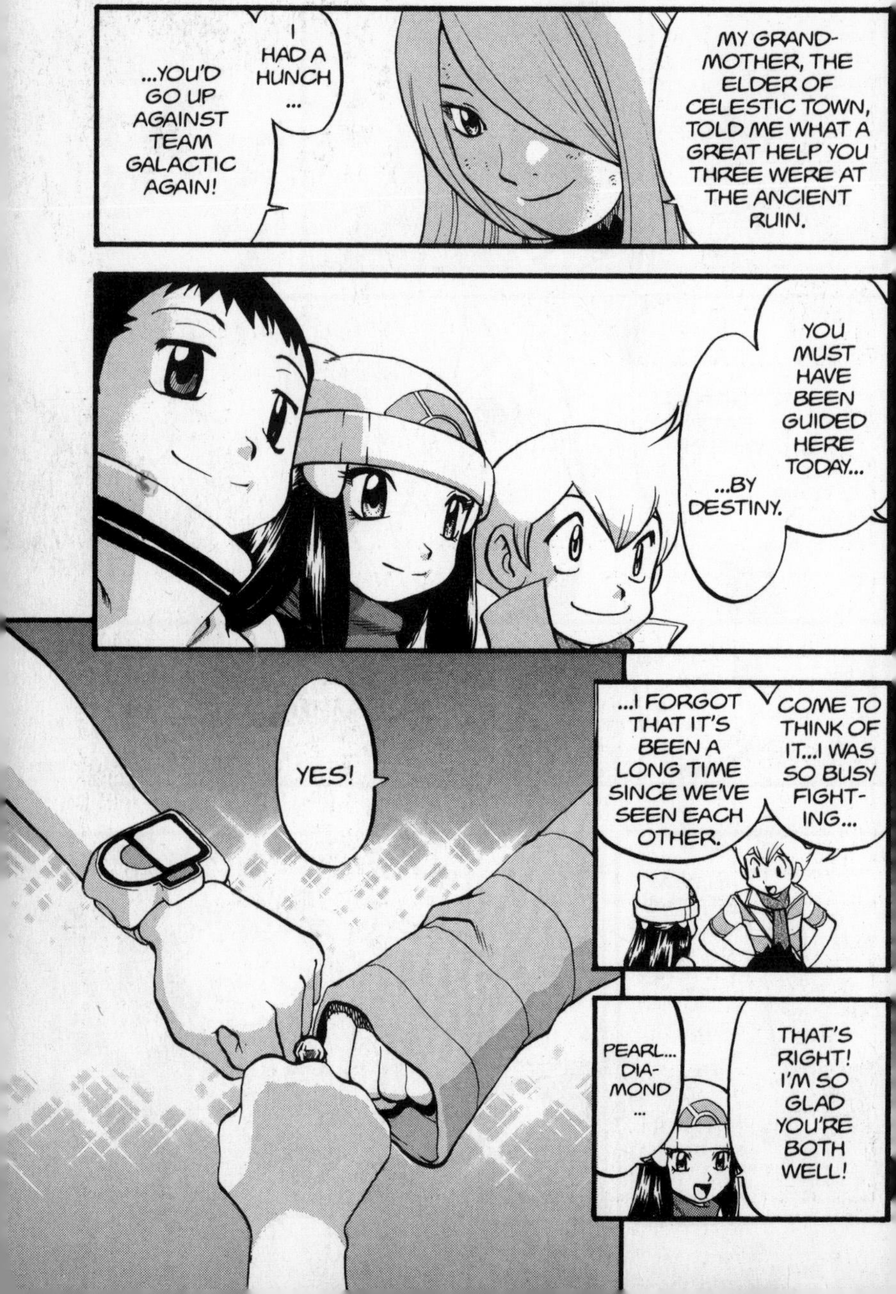
MY GRANDMOTHER, THE ELDER OF CELESTIC TOWN, TOLD ME WHAT A GREAT HELP YOU THREE WERE AT THE ANCIENT RUIN.
I HAD A HUNCH...
...YOU'D GO UP AGAINST TEAM GALACTIC AGAIN!
YOU MUST HAVE BEEN GUIDED HERE TODAY...
...BY DESTINY.
COME TO THINK OF IT...I WAS SO BUSY FIGHTING...
...I FORGOT THAT IT'S BEEN A LONG TIME SINCE WE'VE SEEN EACH OTHER.
THAT'S RIGHT! I'M SO GLAD YOU'RE BOTH WELL!
PEARL... DIAMOND...
YES!

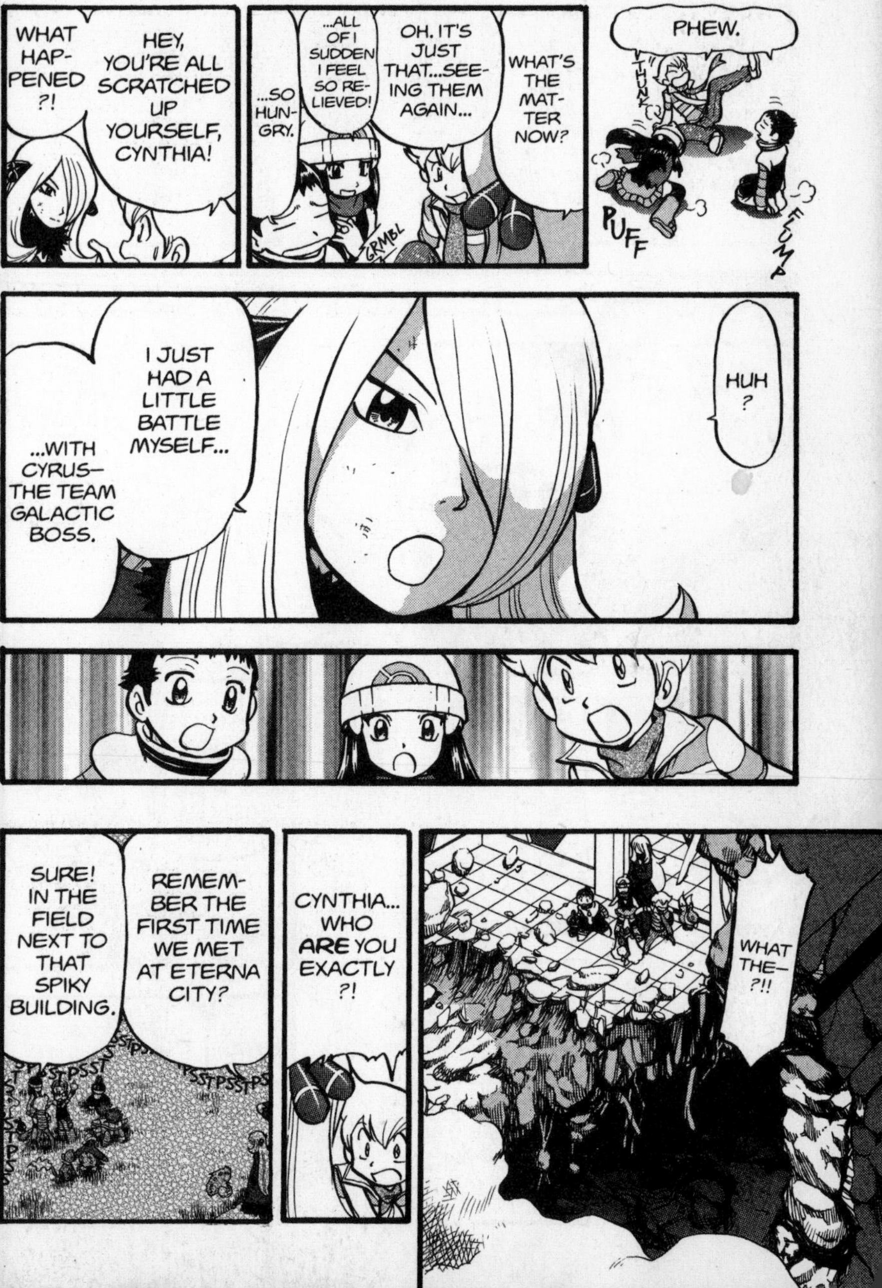
PHEW.
THUNK
PUFF
FLUMP
WHAT'S THE MATTER NOW?
OH. IT'S JUST THAT...SEEING THEM AGAIN...
...ALL OF I SUDDEN I FEEL SO RELIEVED!
...SO HUNGRY.
GRMBL
HEY, YOU'RE ALL SCRATCHED UP YOURSELF, CYNTHIA!
WHAT HAPPENED?!
HUH?
I JUST HAD A LITTLE BATTLE MYSELF...
...WITH CYRUS—THE TEAM GALACTIC BOSS.
WHAT THE—?!!
CYNTHIA... WHO **ARE** YOU EXACTLY?!
REMEMBER THE FIRST TIME WE MET AT ETERNA CITY?
SURE! IN THE FIELD NEXT TO THAT SPIKY BUILDING.
PSST PSST PSST PSST

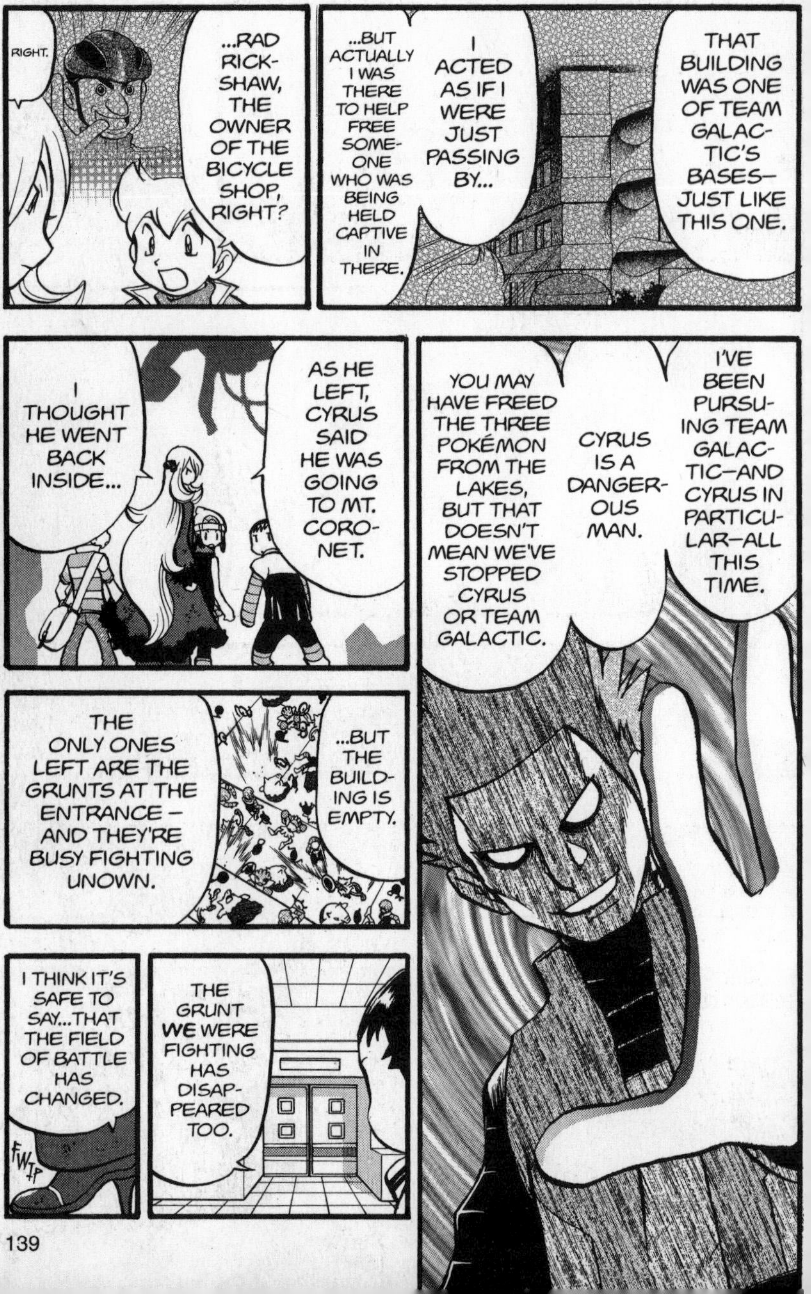
THAT BUILDING WAS ONE OF TEAM GALACTIC'S BASES—JUST LIKE THIS ONE.
I ACTED AS IF I WERE JUST PASSING BY...
...BUT ACTUALLY I WAS THERE TO HELP FREE SOMEONE WHO WAS BEING HELD CAPTIVE IN THERE.
...RAD RICKSHAW, THE OWNER OF THE BICYCLE SHOP, RIGHT?
RIGHT.
I'VE BEEN PURSUING TEAM GALACTIC—AND CYRUS IN PARTICULAR—ALL THIS TIME.
CYRUS IS A DANGEROUS MAN.
YOU MAY HAVE FREED THE THREE POKÉMON FROM THE LAKES, BUT THAT DOESN'T MEAN WE'VE STOPPED CYRUS OR TEAM GALACTIC.
AS HE LEFT, CYRUS SAID HE WAS GOING TO MT. CORONET.
I THOUGHT HE WENT BACK INSIDE...
...BUT THE BUILDING IS EMPTY.
THE ONLY ONES LEFT ARE THE GRUNTS AT THE ENTRANCE—AND THEY'RE BUSY FIGHTING UNOWN.
THE GRUNT **WE** WERE FIGHTING HAS DISAPPEARED TOO.
I THINK IT'S SAFE TO SAY...THAT THE FIELD OF BATTLE HAS CHANGED.
FWIP

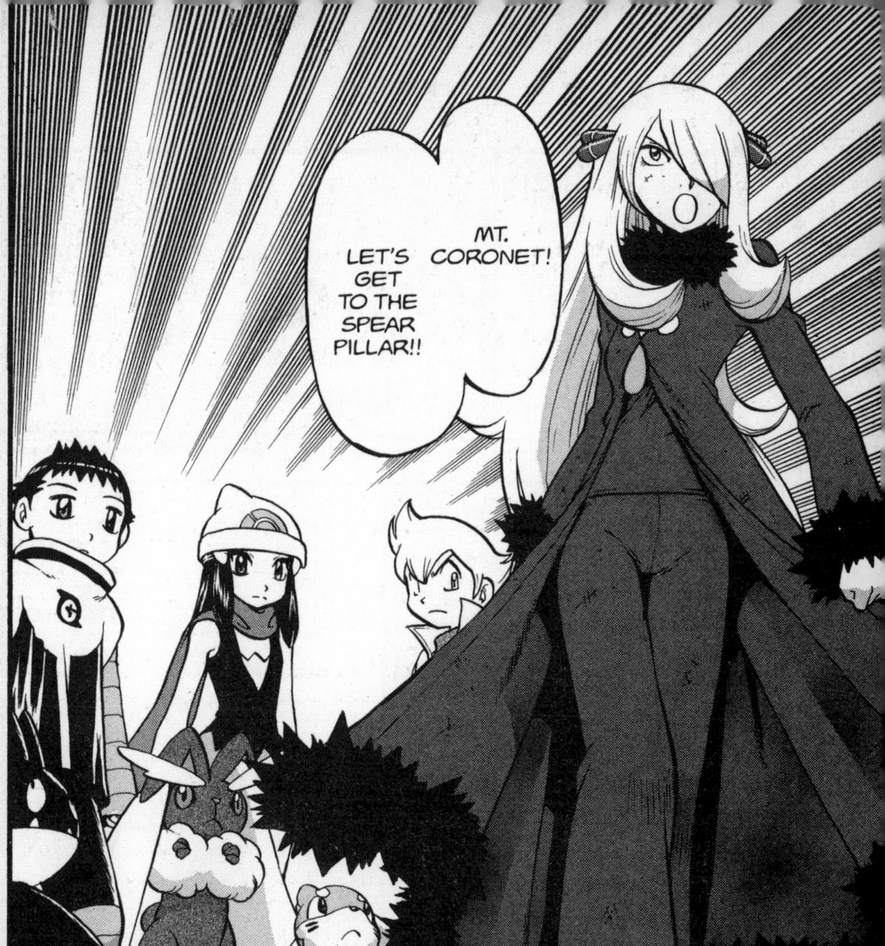
MT. CORONET! LET'S GET TO THE SPEAR PILLAR!!
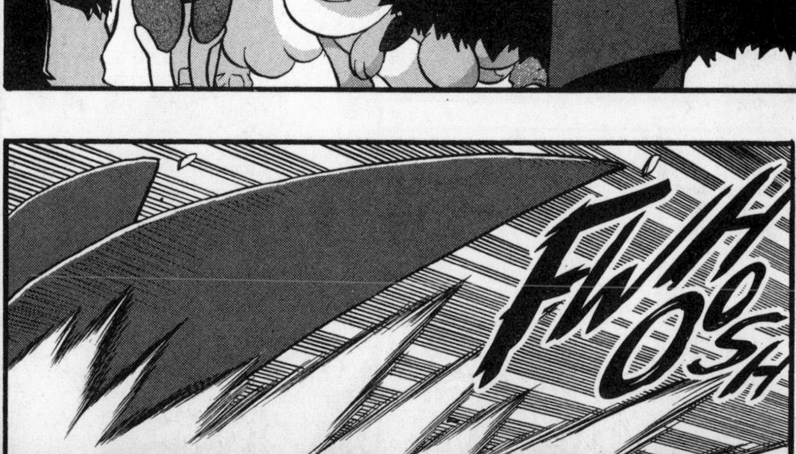
FWHOOSH

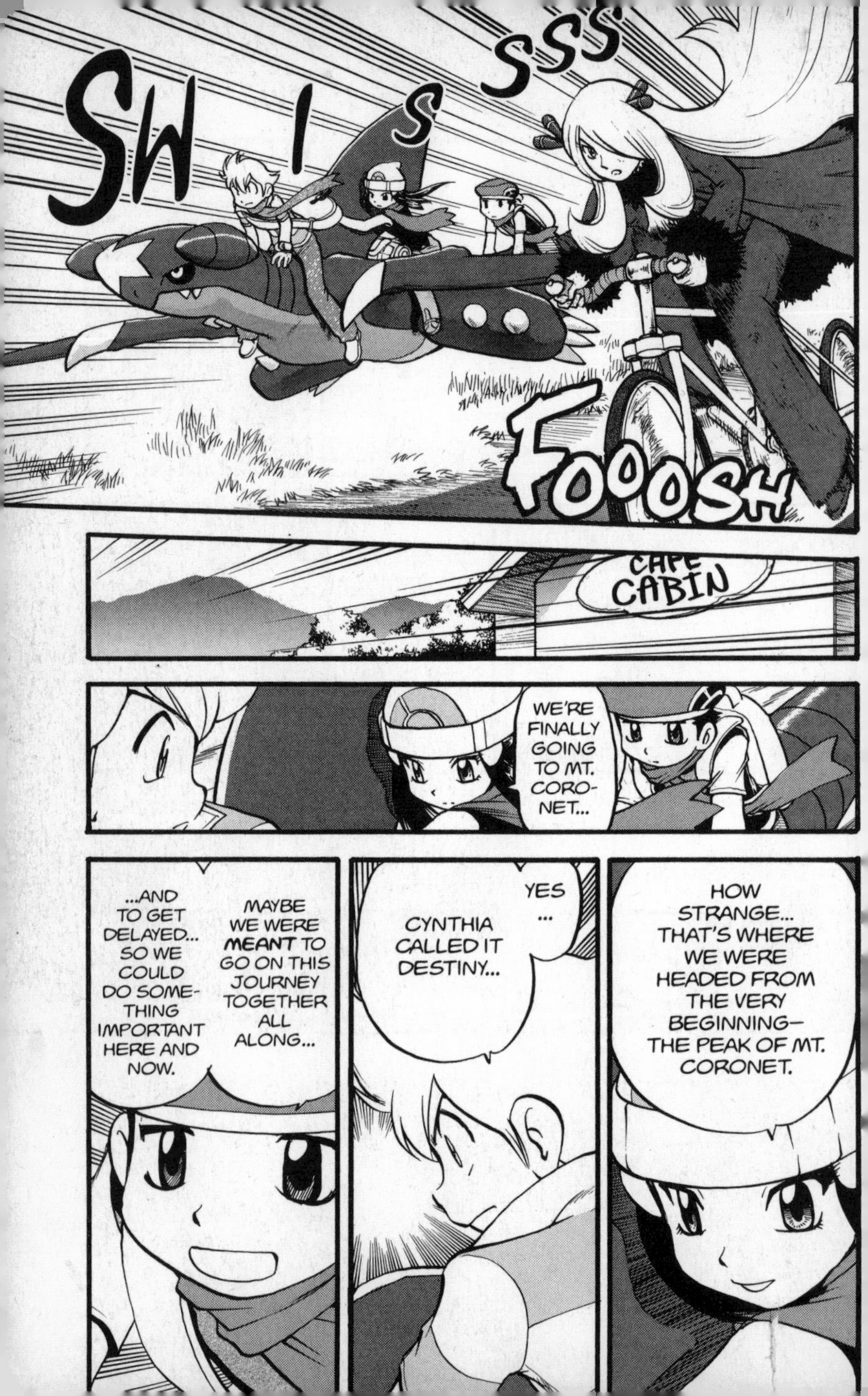

SWISSSS
FOOOSH
CAPE CABIN
WE'RE FINALLY GOING TO MT. CORONET...
HOW STRANGE... THAT'S WHERE WE WERE HEADED FROM THE VERY BEGINNING—THE PEAK OF MT. CORONET.
YES...
CYNTHIA CALLED IT DESTINY...
MAYBE WE WERE **MEANT** TO GO ON THIS JOURNEY TOGETHER ALL ALONG...
...AND TO GET DELAYED... SO WE COULD DO SOMETHING IMPORTANT HERE AND NOW.

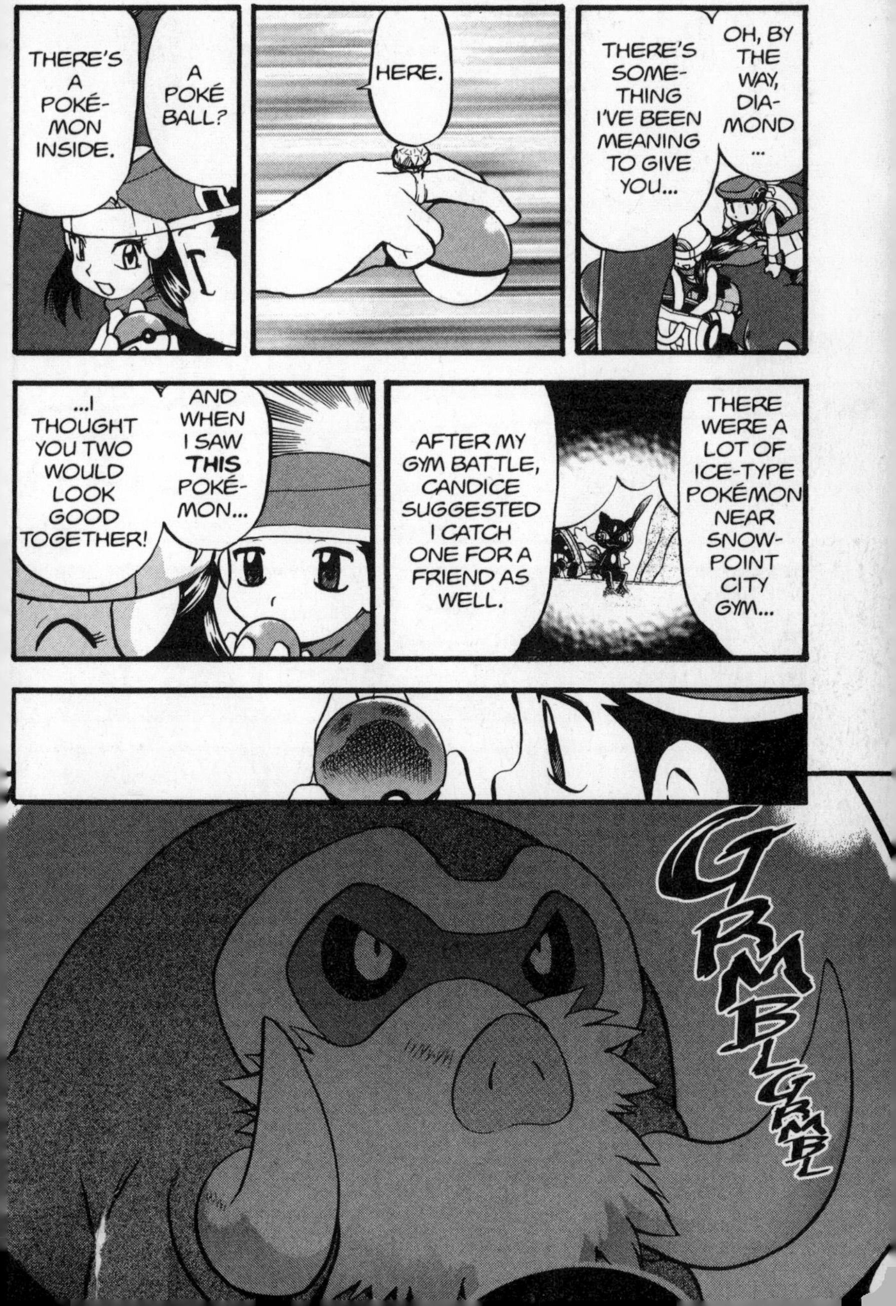
OH, BY THE WAY, DIAMOND...
THERE'S SOMETHING I'VE BEEN MEANING TO GIVE YOU...
HERE.
A POKÉ BALL?
THERE'S A POKÉMON INSIDE.
THERE WERE A LOT OF ICE-TYPE POKÉMON NEAR SNOWPOINT CITY GYM...
AFTER MY GYM BATTLE, CANDICE SUGGESTED I CATCH ONE FOR A FRIEND AS WELL.
AND WHEN I SAW **THIS** POKÉMON...
...I THOUGHT YOU TWO WOULD LOOK GOOD TOGETHER!
GRMBLGRMBL

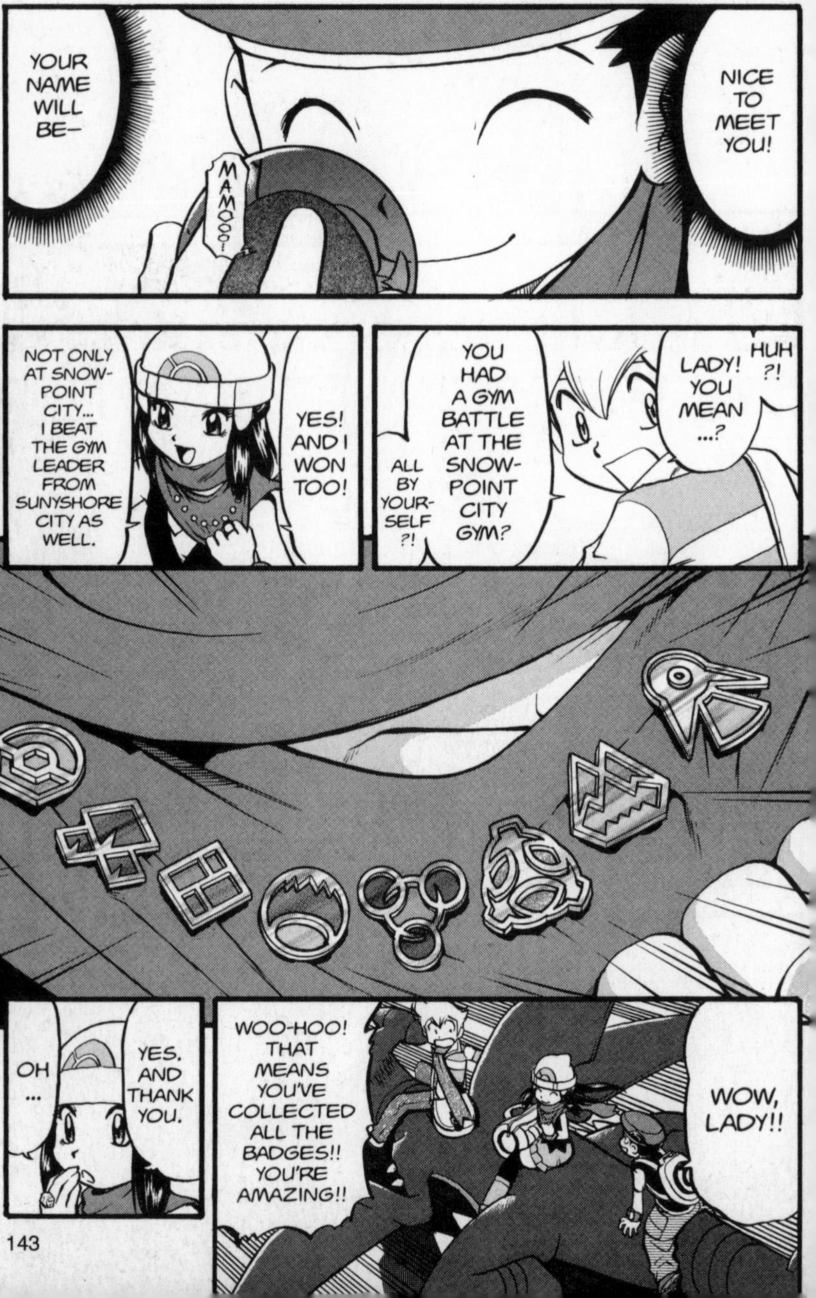
NICE TO MEET YOU!
YOUR NAME WILL BE—
MAMOOO!
HUH ?!
LADY! YOU MEAN ...?
YOU HAD A GYM BATTLE AT THE SNOW-POINT CITY GYM?
ALL BY YOUR-SELF ?!
YES! AND I WON TOO!
NOT ONLY AT SNOW-POINT CITY... I BEAT THE GYM LEADER FROM SUNYSHORE CITY AS WELL.
WOW, LADY!!
WOO-HOO! THAT MEANS YOU'VE COLLECTED ALL THE BADGES!! YOU'RE AMAZING!!
YES. AND THANK YOU.
OH ...

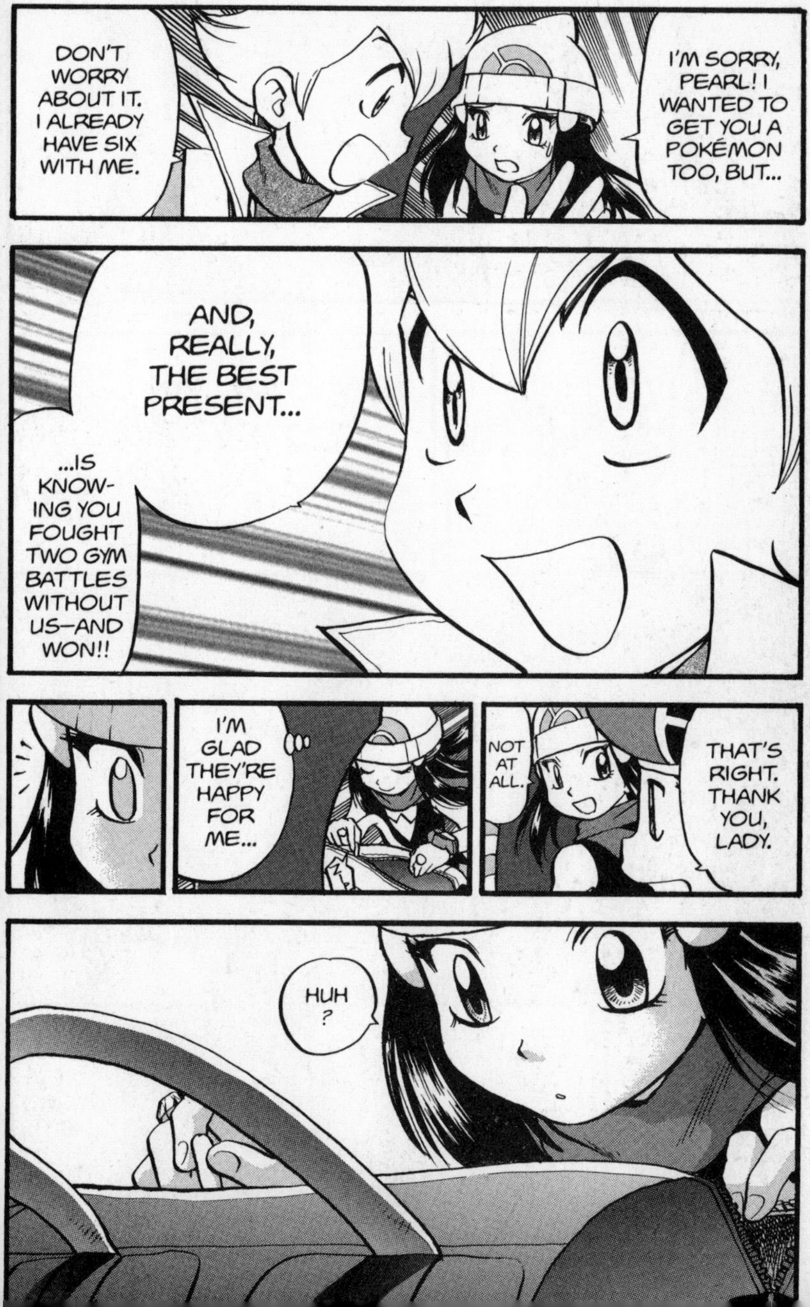
I'M SORRY, PEARL! I WANTED TO GET YOU A POKÉMON TOO, BUT...
DON'T WORRY ABOUT IT. I ALREADY HAVE SIX WITH ME.
AND, REALLY, THE BEST PRESENT...
...IS KNOWING YOU FOUGHT TWO GYM BATTLES WITHOUT US—AND WON!!
THAT'S RIGHT. THANK YOU, LADY.
NOT AT ALL.
I'M GLAD THEY'RE HAPPY FOR ME...
HUH?

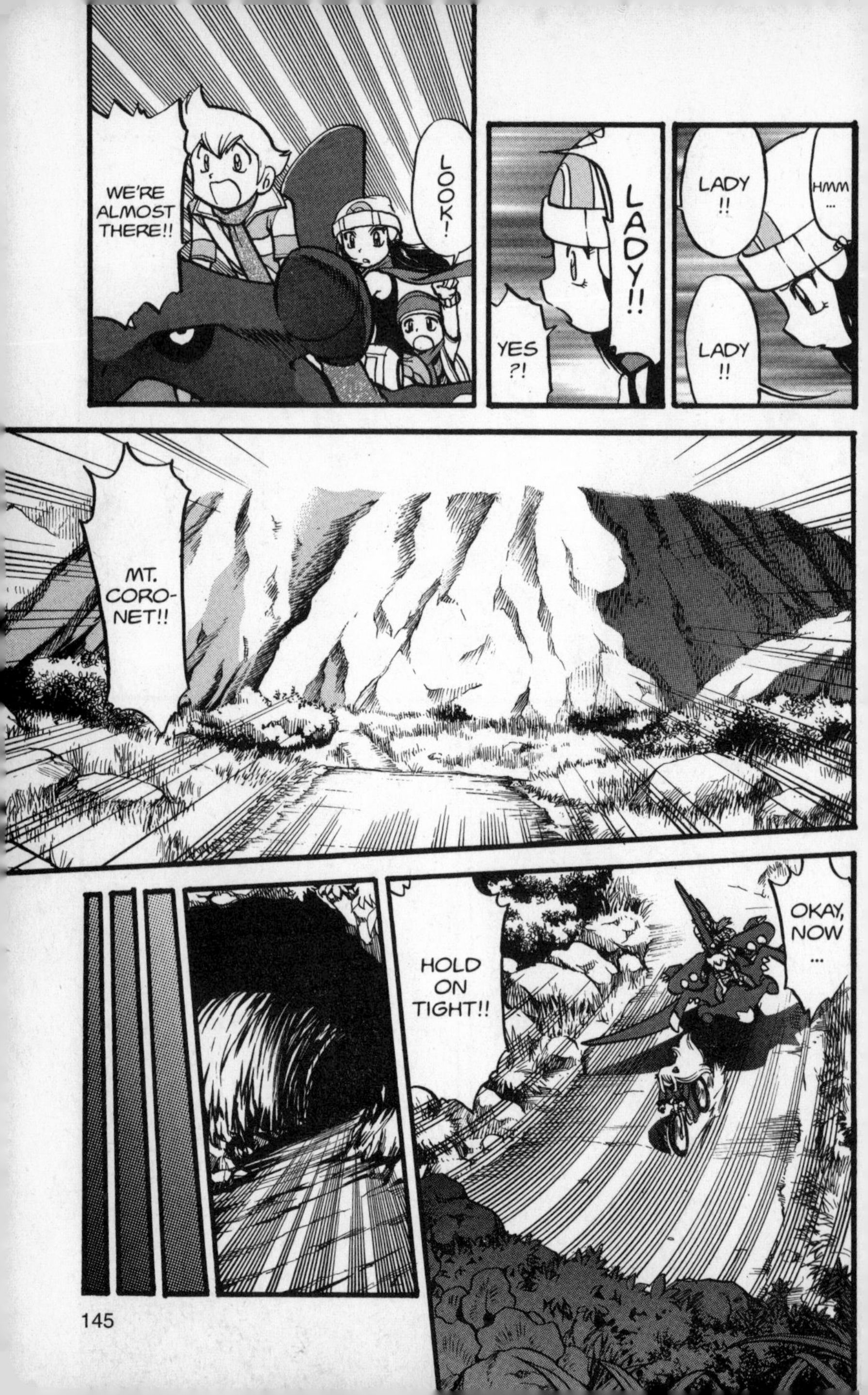
HMM...
LADY!!
LADY!!
LADY!!
YES?!
LOOK!
WE'RE ALMOST THERE!!
MT. CORO-NET!!
OKAY, NOW...
HOLD ON TIGHT!!

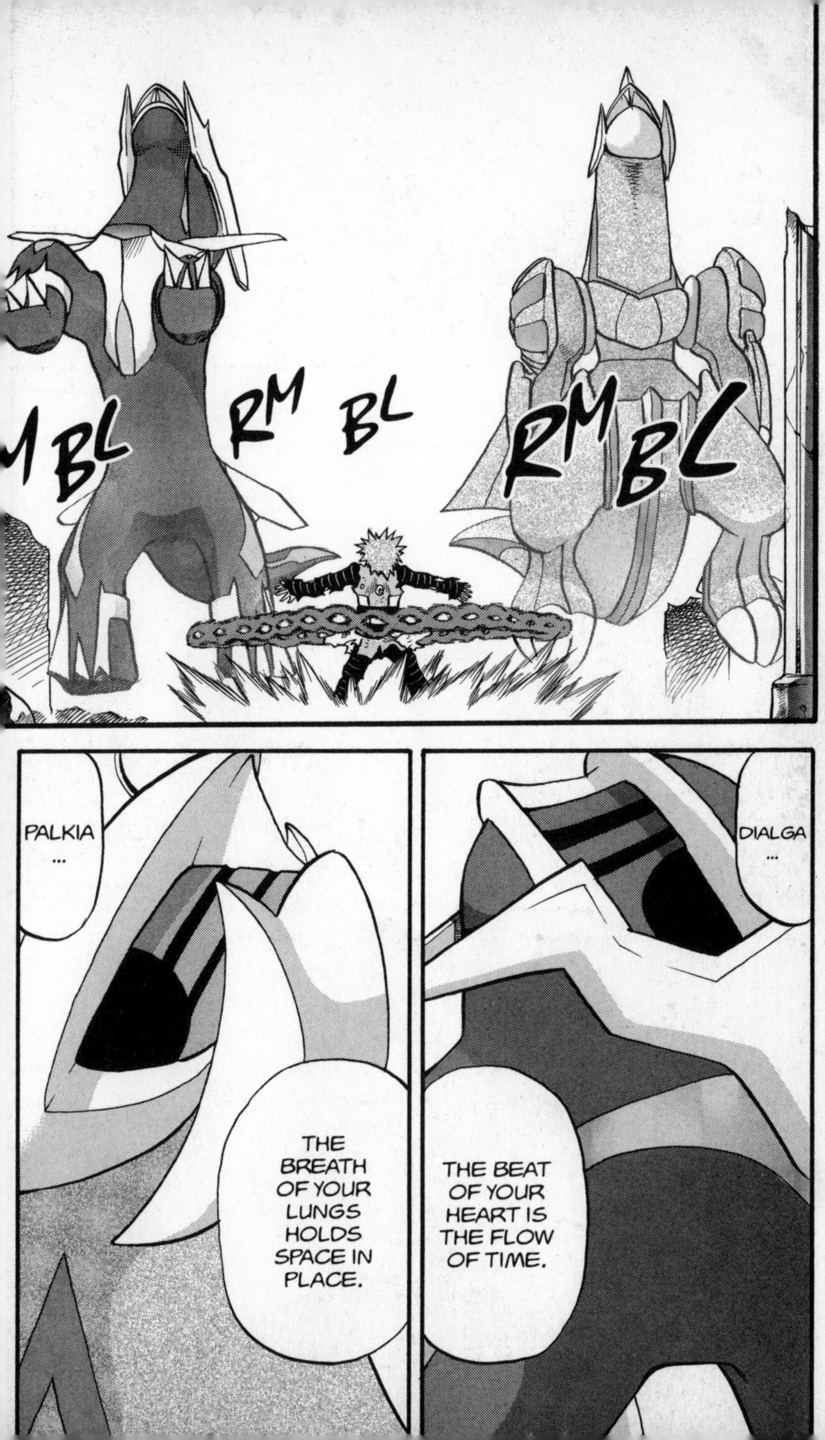

RM BL
RM BL
BL
DIALGA ...
THE BEAT OF YOUR HEART IS THE FLOW OF TIME.
PALKIA ...
THE BREATH OF YOUR LUNGS HOLDS SPACE IN PLACE.

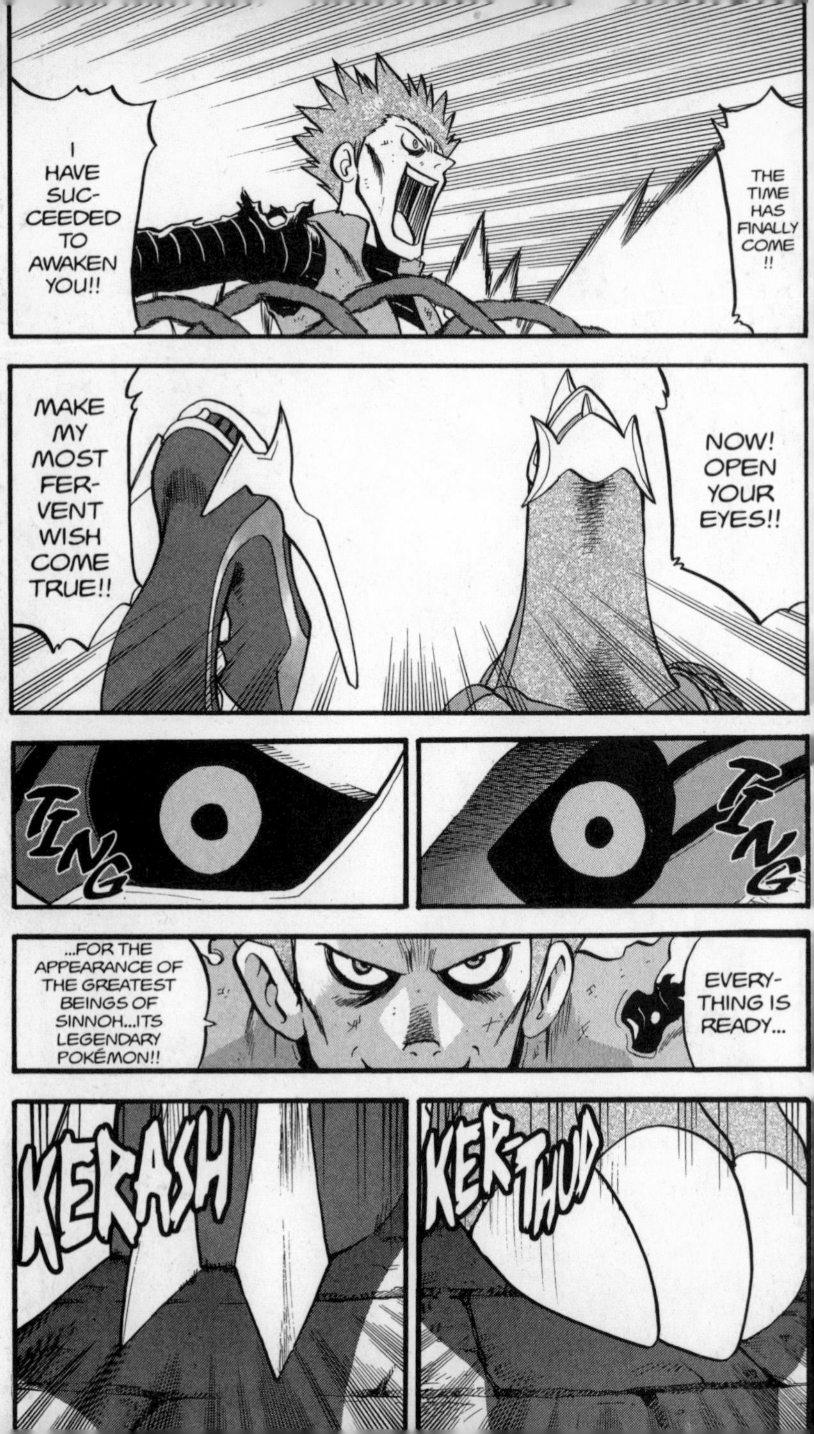
THE TIME HAS FINALLY COME!!
I HAVE SUCCEEDED TO AWAKEN YOU!!
NOW! OPEN YOUR EYES!!
MAKE MY MOST FERVENT WISH COME TRUE!!
TING
TING
EVERYTHING IS READY...
...FOR THE APPEARANCE OF THE GREATEST BEINGS OF SINNOH...ITS LEGENDARY POKÉMON!!
KER-THUD
KERASH

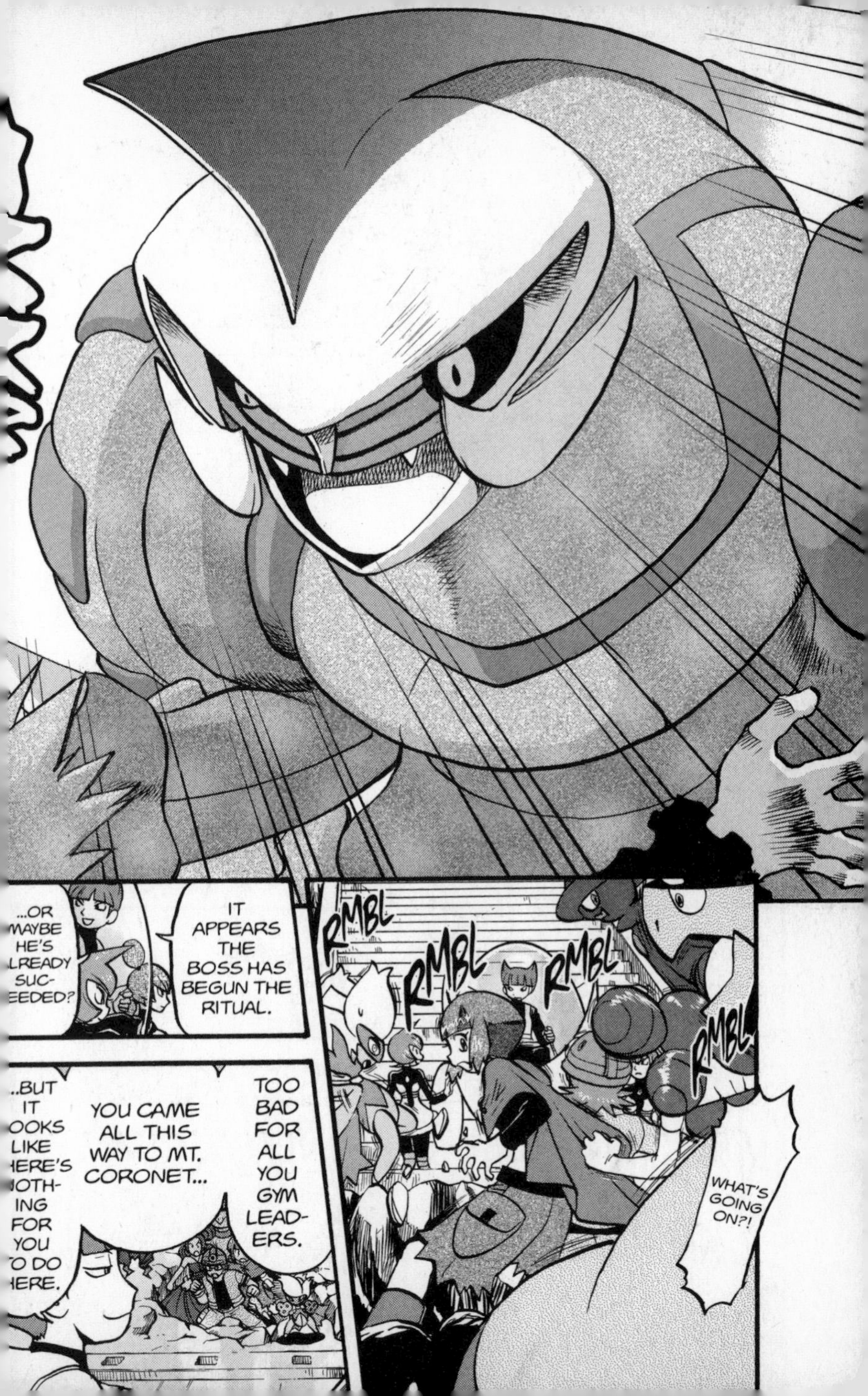
RMBL
RMBL
RMBL
RMBL
WHAT'S GOING ON?!
IT APPEARS THE BOSS HAS BEGUN THE RITUAL.
...OR MAYBE HE'S LREADY SUC-EEDED?
TOO BAD FOR ALL YOU GYM LEADERS.
YOU CAME ALL THIS WAY TO MT. CORONET...
..BUT IT OOKS LIKE HERE'S OTHING FOR YOU O DO HERE.

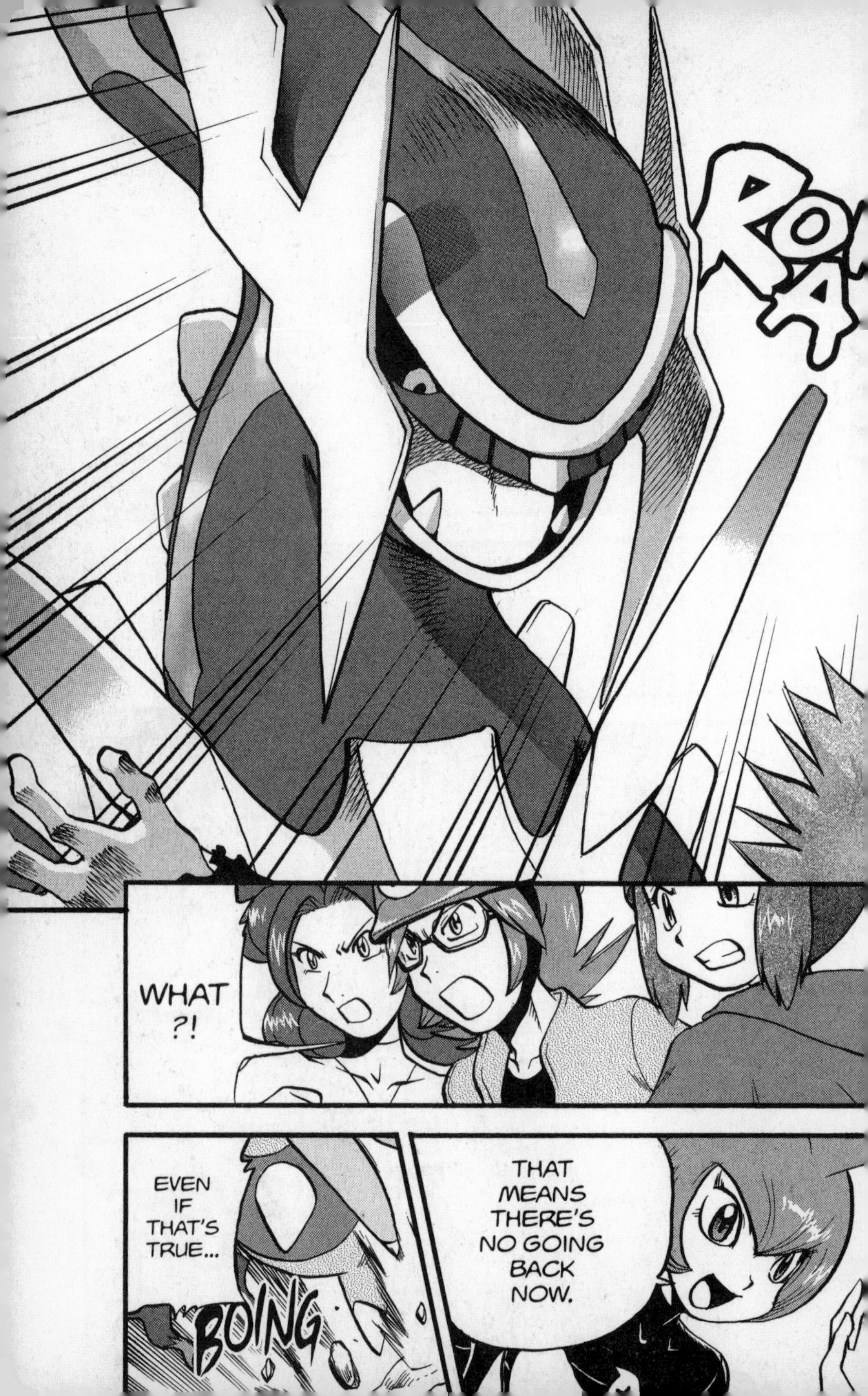
ROA
WHAT ?!
THAT MEANS THERE'S NO GOING BACK NOW.
EVEN IF THAT'S TRUE...
BOING

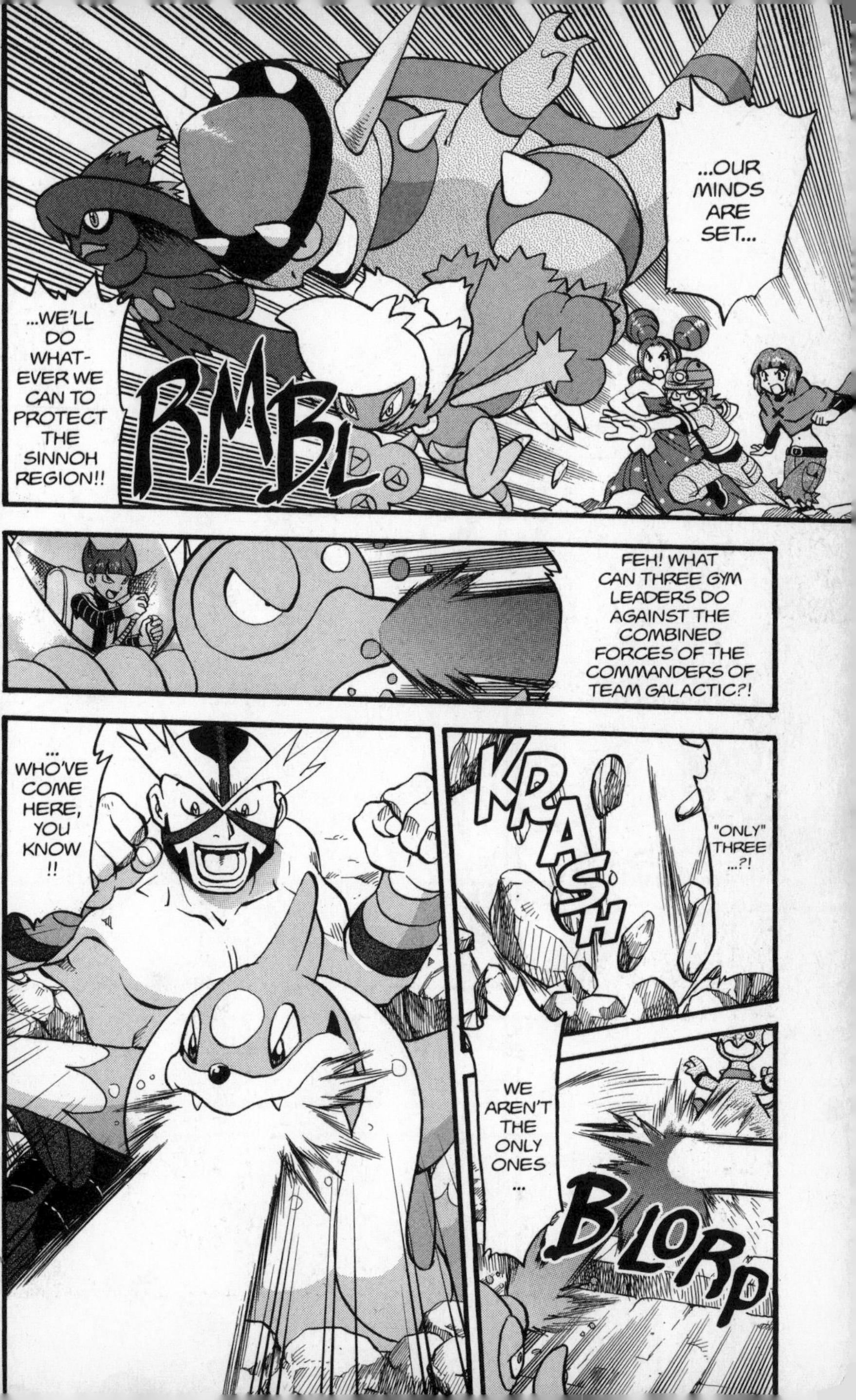
...OUR MINDS ARE SET...
...WE'LL DO WHAT-EVER WE CAN TO PROTECT THE SINNOH REGION!!
RMBL
FEH! WHAT CAN THREE GYM LEADERS DO AGAINST THE COMBINED FORCES OF THE COMMANDERS OF TEAM GALACTIC?!
KRASH
"ONLY" THREE ...?!
WE AREN'T THE ONLY ONES ...
BLORP
... WHO'VE COME HERE, YOU KNOW !!

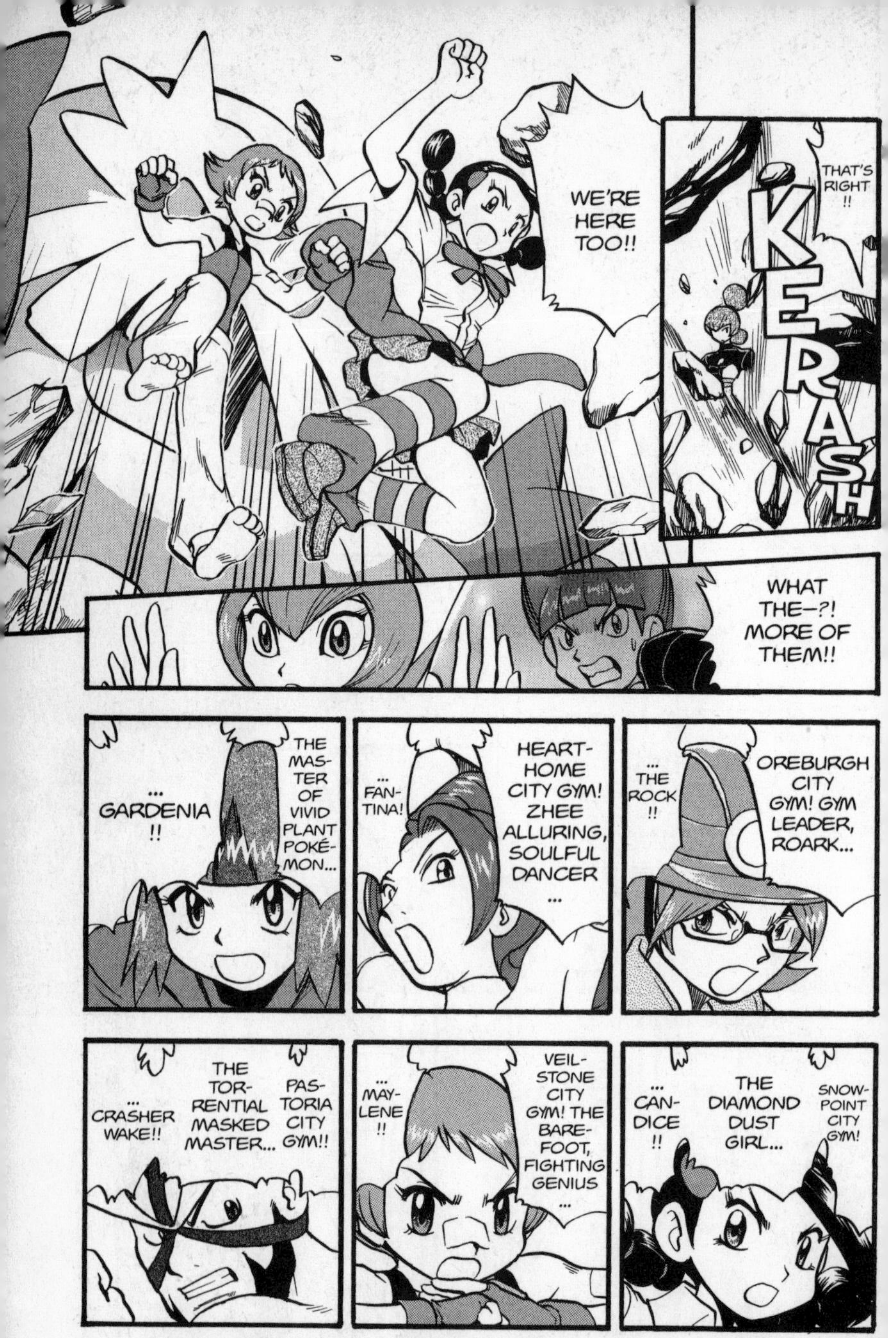
THAT'S RIGHT!!
KERASH
WE'RE HERE TOO!!
WHAT THE—?! MORE OF THEM!!
OREBURGH CITY GYM! GYM LEADER, ROARK...
...THE ROCK!!
HEARTHOME CITY GYM! ZHEE ALLURING, SOULFUL DANCER...
...FANTINA!
THE MASTER OF VIVID PLANT POKÉMON...
...GARDENIA!!
SNOWPOINT CITY GYM!
THE DIAMOND DUST GIRL...
...CANDICE!!
VEILSTONE CITY GYM! THE BAREFOOT, FIGHTING GENIUS...
...MAYLENE!!
PASTORIA CITY GYM!!
THE TORRENTIAL MASKED MASTER...
...CRASHER WAKE!!

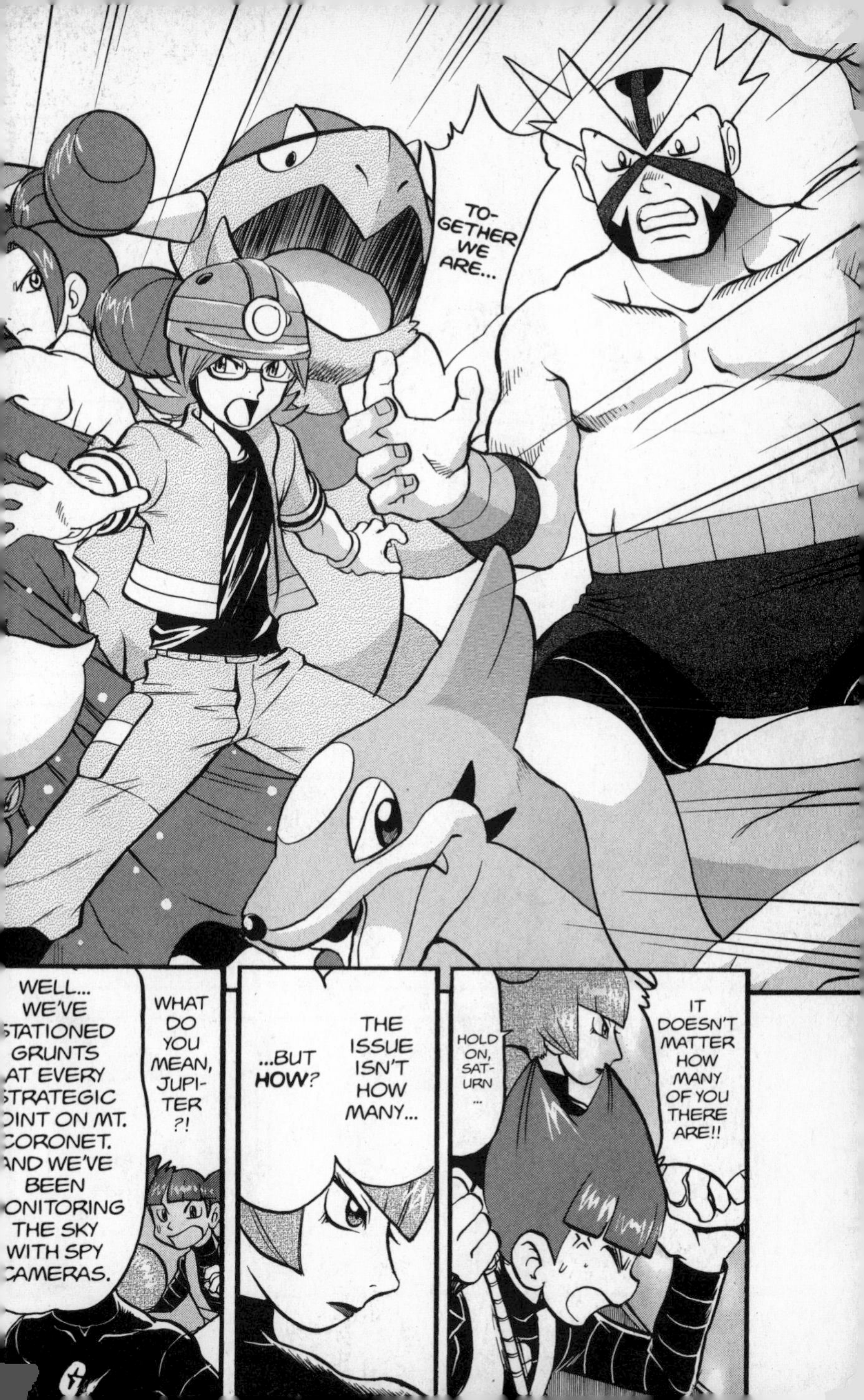
TO-GETHER WE ARE...
IT DOESN'T MATTER HOW MANY OF YOU THERE ARE!!
HOLD ON, SAT-URN...
THE ISSUE ISN'T HOW MANY...
...BUT **HOW**?
WHAT DO YOU MEAN, JUPI-TER?!
WELL... WE'VE STATIONED GRUNTS AT EVERY STRATEGIC POINT ON MT. CORONET. AND WE'VE BEEN MONITORING THE SKY WITH SPY CAMERAS.

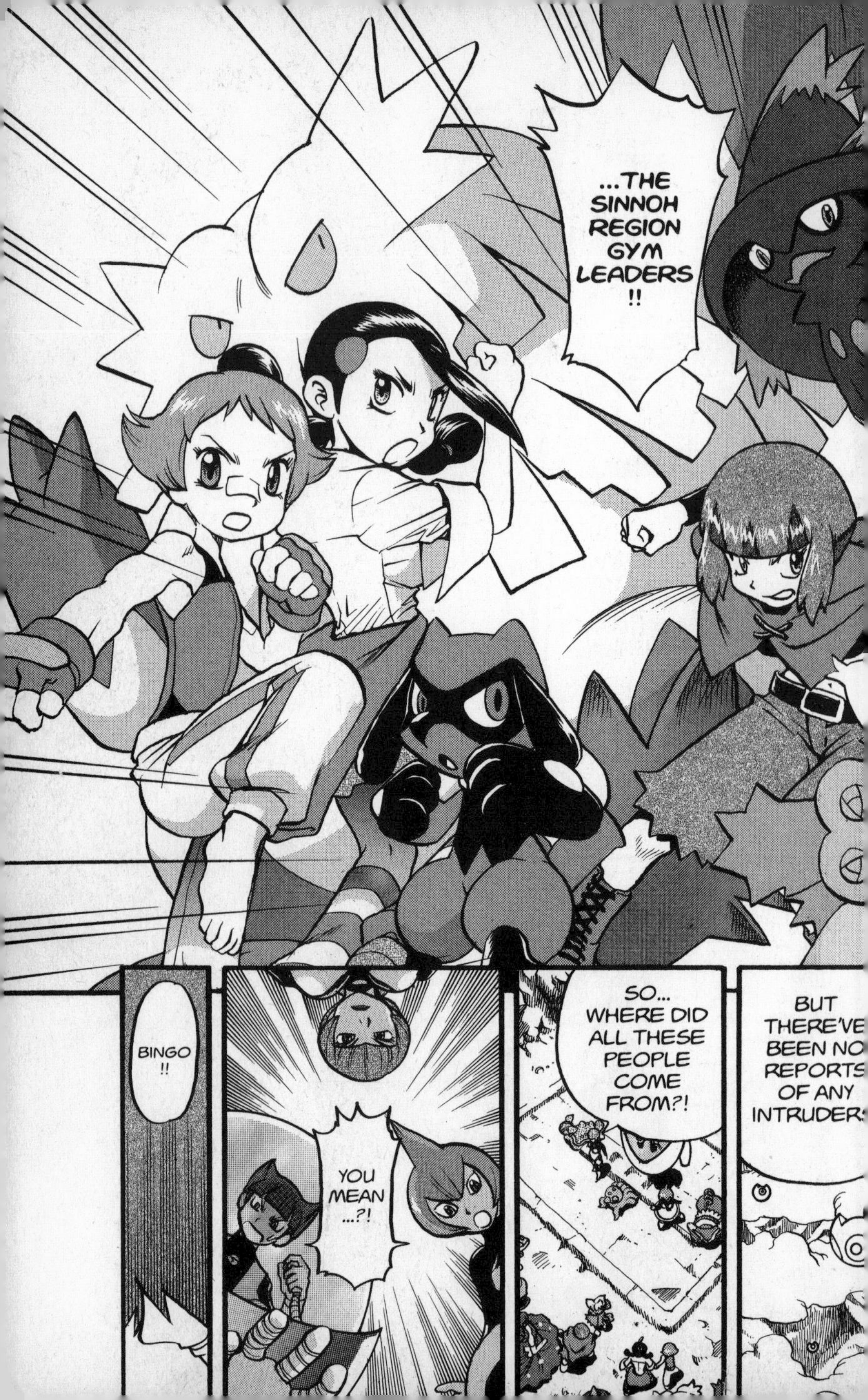
...THE SINNOH REGION GYM LEADERS !!
BUT THERE'VE BEEN NO REPORTS OF ANY INTRUDERS
SO... WHERE DID ALL THESE PEOPLE COME FROM?!
YOU MEAN ...?!
BINGO !!

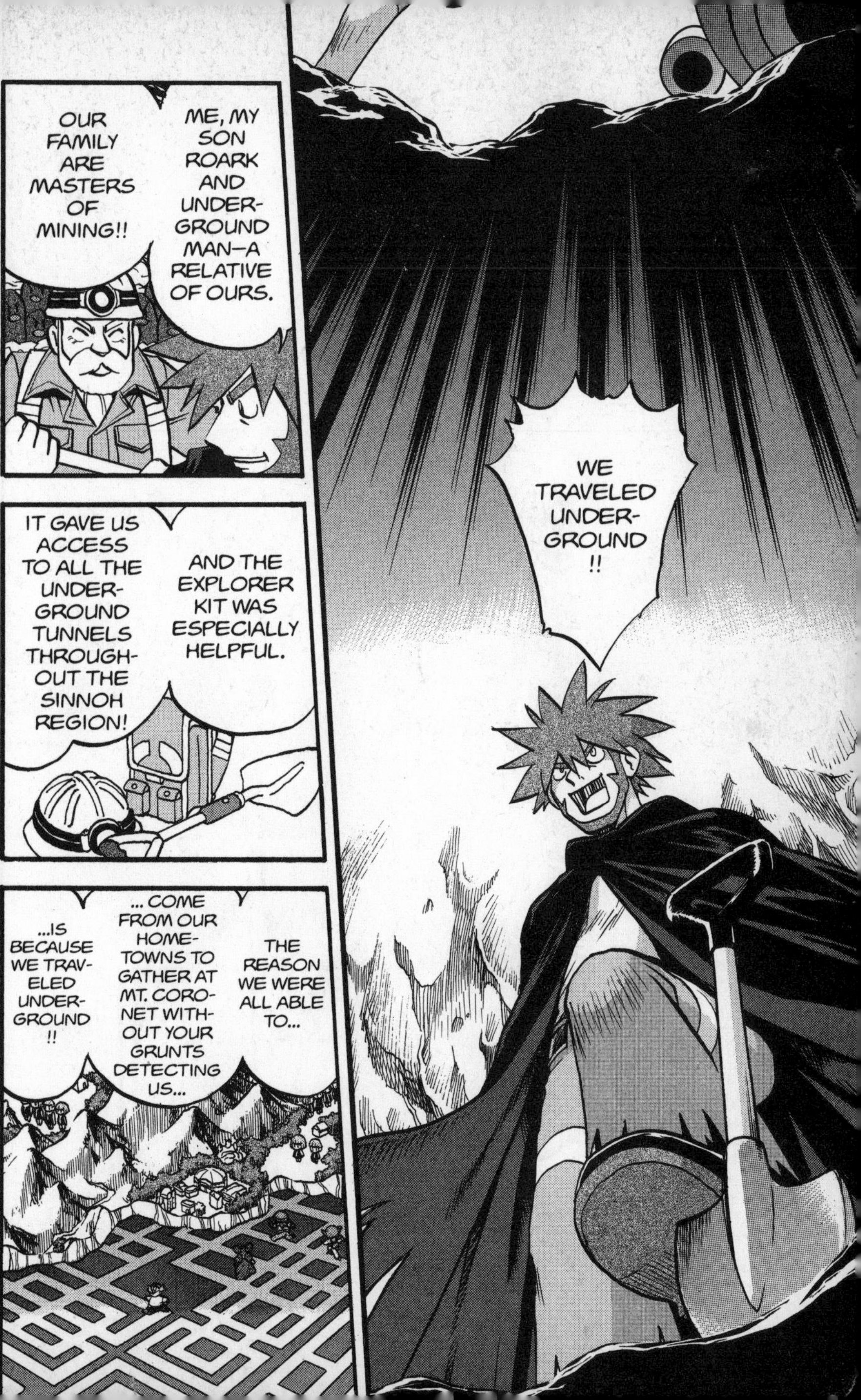
WE TRAVELED UNDER-GROUND !!
ME, MY SON ROARK AND UNDER-GROUND MAN—A RELATIVE OF OURS.
OUR FAMILY ARE MASTERS OF MINING!!
AND THE EXPLORER KIT WAS ESPECIALLY HELPFUL.
IT GAVE US ACCESS TO ALL THE UNDER-GROUND TUNNELS THROUGH-OUT THE SINNOH REGION!
THE REASON WE WERE ALL ABLE TO...
...COME FROM OUR HOME-TOWNS TO GATHER AT MT. CORO-NET WITH-OUT YOUR GRUNTS DETECTING US...
...IS BECAUSE WE TRAV-ELED UNDER-GROUND !!

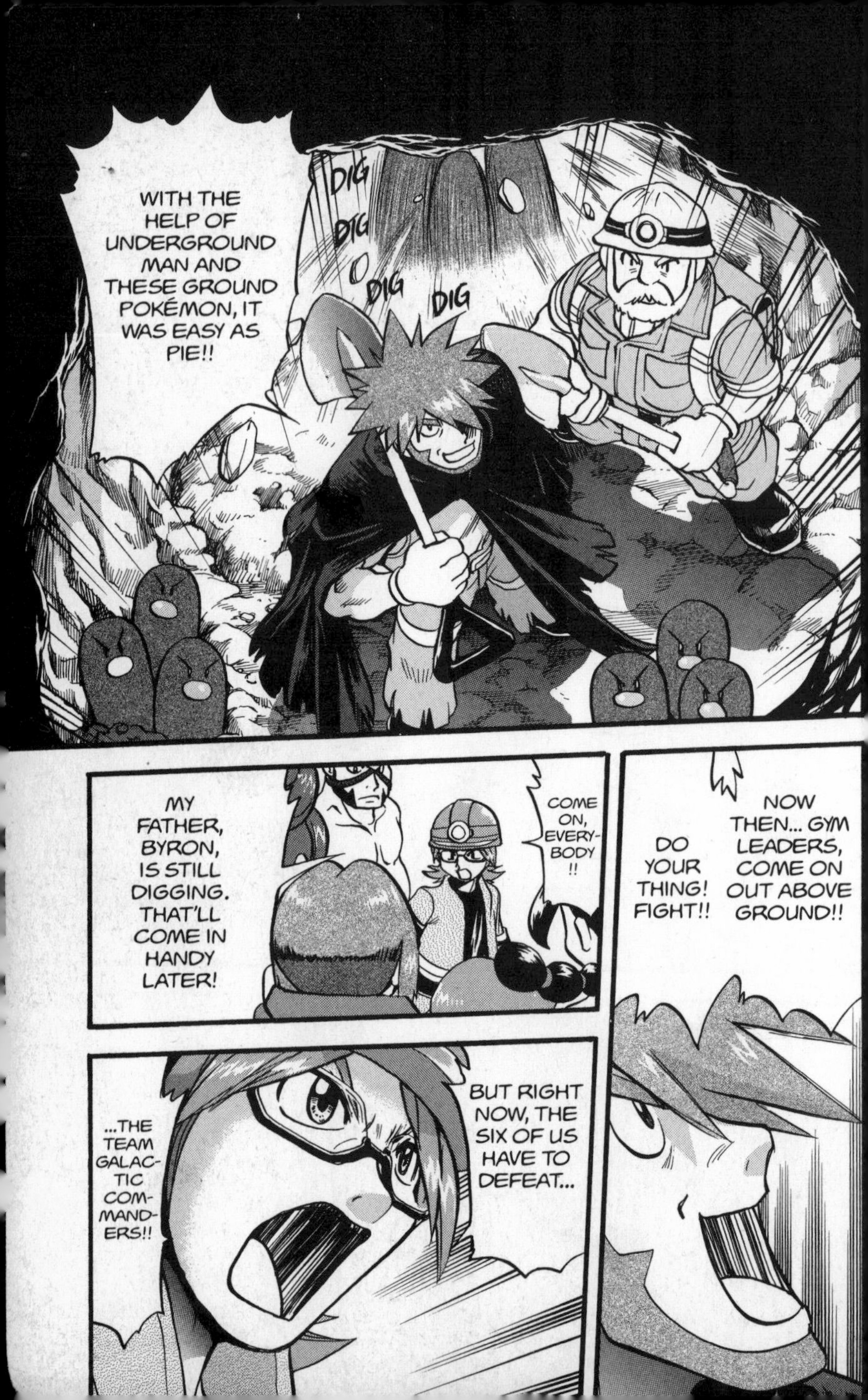
WITH THE HELP OF UNDERGROUND MAN AND THESE GROUND POKÉMON, IT WAS EASY AS PIE!!
DIG DIG DIG DIG
NOW THEN... GYM LEADERS, COME ON OUT ABOVE GROUND!!
DO YOUR THING! FIGHT!!
COME ON, EVERYBODY!!
MY FATHER, BYRON, IS STILL DIGGING. THAT'LL COME IN HANDY LATER!
BUT RIGHT NOW, THE SIX OF US HAVE TO DEFEAT...
...THE TEAM GALACTIC COMMANDERS!!

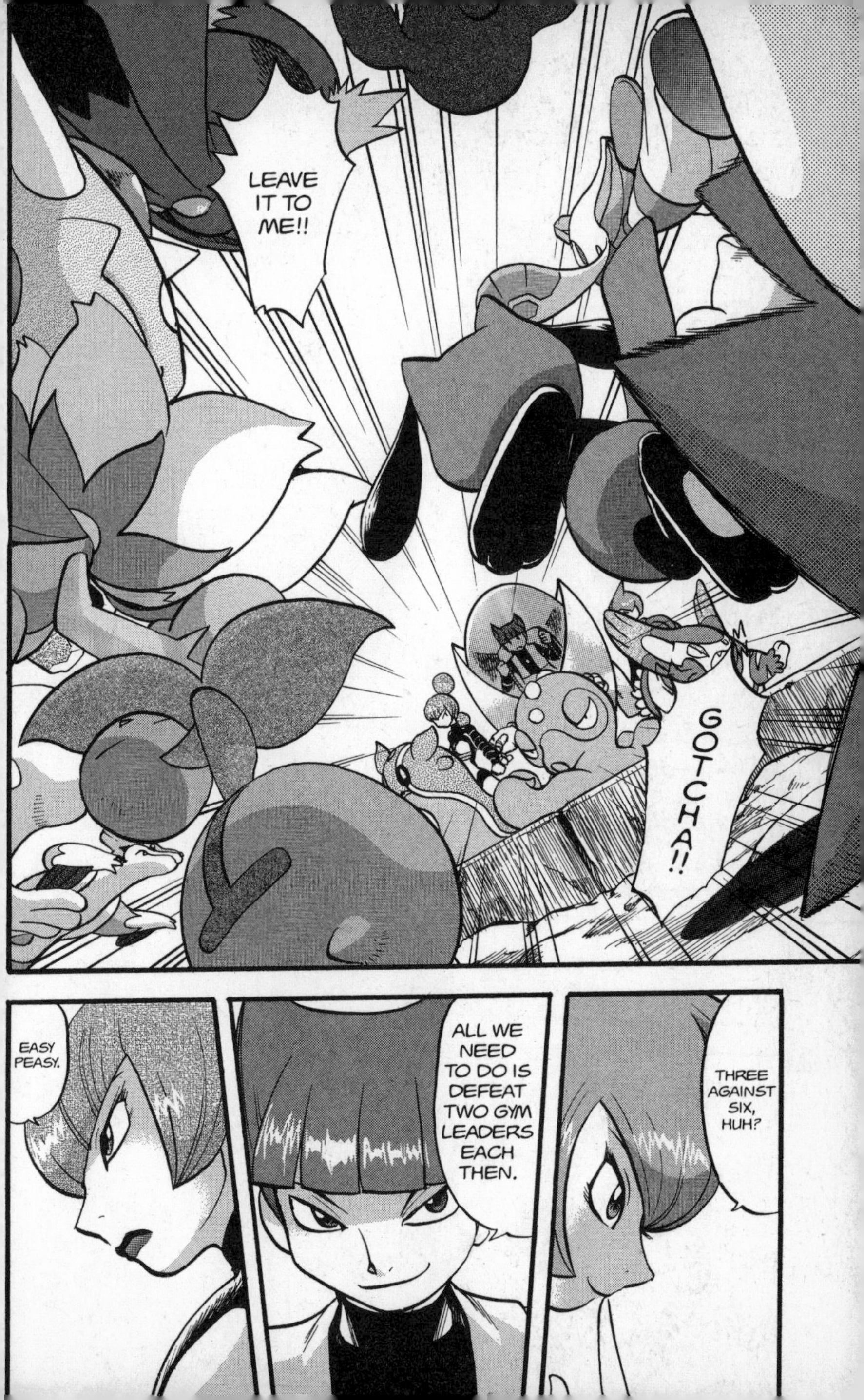
LEAVE IT TO ME!!
GOTCHA!!
THREE AGAINST SIX, HUH?
ALL WE NEED TO DO IS DEFEAT TWO GYM LEADERS EACH THEN.
EASY PEASY.

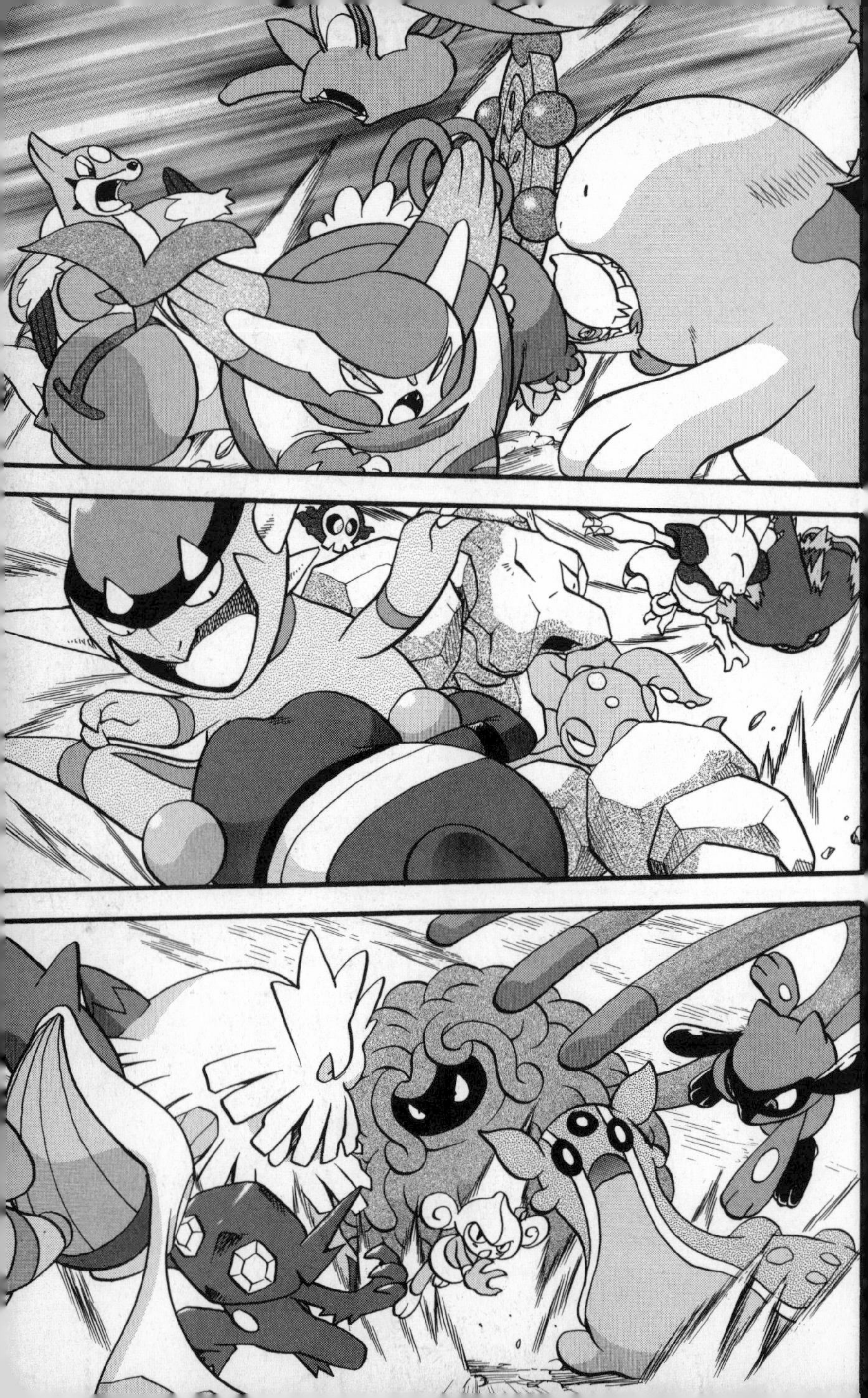

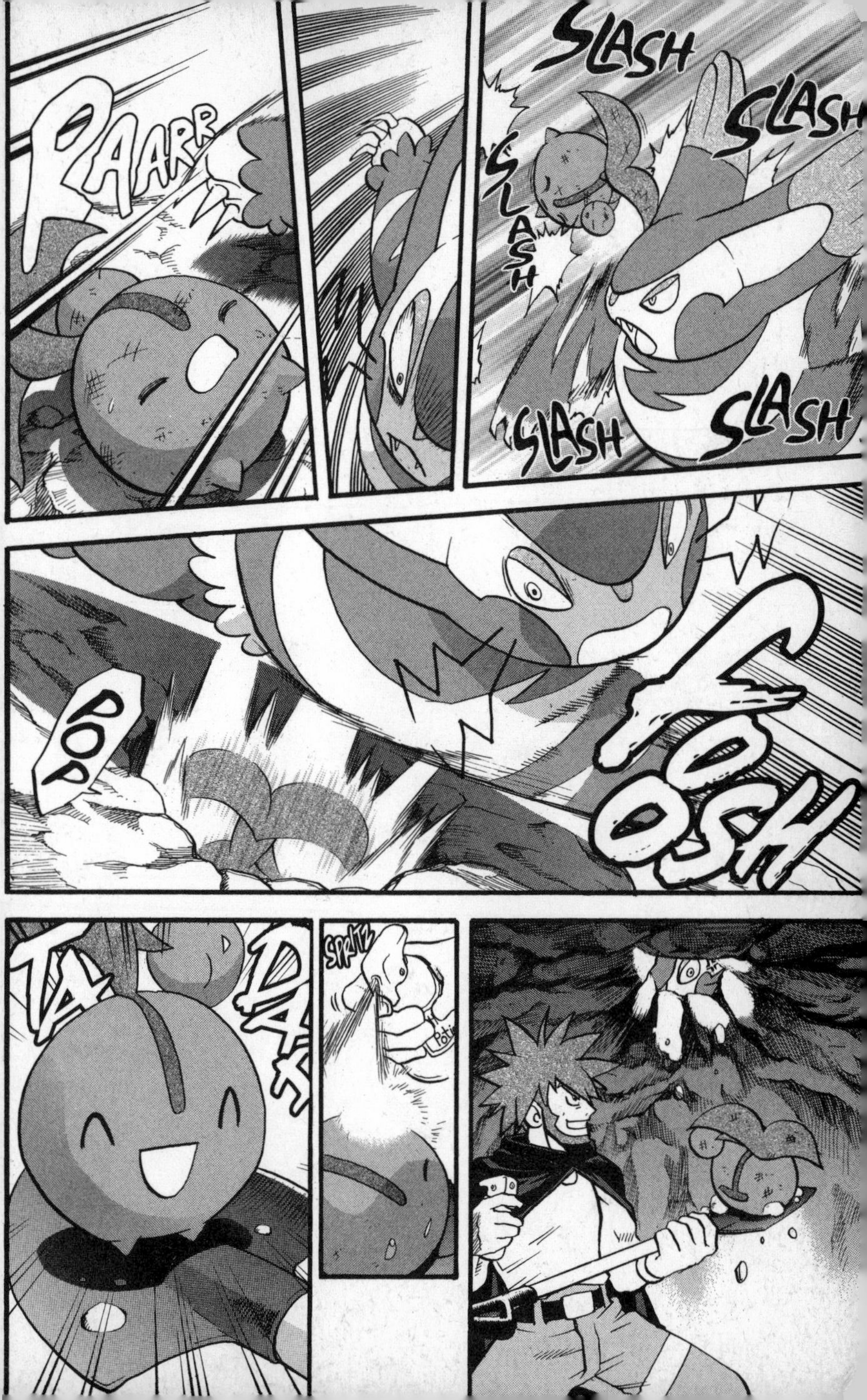
SLASH
SLASH
SLASH
SLASH
SLASH
RAARR
FOOSH
POP
spritz
TA
DA

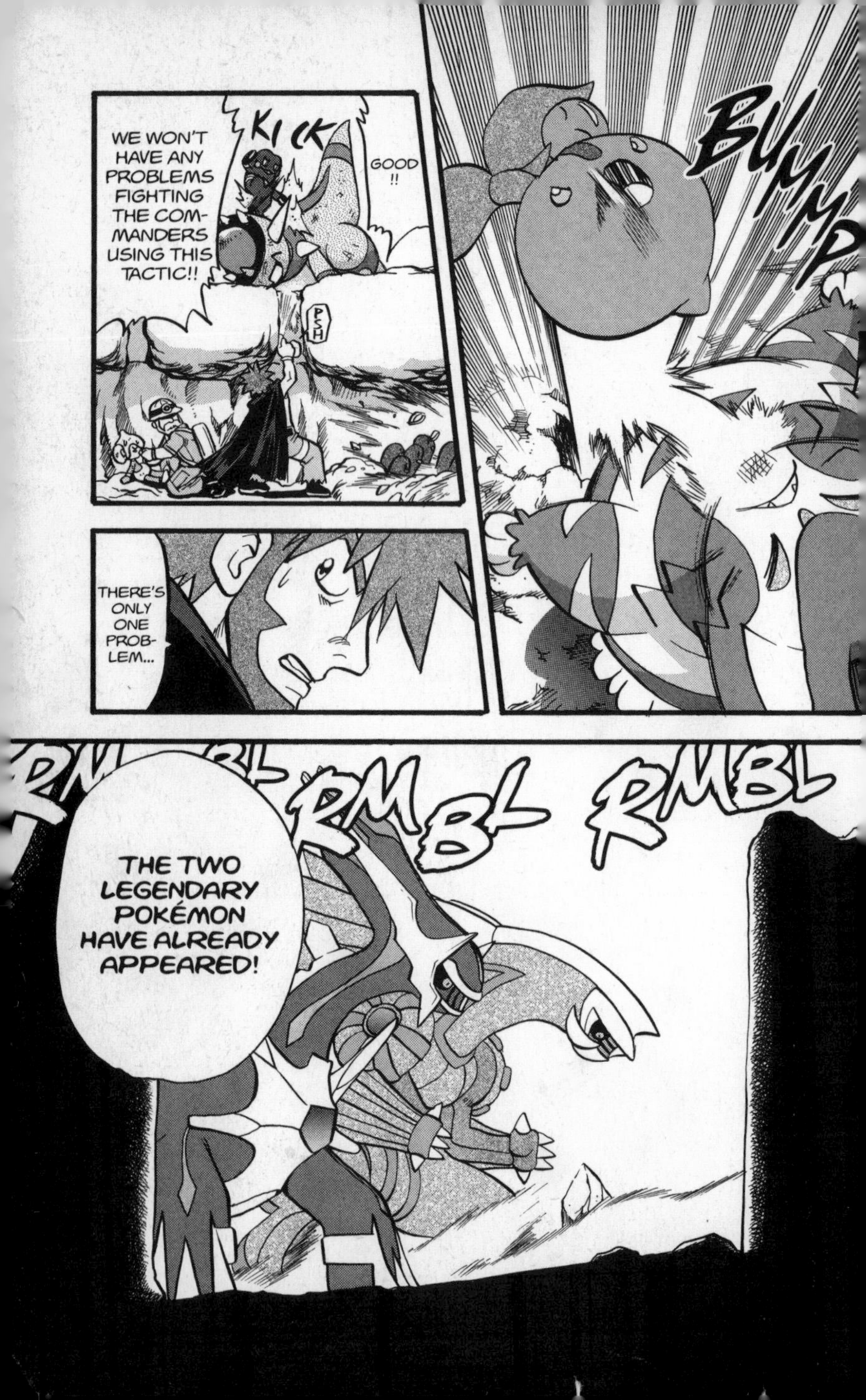
BUMMP
GOOD!!
KICK
WE WON'T HAVE ANY PROBLEMS FIGHTING THE COMMANDERS USING THIS TACTIC!!
PSH
THERE'S ONLY ONE PROBLEM...
RMBL RMBL RMBL
THE TWO LEGENDARY POKÉMON HAVE ALREADY APPEARED!

75

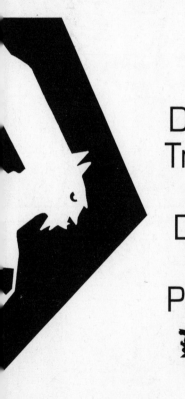

Double
Trouble
with
Dialga
and
Palkia II

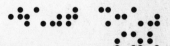

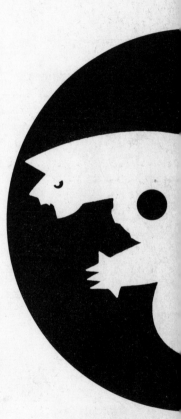

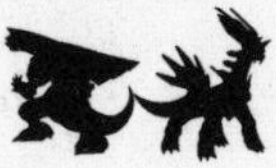

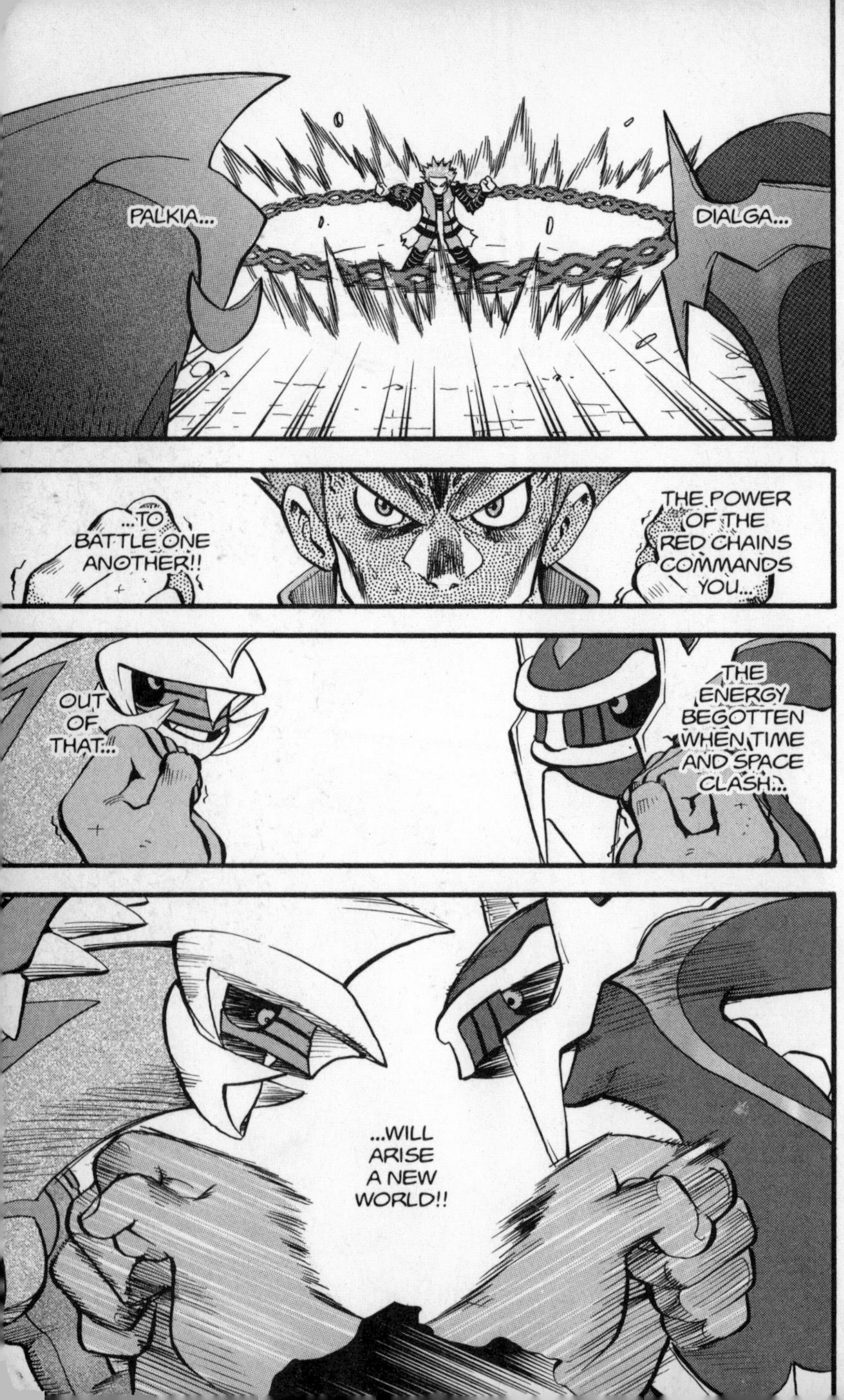
DIALGA...
PALKIA...
THE POWER OF THE RED CHAINS COMMANDS YOU...
...TO BATTLE ONE ANOTHER!!
THE ENERGY BEGOTTEN WHEN TIME AND SPACE CLASH...
OUT OF THAT...
...WILL ARISE A NEW WORLD!!

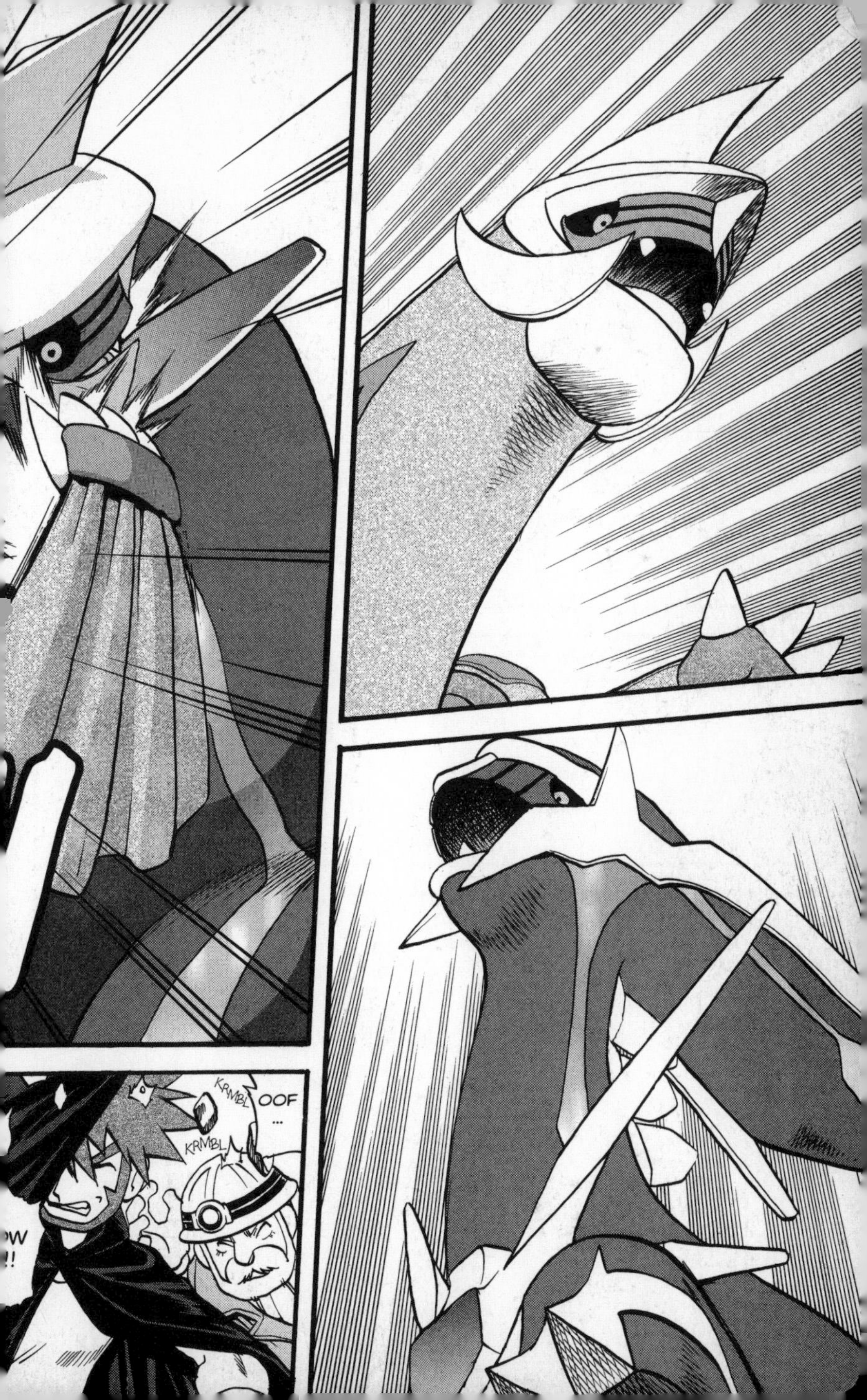
KRMBL
OOF
...
KRMBL

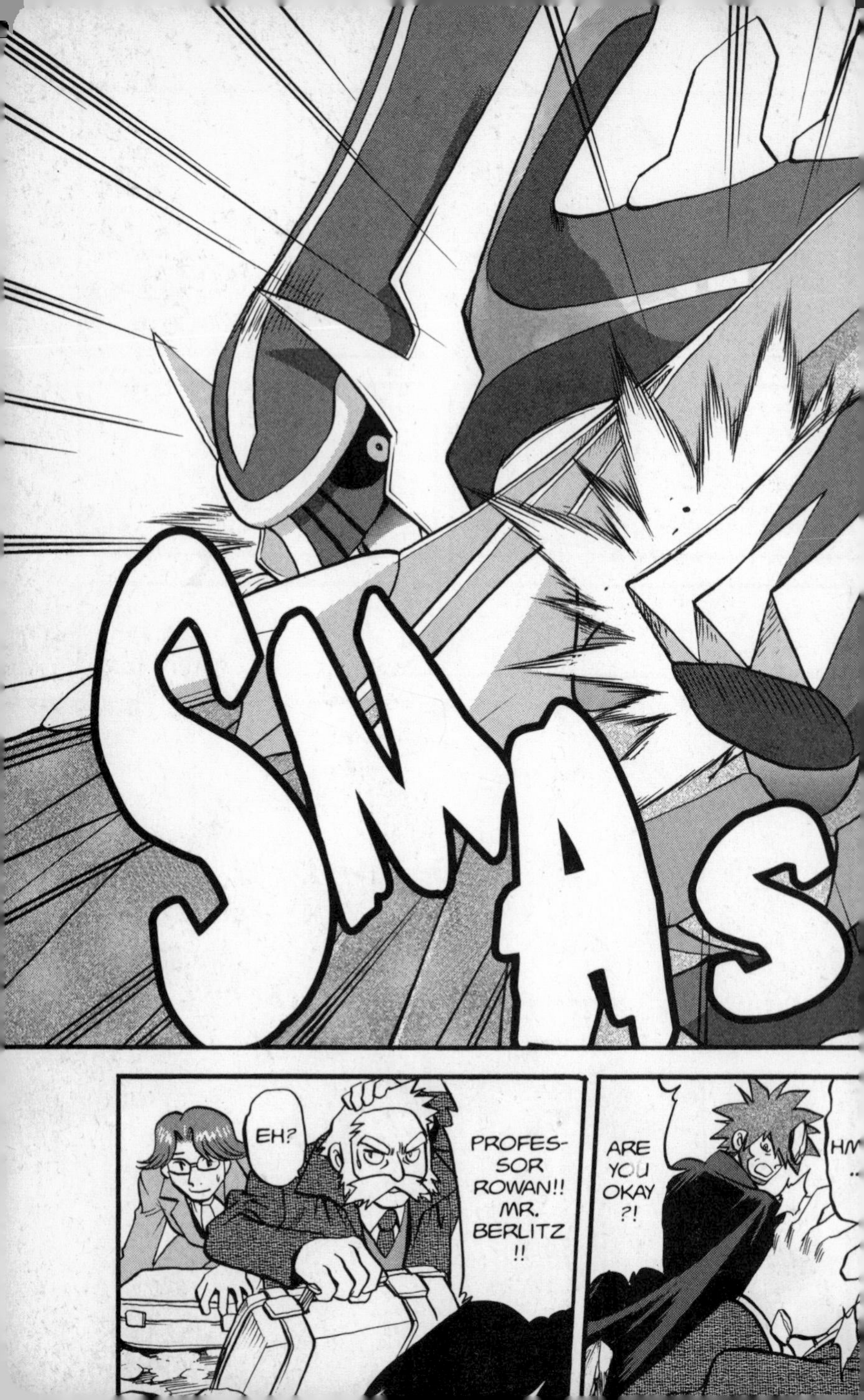
SMAS
HM
..
ARE YOU OKAY?!
PROFESSOR ROWAN!! MR. BERLITZ!!
EH?

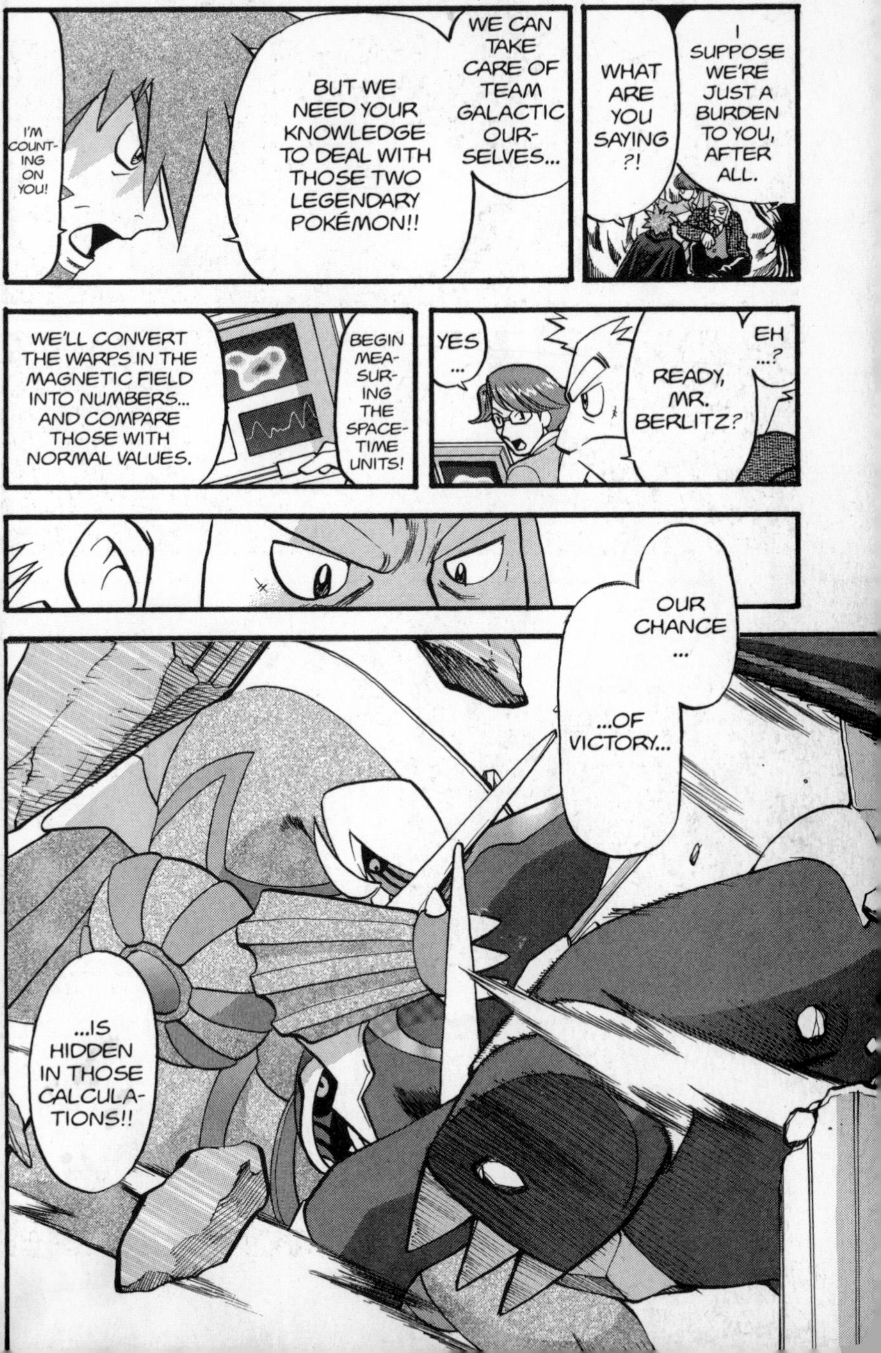
I SUPPOSE WE'RE JUST A BURDEN TO YOU, AFTER ALL.
WHAT ARE YOU SAYING?!
WE CAN TAKE CARE OF TEAM GALACTIC OURSELVES...
BUT WE NEED YOUR KNOWLEDGE TO DEAL WITH THOSE TWO LEGENDARY POKÉMON!!
I'M COUNTING ON YOU!
EH ...?
READY, MR. BERLITZ?
YES ...
BEGIN MEASURING THE SPACE-TIME UNITS!
WE'LL CONVERT THE WARPS IN THE MAGNETIC FIELD INTO NUMBERS... AND COMPARE THOSE WITH NORMAL VALUES.
OUR CHANCE ...
...OF VICTORY...
...IS HIDDEN IN THOSE CALCULATIONS!!

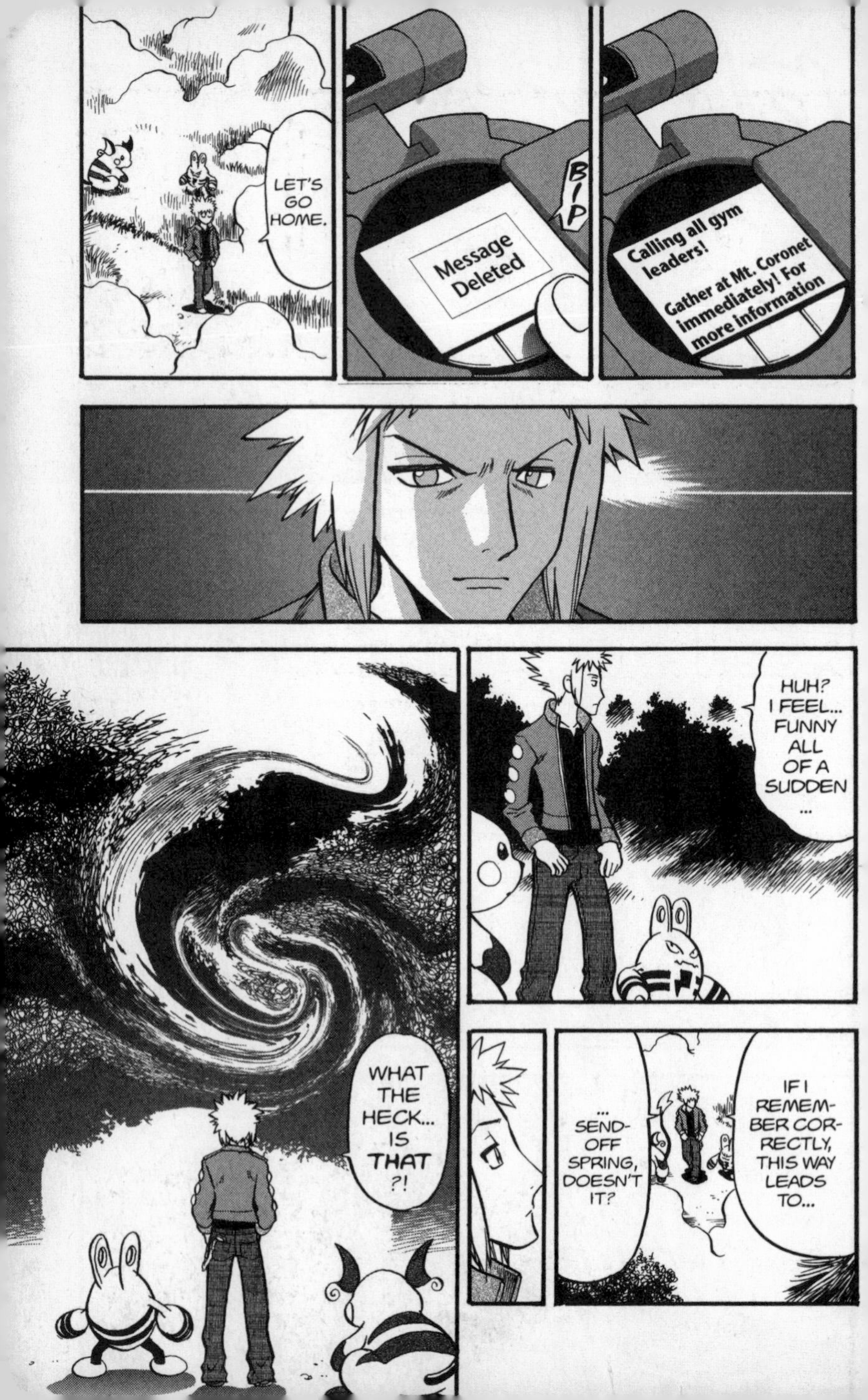
Calling all gym leaders! Gather at Mt. Coronet immediately! For more information
BIP
Message Deleted
LET'S GO HOME.
HUH? I FEEL... FUNNY ALL OF A SUDDEN ...
IF I REMEMBER CORRECTLY, THIS WAY LEADS TO...
... SEND-OFF SPRING, DOESN'T IT?
WHAT THE HECK... IS THAT?!

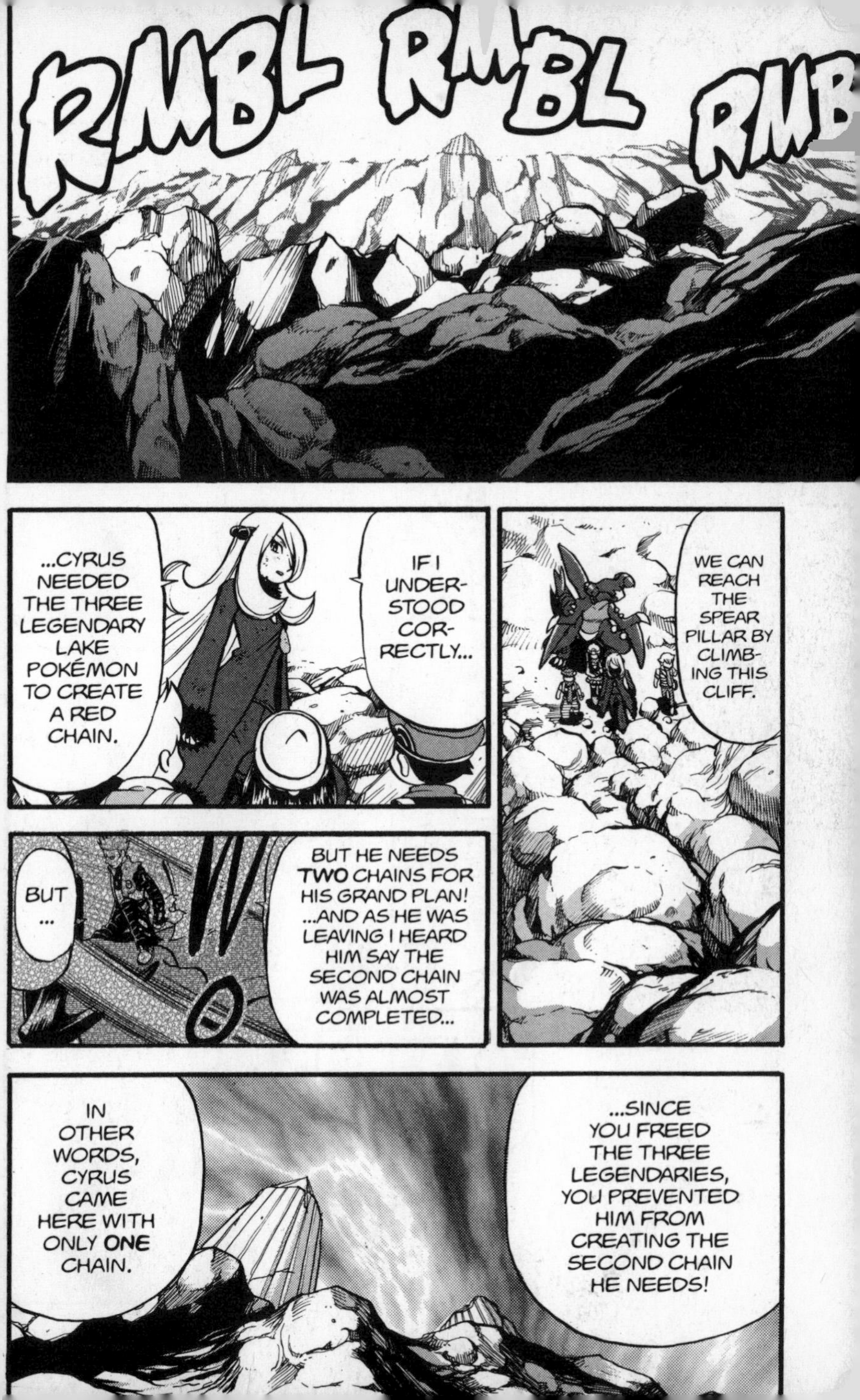
RMBL RMBL RMB
WE CAN REACH THE SPEAR PILLAR BY CLIMBING THIS CLIFF.
IF I UNDERSTOOD CORRECTLY...
...CYRUS NEEDED THE THREE LEGENDARY LAKE POKÉMON TO CREATE A RED CHAIN.
BUT HE NEEDS **TWO** CHAINS FOR HIS GRAND PLAN! ...AND AS HE WAS LEAVING I HEARD HIM SAY THE SECOND CHAIN WAS ALMOST COMPLETED...
BUT ...
...SINCE YOU FREED THE THREE LEGENDARIES, YOU PREVENTED HIM FROM CREATING THE SECOND CHAIN HE NEEDS!
IN OTHER WORDS, CYRUS CAME HERE WITH ONLY **ONE** CHAIN.

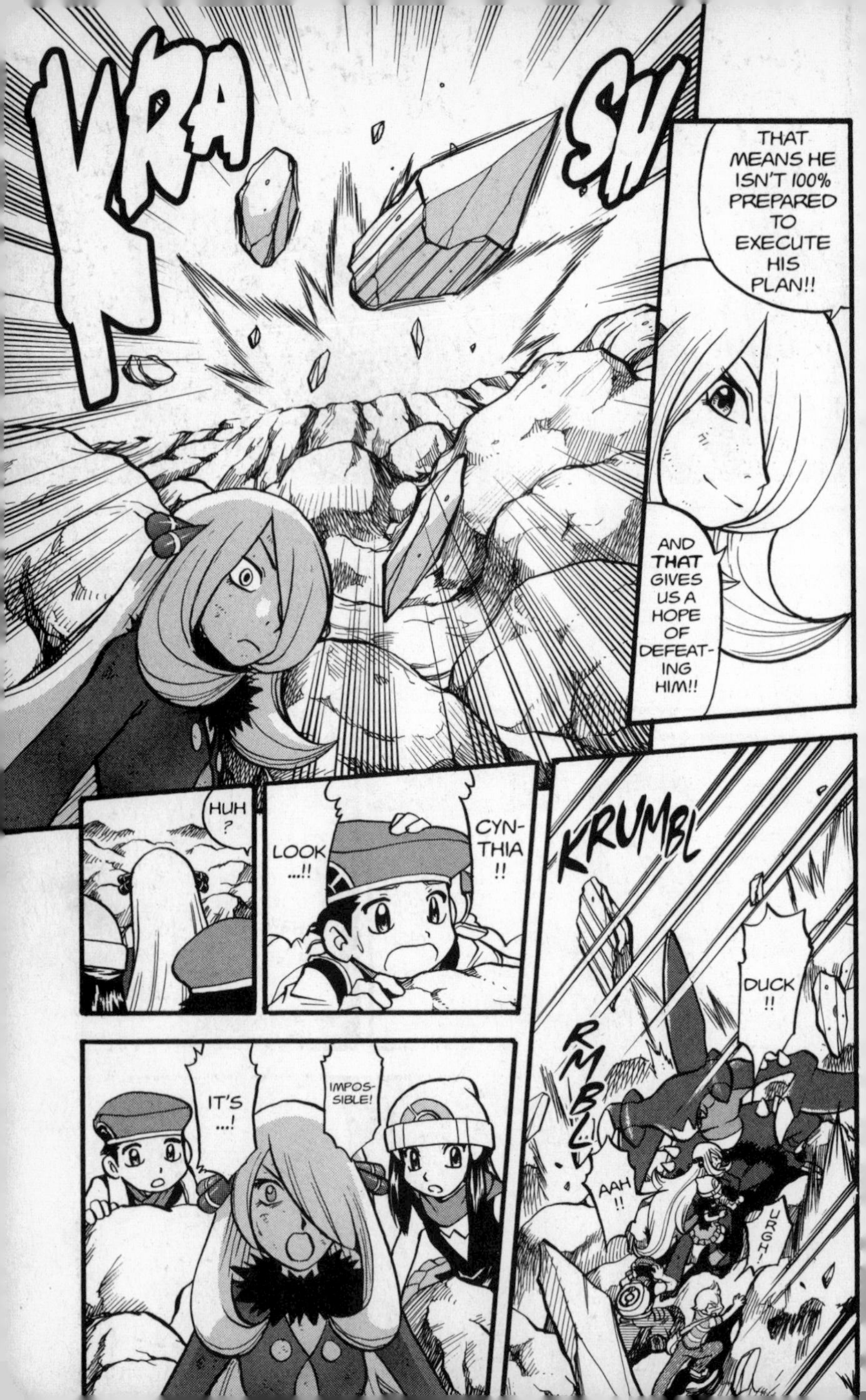
THAT MEANS HE ISN'T 100% PREPARED TO EXECUTE HIS PLAN!!
AND THAT GIVES US A HOPE OF DEFEATING HIM!!
KRA
SH
KRUMBL
DUCK!!
RMBL
AAH!!
URGH!
CYN-THIA!!
LOOK...!!
HUH?
IMPOS-SIBLE!
IT'S...!

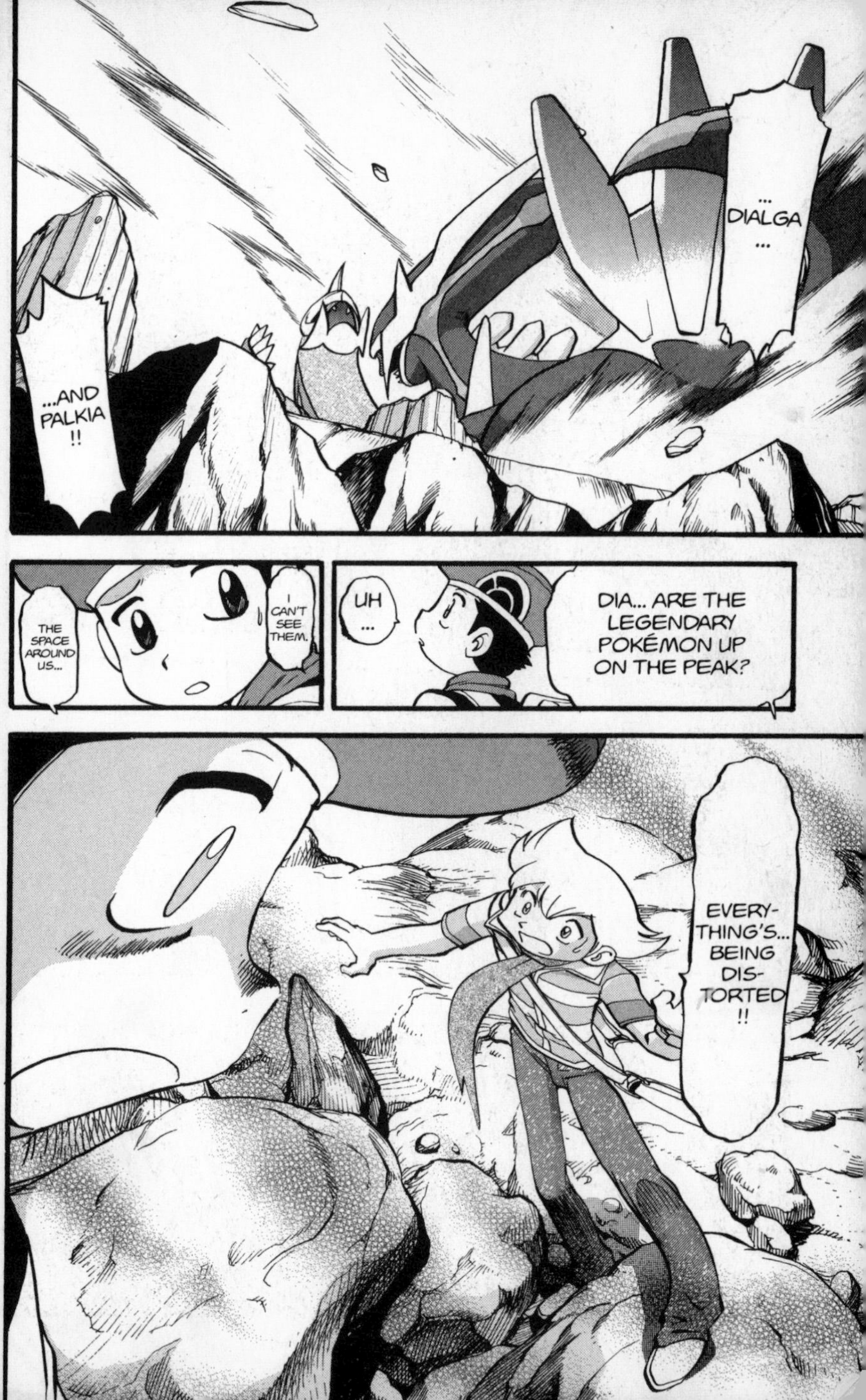
... DIALGA ...
...AND PALKIA !!
DIA... ARE THE LEGENDARY POKÉMON UP ON THE PEAK?
UH ...
I CAN'T SEE THEM.
THE SPACE AROUND US...
EVERY-THING'S... BEING DIS-TORTED !!

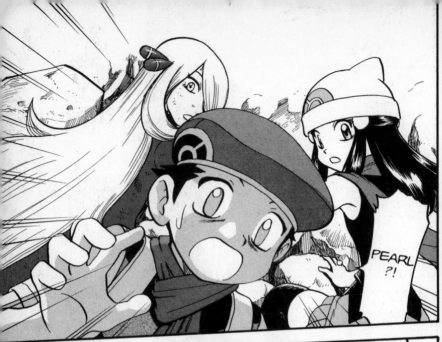

PEARL ?!

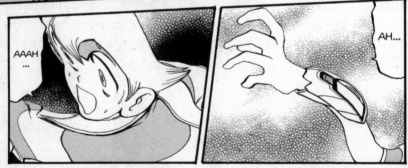

AAAH ...

AH...

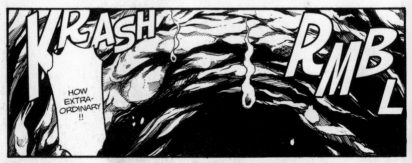

HOW EXTRA- ORDINARY !!

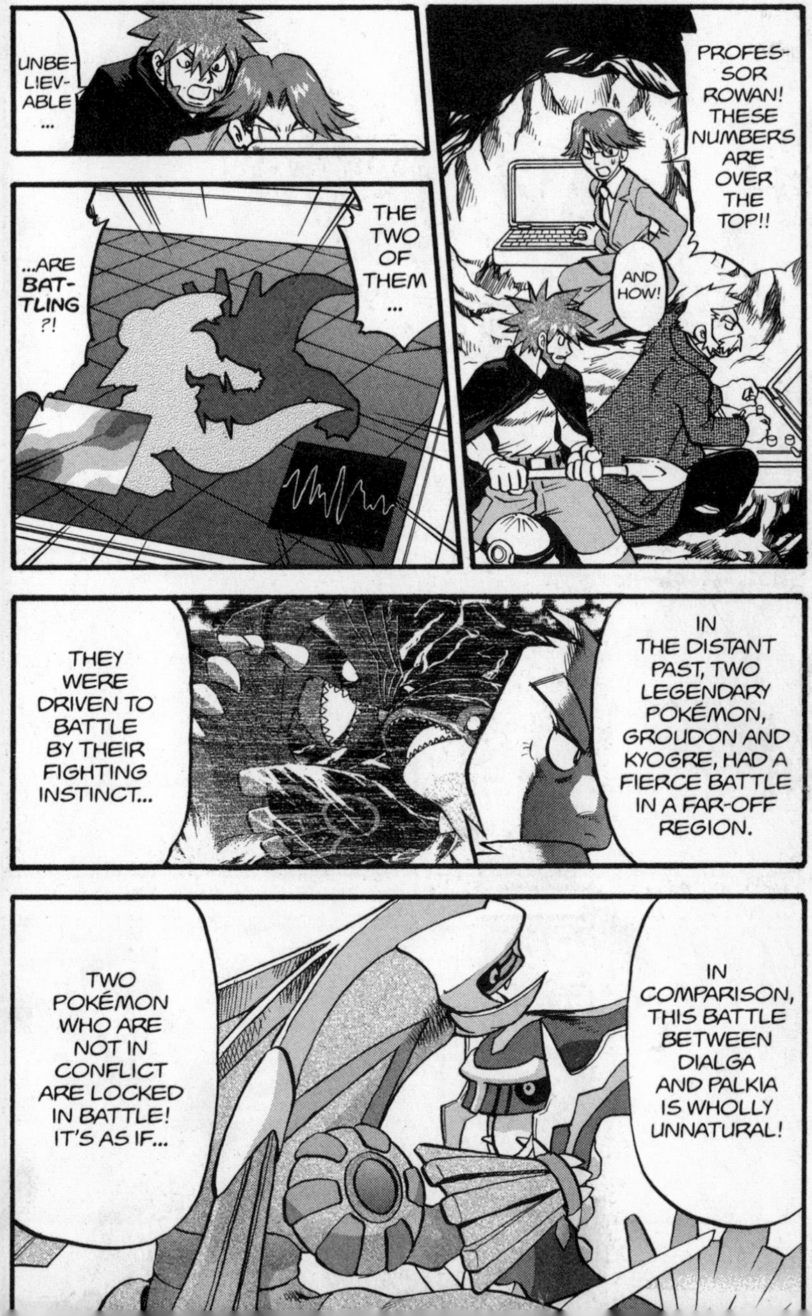
PROFESSOR ROWAN! THESE NUMBERS ARE OVER THE TOP!!
AND HOW!
UNBELIEVABLE...
THE TWO OF THEM...
...ARE BATTLING?!
IN THE DISTANT PAST, TWO LEGENDARY POKÉMON, GROUDON AND KYOGRE, HAD A FIERCE BATTLE IN A FAR-OFF REGION.
THEY WERE DRIVEN TO BATTLE BY THEIR FIGHTING INSTINCT...
IN COMPARISON, THIS BATTLE BETWEEN DIALGA AND PALKIA IS WHOLLY UNNATURAL!
TWO POKÉMON WHO ARE NOT IN CONFLICT ARE LOCKED IN BATTLE! IT'S AS IF...

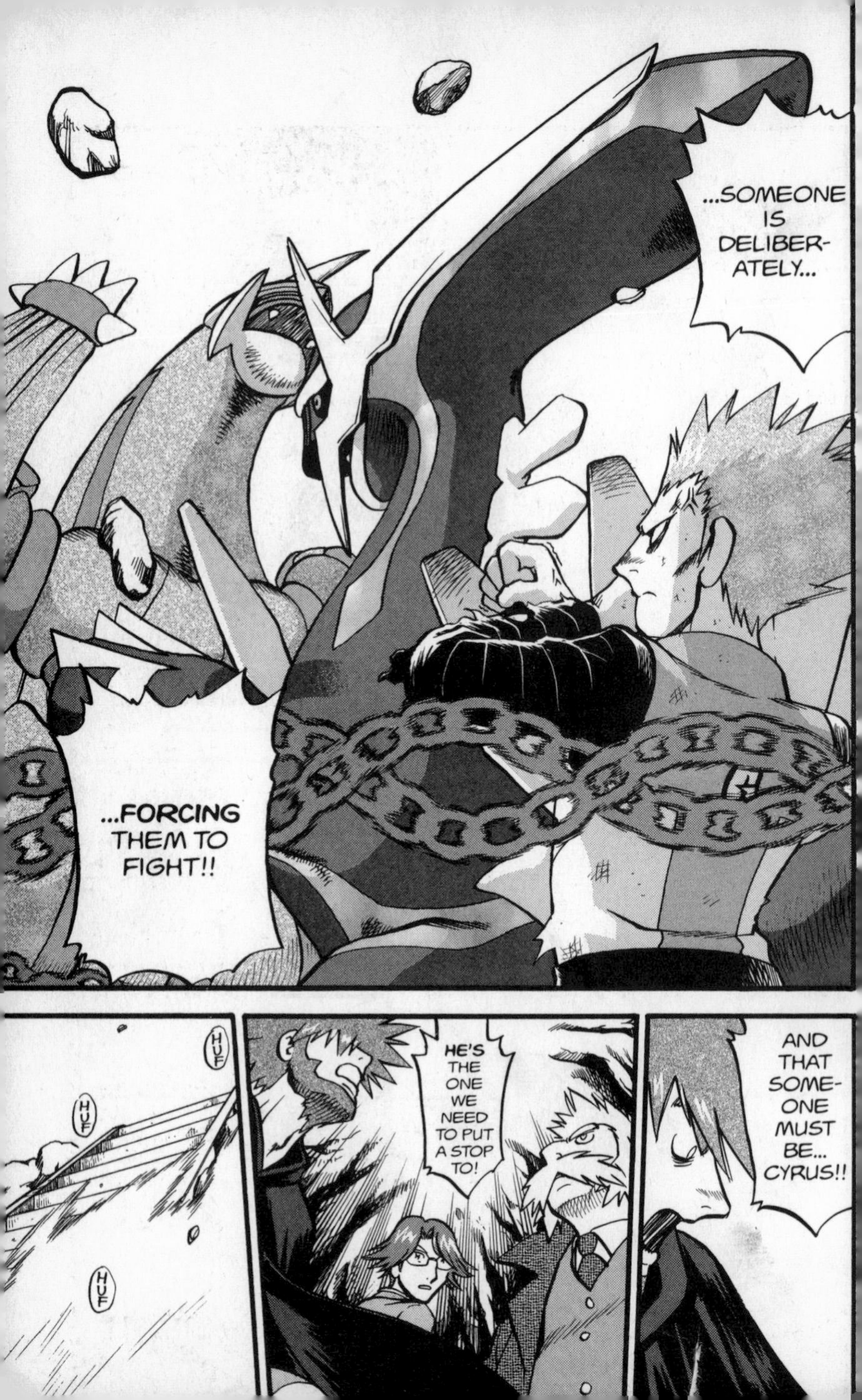
...SOMEONE IS DELIBER-ATELY...
...FORCING THEM TO FIGHT!!
AND THAT SOMEONE MUST BE... CYRUS!!
HE'S THE ONE WE NEED TO PUT A STOP TO!
HUF
HUF
HUF

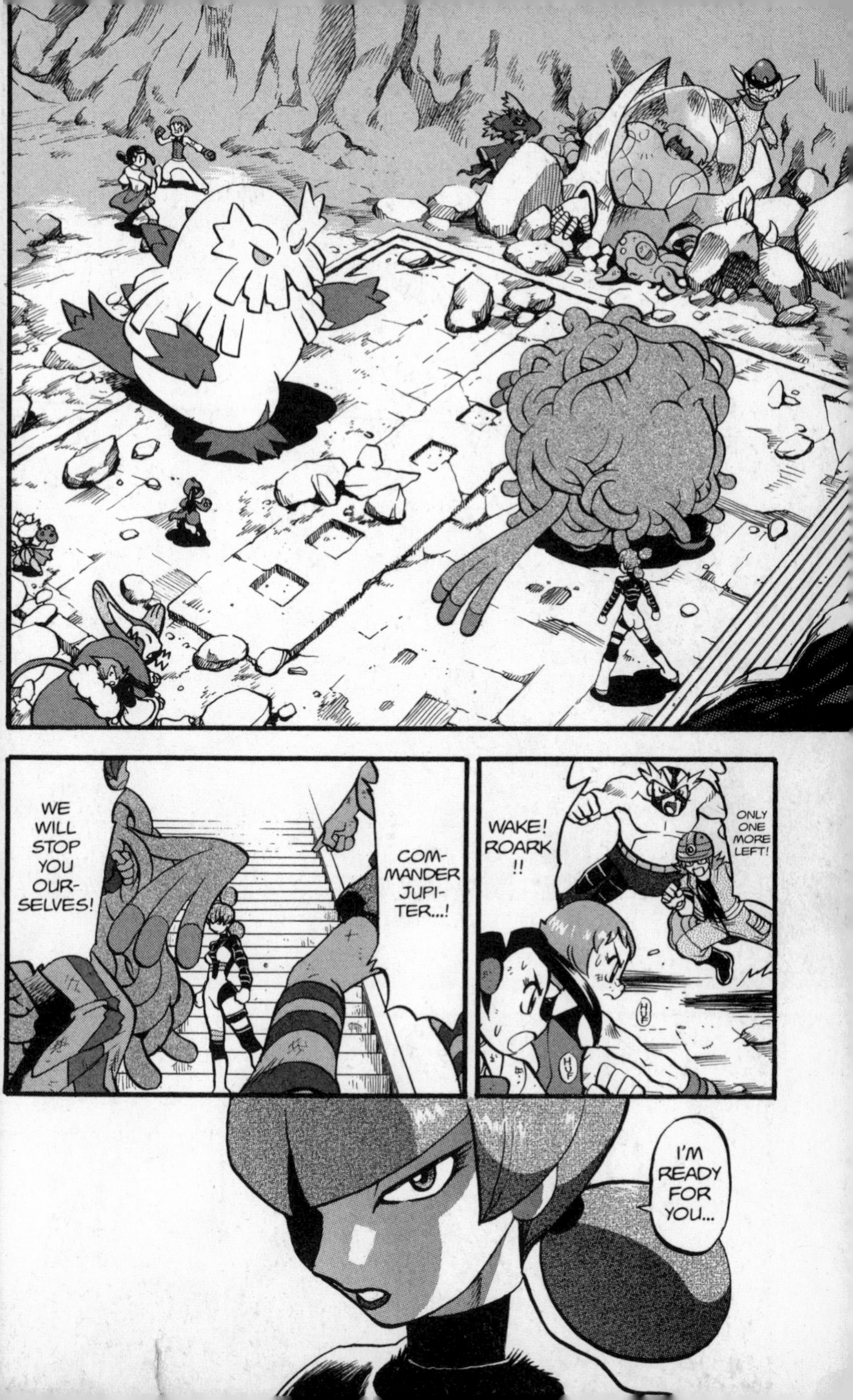
ONLY ONE MORE LEFT!
WAKE! ROARK !!
HUF
HUF
COM-MANDER JUPI-TER...!
WE WILL STOP YOU OUR-SELVES!
I'M READY FOR YOU...

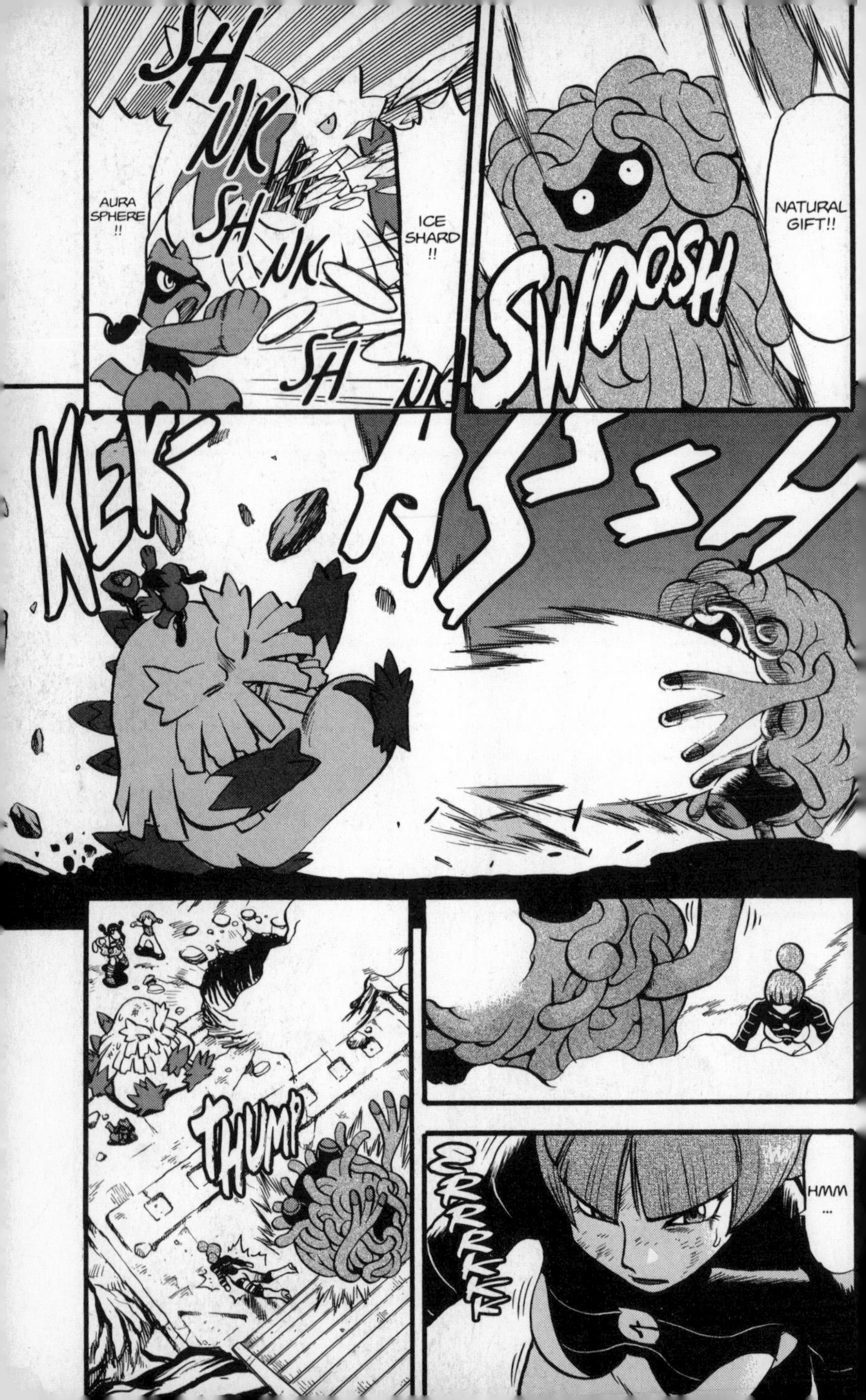
NATURAL GIFT!!
SWOOSH
ICE SHARD !!
AURA SPHERE !!
SHUNK
SHUNK
SHUNK
KEKASSH
HMM ...
CRRRRKKKT
THUMP

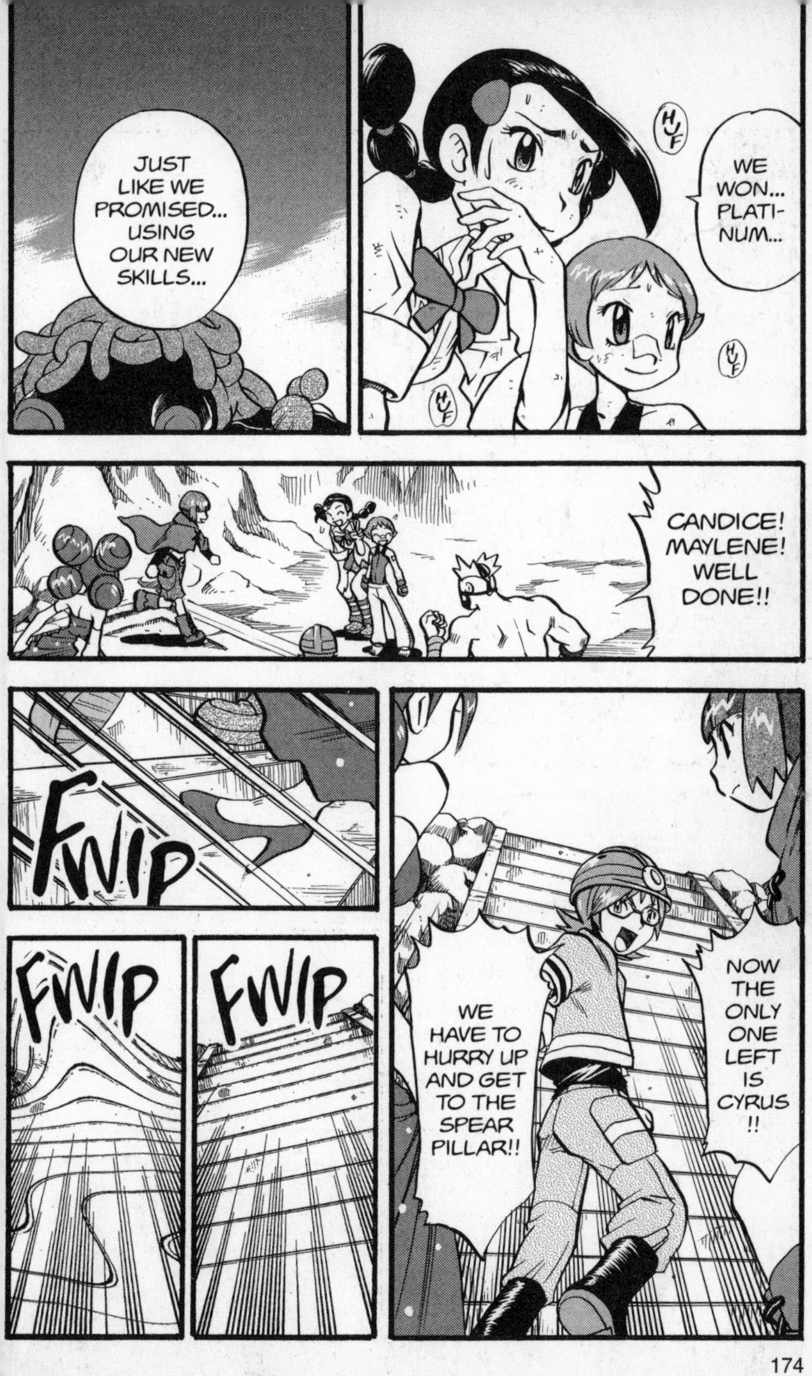
HUF
WE WON... PLATI-NUM...
HUF
HUF
JUST LIKE WE PROMISED... USING OUR NEW SKILLS...
CANDICE! MAYLENE! WELL DONE!!
NOW THE ONLY ONE LEFT IS CYRUS!!
WE HAVE TO HURRY UP AND GET TO THE SPEAR PILLAR!!
FWIP
FWIP
FWIP

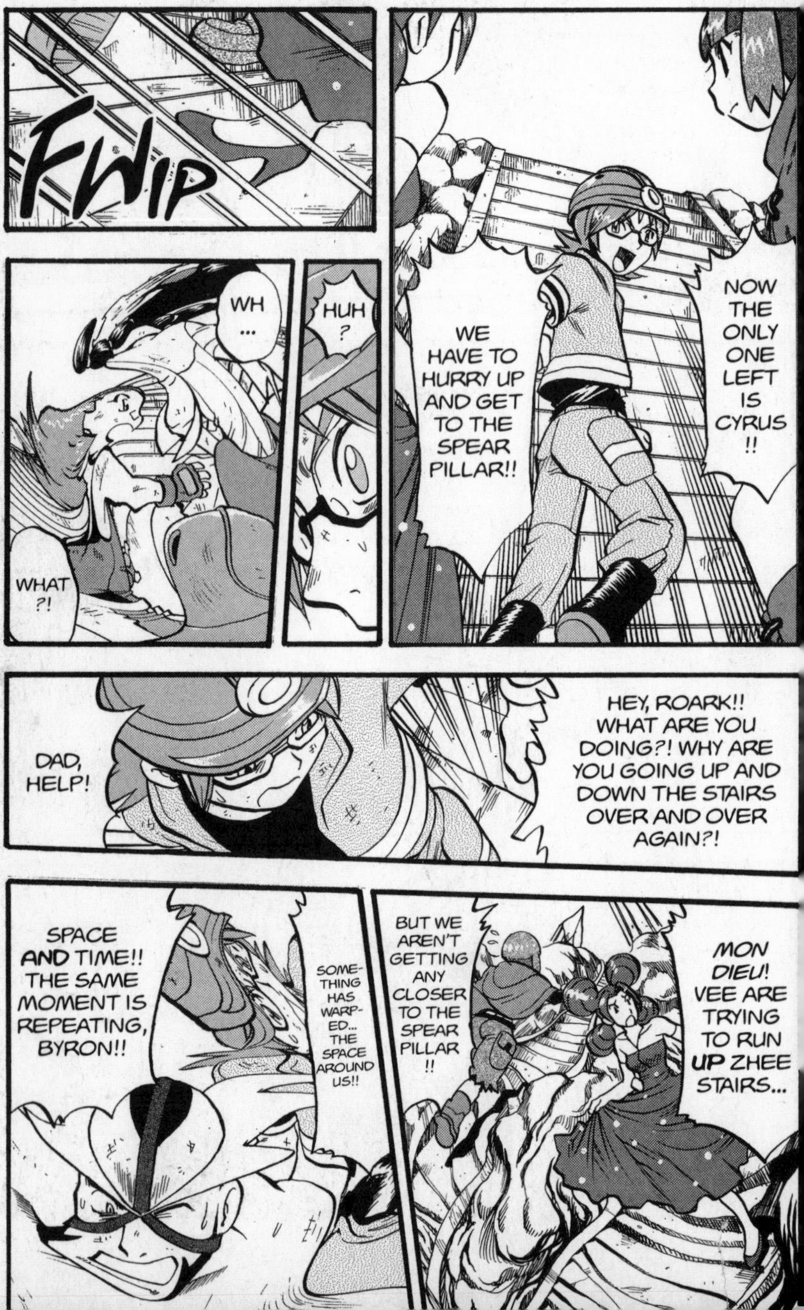
NOW THE ONLY ONE LEFT IS CYRUS!!
WE HAVE TO HURRY UP AND GET TO THE SPEAR PILLAR!!
FWIP
HUH?
WH...
WHAT?!
HEY, ROARK!! WHAT ARE YOU DOING?! WHY ARE YOU GOING UP AND DOWN THE STAIRS OVER AND OVER AGAIN?!
DAD, HELP!
MON DIEU! VEE ARE TRYING TO RUN UP ZHEE STAIRS...
BUT WE AREN'T GETTING ANY CLOSER TO THE SPEAR PILLAR!!
SOMETHING HAS WARPED... THE SPACE AROUND US!!
SPACE AND TIME!! THE SAME MOMENT IS REPEATING, BYRON!!

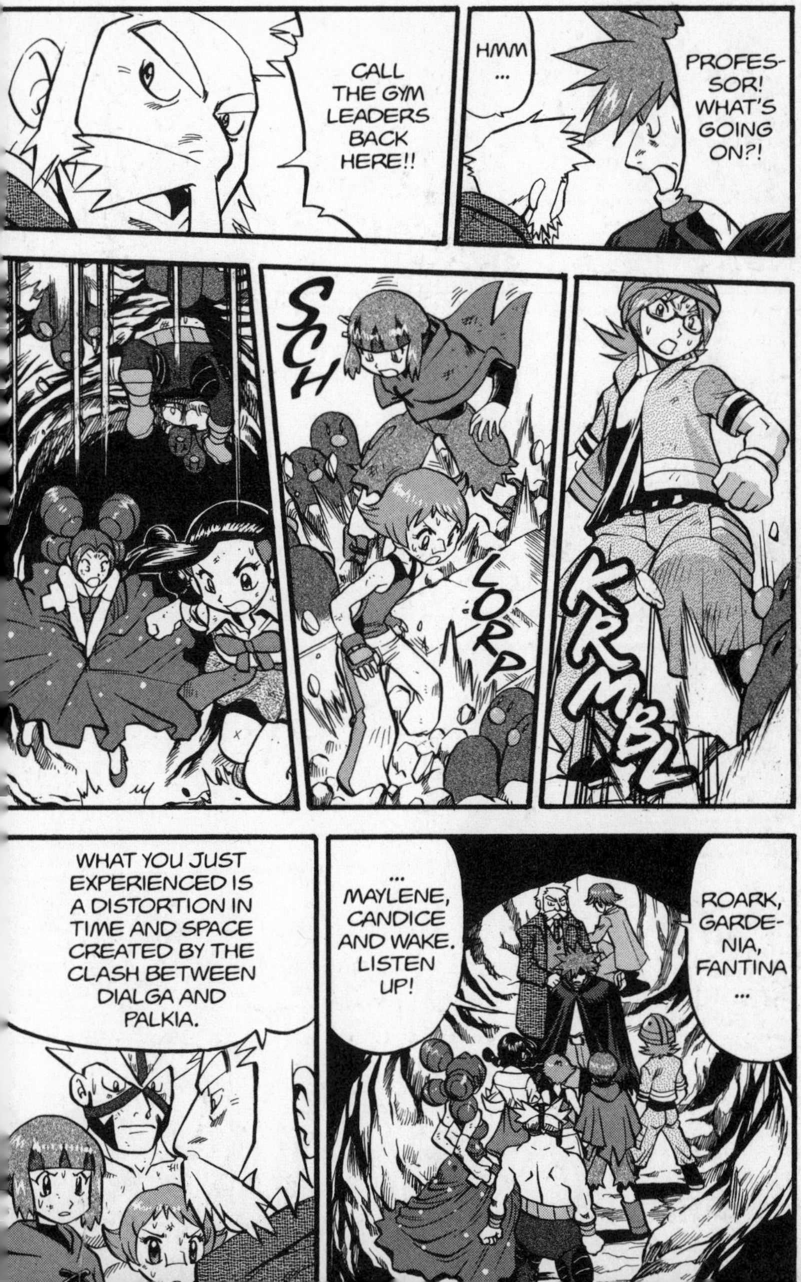
PROFES-
SOR! WHAT'S GOING ON?!
HMM ...
CALL THE GYM LEADERS BACK HERE!!
KRMBL
LORP
SCH
RORAK, GARDE-
NIA, FANTINA ...
... MAYLENE, CANDICE AND WAKE. LISTEN UP!
WHAT YOU JUST EXPERIENCED IS A DISTORTION IN TIME AND SPACE CREATED BY THE CLASH BETWEEN DIALGA AND PALKIA.

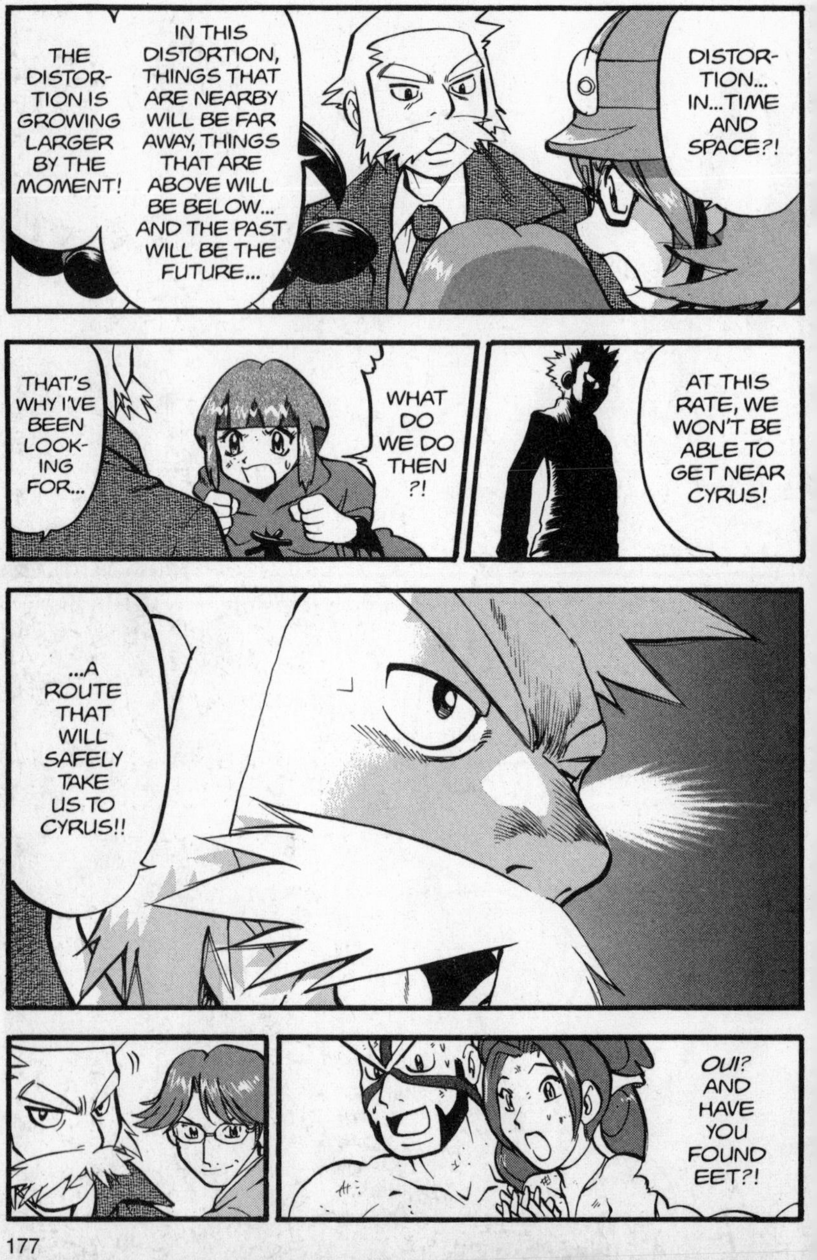
DISTORTION... IN...TIME AND SPACE?!
IN THIS DISTORTION, THINGS THAT ARE NEARBY WILL BE FAR AWAY, THINGS THAT ARE ABOVE WILL BE BELOW... AND THE PAST WILL BE THE FUTURE...
THE DISTORTION IS GROWING LARGER BY THE MOMENT!
AT THIS RATE, WE WON'T BE ABLE TO GET NEAR CYRUS!
WHAT DO WE DO THEN?!
THAT'S WHY I'VE BEEN LOOKING FOR...
...A ROUTE THAT WILL SAFELY TAKE US TO CYRUS!!
OUI? AND HAVE YOU FOUND EET?!

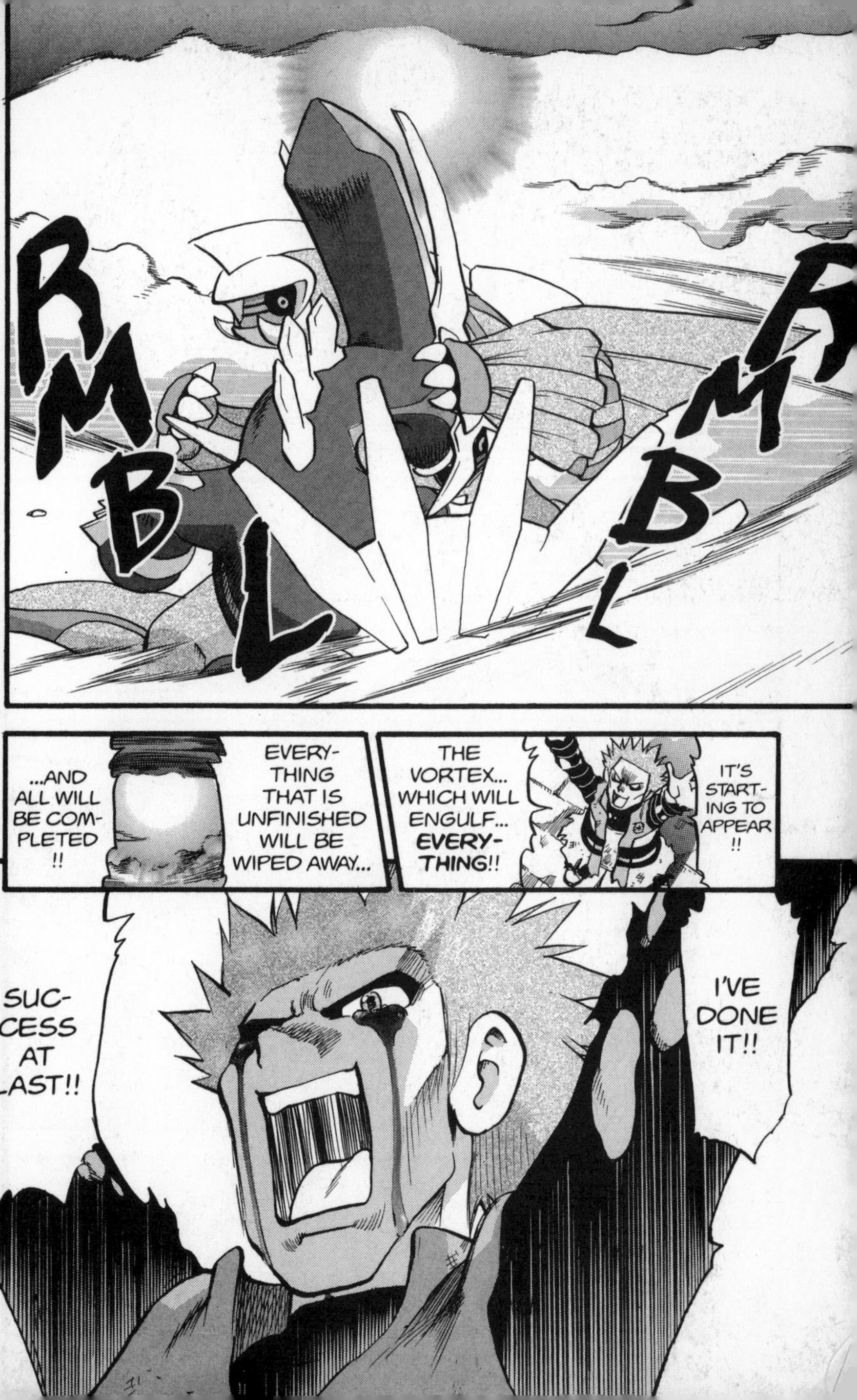
RMBL
RMBL
IT'S STARTING TO APPEAR!!
THE VORTEX... WHICH WILL ENGULF... EVERYTHING!!
EVERYTHING THAT IS UNFINISHED WILL BE WIPED AWAY...
...AND ALL WILL BE COMPLETED!!
I'VE DONE IT!!
SUCCESS AT LAST!!

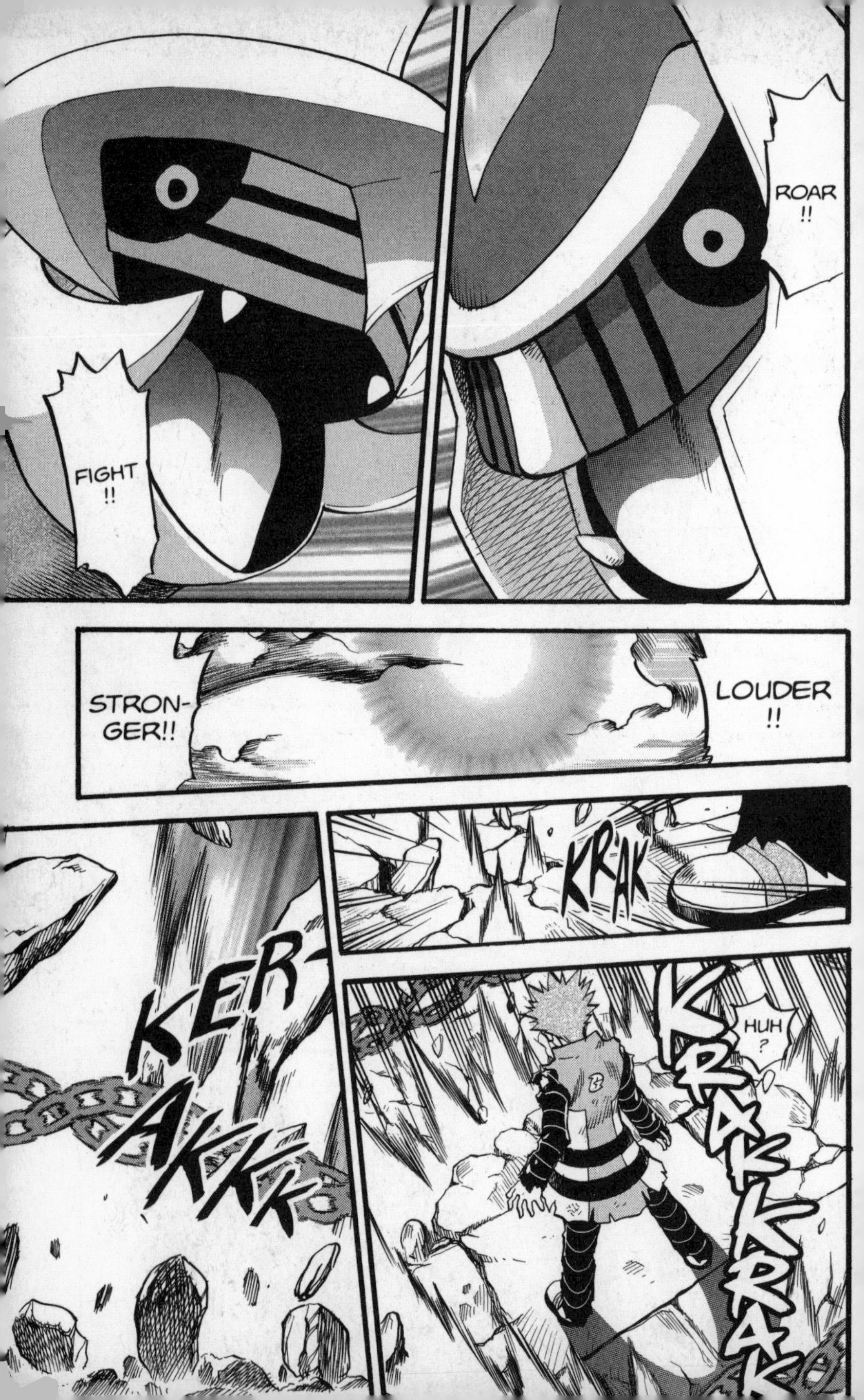
ROAR!!
FIGHT!!
LOUDER!!
STRONGER!!
KRAK
HUH?
KRAKKRAK
KER-AKKKK

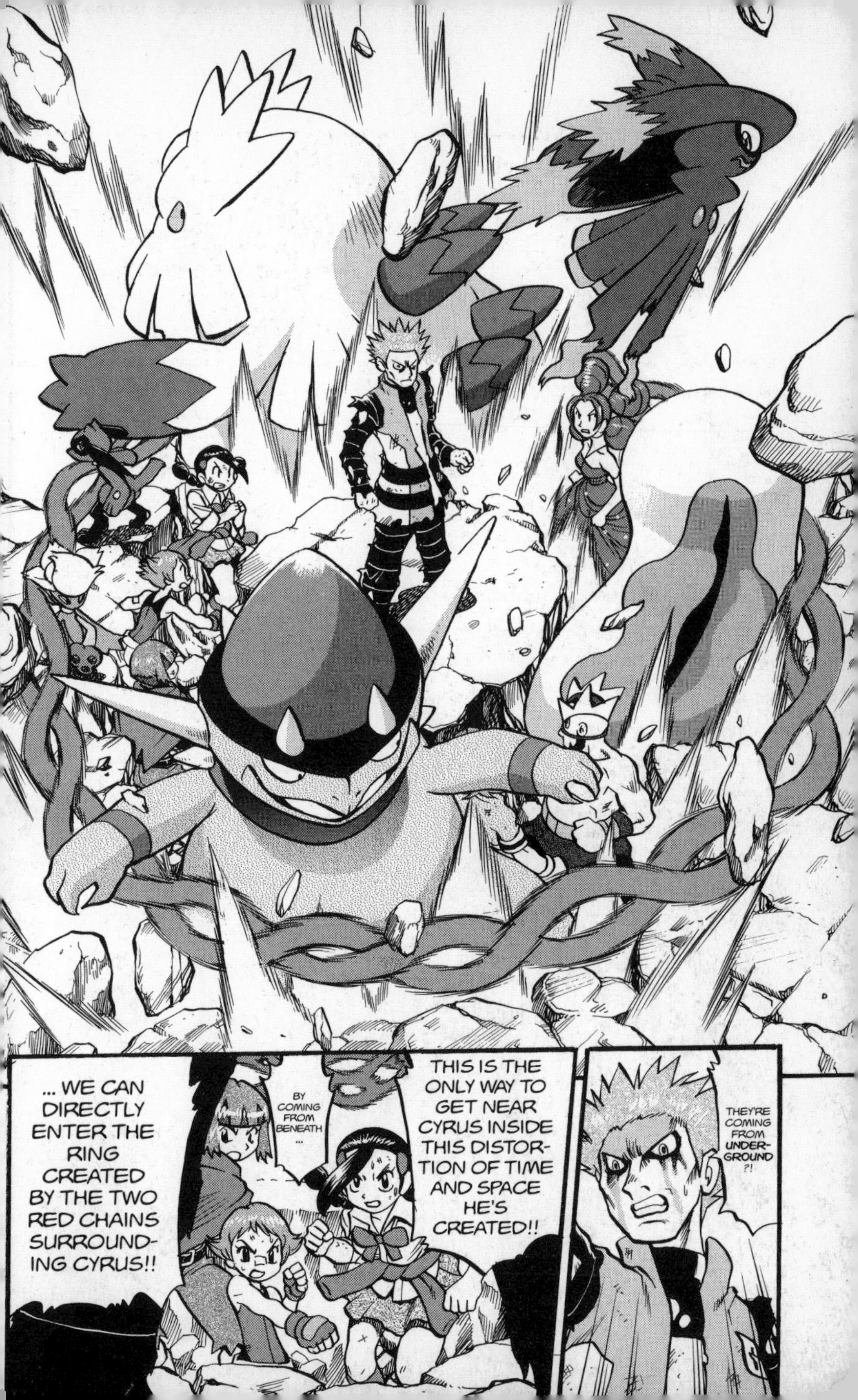
THEY'RE COMING FROM UNDER-GROUND?!
THIS IS THE ONLY WAY TO GET NEAR CYRUS INSIDE THIS DISTORTION OF TIME AND SPACE HE'S CREATED!!
BY COMING FROM BENEATH...
... WE CAN DIRECTLY ENTER THE RING CREATED BY THE TWO RED CHAINS SURROUND-ING CYRUS!!

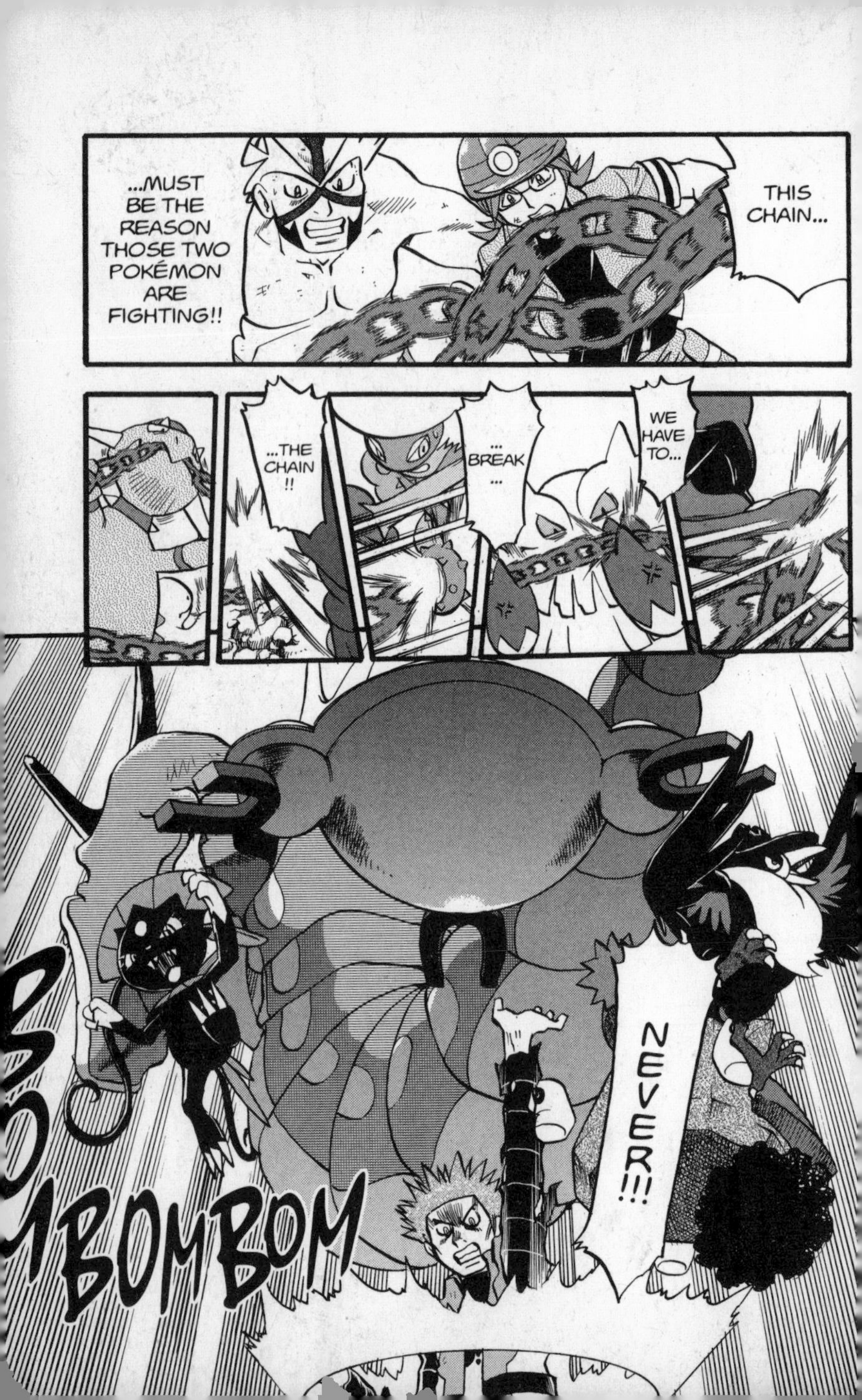
THIS CHAIN...
...MUST BE THE REASON THOSE TWO POKÉMON ARE FIGHTING!!
WE HAVE TO...
... BREAK ...
...THE CHAIN !!
NEVER!!!
BOMBOM

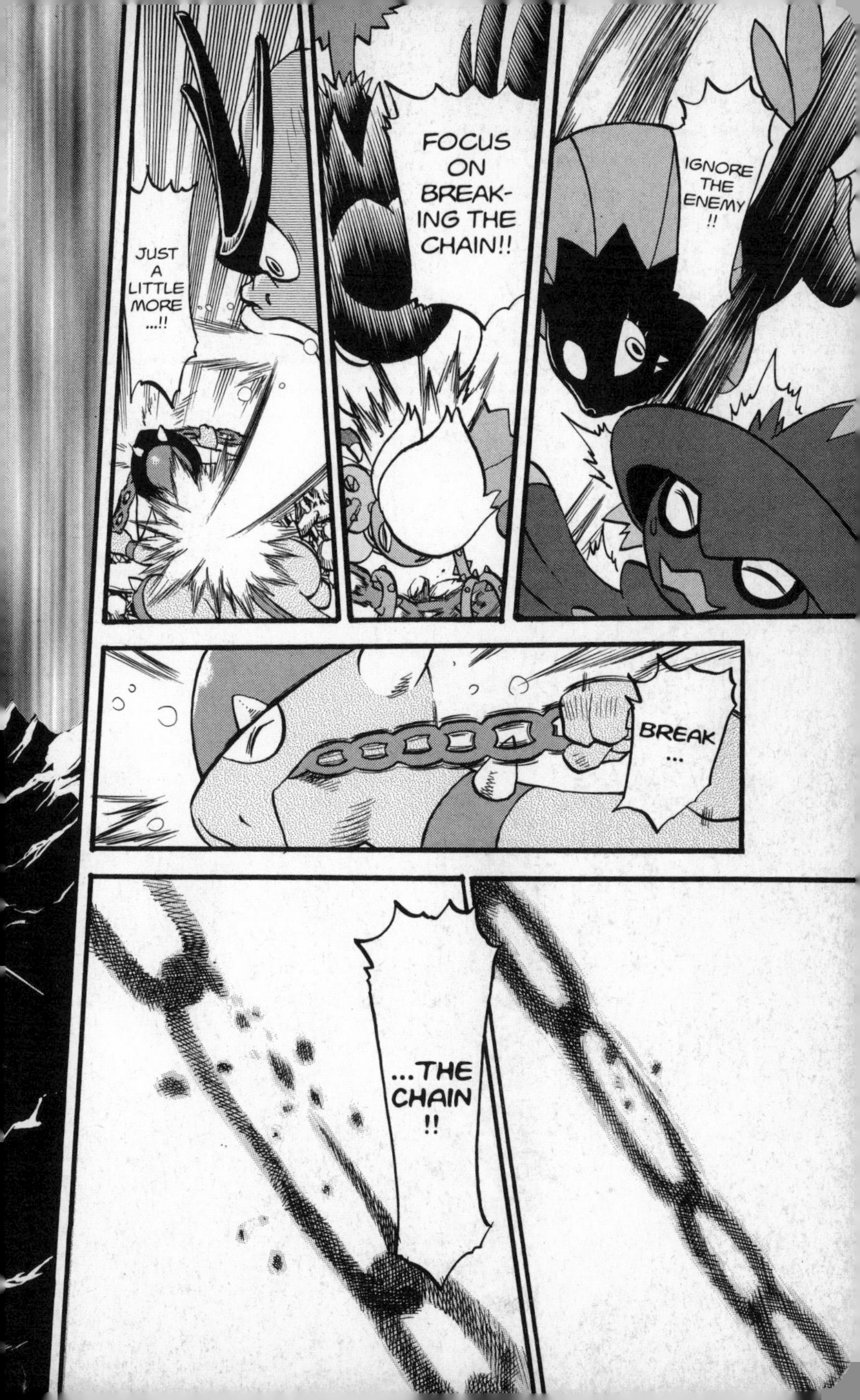
IGNORE THE ENEMY!!
FOCUS ON BREAK-ING THE CHAIN!!
JUST A LITTLE MORE ...!!
BREAK ...
...THE CHAIN!!

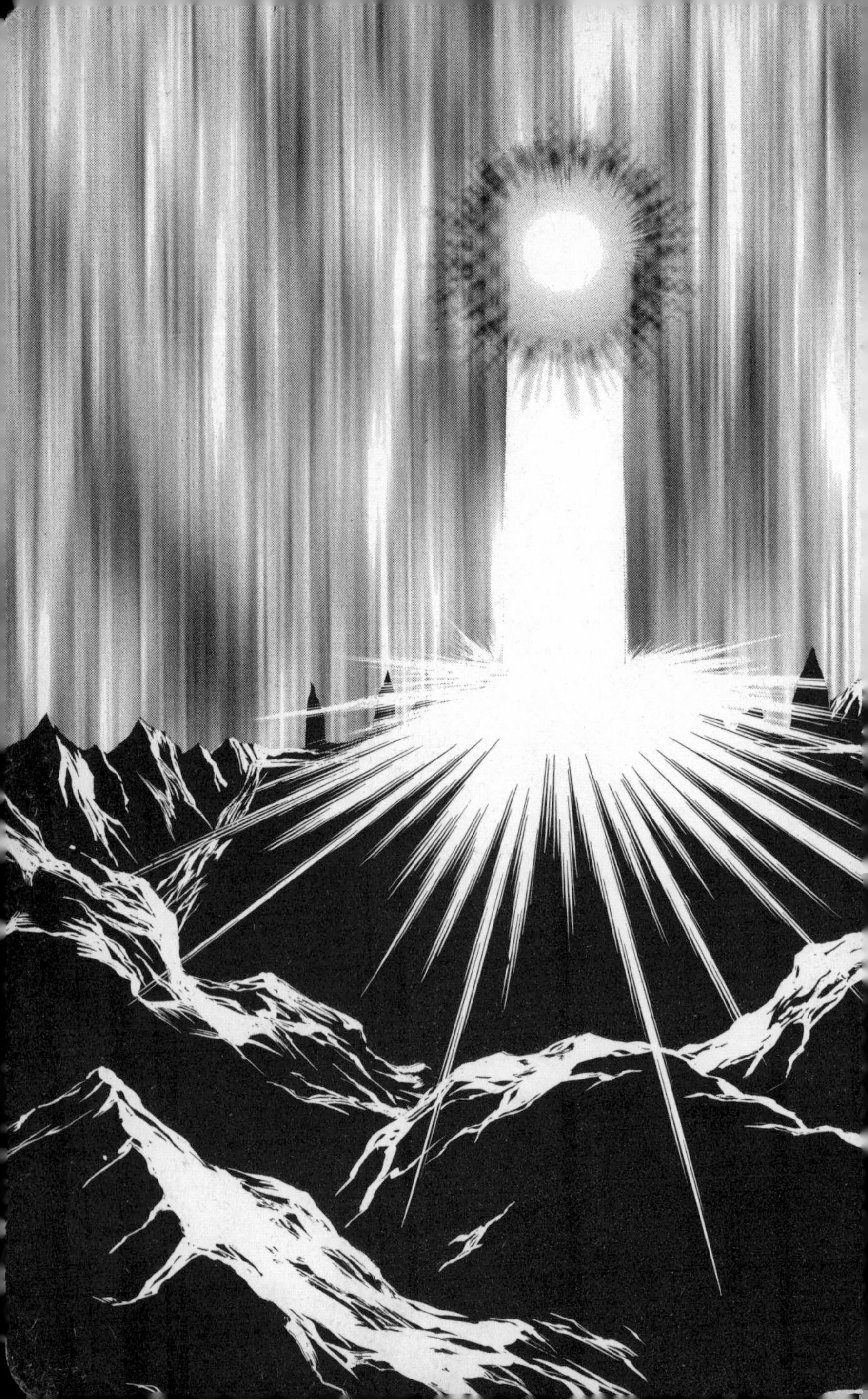

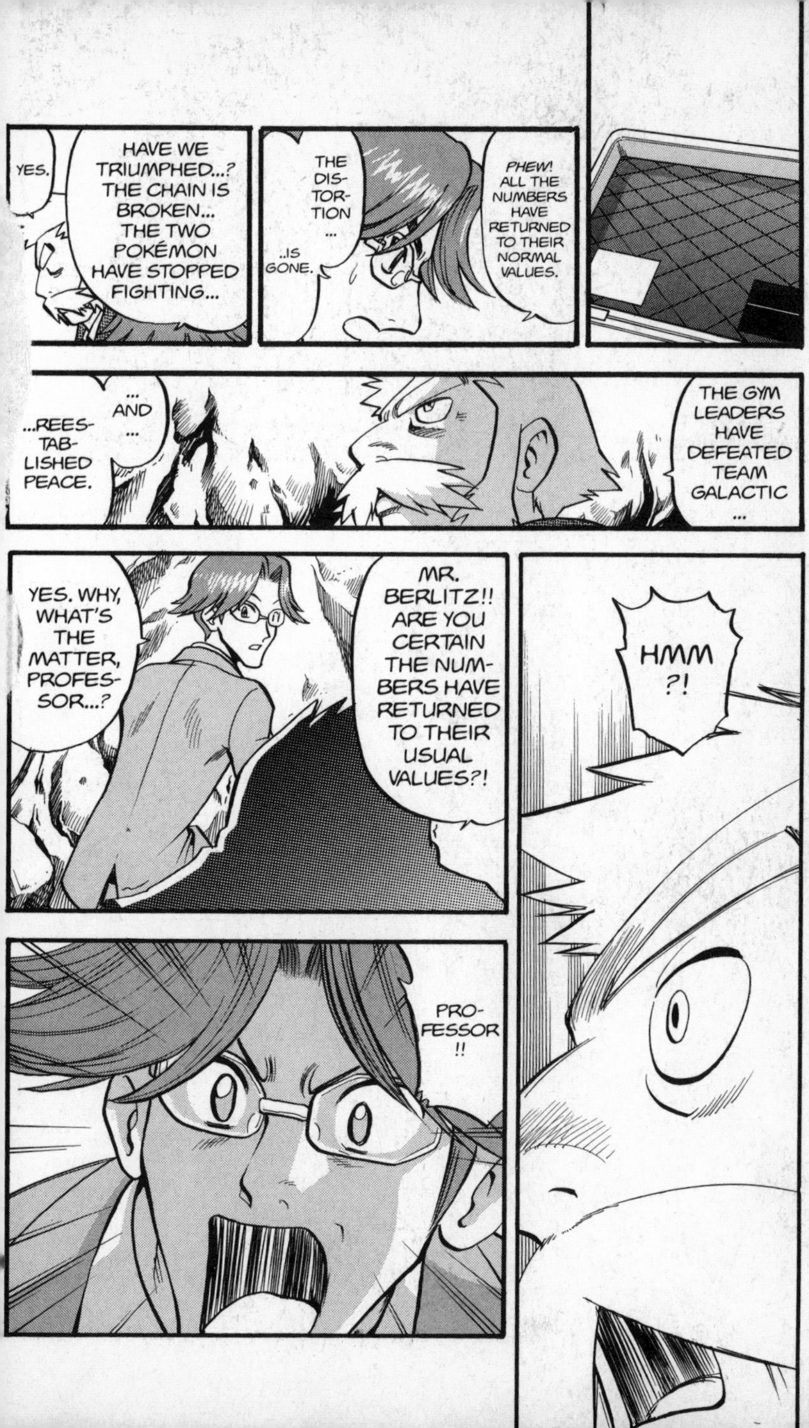
PHEW! ALL THE NUMBERS HAVE RETURNED TO THEIR NORMAL VALUES.
THE DISTORTION ...
..IS GONE.
HAVE WE TRIUMPHED...? THE CHAIN IS BROKEN... THE TWO POKÉMON HAVE STOPPED FIGHTING...
YES.
THE GYM LEADERS HAVE DEFEATED TEAM GALACTIC ...
... AND ...
...REESTABLISHED PEACE.
HMM ?!
MR. BERLITZ!! ARE YOU CERTAIN THE NUMBERS HAVE RETURNED TO THEIR USUAL VALUES?!
YES. WHY, WHAT'S THE MATTER, PROFESSOR...?
PROFESSOR !!

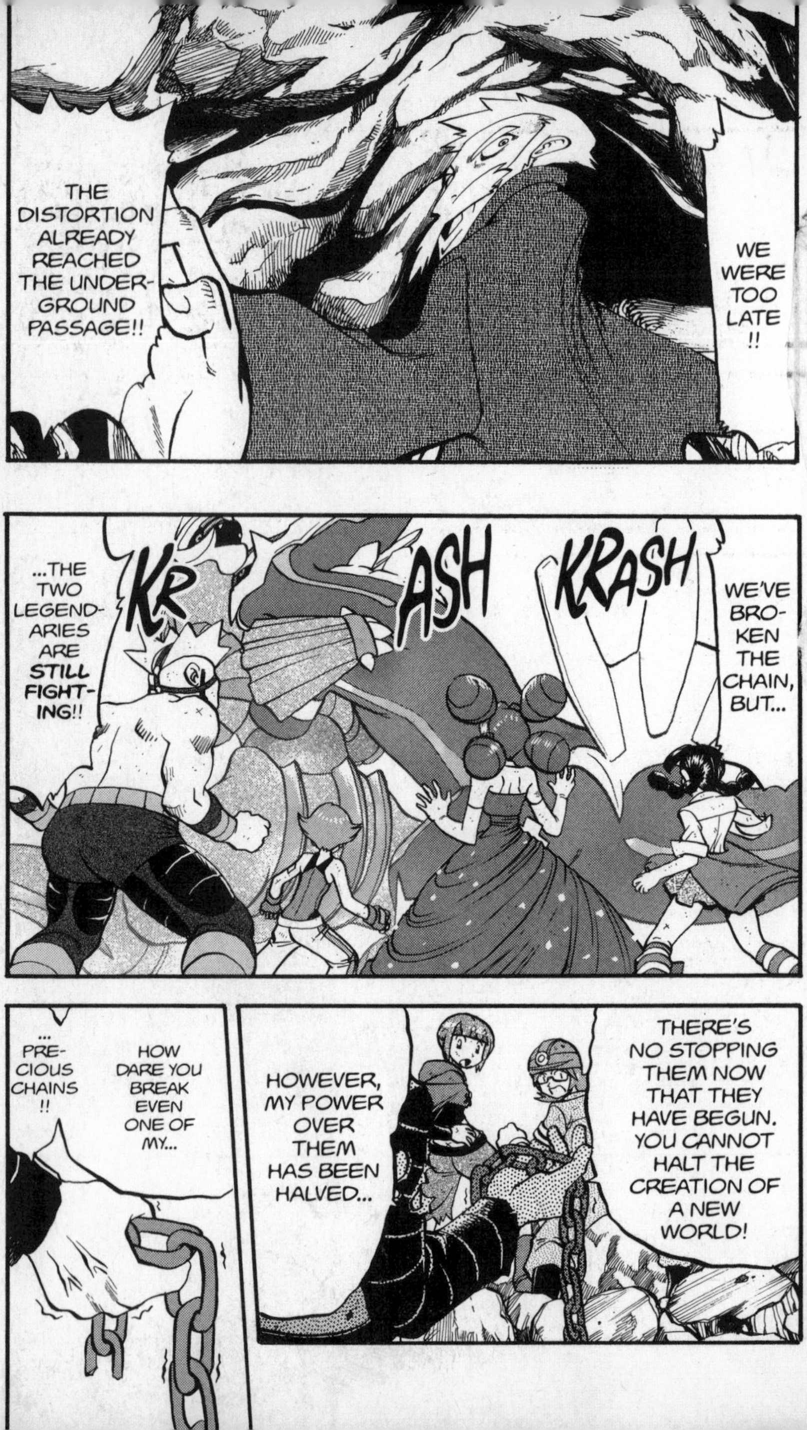
WE WERE TOO LATE!!
THE DISTORTION ALREADY REACHED THE UNDERGROUND PASSAGE!!
WE'VE BROKEN THE CHAIN, BUT...
KRASH
KR
ASH
...THE TWO LEGENDARIES ARE **STILL FIGHTING**!!
THERE'S NO STOPPING THEM NOW THAT THEY HAVE BEGUN. YOU CANNOT HALT THE CREATION OF A NEW WORLD!
HOWEVER, MY POWER OVER THEM HAS BEEN HALVED...
HOW DARE YOU BREAK EVEN ONE OF MY...
...PRECIOUS CHAINS!!

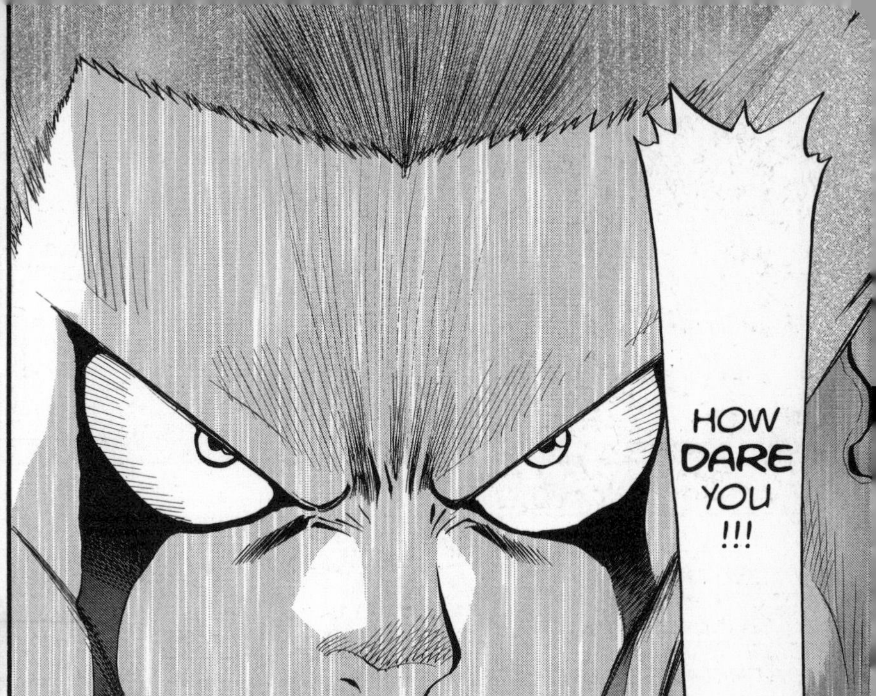
HOW DARE YOU !!!

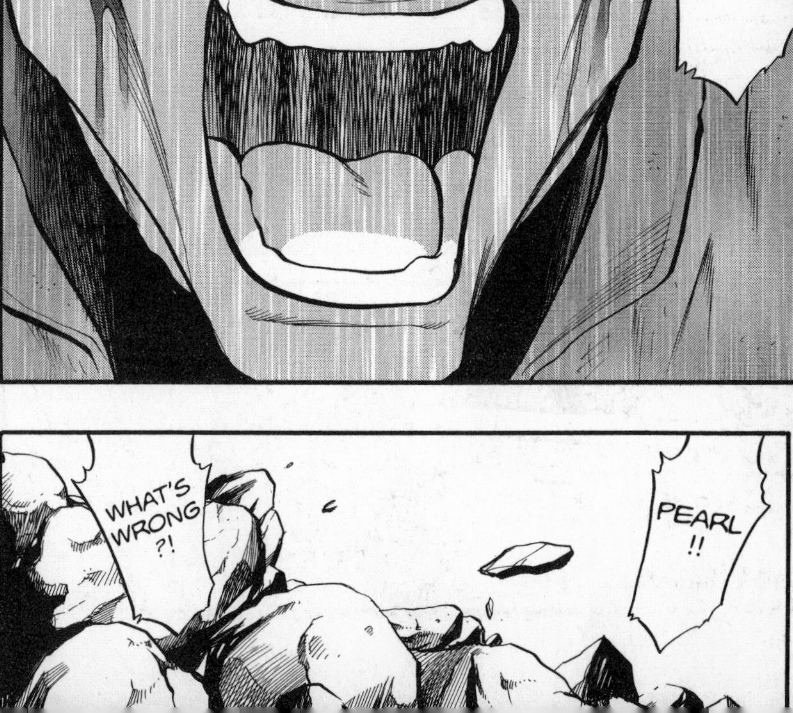
PEARL !!
WHAT'S WRONG ?!

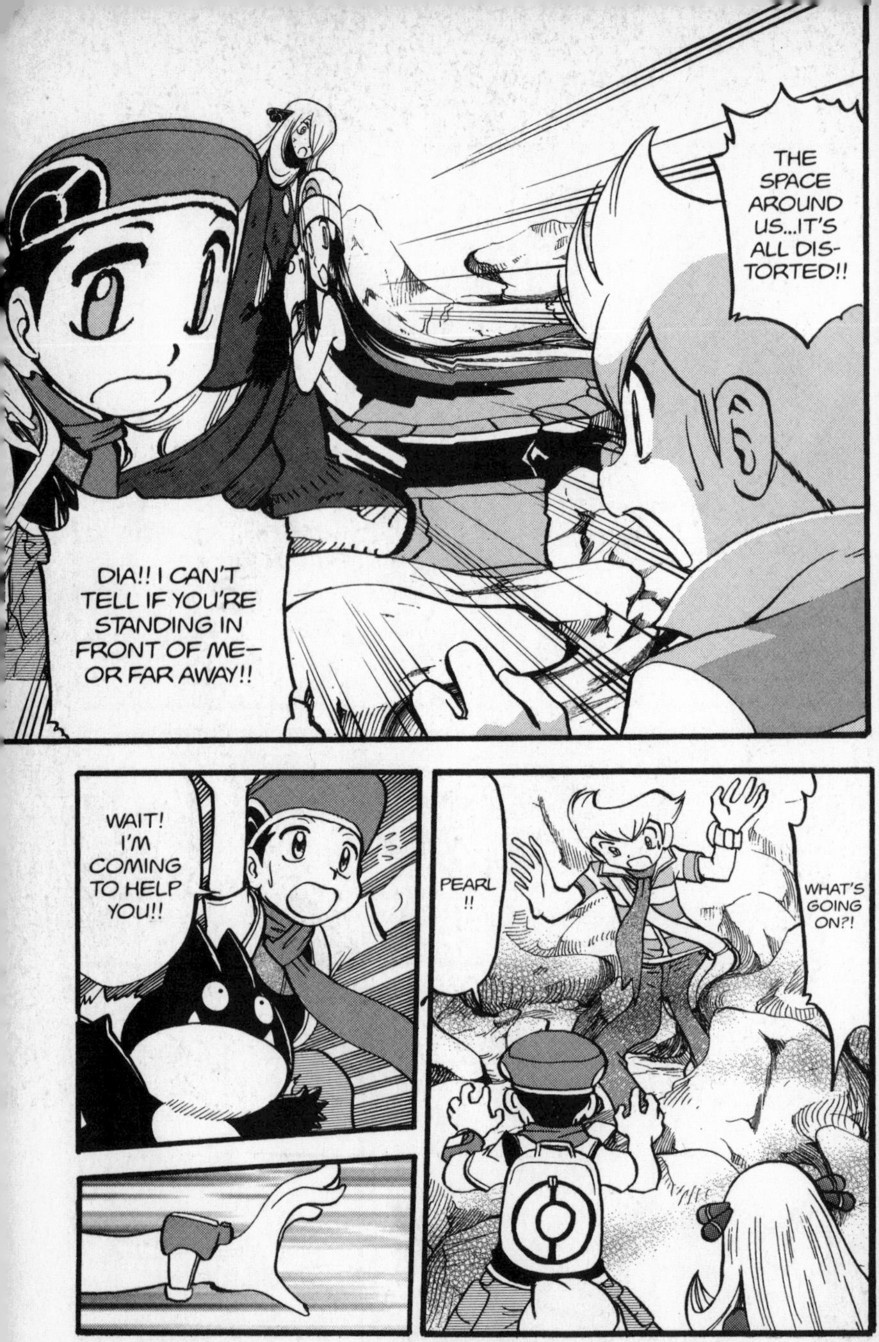
THE SPACE AROUND US...IT'S ALL DISTORTED!!
DIA!! I CAN'T TELL IF YOU'RE STANDING IN FRONT OF ME—OR FAR AWAY!!
WHAT'S GOING ON?!
PEARL!!
WAIT! I'M COMING TO HELP YOU!!

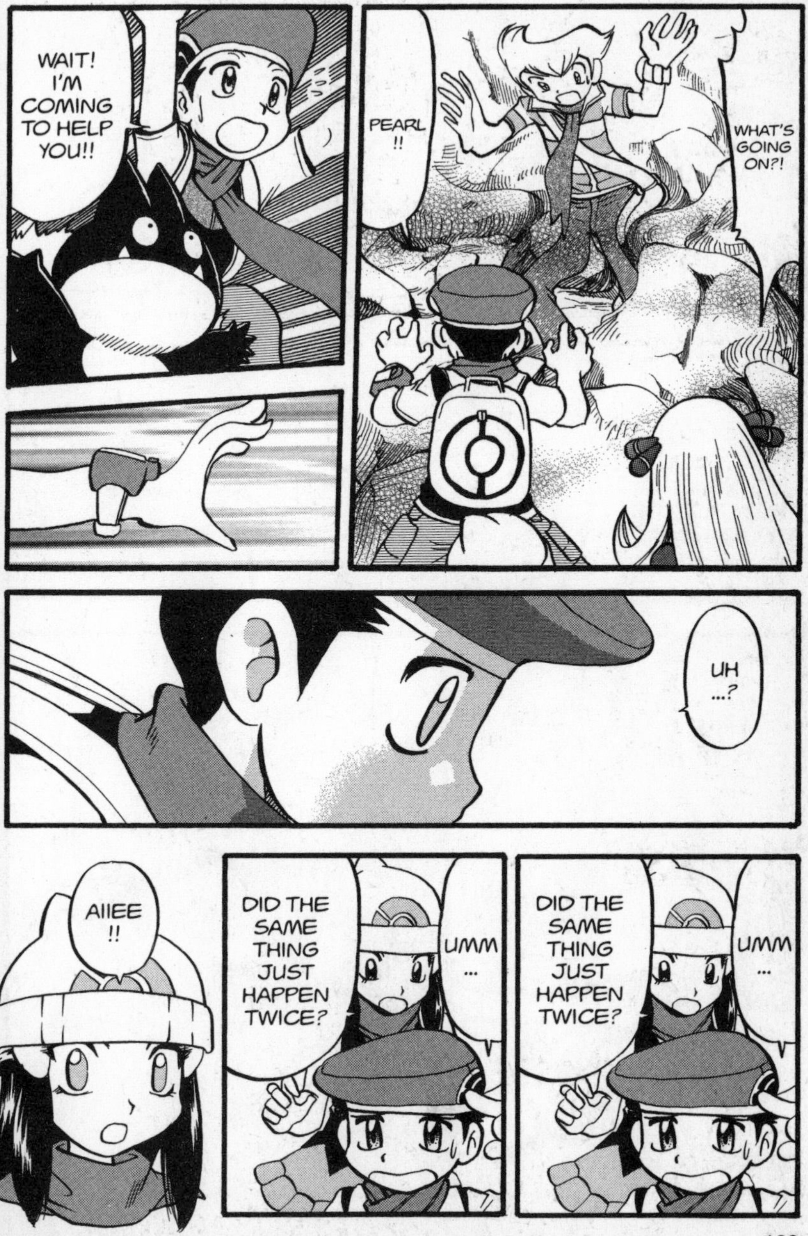
WHAT'S GOING ON?!
PEARL !!
WAIT! I'M COMING TO HELP YOU!!
UH ...?
UMM ...
DID THE SAME THING JUST HAPPEN TWICE?
UMM ...
DID THE SAME THING JUST HAPPEN TWICE?
AIIEE !!

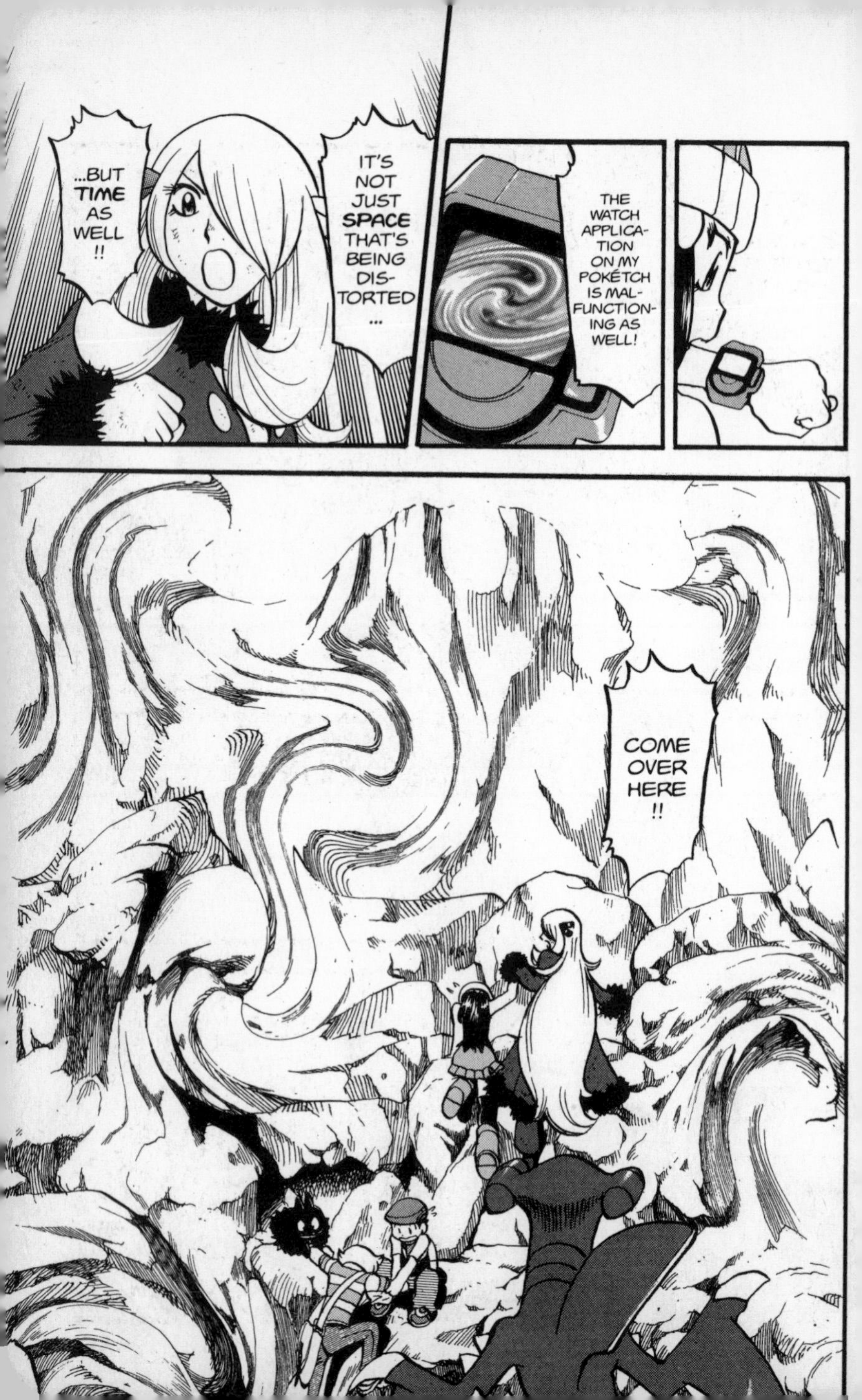
THE WATCH APPLICATION ON MY POKÉTCH IS MALFUNCTIONING AS WELL!
IT'S NOT JUST SPACE THAT'S BEING DISTORTED...
...BUT TIME AS WELL!!
COME OVER HERE!!

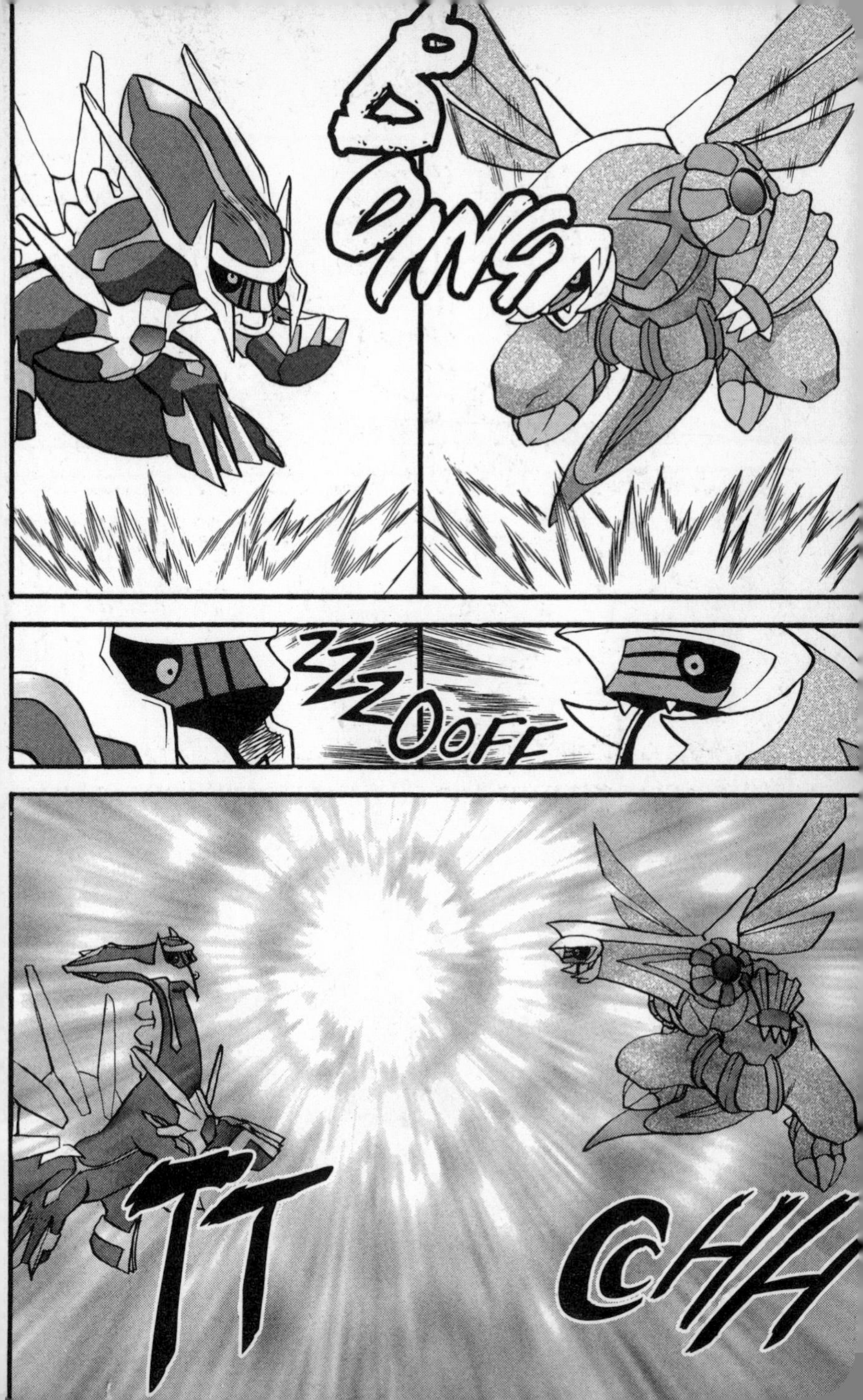
BOING
ZZZOOFF
CHH
TT

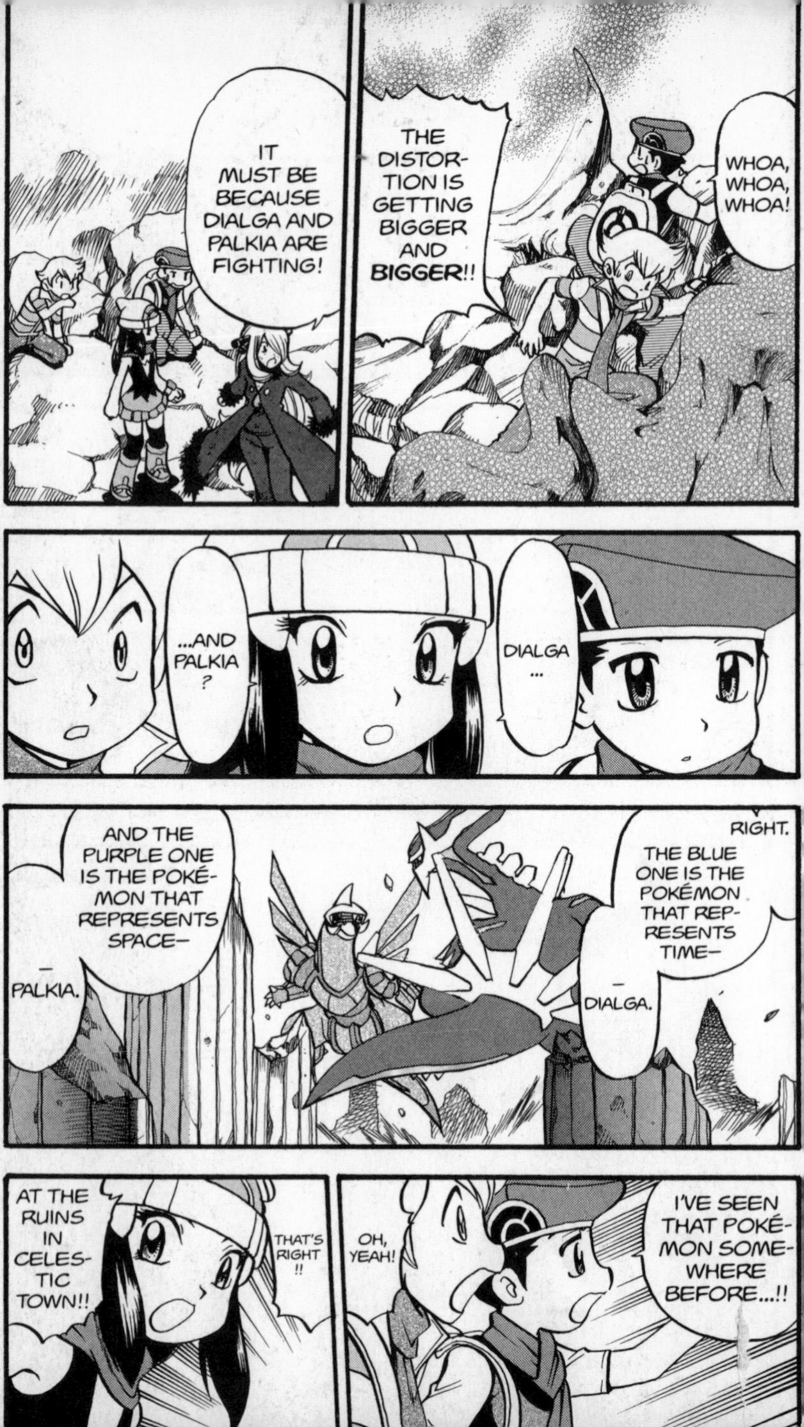
WHOA, WHOA, WHOA!
THE DISTORTION IS GETTING BIGGER AND BIGGER!!
IT MUST BE BECAUSE DIALGA AND PALKIA ARE FIGHTING!
DIALGA...
...AND PALKIA?
RIGHT. THE BLUE ONE IS THE POKÉMON THAT REPRESENTS TIME—
—DIALGA.
AND THE PURPLE ONE IS THE POKÉMON THAT REPRESENTS SPACE—
—PALKIA.
I'VE SEEN THAT POKÉMON SOMEWHERE BEFORE...!!
OH, YEAH!
THAT'S RIGHT!!
AT THE RUINS IN CELESTIC TOWN!!

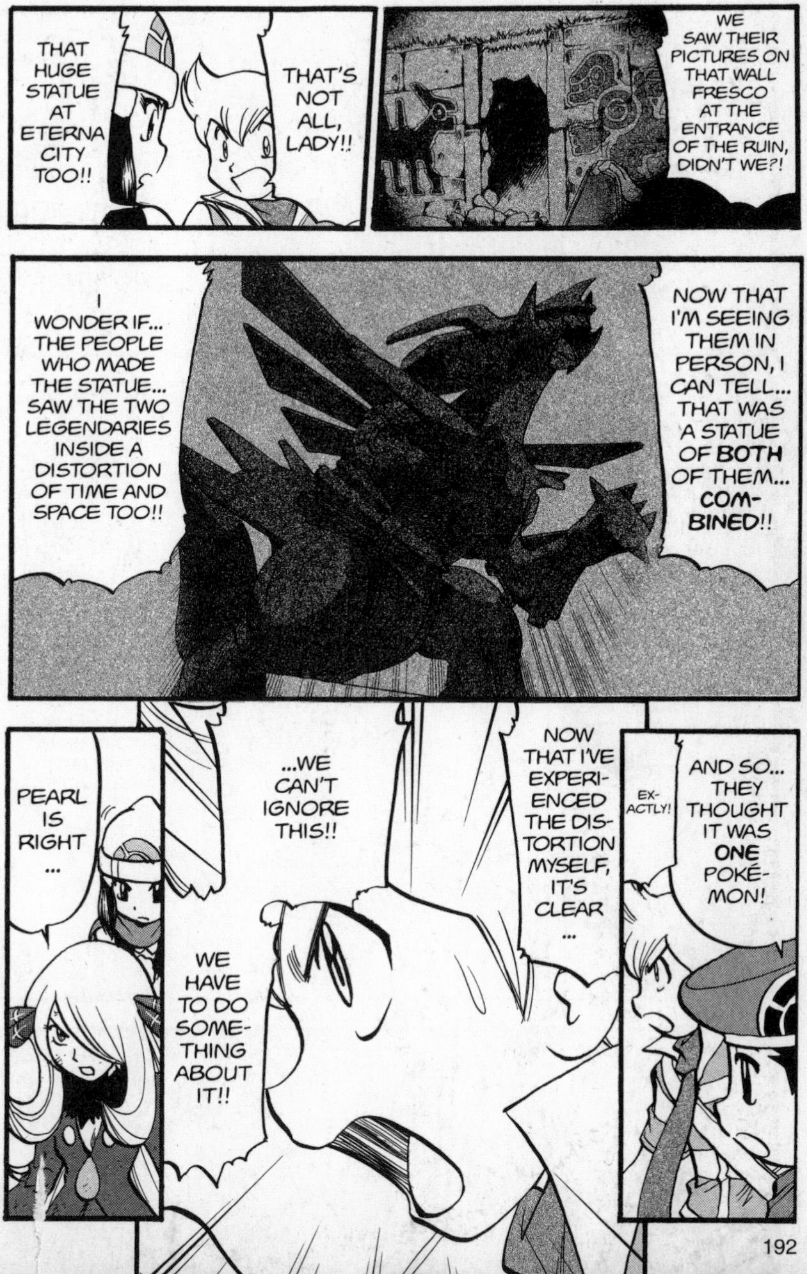
WE SAW THEIR PICTURES ON THAT WALL FRESCO AT THE ENTRANCE OF THE RUIN, DIDN'T WE?!
THAT'S NOT ALL, LADY!!
THAT HUGE STATUE AT ETERNA CITY TOO!!
NOW THAT I'M SEEING THEM IN PERSON, I CAN TELL... THAT WAS A STATUE OF **BOTH** OF THEM... **COMBINED**!!
I WONDER IF... THE PEOPLE WHO MADE THE STATUE... SAW THE TWO LEGENDARIES INSIDE A DISTORTION OF TIME AND SPACE TOO!!
AND SO... THEY THOUGHT IT WAS **ONE** POKÉMON!
EXACTLY!
NOW THAT I'VE EXPERIENCED THE DISTORTION MYSELF, IT'S CLEAR...
...WE CAN'T IGNORE THIS!!
WE HAVE TO DO SOMETHING ABOUT IT!!
PEARL IS RIGHT...

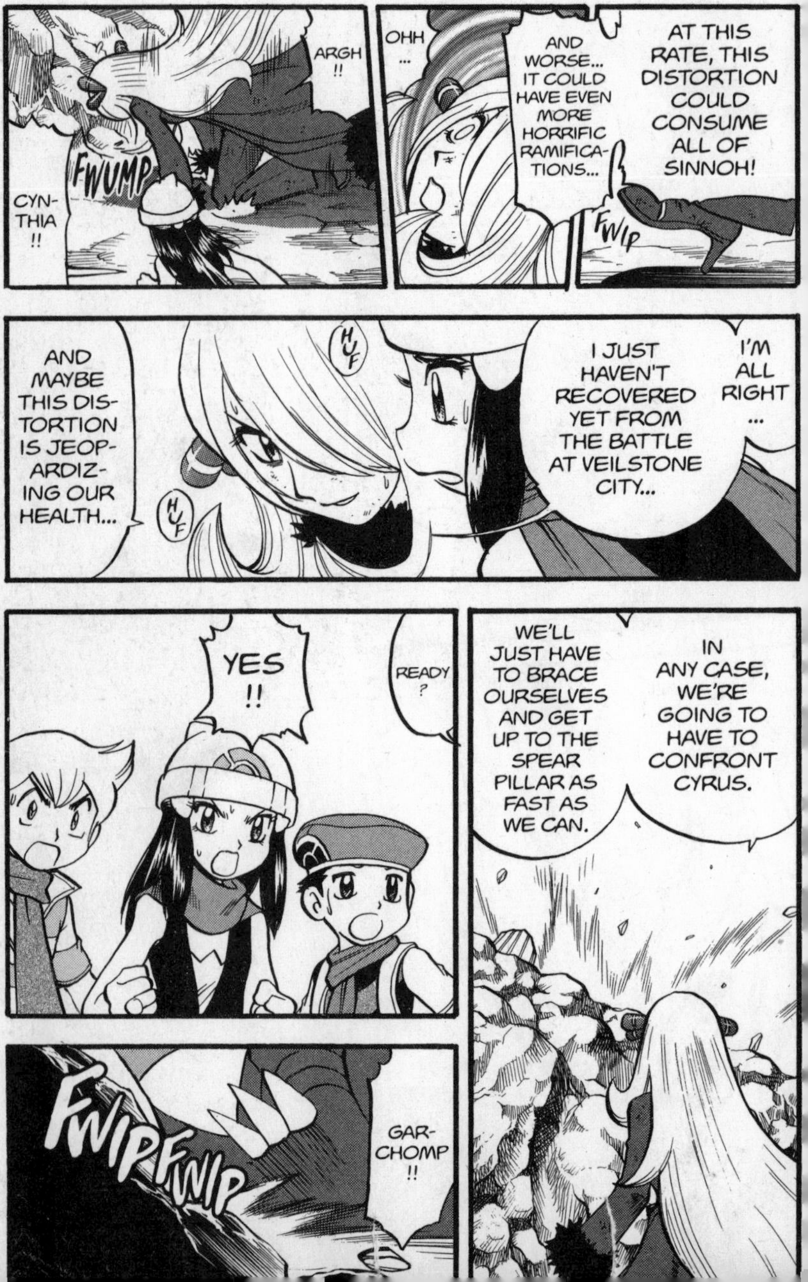
AT THIS RATE, THIS DISTORTION COULD CONSUME ALL OF SINNOH!
AND WORSE... IT COULD HAVE EVEN MORE HORRIFIC RAMIFICATIONS...
FWIP
OHH ...
ARGH !!
FWUMP
CYNTHIA !!
I'M ALL RIGHT ...
I JUST HAVEN'T RECOVERED YET FROM THE BATTLE AT VEILSTONE CITY...
HUF
HUF
AND MAYBE THIS DISTORTION IS JEOPARDIZING OUR HEALTH...
IN ANY CASE, WE'RE GOING TO HAVE TO CONFRONT CYRUS.
WE'LL JUST HAVE TO BRACE OURSELVES AND GET UP TO THE SPEAR PILLAR AS FAST AS WE CAN.
READY ?
YES !!
GARCHOMP !!
FWIP FWIP

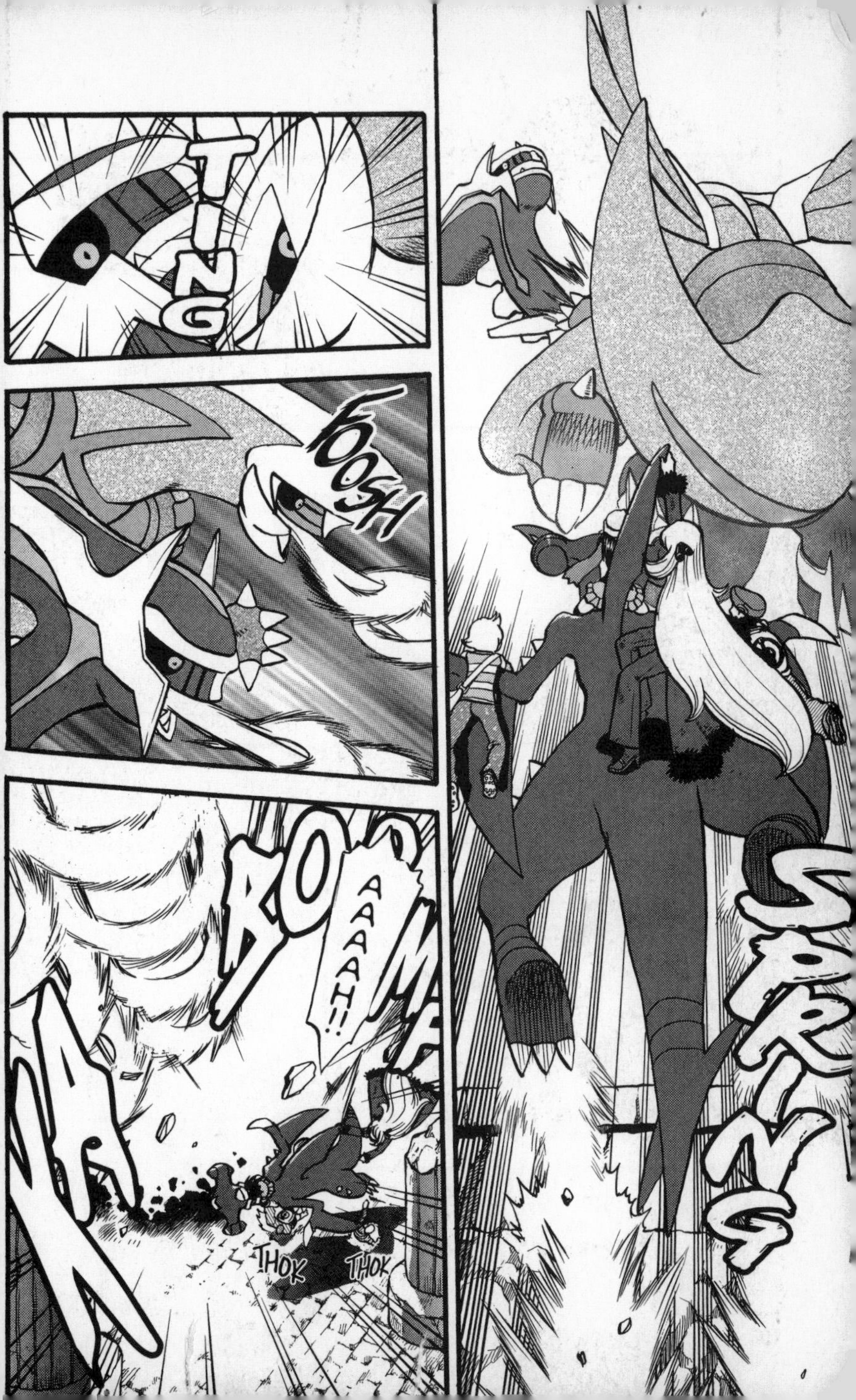
SPRINGS
TING
FOOSH
BOOM
AAAAAH!!
THOK
THOK

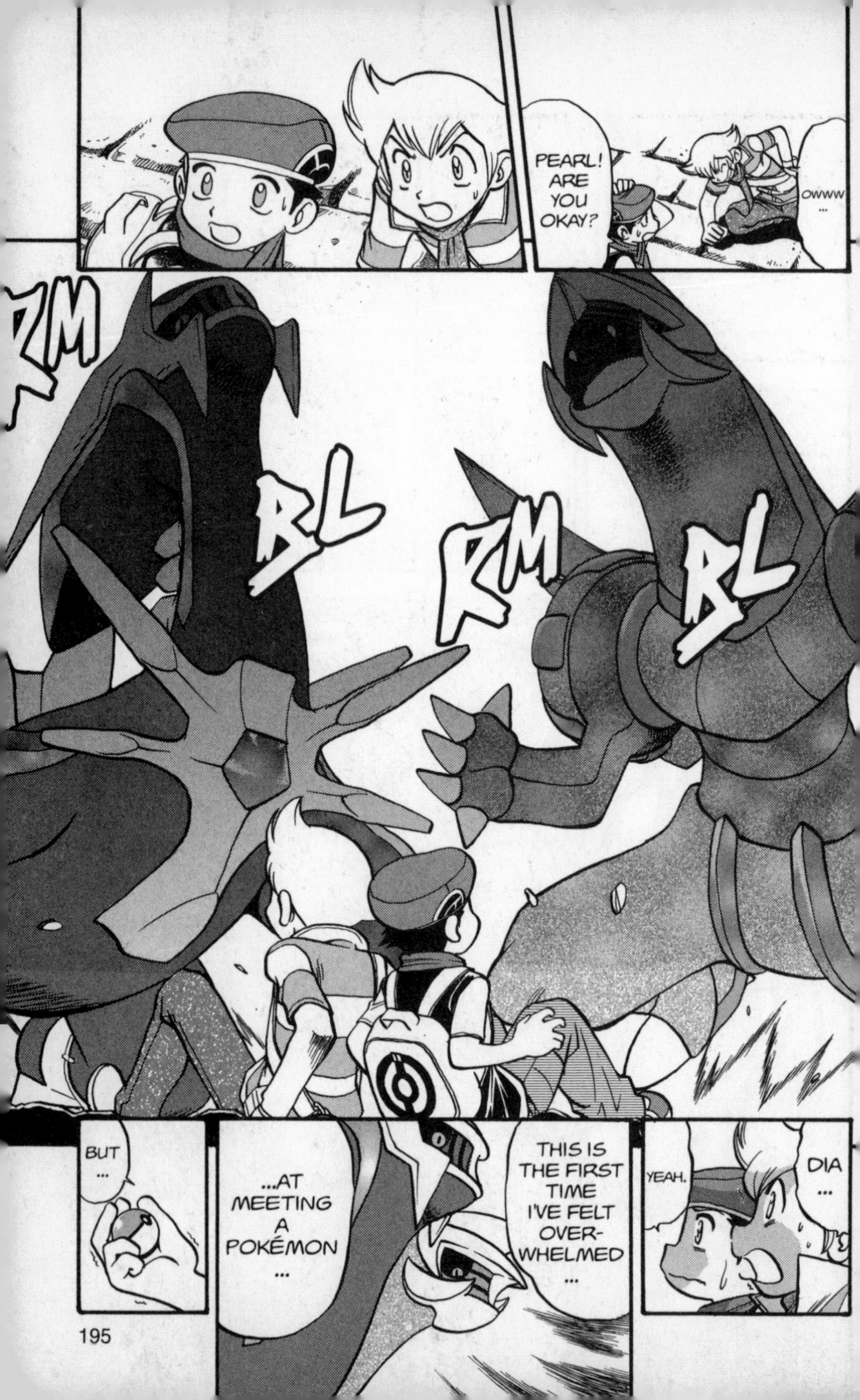
OWWW ...
PEARL! ARE YOU OKAY?
BL
RM
BL
RM
DIA ...
YEAH.
THIS IS THE FIRST TIME I'VE FELT OVER-WHELMED ...
...AT MEETING A POKÉMON ...
BUT ...

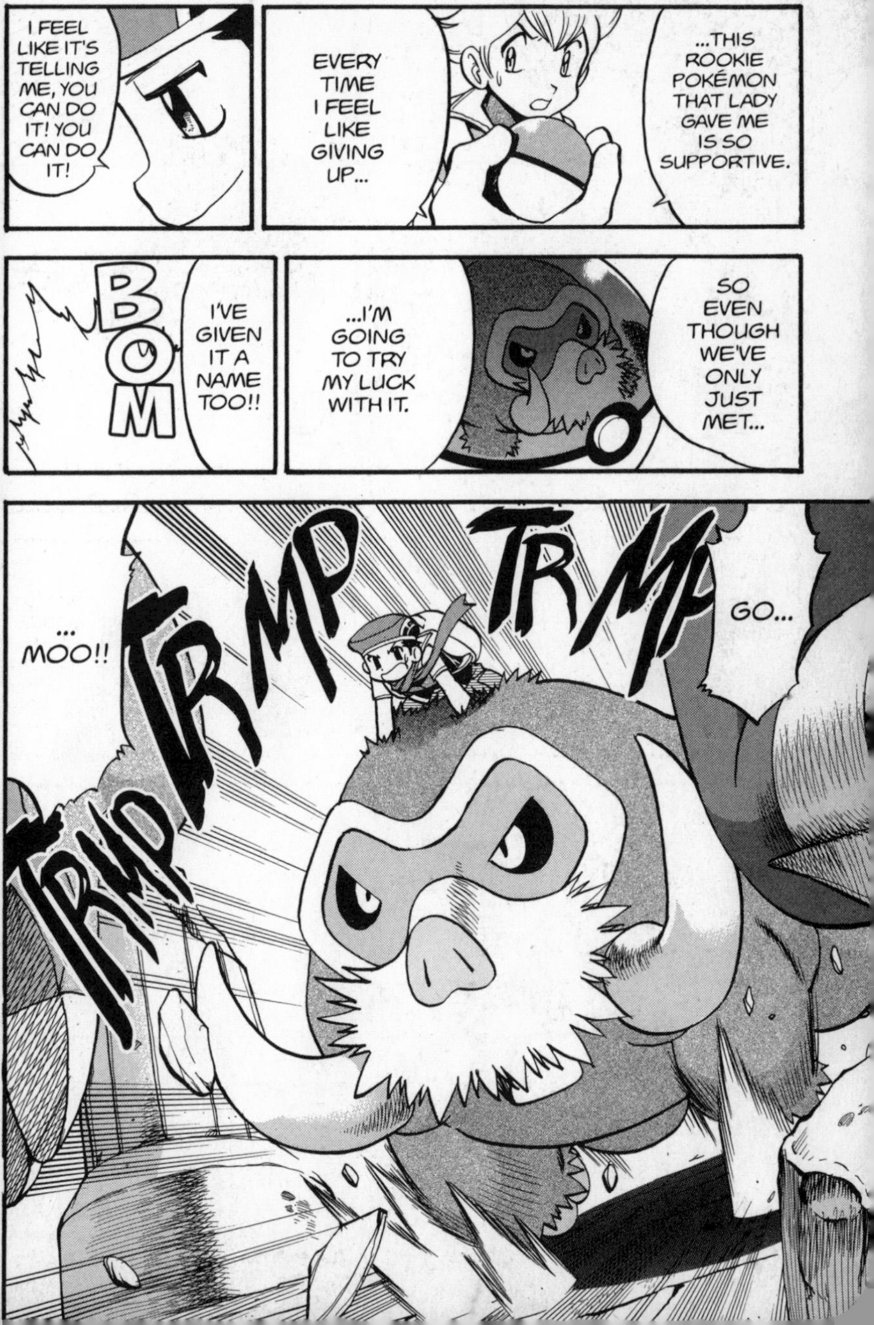
...THIS ROOKIE POKÉMON THAT LADY GAVE ME IS SO SUPPORTIVE.
EVERY TIME I FEEL LIKE GIVING UP...
I FEEL LIKE IT'S TELLING ME, YOU CAN DO IT! YOU CAN DO IT!
SO EVEN THOUGH WE'VE ONLY JUST MET...
...I'M GOING TO TRY MY LUCK WITH IT.
I'VE GIVEN IT A NAME TOO!!
BOM
GO...
TRM
TRMP
... MOO!!
TRMP
TRMP

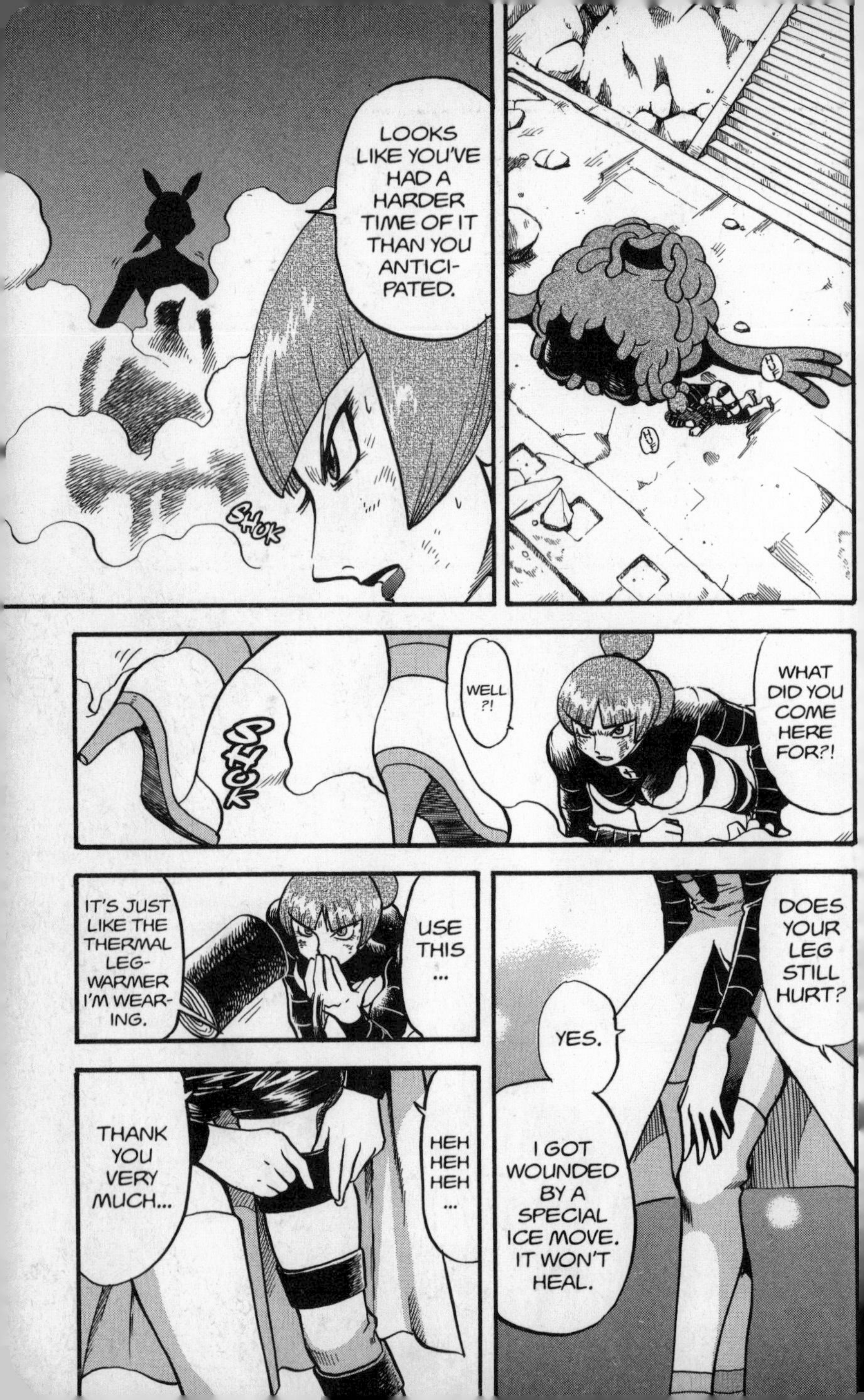
HUF
HUF
LOOKS LIKE YOU'VE HAD A HARDER TIME OF IT THAN YOU ANTICI-PATED.
SHOK
WHAT DID YOU COME HERE FOR?!
WELL ?!
SHOK
DOES YOUR LEG STILL HURT?
YES.
I GOT WOUNDED BY A SPECIAL ICE MOVE. IT WON'T HEAL.
USE THIS...
IT'S JUST LIKE THE THERMAL LEG-WARMER I'M WEAR-ING.
HEH HEH HEH...
THANK YOU VERY MUCH...

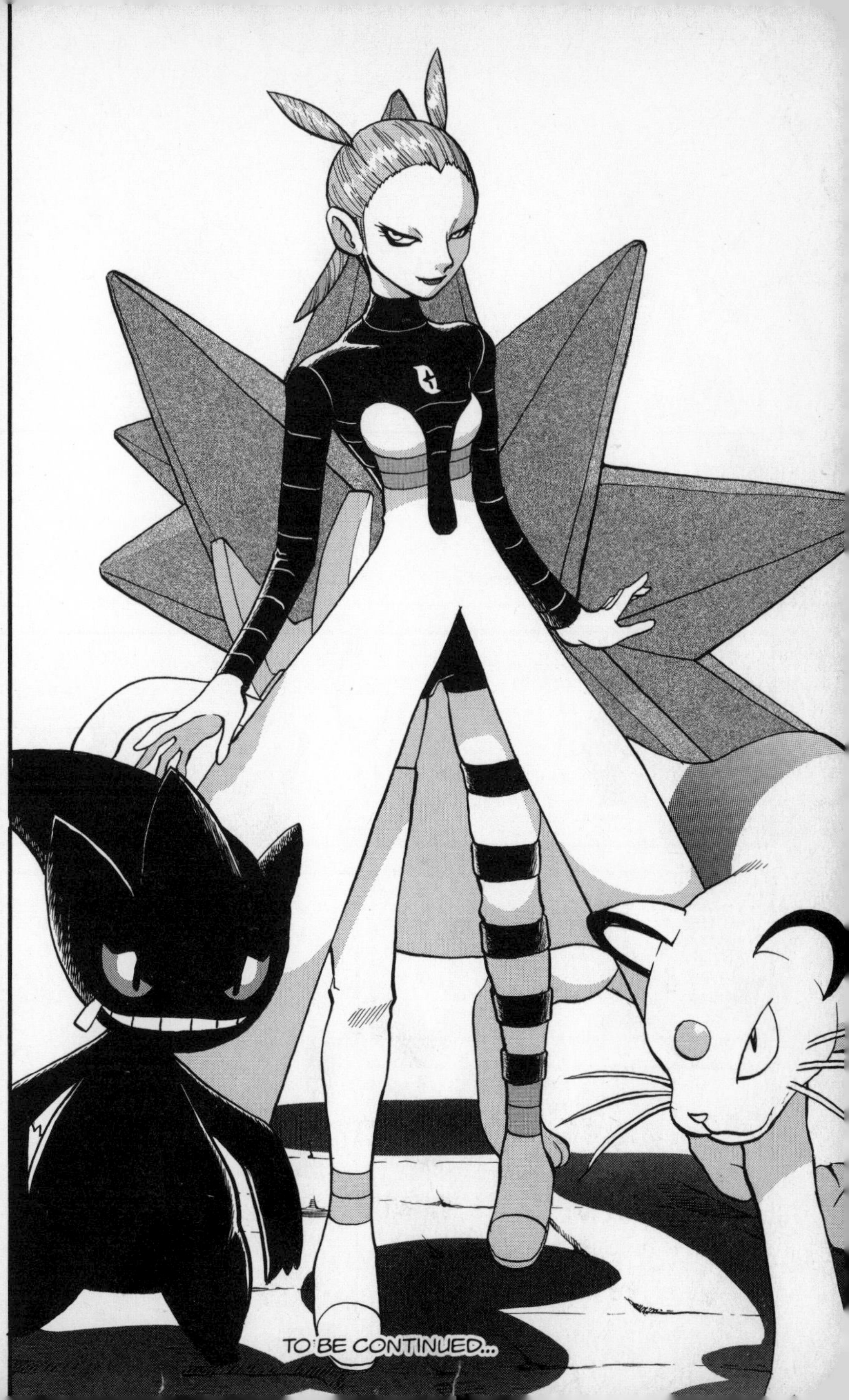
TO BE CONTINUED...

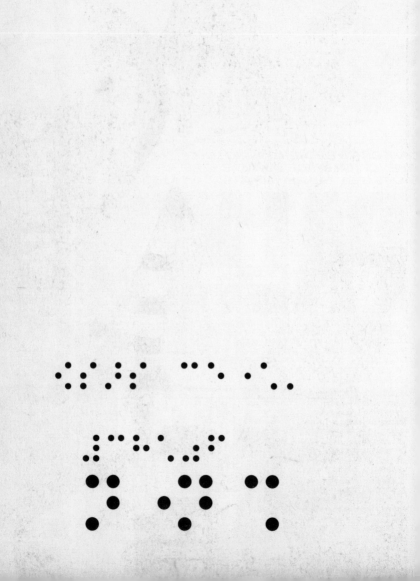

The Legendary Pokémon of Sinnoh!

DIALGA • PALKIA

An epic battle is rocking the Sinnoh region! The only way to end it is to calm these two Legendary Pokémon. But how does one communicate with such powerful creatures...?! Let's examine them more closely in hopes of finding a solution!!

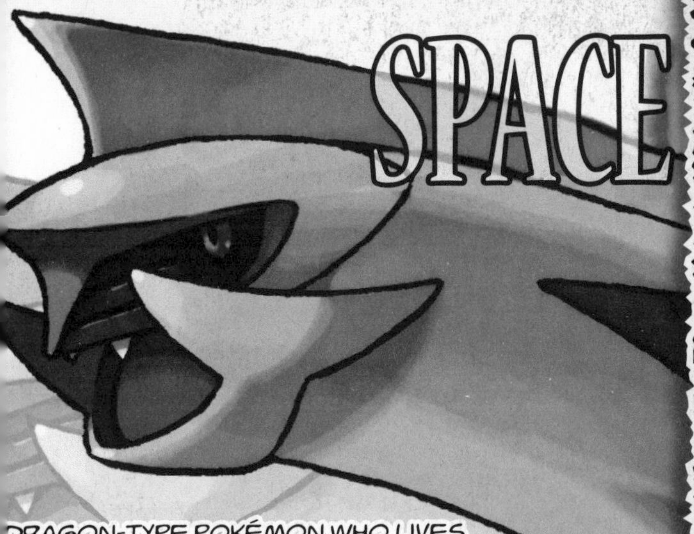

SPACE

DRAGON-TYPE POKÉMON WHO LIVES THE VOID OF SPACE. ITS MOVE SPACIAL END TEARS ITS ENEMY APART!!

PALKIA

Palkia

A LEGENDARY POKÉMON WITH THE POWER TO DISTORT SPACE. IT IS DEPICTED AS A PAIR WITH DIALGA IN LEGENDS AND ITS IMAGE APPEARS IN ANCIENT WALL FRESCOS. IT IS SAID THAT EVERY BREATH PALKIA TAKES STABILIZES SPACE, AND THUS IT CAN CONTROL SPACE AND TRAVEL TO FAR-OFF PLACES AND ALTERNATE DIMENSIONS. ITS MOVE SPACIAL REND TEARS AN ENEMY APART ALONG WITH THE SPACE AROUND IT. THIS MOVE CAN ONLY BE USED BY PALKIA.

Height	13′ 09″
Weight	740.8 lbs.
Species	Spatial Pokémon
Gender	Unknown
Type	Water-Dragon
Ability	Pressure
Pokédex Number	Sinnoh: 150, National: 484
Items	Lustrous Orb

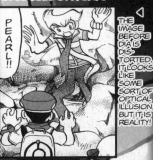

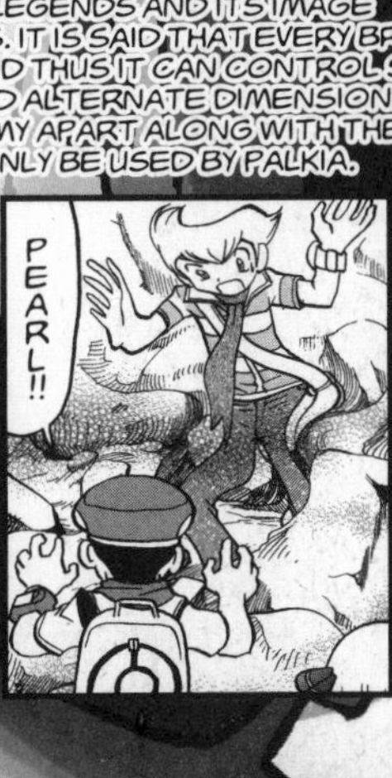
PEARL!!

◁ THE IMAGE BEFORE DIA IS DISTORTED. IT LOOKS LIKE SOME SORT OF OPTICAL ILLUSION, BUT IT IS REALITY!

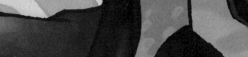

TIME

A DRAGON THAT CONTROLS TIME!
HEAR ITS ROAR OF TIME!!

Dialga

DIALGA

THE OTHER LEGENDARY POKÉMON OF THE SINNOH REGION. IT IS SAID THAT TIME BEGAN TO FLOW WHEN DIALGA WAS BORN, AND THAT THE BEAT OF ITS HEART MATCHES THE FLOW OF TIME. IT HAS THE ABILITY TO TRAVEL TO THE PAST AND FUTURE. ITS MOVE THE ROAR OF TIME IS SO POWERFUL THAT IT DISTORTS THE FLOW OF TIME AROUND IT.

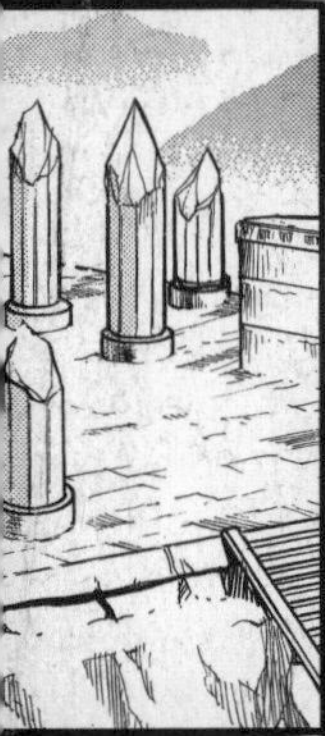

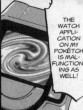

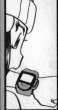

THE WATCH APPLI-CATION ON MY POKÉTCH IS MAL-FUNCTION-ING AS WELL!

▲TIME IS STARTING TO TURN BACK?! JUST STEPPING INTO THIS AREA WILL THROW YOU INTO A RAPID DISTORTION OF TIME!

Height	17' 09"
Weight	1505.8 lbs.
Species	Temporal Pokémon
Gender	Unknown
Type	Steel-Dragon
Ability	Pressure
Pokédex Number	Sinnoh: 149, National: 483
Items	Adamant Orb

SPEAR PILLAR

They appeared at the peak of Mt. Coronet.

The great Mt. Coronet divides the Sinnoh region in half from east to west. If you climb to its peak, you will find a strange ruin with sharp pillars that look like spears pointing up to the sky. This ormation is known as the Spear Pillar and is the location Cyrus chose to perform his mysterious ritual. What will the conclusion of his ritual lead to? Let's examine he possibilities on the next page.

TIME × SPACE = UNIVERSE?!!

"And when time and space intertwine to create a double spiral...a new and perfect creation will be born!!" Cyrus's scheme has become a reality! The two legendary Pokémon were summoned by his ritual and have obeyed his command to battle one another. What will the outcome of this epic struggle be...?!

Red Chain

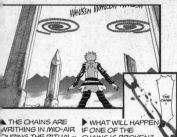

DIALGA AND PALKIA HAVE APPEARED IN FRONT OF THE SPEAR PILLAR. EACH OF CYRUS'S CHAINS HAS THE POWER TO SUMMON THESE POKÉMON FROM THE DIMENSION WHERE THEY LIVE AND BIND THEM TO THE PERSON WHO SUMMONED THEM. THE CHAINS ALSO FUNCTION AS WHIPS TO FORCE THE TWO POKÉMON TO OBEY COMMANDS.

...THE CHAIN !!

▶ WHAT WILL HAPPEN IF ONE OF THE CHAINS IS BROKEN?

WHUSSH

▲ THE CHAINS ARE WRITHING IN MID-AIR DURING THE RITUAL—AS IF THEY ARE ALIVE.

The Battle Begins

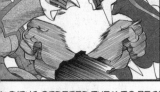

PROFESSOR ROWAN CLAIMS THAT DIALGA AND PALKIA ARE NOT IN CONFLICT. IN FACT, THESE TWO HARDLY SEE EACH OTHER SINCE THEY LIVE IN DIFFERENT DIMENSIONS! WHAT WILL HAPPEN WHEN THESE TWO POKÉMON FIGHT...?

▲ CYRUS ORDERED THEM TO BEGIN FIGHTING BY RINGING A GONG.

The Distortion of Time and Space

AS SOON AS THE TWO POKÉMON STARTED BATTLING, TIME AND SPACE BEGAN TO WARP AROUND THEM! TIME CONTINUES TO WIND BACK AND REPEAT ITSELF, AND THE DISTANCE BETWEEN OBJECTS IS BECOMING UNCLEAR! THIS IS WHAT CYRUS WISHED TO CREATE! THIS DISTORTION IS THE KEY TO CYRUS'S "NEW UNIVERSE."

THE TWO OF THEM ...
...ARE BATTLING?!

▶ THIS CHINE CON-INUES TO SURE NNAT-RALLY HIGH BERS WHILE THE TWO FIGHT.

The Creation of a Universe!!

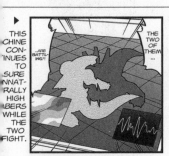

THE LAST TIME HE CAME TO MT. CORONET, CYRUS DECLARED HE WANTED TO "EXPERIENCE THE ENERGY OF THE CREATION OF THE WORLD." HE WAS TALKING ABOUT THE CREATION OF A NEW UNIVERSE—AND THAT SEEMS TO BE WHAT'S OCCURRING NOW. CYRUS DREAMS OF CREATING A PERFECT WORLD, AND IN ORDER TO ACHIEVE THAT, HE'LL GO TO THE EXTREME OF ERASING THE CURRENT WORLD'S EXISTENCE!!

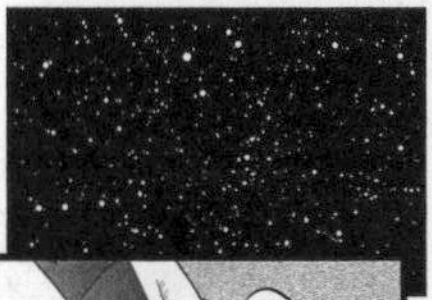

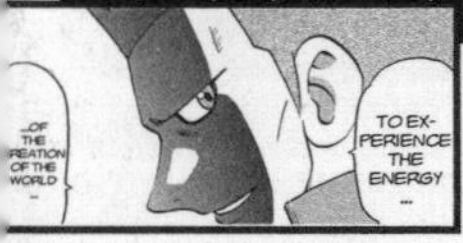

TO EXPERIENCE THE ENERGY ...
...OF THE CREATION OF THE WORLD ...

▲ MT. CORONET IS SAID TO BE THE FIRST PLACE CREATED IN THE SINNOH REGION. THAT'S WHY CYRUS CHOSE THIS SPOT AS HIS STAGE TO CREATE A NEW UNIVERSE.

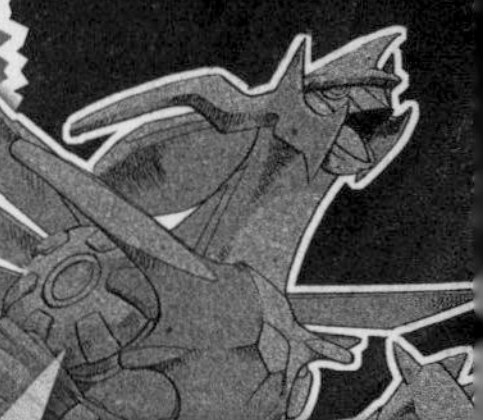

ANCIENT HISTORICAL RECORDS REVEAL THAT DIALGA AND PALKIA HAVE APPEARED IN THE PAST. BUT THE ANCIENT PEOPLES WHO SAW THEM WERE UNABLE TO GET A CLEAR VIEW OF THE TWO DUE TO THE DISTORTION EFFECT. AS A RESULT, THEY MISREPRESENTED THEM IN A STATUE THAT IS A COMBINATION OF BOTH POKÉMON!

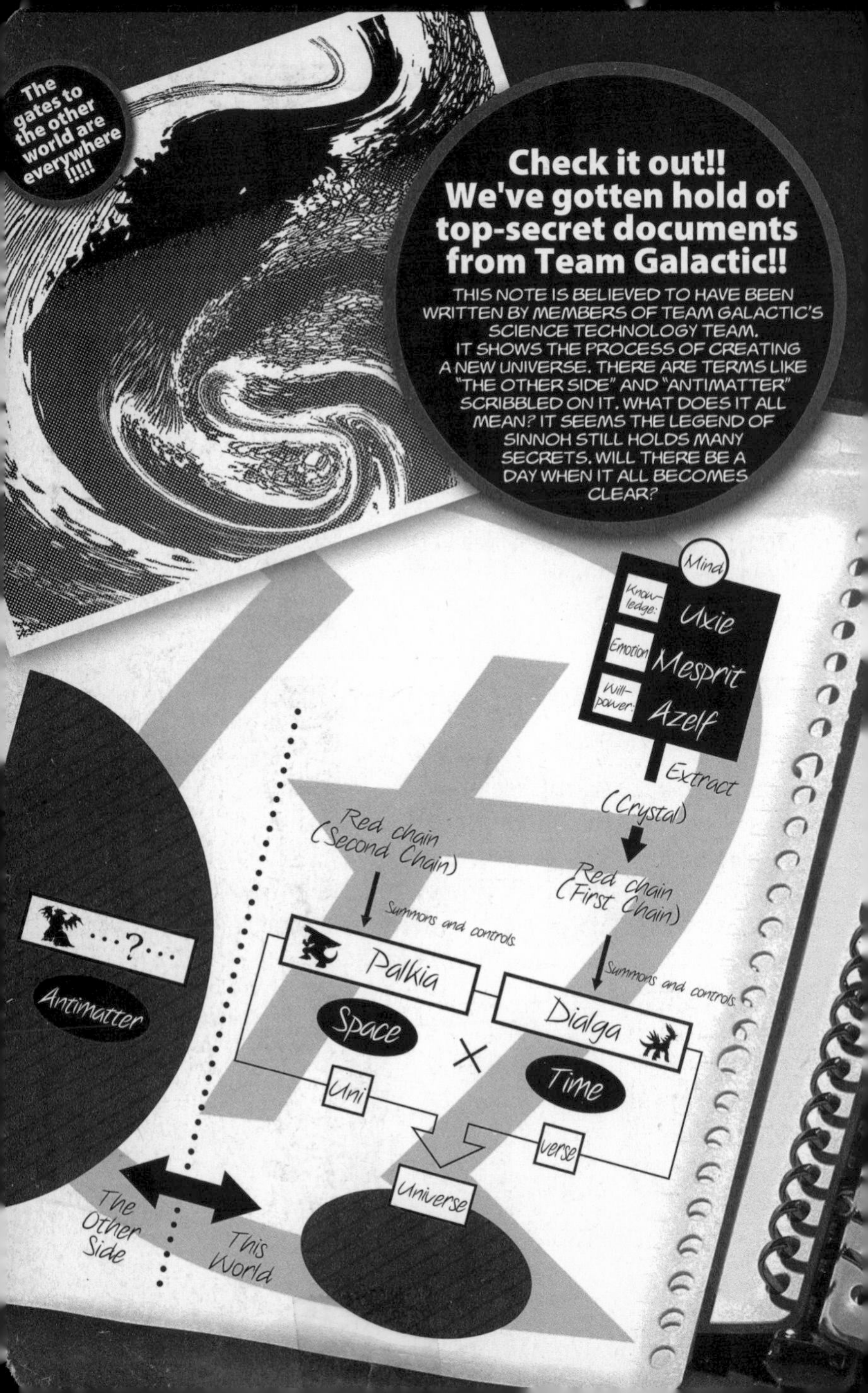
The gates to the other world are everywhere !!!!!
Check it out!! We've gotten hold of top-secret documents from Team Galactic!!
THIS NOTE IS BELIEVED TO HAVE BEEN WRITTEN BY MEMBERS OF TEAM GALACTIC'S SCIENCE TECHNOLOGY TEAM. IT SHOWS THE PROCESS OF CREATING A NEW UNIVERSE. THERE ARE TERMS LIKE "THE OTHER SIDE" AND "ANTIMATTER" SCRIBBLED ON IT. WHAT DOES IT ALL MEAN? IT SEEMS THE LEGEND OF SINNOH STILL HOLDS MANY SECRETS. WILL THERE BE A DAY WHEN IT ALL BECOMES CLEAR?
Mind
Know-ledge: Uxie
Emotion: Mesprit
Will-power: Azelf
Extract
(Crystal)
Red chain (First Chain)
Summons and controls
Red chain (Second Chain)
Summons and controls
Palkia
Dialga
Space
×
Time
Uni
verse
Universe
...?...
Antimatter
The Other Side
This World

Message from
Hidenori Kusaka

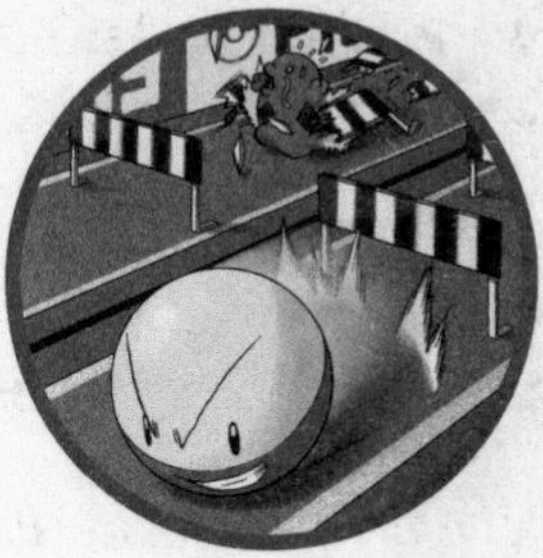

This is how I bought a car: I don't know a lot about them, so when I went to the car dealer I shopped by color. And the colors weren't simply "gray" or "white"—they had fancy names like "Meteor Metallic" and "Premium White." I found myself attracted to a nice red color, so I asked the dealer, "What's the name of that color?" The dealer replied, "Royal Ruby Red Pearl"! "Ruby" and "Red" and "Pearl," huh...? (laugh) Obviously, that's the one I bought!

Message from
Satoshi Yamamoto

Teamwork and a sigh of relief! That's the best way to describe this volume. I bet some fans would like every *Pokémon Adventures* story arc to end like that. But there are some manga characters (guess who!) that just don't play well with others (*laugh*). I've never been good at that myself. (Also, I'm envious of how strong he is...)

Pokémon

BLACK AND WHITE

MEET POKÉMON TRAINERS BLACK AND WHITE

THE WAIT IS FINALLY OVER!
Meet Pokémon Trainer Black!
entire life, Black has dreamed
winning the Pokémon Leag
Now Black embarks on a
journey to explore the Ur
region and fill a Pokéde
Professor Juniper. Tim
Black's first Pokémon
Trainer Battle ever!

Who will Black choo
as his next Pokémo
Who would *you*
choose?

Plus, meet
Pokémon Sn
Tepig, Osha
and many m
new Pokémo
the unexplo
Unova regior

Story by
HIDENOF
KUSAK

Art by
SATOSH
YAMAMO

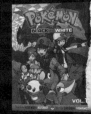

Inspired by the hit video games
Pokémon Black Version and *Pokémon White Version!*

$4.99 USA | $6.99 C

Available Now
at your local bookstore or comic store

© 2011 Pokémon.
©1995-2011 Nintendo/Creatures Inc. /GAME FREAK inc.
Pokémon properties are trademarks of Nintendo.
POCKET MONSTER SPECIAL © 1997 Hidenori KUSAKA

vizkids

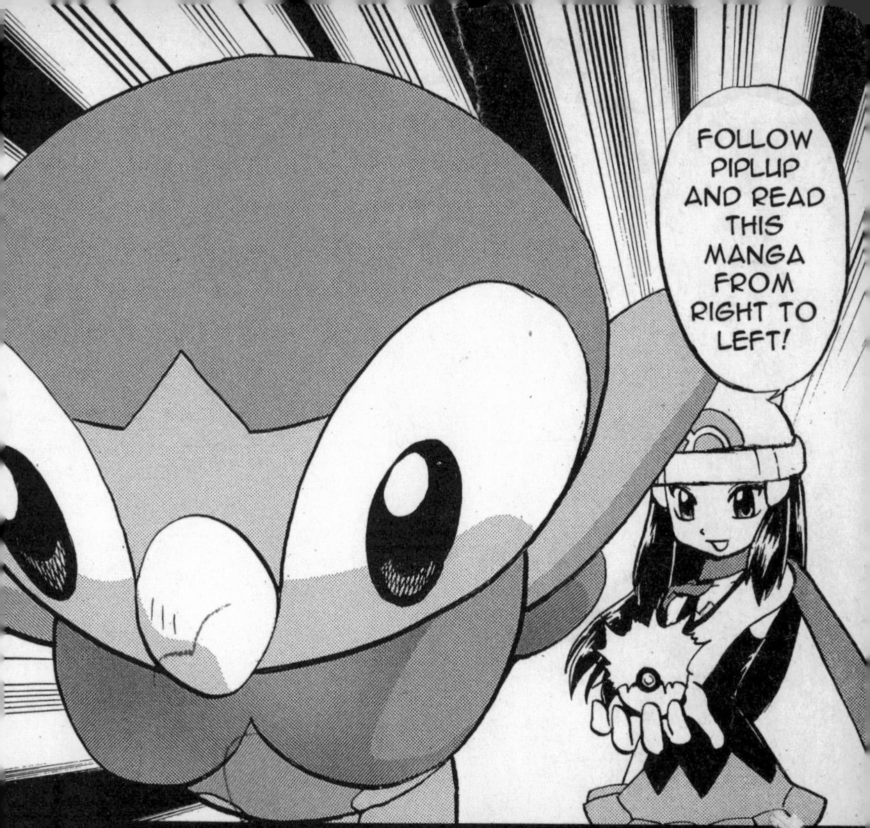
FOLLOW PIPLUP AND READ THIS MANGA FROM RIGHT TO LEFT!

THIS IS THE END OF THIS GRAPHIC NOVEL!

To properly enjoy this VIZ Media graphic novel, please turn it around and begin reading from right to left.

This book has been printed in the original Japanese format in order to preserve the orientation of the original artwork. Have fun with it!

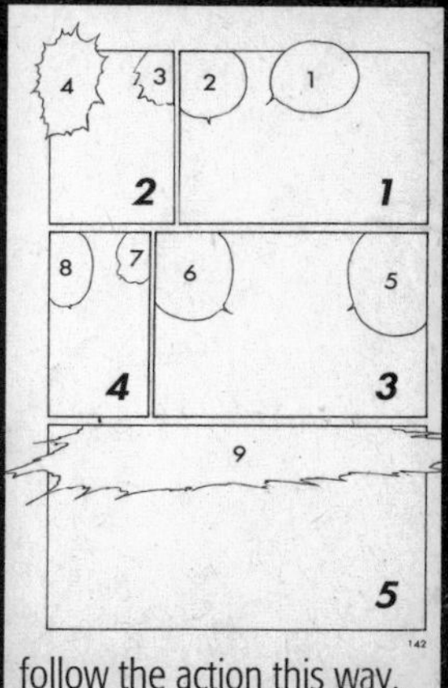

follow the action this way.

More Adventures Coming Soon...

Finally together again, Dia, Pearl, and Platinum must battle Legendary Pokémon Dialga and Palkia, who are being controlled by Cyrus, the powerful boss of Team Galactic! Then a new Legendary Pokémon leaps into the fray! Whose side is it on...?

And who will rescue Platinum's hapless bodyguards from the mysterious Distortion World they've been banished to...?

Plus, hang with Lopunny and meet Porygon-Z, Gallade, and...Looker?!

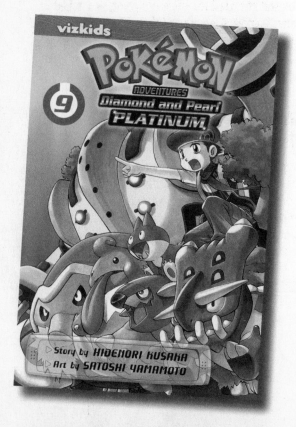

AVAILABLE OCTOBER 2013!

P9-DXN-369

mameshiba
On the LOOSE!

stories by **james turner**
art by **jorge monlongo**
"Mameshiba Shorts" by **gemma correll**

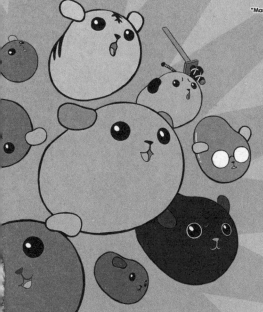

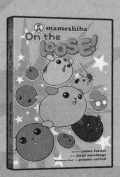

PRICE: $6.99 USA $7.99 CAN
ISBN: 9781421538808
Available NOW!
in your local
bookstore or comic shop

It's a BEAN! It's a DOG! It's...*BOTH*?!

Meet **Mameshiba**, the cute little bean dogs with bite! Starring in their first-ever adventures, they rescue friends, explore outer space and offer interesting bits of trivia when you least expect it! Hold on tight–Mameshiba are on the **LOOSE**!

© DENTSU INC.
www.viz.com   www.vizkids.com